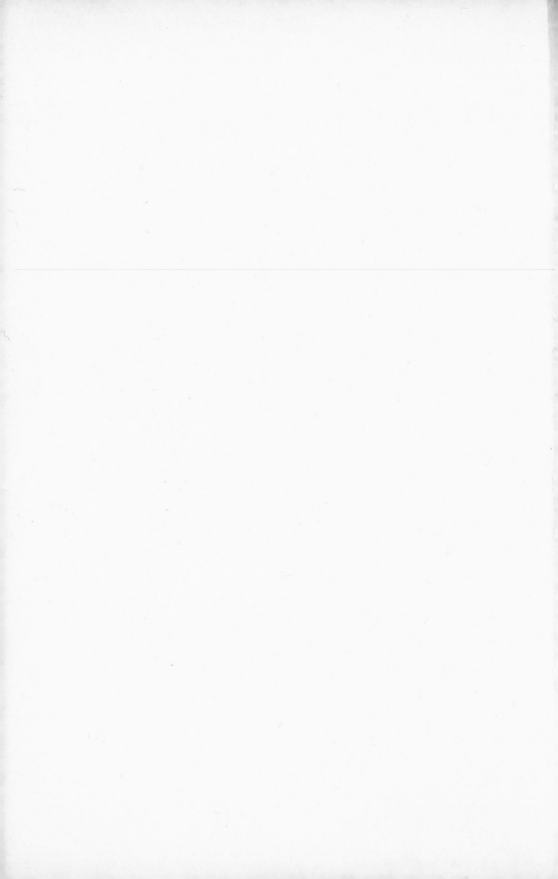

Tangled Web

Tangled Web

KEN McCLURE

SIMON & SCHUSTER
A VIACOM COMPANY

First published in Great Britain by Simon & Schuster UK Ltd, 2000
A Viacom company

1 3 5 7 9 10 8 6 4 2

Simon & Schuster UK Ltd
Africa House
64–78 Kingsway
London WC2B 6AH

Simon & Schuster Australia
Sydney

A CIP catalogue record for this book is available from the British Library

ISBN 0-684-86044-9

Typeset in Goudy Modern by
Palimpsest Book Production Limited, Polmont, Stirlingshire
Printed in Great Britain by Butler & Tanner Ltd.,
Frome and London

O what a tangled web we weave, When first we practise to deceive!

Sir Walter Scott (1771–1832) *Marmion*
(1808) canto 6, st. 17

~ *Prologue* ~

John Palmer came into the room and placed another log on the fire. He made sure it was stable before turning round and looking at his wife, Lucy, who sat with their baby daughter on her knee.

'You know, Lucy, this is how I always hoped it would be,' he said. 'You, me and our baby in our own home.'

'You're just a big softy when it comes right down to it,' she smiled. 'But it's not going to be easy, you know.'

John knelt down beside them and gently stroked the baby's cheek. 'She's our daughter,' he said. 'That's all that really matters. We'll cope with the problems as they come along.'

'We will,' agreed his wife.

John tickled the baby's tummy and she responded with a gurgle. 'See?' he said fondly. 'She knows it too.'

'You smell of sawdust,' said Lucy, sniffing at his hair.

'I've been cutting logs – I'm entitled to smell all woody,' John told her with a grin.

'I didn't say it was unpleasant,' she countered. 'It's quite macho really, in a lumberjack sort of a way. Is it still snowing outside?'

'A little, but this'll be the last snow of the winter, I'm sure.' John moved over to the window, leaning both hands on the sill to look out at the garden.

'The weather forecast said it was going to get warmer towards the end of the week,' said Lucy.

'If it's going to thaw then maybe I should build Anne-Marie a snowman today.' John sounded thoughtful.

'A snowman?' exclaimed Lucy through stifled laughter. 'Come on – she's only three months old!'

'No matter. We can take her out into the garden and show it to her – make sure she appreciates the finer points of her father's artistic talents.' John turned round, his face filled with growing enthusiasm for the idea. 'Tell you what, you have a hunt for clothes for the snowman and I'll get started. Play your cards right and you can have the honour of naming him. Come on, let's get cracking!'

'Oh, all right.' Lucy knew that any argument was pointless once her husband got a bee in his bonnet. 'I'll put Anne-Marie down for her sleep and then have a hunt through the wardrobes, see what I can come up with.'

'We'll also need a carrot for a nose and buttons for eyes and—'

'One thing at a time,' protested Lucy.

'C'mon, chop, chop!'

'First, your daughter is going down for a nice nap.' Lucy cradled Anne-Marie in her arms and stood up. 'So don't make too much of a racket.'

'Maybe I should build it in the front garden instead,' said John, hesitating at the door.

'Good idea – you do that.'

'I'll expect you outside in ten minutes if not before.'

'You took your time,' said John but not unkindly, when Lucy finally reappeared a good half-hour later, carrying a laundry basket full of bits and pieces. 'I've practically finished. What kept you?'

'It's amazing what you find when you start emptying out

the wardrobes,' said Lucy, propping the front door open a couple of inches to listen out for the baby. 'I came across things I hadn't seen for years – stuff I'd completely forgotten about. This is the blue dress I wore to your sister's wedding, remember? Here are the beach sandals I bought in Greece, and that top I spilled spaghetti down – I've never been able to get the marks out. I found lots of things, including some of yours. I'll show you later.'

'All right. Look, I'm just about finished here. You can dress him and put the final touches to his face, if you like.'

'Thank you – I shall enjoy that,' said Lucy. Carefully she inserted the button eyes and carrot nose, and stuck a little piece of red material below them as a mouth. She adjusted it into a crescent shape. 'Let's give him a nice big smile,' she said. There was an old cap in her laundry basket; she patted it into place on the snowman's broad head. His sloping shoulders looked quite dashing with an elderly yellow cycling cape tied round them.

'Handsome devil, isn't he?' Lucy stood back to admire her handiwork. John put his arm around her shoulders. He said enthusiastically 'This is fun. It's like being a kid all over again. I can't wait to go to the zoo and have picnics at the beach. I'll build her a little house in the garden too, and she can keep her dolls in it. Maybe we can get a dog when she's a bit older.

'Steady on,' smiled Lucy. 'She's only little.'

'It's going to be great,' said John. 'You'll see.'

Lucy smiled but her eyes held a hint of sadness. She tilted her head so that her cheek touched John's hand on her shoulder. After a few moments, she said, 'I've just remembered, I've got a red scarf somewhere – hall cupboard, I think. I'll get it.'

Lucy went into the house and returned a few moments

later with a scarlet woollen scarf which she wrapped round the snowman's neck. Then she and John stepped back again to eye the garishly-dressed rotund white figure standing proudly in their front garden.

'What have you decided to call him?' asked John.

'Captain Mainwaring,' replied Lucy, then burst out laughing.

'Perfect!' John could see a definite resemblance to the pompous *Dad's Army* TV character. 'Captain Mainwaring it is then. Is it too soon to wake Anne-Marie?'

'Let's have a cup of tea first,' said Lucy. 'She needed a nice long nap, she's been restless all day. I'm longing for the time when she sleeps through the night. I feel completely wiped out. Come on – I'll put the kettle on.'

They trudged inside, leaving their snowy boots by the front door to drip puddles on a piece of newspaper, and had tea and biscuits in the kitchen, warming their hands by the wood-burning stove.

'Anything good on telly tonight?' John yawned. He was feeling sleepy now after his labours.

'Haven't looked.'

'Saturday night – let me think. There's a Ruth Rendell thing on at eight if I remember right, but that's going to be a bit too early for me. I've still got some marking to do. I've skived off long enough making Captain Mainwaring.'

'Have you got a lot?'

'Well, all of Class 3c's thoughts on the biological basis of life. In terms of intellectual ability, I think Captain Mainwaring might make the middle of that lot if he put his mind to it.'

'You don't mean that,' said Lucy.

'Maybe not,' admitted John, 'but they can be exasperating. Come on, let's wake the baby and introduce her to the Captain.'

'All right,' Lucy said. 'But I'll have to wrap her up warmly. We don't want her catching cold.' She left the room and John washed out the mugs they'd been using.

Suddenly a scream tore through the air, making him drop the second one in the sink, where it smashed into three pieces. His blood ran cold as he ran through the house to Anne-Marie's room, where he found Lucy staring at an open window. The Disney pattern curtains were billowing gently in the icy breeze.

'She's gone!' Lucy said hoarsely, her whole body beginning to shake.

'But how?' protested John. 'Where? How could she?'

'Someone's taken her!'

'Oh my God,' John looked disbelievingly from the window to the empty cot with its covers thrown back and its sidebars dropped. Coming quickly to his senses, he flew out of the back door, not stopping to put on his boots. He was hoping to look for footprints in the snow, but his heart fell as he discovered that he couldn't make anything out: he himself had trampled down most of the area when he'd been out there earlier chopping logs. There was no trail to follow.

'The police,' he exclaimed. 'We must get the police!' Lucy was standing at the window, staring into the distance, seemingly paralysed with shock. John stumbled inside and grabbed at the phone in the hall. His frozen fingers jabbed out 999. 'Police? Come quickly! Our baby daughter's been kidnapped.'

~ One ~

Dr Tom Gordon looked down from the top of the hill behind Felinbach, the small North Wales coastal village that had become his home over the past two years. Out in the Menai Strait, the wintry sun was setting over Anglesey and a clear sky suggested that there might be a frost tonight. It was fast approaching the middle of March so he took comfort from the thought that spring could not be far away.

Weather was an important factor in the life of a GP in rural North Wales, and Tom felt he'd just about had enough of coaxing his Land Rover over icy roads and up snow-covered mountain tracks for one year. Today it had taken him longer than he had anticipated to get through his outlying calls because of a sudden fall of snow on the Llanberis Pass, but he had still managed to complete his list and get back on time for evening surgery. Not that this would have been a major problem because his colleague and senior partner, Dr Julie Rees, herself a native of Snowdonia, understood the vagaries of travel on local roads in winter only too well: she would be ready to cope on her own if need be.

The sun was now very low and its glow was reflected off the calm sea, bathing the village below in a pleasing orange light. Felinbach was home to some 1500 inhabitants who lived in a variety of houses clinging to the steep hillside leading down to the harbour. Main Street boasted six shops and two pubs — one at either end — and a third pub nestled down by the harbour wall next to the yacht chandlers. There were two bus stops on Main Street, one on either side depending on whether you wanted to go to Caernarfon in one direction or Bangor in the other.

The village had a primary school, two churches and a chapel, all of them built in Victorian times. In fact, the sepia-tint photograph of the village, displayed in the Post Office window and taken in 1898, showed Main Street pretty much as it looked today, apart from the lamp-posts. The harbour area, however, had changed out of all recognition in recent times, with the construction of a modern marina to accommodate the smart yachts belonging to wealthy visitors. Where once, grimy barges had filled their holds with slate from Welsh quarries, sleek catamarans with quirky names now huddled in safety while their owners enjoyed the hospitality and laundry facilities of the local yacht club.

A white baker's van drew up alongside Tom's vehicle and a plump, red-faced man wound down his window to ask, 'Everything all right, Doc?'

'Fine thanks, Glyn,' he replied. 'Just stopped to enjoy the view for a couple of minutes.'

'You'd be hard pushed to find a better one,' agreed Glyn Morris, the local baker.

'Outside of Scotland, that is,' said Tom, tongue in cheek.

'Oh, I'd quite forgotten you were a Scot,' exclaimed Morris. 'You've been here a while now.'

'Two and a half years,' the young GP told him.

'Can't be that bad then?'

Tom answered with a grin and Morris put his van into gear. 'See you around, Doc.'

Tom wound up his own window and prepared to move off. He supposed what Morris had said was true. It couldn't have been 'that bad' or he wouldn't have stayed so long. But was that entirely true? he wondered. People often imagine that they do things out of personal choice when that is rarely the case. Most of us tend to move with the flow of events in and around our lives, and those who sing the pub anthem 'My Way' are taking harmless liberties with the truth. Doing things the government's way, the family's way, society's way or even the Church's way, is usually a much more realistic appraisal.

Tom had originally come to Felinbach to work as a locum in general practice after the trauma of divorce back home in Edinburgh. He had seen the advert for the job in the *British Medical Journal* and it had come up at a time when he had felt the need to be away from the trappings of his old life. He wanted to take a look at things from a distance before even thinking about making any plans for the future. North Wales had seemed like a good idea at the time.

The fact that he was still here over two years later was down to changing circumstance. He'd only been at the practice for four months when the senior partner, Dr Glyn Williams, the man who'd taken him on in the first place to help smooth his own passage into semi-retirement, had collapsed and died. Dr Julie Rees, his married daughter, had taken over the running of her father's practice and had surprised him by offering Tom a full partnership if he agreed to stay on. He in turn had surprised her by agreeing almost without a second thought.

He supposed on reflection that there might have been an element of not having quite got over the pain of divorce at the time, but on the other hand he had been sure that he liked Julie and felt they'd get on, as indeed they had. He also liked the village and admired its breathtaking scenery.

He'd come to love the mountains of Snowdonia as much as he used to love the Cairngorms and the Cuillins of home. In many ways North Wales was like Scotland in miniature. Only the great tracts of featureless moorland were missing, a blessing that rendered everything more accessible.

At the age of thirty-two, Tom supposed he should be thinking more about the future than he actually did, but there was a certain comfort to be had from just living each day as it came. Realistically, it would be very difficult for him to return to hospital medicine after having been away for such a long time: the competition for jobs was so fierce. He had more or less resigned himself to a career in general practice but this was no great problem; he enjoyed it a lot.

There was no serious love interest in his life at the moment but mainly because he didn't want there to be. He had enjoyed one or two casual relationships with young women in the area and hoped that he might do so again, but the scars left by his divorce made him steer well clear of anything resembling commitment. Besides, thirty-two wasn't old; there was no need for him to rush into anything.

Dr Tom Gordon was six feet tall, athletic and blessed with looks and a quiet charm that women found attractive. They tended to seek him out rather than the other way around. This of course, in a small community, held certain dangers in that anyone he met was liable to be his patient. It was something he was acutely aware of and constantly on guard against.

Felinbach Medical Centre was situated in a small side street to the north of Main Street; it stood next door but one to the Methodist chapel, on the corner of a hill that led down to the marina. The only modern thing about it was the sign designating it a 'medical centre' when everyone still knew it as 'the surgery'. Like the other buildings around here, it was built of Victorian stone, darkened by time and the elements, although it did have a concrete extension built on to the back, something that had been added in the 1960s.

Tom parked his Land Rover in the space next to Julie's Vauxhall Frontera and entered the building. A pleasing warmth engulfed him and he saw that Julie had lit the butane gas heater in the hallway to augment a central-heating system that often created more noise than it did heat. He could see that she already had a patient with her so he did not announce his return but instead, looked into the waiting room where he found some eight people sitting there, reading magazines of varying antiquity. He smiled and said good evening before going along to his room in the concrete extension and taking his coat off. He settled himself behind his desk, glanced briefly at the pile of patients' records then pressed the buzzer to summon his first patient.

A small woman dressed entirely in black came through the door and gave a half-hearted smile as she sat down. The wrinkles on her face spoke of a life that had been none too easy.

'Mrs Lloyd, isn't it?' said Tom. 'What can I do for you?'

'I'm not sleeping, Doctor. I thought maybe you could give me something?'

'Nothing easier,' agreed Tom, then he leaned forward on the desk and said, 'Any idea why you're not sleeping?'

'A lot on my mind, I suppose,' replied the woman uncertainly.

'It must be over a year now since Owen died?' said Tom gently, remembering that her husband had died of cancer.

The woman nodded. 'On the third of last month.'

'And the boys, do you see much of them these days?'

'It's difficult for them. They've got jobs and families and it's such a long way to come up here from Swansea.'

Tom nodded. He didn't say anything: he wanted the woman to continue speaking. Instead, she started to cry. He got out of his seat and came round the desk to put an arm round her shoulders. 'There, there now,' he comforted her. 'Why don't you tell me all about it. What's really troubling you?'

'It's stupid, Doctor,' she wept. 'I can see it is but I just can't seem to help myself.'

'What is?'

'Silver. He died a month ago and I just can't stop thinking about him. I know it's silly, he was only a cat, but . . .'

'It's not silly at all,' said Tom kindly. 'He was your pet and you loved him. There's nothing to be ashamed of.'

The widow's shoulders heaved as she sobbed into her handkerchief. Tom returned to his side of the desk and took out his prescription pad. 'I'll give you something to help you sleep, but only for a few nights. Then I'd like you to consider something else.'

The woman sniffed and pocketed her handkerchief. 'What's that, Doctor?'

'Silver doesn't need you any more,' said Tom. 'He's had his time and now he's gone. He doesn't need the care and love you gave him, but I suspect a lot of other cats out there do. I think you should at least consider getting another one.'

'I don't think I could . . . not after my old Silver.'

'You don't have to rush into anything, and don't think of it as a replacement for Silver. It will be a new cat with a different personality and problems of its own. Promise me you'll consider it?'

Mrs Lloyd managed a small smile and said that she

would. Tom showed her to the door and pressed the buzzer for the next patient. A man with chronic bronchitis, a retired miner, came in to ask for a repeat prescription for antibiotics. He was followed by a middle-aged woman who wanted information about hormone replacement therapy: her sister over in Bangor swore by it. An elderly man with a lump on his elbow was given assurance that it was nothing serious, and a younger man, who reported recurrent stomach pains, was prescribed something for the pain, but Tom also referred him to Caernarfon General Hospital for further investigation.

Tom was just thinking that he had seen the last of the evening's patients when a stocky young man with closely clipped fair hair knocked and came into the room. 'Dr Gordon? DS Walters, sir, North Wales Police. I need to talk to you.'

Tom invited him to sit. 'What can I do for you, Sergeant?'

'I understand that you are John and Lucy Palmer's GP, sir?'

'I am,' Tom agreed, a note of concern creeping into his voice. 'They're also good friends of mine. What's wrong?'

'It's their daughter, sir. She's gone missing.'

'Anne-Marie missing?' exclaimed Tom. 'How can she go missing? She's only three months old.'

'She appears to have been kidnapped, sir.'

'Kidnapped! Who'd want to kidnap the Palmer baby, for God's sake?'

'That's what we're trying to establish at the moment, sir. Money's rarely a motive in cases like this so, although we're keeping an open mind, we're not thinking along the lines of a ransom. We were wondering more if perhaps you or your colleague might know of any woman in the area who's recently lost a baby . . . or suffered some kind of upset that might have led to her into taking someone else's baby?'

'I see,' said Tom, accepting that this would be a more likely scenario. He thought for a moment. 'No one springs immediately to mind, but we'd better ask Julie when she's through with evening surgery. She should be finished any time now. When did all this happen?'

'This afternoon, sir.'

'In broad daylight? What were John and Lucy doing?'

'I believe they were building a snowman. Mrs Palmer had put the baby down for an afternoon nap. When she went to wake her up, the bedroom window was open and the baby had gone.'

'It's unbelievable! My God, they must be beside themselves with worry,' Tom said. He found the news hard to take in. 'I'd better get over there, see what I can do.'

'There's a WPC with Mrs Palmer at the moment, sir, but you're right, the couple are pretty upset. She's their only child, I believe?'

Tom nodded. 'Have you got anything to go on at all?' he asked.

'To be quite honest, sir, not at the moment, but Detective Chief Inspector Davies is with the couple, searching for possible motives. Once money and malicious grudges have been ruled out, there's not much left. We'll be looking at a disturbed mind, I'm afraid.'

A knock came on the door and Julie Rees put her head round. 'Sorry, I didn't realise you had someone with you,' she said.

'Come in, Julie, we've been waiting for you,' Tom said. 'This is Detective Sergeant Walters of the North Wales Police. The Palmer baby has gone missing and it looks as if she's been kidnapped.'

Julie Rees, an attractive woman in her early forties,

smartly dressed in dark green sweater and skirt and still with her stethoscope slung round her neck, looked shocked. 'Good Lord,' she exclaimed as she stepped into the room. 'Where from? How did it happen?'

Tom let Walters tell her what had happened. Then: 'The police are thinking along the lines of a disturbed, would-be mother having snatched her for herself. What d'you think? Do we know anyone like that?'

Julie considered for a few moments before saying, 'I can think of two ladies in the area who've had miscarriages recently and there's been a cot death baby, but honestly I don't see any of them doing anything like this. That doesn't mean to say that they weren't very upset, of course, particularly Mrs Griffiths, the cot death mother — it was such a tragic thing to happen — but we're talking about grief here not psychiatric disorder. Apart from that, all three ladies have supportive husbands and stable homes. Why the Palmer baby? It doesn't make any sense.'

'I know.' Tom was as baffled as she was.

'Why *not* the Palmer baby?' asked Walters, wondering whether he was missing something.

Julie and Tom looked at each other. 'You don't know?' said Tom.

'Know what?'

'Anne-Marie Palmer is quite badly disabled.'

Walters gave a low whistle. 'I didn't know that,' he said. 'The parents didn't mention it.'

'She's a much-loved baby,' said Tom defensively, not liking what he thought might be going through Walters's mind.

'Of course, sir,' said Walters, backing off slightly. He turned to Julie. 'I wonder if I might just get a note of the names and addresses of the ladies you mentioned, Dr Rees?'

'Of course,' shrugged Julie. 'But I really think you'll be barking up the wrong tree.'

'It'll just be a routine check, Doctor. We have to begin somewhere. It's what DCI Davies terms "dotting our is and crossing our ts" – doing all the routine things so that no one can accuse us later of neglecting them. I should think it's probably the same in your job? You carry out a whole series of tests on autopilot while you consider what's *really* wrong with your patient.'

Tom nodded his agreement with a smile.

'Perhaps the kidnapper didn't know about Anne-Marie's disability when he or she took her,' suggested Julie.

'I suppose that's possible,' Walters said, 'but she was taken from home. It wasn't as if she was snatched from a nursery or from her pram outside a supermarket in a shopping mall.'

To Tom, the idea that someone had specifically targeted the Palmers' baby for abduction seemed hard to fathom. The lurking suspicion in the air of a more sinister explanation for the baby's disappearance made him want to help redress the balance. 'The Palmers have been trying for years to have children,' he told the policeman. 'It was what they wanted above all else; they kept on trying against all the odds.'

'All the odds, sir?'

'Mrs Palmer couldn't conceive in the normal fashion,' said Tom, choosing to ignore the warning look from Julie. Doctor/patient confidentiality was important but so was common sense. 'The details don't concern you, Sergeant,' he continued, as a sop to Julie's unease, 'but she and her husband persisted over several years with specialised help from various clinics. They had setback after setback, but still they kept on trying. In the end, their baby was conceived through *in vitro* fertilisation carried out in Professor Carwyn Thomas's unit at Caernarfon General Hospital.'

'A famous clinic,' said Walters.

'And rightly so. It's helped more childless couples than practically any other unit in the country bar Robert Winston's.'

'Yes, sir.'

'The point is,' continued Tom, 'that if you go to all that trouble to have children, Sergeant, you really *want* to have them.'

'But,' said Walters, diverting his gaze for a moment, 'it must have been a terrible disappointment for them when their child was born with problems.'

'It was,' agreed Tom quietly. 'It was a bloody shame.'

'How did the couple take it?' Walters asked.

Tom's spirits sank again as he saw where this line of questioning was leading. 'Not well,' he confessed.

Walters remained silent but obviously expected more.

'The baby's condition came as a terrible shock to them, naturally.'

'They hadn't been warned beforehand?' exclaimed Walters.

Tom shook his head. 'The pre-natal scans didn't pick up on the problem, I'm afraid.'

'What exactly *was* the problem, sir?' asked Walters, leaning forward in his seat.

'The bones in Anne Marie's legs didn't develop properly, in fact, they didn't really develop at all. Her lower limbs were useless.'

Walters grimaced.

'Surgical intervention was required to save her life.'

'Intervention, sir?'

'They had to amputate her legs.'

'I see,' said Walters, after a pause. 'Must have been awful for the parents.'

'Lucy rejected her baby when she first saw it, quite natural in the circumstances, I think.'

'And Mr Palmer?'

'John must have found it difficult too, but he didn't show it; he was a tower of strength to Lucy throughout.'

Walters nodded.

'It was only a short-term problem, I assure you,' insisted Tom. 'They both came to terms with the situation quite quickly and now they love their baby as much as any other couple I know.'

'I see, sir. Well, thank you both for your help. I'd better report back to DCI Davies. He'll be wondering where I've got to.'

And very interested in what you have to tell him, thought Tom. He was left with an uncomfortable feeling inside of him.

Walters left and Julie said thoughtfully, 'Well, what d'you think?'

'Just what I told him,' Tom said, slightly annoyed at the question. 'I *know* that the Palmers love their baby; if they say that Anne-Marie's been kidnapped then that's exactly what's happened. And you? What do you think?'

'I don't know them well enough,' replied Julie guardedly. 'They were Dad's patients and then they became yours, but it does seem odd that anyone would snatch Anne-Marie from home like that . . .'

'I'd better get over to the house,' said Tom. He was anxious for the conversation to end.

The Palmers lived in a comfortable modern house on a small, private housing development, just outside Felinbach on the way to Caernarfon. Although the snow had started to melt on the main road, Tom was glad of the Land Rover's four-wheel drive as he coaxed it up the steep hill leading to the estate. He parked it in front of the Palmers' house, behind the two police cars that were already sitting there, and walked up the path. As he did so, the front door opened and two men emerged: one was DS Walters who introduced him to the other man, Detective Chief Inspector Davies.

'Well, Doctor,' said Davies. 'I think Mrs Palmer could do with some medical help. She's a very distraught lady.'

Tom had the distinct impression that Davies had said this in order to measure his reaction. He looked directly back at the man and thought he knew the type – physically big, a bit of a bully who probably thought he was a lot brighter than he actually was, an illusion reinforced by his position of authority.

'I'm not surprised,' Tom said briskly. 'Have you anything to go on at all, Chief Inspector?'

'We're currently checking out the women your colleague mentioned to the Sergeant here, although bearing in mind what she said, we're not too hopeful. We're also in the process of asking the hospitals if they've had any dealings with likely candidates for child abduction in the last few weeks. Apart from that, our lines of investigation are somewhat limited. Do you have any ideas yourself, Doctor?'

There it was again, that appraising gaze. 'Absolutely none at all,' replied Tom, shaking his head. 'I suppose my fear . . .' He broke off.

'Yes, Doctor?'

'It was something your Sergeant said,' confessed Tom. 'I was going to say my great fear is that Anne-Marie has been taken away by someone with a deranged mind.'

'A *real* nutter, you mean,' Davies grunted. 'A psycho, not just some woman who thinks she's found a new doll to play with and will look after it until we find her alive and well-cared for, as is usually the case with missing babies?'

'Yes,' Tom said reluctantly. 'A *real* nutter.'

'God forbid. Such people are notoriously difficult to trace because neither rhyme nor reason comes into their thinking.

Motive is usually non-existent or so convoluted as to be beyond normal comprehension,' said Davies. 'Happily, such people are far fewer on the ground than many of the papers would have us believe, Doctor. Chances are, that's not what we're dealing with here.'

'In that case, I hope you find her soon,' said Tom. 'Right – I'd better see to my patients.' He squeezed past, feeling uncomfortable in Davies's presence, although he recognised that it wasn't entirely the policeman's fault. There was an element of conflict going on inside his own head that was contributing to his unease.

'Tom! Good of you to come,' said a relieved-sounding John Palmer, getting up when Tom entered the room. A WPC was sitting on the couch next to Lucy, who looked up and smiled wanly. 'Hello, Tom,' she whispered.

'This is a nightmare,' he said, 'but I'm sure the police will find her soon and bring her back unharmed.'

'I hope to Christ you're right,' burst out John Palmer. 'Why on earth would anyone do this? It's like some kind of sick punishment. We wait for years to have a baby then we get one, only to have her taken away like this . . .' Palmer broke down, putting his hands to his face to hide his silent sobs; only his heaving shoulders gave him away.

Tom ushered him to a chair. 'You both need some help to get you through this,' he said. 'So no protests please, there's nothing noble about unnecessary suffering. Just take the sedatives I'm going to prescribe for you and think positive thoughts. The police will pull out all the stops. They'll find her.'

~ Two ~

Three Days Later

For a big man, Chief Inspector Alan Davies could appear disarmingly tender and considerate. His voice dropped to a whisper and he clasped his hands in front of him as he leaned forward solicitously in his chair. He was in John and Lucy Palmer's living room, sitting opposite them on the floral patterned couch that filled the window alcove. The fourth person in the room, Detective Sergeant Walters, sat away from the other three, on a dining-room chair by the door. He watched the proceedings, notebook in hand but held discreetly out of sight for the time being in deference to the ambience of sympathy and understanding being fostered by his superior officer.

'What more is there to tell?' said John Palmer, letting go of his wife's hand to spread his own in a gesture of bewilderment. 'You must know absolutely everything there is to know about us by now. We'd been married for eight years and there wasn't a day when we didn't hope for a child of our own.' He took hold of his wife's hand again and kissed it gently before continuing. He did it in an unself-conscious way, suggesting that it was nothing out of the ordinary. 'Then, quite suddenly, Lucy fell pregnant with Ann-Marie and it seemed like a dream come true. All our prayers were answered; a real true-to-life miracle had happened. Sounds soppy but that's the way it was.'

'This was after you were referred to Professor Thomas's clinic at Caernarfon General?'

'Yes. We'd tried everything else. The doctors had just about given up on us: they kept trying to persuade us to consider adoption when Professor Thomas said he'd like to try out a new IVF technique.'

'What kind of new technique?'

Palmer gave Davies a look that suggested it was really none of his business but he scratched his head and answered anyway. 'It's actually a modification to the standard *in vitro* fertilisation method called ICSI – that stands for intra-cytoplasmic sperm injection. Instead of just mixing sperm and ova in a test tube and hoping for the best, the doctor actually picks up a single sperm in a very fine needle and injects it into an ovum. Then the fertilised egg is implanted in the mother's womb.'

Davies shook his head and smiled. 'Amazing what they can do these days,' he said.

'Professor Thomas warned us that there were risks attached to the technique, and it was something they wouldn't use for everyone, but they were keen to try it for particularly difficult cases: we certainly qualified on that score – or rather, I did.'

Davies noticed Lucy give her husband's arm a little rub, a simple gesture of support. He patted her hand in return.

'Didn't you have any qualms at all about the risks?' asked Davies carefully.

'Not really,' shrugged Palmer, looking at his wife who gave a slight shake of the head. 'We were desperate, Chief Inspector. We were willing to try anything to have a child of our own.'

Davies nodded understandingly and said, 'And it paid off in the end. You finally fell pregnant, Mrs Palmer.'

Lucy Palmer smiled distantly. 'It was the best day of my life,' she said, obviously remembering it with pleasure. 'When the Professor told me the implant had taken and I was going to have a baby I felt so happy I almost burst with pride. I wanted to tell everyone. I wanted to stand on street corners and shout out the news. I wanted everyone in the world to feel that good.' As the memory faded and reality started to reassert itself, Lucy's smile disappeared and emotion threatened to overwhelm her. John put his arm round her shoulders and hugged her to him, whispering reassurance in her ear.

'Would you say it was an uneventful pregnancy, Mrs Palmer?'

John Palmer furrowed his brow at the question and interrupted, 'I'm sorry, Chief Inspector, but I really don't see the relevance of the details of Lucy's pregnancy to our daughter's disappearance.'

'If you'll just bear with me, sir.'

Lucy shrugged her shoulders. 'There were a couple of scares along the way when I thought I might lose the baby – a bit of bleeding around three months – but nothing too out of the ordinary, I don't think.'

'Morning sickness? Cravings for strange food?'

'Look, Chief Inspector, I really must—'

Davies held up his hand without breaking eye-contact with Lucy. Palmer stopped his protest.

'I *was* sick and yes, I *did* develop a liking for beetroot sandwiches and tuna with jam somewhere along the way, but I fail to see what this has to do with Anne-Marie's kidnapping. Why are you asking these questions, Inspector?' said Lucy, becoming agitated.

Davies appeared to remain deep in thought for a moment,

then he said, 'I'm just trying to get an idea of how you felt about your baby while you were carrying her, Mrs Palmer.'

An uneasy silence fell on the room. It seemed to go on for ever until Lucy asked slowly and coldly, 'How I felt about my baby, Inspector? How d'you *think* I felt about her? How does any mother feel about her baby when she's carrying it? Anne-Marie was the most precious thing in the world; I loved her completely, as I do now.'

Davies held up his palms in a gesture of appeasement and apologised. 'Of course, I'm sorry, I probably put it badly. It's just that sometimes pregnancy brings about changes in a woman. Unaccountable psychological changes.'

The Palmers looked puzzled.

'Feelings of resentment are not unknown, even . . . hatred in some cases,' said Davies. His eyes never left the Palmers.

'There has never been a moment when I hated my daughter, Inspector,' said Lucy flatly.

'I see,' said Davies quietly. 'So Ann-Marie was born three months ago on December the fourteenth at Caernarfon General?'

'Yes.'

'But very badly deformed.'

John Palmer winced and rubbed nervously at his forehead at Davies's summation. Lucy looked down at the floor, unwilling to have her emotions scrutinised. The words hung in the air like a dark challenge.

'Our baby is *disabled*, Chief Inspector. She was left without legs after surgical measures necessary to save her life. Now, where is all this leading, may I ask?' said John Palmer when he'd recovered his composure. The tone of his voice suggested he was struggling to remain civil.

'No legs,' said Davies with a slow shake of the head.

'Poor mite didn't have much of a future to look forward to.'

'Nonsense! And what on earth has our daughter's future got to do with you investigating her kidnap?' demanded Palmer.

Davies ignored the question and pressed on. 'Her deformation was such that you, Mrs Palmer, completely rejected her when she was born, I understand.'

Lucy buried her face in her hands and started sobbing. John put his arm round her and said through gritted teeth, 'We were both very upset at the time: it came as a complete shock. We had absolutely no warning that anything was amiss with Anne-Marie.'

'I thought medical science could predict just about everything these days,' said Davies sourly.

'Foetal monitoring failed to pick up the problem with her leg bones.'

'I see, sir.'

'You can appreciate, I'm sure, that it took us a little time to come to terms with Ann-Marie's condition, but that's all we needed . . . just a little time. I think that would be the case for most people in similar circumstances, don't you?'

'All the same, I was given to understand that you refused to have anything to do with your daughter after she was born, Mrs Palmer,' persisted Davies. 'Is that correct? You were quite adamant that you were not going to look after her? In fact, you insisted that the nursing staff take her away. "Get her out of my sight" were the words you used.'

'For God's sake, man, why are you doing this to us at a time like this?' exclaimed John Palmer angrily. 'I've already told you we were both very upset. It was a tremendous shock to both of us. We needed time to come to terms with it.'

'"It", Sir?'

'The situation!' exploded Palmer angrily. 'How many times must I say it? We were upset. We needed help and we got it.'

'Go on, sir.'

Palmer took a deep breath as if reluctant to say any more but in the end he continued, 'The staff at the clinic were very understanding and the nurses were kindness itself. Lucy underwent a course of counselling, which did her the world of good, and Professor Thomas put us in touch with a support organisation, which was – and is – run by wonderful people. They're the kind of people who restore your faith in human nature and make you feel quite inadequate by comparison. Professor Thomas also arranged for us to contact parents in the same situation as ourselves so we didn't feel so alone. We came to terms with our daughter's condition quite quickly, Chief Inspector: we stopped seeing her as being disabled. She's now just our Anne-Marie and we love her very much.' There were tears in his eyes.

Davies took a few moments to digest what he'd been told then asked, 'What sort of person would you say has kidnapped your child, sir?'

'How the hell should I know?' John Palmer exclaimed. 'That's your job, isn't it? Why aren't you out there trying to find our baby instead of sitting here on your backside asking us damn fool questions?'

Davies remained impassive and Palmer, unhappy with the ensuing silence, added, 'It's usually some sort of woman with a problem, isn't it? Someone who has lost her own child . . . something like that.'

'So you wouldn't expect a ransom demand then?'

The man looked astonished. 'We're not rich people and nothing about us suggests that we are. No one in their right mind would think of kidnapping our baby for money.'

'You're not even a bank manager,' said Davies.

Palmer looked puzzled.

Davies explained, 'You're not in a position to give kidnappers access to other people's money.'

' I'm a science teacher, for God's sake, I earn twenty-two thousand pounds a year. I've got a fifty-thousand-pound mortgage and a bank loan for a three-year-old car.'

'And you, Mrs Palmer?'

'I was a teacher too until I gave up work after the birth of my daughter. I taught Modern Studies.'

Davies smiled nastily. 'Didn't have that in my schooldays. Still, I don't suppose it involves earning large sums of money.'

'Of course not,' snapped Lucy.

'So, as you said, Mr Palmer, no one in their right mind would want to kidnap your daughter . . .'

'For money,' added Palmer.

'What about any other reason?'

'What are you getting at now?' John Palmer was reaching the end of his tether with these questions.

'She *is* badly disabled.'

'So what? Why are we discussing the feasibility of it all when our daughter already *has* been kidnapped? She's been gone three days and we are climbing the walls with worry.'

'Indeed, sir,' said Davies slowly and deliberately.

'What's that supposed to mean?'

Davies screwed up his face as if wrestling with some conundrum. 'You see, sir, I have a problem with all of this,' he said. 'No disrespect, but for the life of me I can't understand why anyone would want to steal a deformed infant.'

'How dare you!' stormed Lucy.

Davies looked surprised. 'I simply meant that she would be readily identifiable wherever she was taken, Mrs Palmer.'

'For God's sake, man, why are you persisting with this? The motivation doesn't matter. Someone *has* taken Anne-Marie — *now will you please do something about getting her back?*'

Davies looked down at his feet for a few moments before saying, 'I fear that may not be possible, sir.'

An awful silence fell on the room before Palmer asked in quiet trepidation, 'What do you mean, not possible?'

Davies looked him straight in the eye and said with sudden, chilling coldness, 'Because I think she's already dead, sir, and I think that you and your wife are responsible for her death. I think you found the prospect of bringing up a severely handicapped child just too much and took matters into your own hands. You came up with your own solution to the problem.'

'This is outrageous!' exclaimed John Palmer in a barely audible whisper. Lucy's eyes opened wide in disbelief at what Davies had said. She tried to find words but none came out. She was dumbstruck with horror.

The Chief Inspector brought out a folded document from his inside pocket and announced, 'I have here a warrant to search your house and its environs.' He turned to DS Walters and nodded; the Sergeant got up and left the room. The following silence only lasted for a few moments before Walters opened the front door and the sound of voices filled the hall as instructions were given to a police search team. The words 'no stone unturned' seemed to detach themselves from the general clamour to drift into the room and break the spell.

John Palmer got to his feet. 'Crazy, crazy, crazy,' he

complained as he started to pace up and down and make gestures of hopelessness with his hands. Lucy maintained a steady sad gaze into the middle distance as if the last few minutes had been too much for her and her brain was refusing to acknowledge what was going on around her. The policewoman who had been detailed to look after her since Anne-Marie's disappearance had come back into the room at Davies's request but her attitude had changed; she remained standing and at a discreet distance.

Outside the sound of a heavy engine starting up made Palmer stop pacing and go over to look out of the window. A yellow JCB digger stood at the entrance to the short drive leading up to their house; its driver was talking to two policemen.

Palmer turned questioningly to Davies. 'What the hell?'

'The garden too,' said Davies without emotion.

Palmer's eyes were tortured pools of disbelief as the digger lurched forward, its huge wheels cracking several of the concrete slabs where he hadn't used enough bedding sand when he'd laid them during the previous summer. The huge vehicle made its way round the side of the house, lowering its shovel as it went and filling the air with blue exhaust fumes.

Time passed slowly as John and Lucy Palmer huddled together on the couch in their own private hell while strangers ransacked their house and destroyed their garden. Words had ceased to be of any use; they sat in disbelieving silence even as junior officers started to come into the room and make their reports to Davies.

'Nothing upstairs, sir.'

'Loft clear, sir.'

'Nothing in the cellar, sir.'

The continual series of negatives gradually got through

to John Palmer. After the third he found the confidence to look at Davies with ill-disguised contempt and said, 'Now will you get your damned circus out of our house and leave us alone?'

'All in good time, sir,' replied Davies automatically and without emotion.

A few minutes later a Police Constable, wearing dark blue overalls and Wellington boots entered the room with scant regard for the carpets he was trailing mud over. 'Can I have a word, sir?'

Davies left the room and was gone for fully ten minutes. When he returned he stood directly in front of the Palmers and announced, 'It's over: we've found her.'

'Don't be ridiculous! How can you have? You're lying,' said John Palmer, springing to his feet.

Lucy Palmer suddenly screamed and made a headlong dash to the door, bursting out of the room past the startled Constable who made a late grab for her but missed.

'Stop her!' cried Davies but she ran round the back of the house to where canvas screens were now being erected around an excavated section of the garden about twenty metres back from the house. Two police officers stepped forward to restrain her but not before she got a good look at what lay in the shallow pit. There was a moment when all of them seemed to freeze like a tableau before Lucy let out a scream that tore at the nerves of all present. Then she collapsed unconscious onto the wet grass at the feet of the officers.

Davies and John Palmer reached the scene and it was Palmer's turn to see what lay there. He was left to stare down at the tiny little legless corpse lying in the mud between the Wellington boots of the officer who had dropped down into the hole to reach it. He shook his head slowly as if unwilling to believe what he was seeing. His eyes didn't blink and he seemed oblivious to everything around him, even his wife's unconscious condition, leaving her welfare entirely to the policewoman who was kneeling beside her, loosening her clothing and trying to bring her round.

Palmer didn't appear to hear the murmured angry comments of the police search team as he moved closer to the edge of the hole and squatted down on his haunches. Davies warned his officers off with a glance. When he judged the time to be right he asked the policewoman if Lucy Palmer was going to be fit to caution in the near future.

John Palmer interrupted her reply. 'No,' he said, turning to look at Davies directly. 'Leave Lucy out of this, she had nothing to do with it. It was me, I did it. I'm sorry, I just couldn't cope any longer.'

As two police officers took hold of his arms John Palmer looked down into the grave and said sadly, 'I'm so sorry, my darling.'

Lucy Palmer was still unconscious as he was led away.

'Well, what d'you make of that?' Davies asked his Sergeant as they drove back to the station.

'Bloody unsatisfying,' Walters replied.

'You're kidding – we've just cleared up a murder.'

'But it's just a mess, isn't it, sir? I mean, it's not like catching a real murderer, is it?'

'Isn't it? That's how the law will see it.'

'I suppose. Maybe that's why it feels, like I said, unsatisfying. I feel for them, don't you? All their prayers were answered, they were so happy and then it all went wrong. The baby is born like that and it all ends in tragedy for everybody.'

'Mark my words, we're in for an emotional sports

day over this one,' said Davies. 'The Bible-thumpers, the disabled lobby, the euthanasia mob, they're all going to start shouting the odds but let's look on the bright side, boyo, we've just cleared up a kidnapping and solved a murder. Not bad for a day's work, wouldn't you say?'

— Three —

Gordon was called out on Tuesday afternoon to a local shop where a middle-aged woman had collapsed on the floor. She had already come round by the time he got there, although it had taken him less than five minutes to sprint up from his own flat near the harbour. He was out of breath from the climb up the steep flight of steps to Main Street — something that caused even the woman herself to smile. She was still sitting on the floor but had been propped up with her back against the counter. One of the shop assistants knelt beside her holding a glass of water in readiness while a small group of onlookers stood in a huddle at a discreet distance.

'I just came over all faint, Doctor,' said the woman. Tom recognised her as Ida Marsh, who did cleaning work in the village. The Palmers were one of her customers.

'Now then, Mrs Marsh, tell me what happened exactly.'

'I think it must have been the fumes, Doctor. They were making me feel light-headed while I was working.'

'What fumes?'

'I was cleaning out the sitting room in the place I do on Tuesday mornings along in Aberlyn when I came over all queer, like. Maybe it's because the windows are never open in that house — it's empty most of the time, but there was a funny smell in the room; made me feel quite sick it did while I was working there. I told the gentleman about it, like, and he apologised – said it was the paint-stripper he'd been using on an old chest of drawers.'

'What man was this?'

'Peggy Grant's tenant. She's rented out her house down on Beach Road while she's away in Australia visiting her son and his family. Nice man, English but a gentleman, like. Works up in Caernarfon.'

'Paint-stripper can be nasty stuff,' said Tom. 'Especially in enclosed spaces.'

'I popped in here when I got off the bus to buy a bottle of lemonade to take away the taste in my mouth and suddenly all the lights went out. I've made a right fool of myself.'

'Nonsense,' said Tom reassuringly. 'It could happen to anyone. Are you sure that's all it is? You've not been overdoing it lately? Taking on too much in the way of cleaning jobs, I mean.'

'No, Doctor, far from it. I've just given up one of them. Dai didn't want me going to the Palmers' house any more, he said.'

There was a murmur of assent from the huddle of women and knowing looks were passed.

Tom felt annoyed but he knew that rumours had been spreading like wildfire in the village over the past couple of days. Julie had said that she'd heard people talking in the bank on Monday morning.

'That baby was never kidnapped,' said one of the women. 'Mark my words.'

'Perhaps you should share your knowledge with the police, Mrs Jones,' snapped Tom who'd recognised the voice as belonging to the wife of the local butcher.

'Don't think I need to, Doctor,' came the reply. 'They were up there this afternoon – in force, I hear.'

'What does that mean?'

'Let's just wait and see, shall we?' said Freda Jones with a self-satisfied nod of the head as she did up the top button of her coat and sought the support of her companions with sideways glances in both directions.

'Who'd want to kidnap a child . . . well, like that,' said one of the others.

'Doesn't make any sense, if you want my opinion.'

'It's just a matter of time before they find her body. You'll see; there was never any kidnapping.'

'Mind you, when you think about it, it must have been a terrible strain on the pair of them. I mean, you've got to have some sympathy.'

'Nonsense,' insisted Freda Jones. 'The good Lord put that little mite here for a purpose. It's not up to anyone else to question what that purpose might be.'

'I suppose.'

'Maybe you should all just hold your malicious tongues!' exploded Tom, who could remain quiet no longer.

'Well, really,' bridled Freda Jones. 'I don't think there's any call for *that* kind of talk. We're just saying what is perfectly obvious to all of us, with the apparent exception of yourself, Doctor.'

Tom bit his tongue this time and turned his attention back to Ida Marsh to finish his examination. He helped her to her feet. 'No real harm done,' he said. 'I don't think you'll have any more trouble but if you do, give me a call at the surgery.'

'Thank you, Doctor. I'm very grateful to you but I'm sure it was just the fumes in that room,' said Ida Marsh. She said it without any real feeling as if unwilling to alienate her friends by appearing too effusive in her thanks to Tom.

Tom closed up his bag and nodded to the huddle as he left. 'Good afternoon, ladies.'

As he walked back down the harbour steps, smarting with anger at the rumour-mongers, he worried in particular about what the woman Jones had said. She'd made the fact that the police were up at the Palmer house sound very sinister. The sight of Sergeant Walters standing outside his building when he turned the corner did nothing to help matters, the expression on his face was serious and he didn't smile as Tom approached him.

'Have you found her? She's not been harmed, has she?' asked Tom, willing the answer to be positive.

'I'm afraid she's dead, Dr Gordon. We found her this afternoon.'

'Oh God, no.' Tom felt so terribly sad. 'Of all the lousy things to happen. Christ, there are some sick bastards out there. Do you know what happened? Where did you find her?'

'She was found buried in the Palmers' own garden, sir. John Palmer has since confessed to murdering his daughter.'

Tom felt a great weight come down on his shoulders. He looked at Walters, as if there must be some mistake in what he was hearing. 'John confessed to murdering Anne-Marie?' he repeated. 'That's the most ridiculous thing I've ever heard. I simply don't believe it! He *loved* that child. They both did. I just can't believe it. If ever the term "good Christian man" could be applied to anyone, it would be John Palmer.'

Walters said flatly, 'Well, your good Christian man has admitted to murdering his own daughter and burying her body in the garden. That's an end to it, as far as we're concerned.'

'How did he do it?' asked Tom quietly.

'We don't know yet. The forensic people are doing their stuff and the pathologist will carry out the PM this evening.

She was in a bit of a mess, badly decomposed if you know what I mean.'

Tom looked at him questioningly. 'She couldn't have been in the ground for more than three days,' he said.

'Maybe something to do with the weather or the soil conditions,' ventured Walters.

Tom thought the very opposite should apply in the cold conditions they'd been having, but didn't pursue the matter; he didn't have the heart. 'Where's Lucy?' he asked.

'Mrs Palmer collapsed when they found the baby: she's staying with her married sister over in Bangor for the time being.'

'Can I see John?'

'I'm afraid not. He's still undergoing interrogation at the moment with Chief Inspector Davies.'

Tom accepted this with a nod.

'We would value your opinion on John Palmer's state of mind over the past few weeks if you feel able to help us,' said Walters. 'As his GP you're probably the best person to judge that – if you'd seen him at all, of course.'

'His state of mind?' Tom echoed.

'Was he under a lot of stress? Did he appear worried, morose, sleeping badly, that sort of thing.'

Tom shook his head slowly. 'I have seen him on more than one occasion over the last fortnight, as it happens, but socially not professionally. The answer to your question is no, no he didn't. And I still find it impossible to believe that he did what you're saying he did.'

'It's not me saying it, sir. It's him.'

'They both doted on that child – if anything, John more than Lucy.'

The two men looked at each other for a moment before Walters asked the question that now hung in the air. 'Do you think he might have confessed to protect his wife?'

'I don't think I know anything any more,' Tom was sounding subdued. 'I'm sorry to keep saying it, but I just can't believe that either of them could have done this.'

'Maybe their child's deformity had a greater effect on them than you imagined,' suggested Walters. 'I mean, it must have been awful for them. That sort of thing could really get to anyone, make you believe the entire world was against you.'

'Anne-Marie was badly disabled; there's no getting away from that,' agreed Tom, 'but John and Lucy loved their daughter. They weren't pretending. You can't fake something like that.'

'You're quite sure about both of them?'

'Yes,' he said after a moment's thought.

Walters noticed the pause. 'You don't seem . . . *absolutely* sure?' he said.

'I'm sure.'

'Do they know why the baby was born the way she was?' asked Walters.

'Just one of these things. Nobody's fault.'

'Seems like a twist of fate too far, if you ask me,' Walters commented.

'What d'you mean?'

'Them trying for a baby so hard then having that happen to them. It just doesn't seem right. Surely they deserved a bit of a break after all they'd been through.'

Tom nodded. The policeman was right. 'They bloody did.'

'I don't suppose it was connected in any way, was it? I mean, their difficulties in conceiving and the abnormality in the baby?'

'No, not as far as I know.'

'Would you say the outlook for the child was bleak, in

terms of future prospects, education, job and that – quality of life, I think the term is.'

'No, I wouldn't,' said Tom firmly. 'She didn't have legs so it would have meant life in a wheelchair, of course, but many people have happy productive lives despite that.'

'They're the only ones you hear about,' Walters said gloomily.

Tom looked at him.

'A friend of mine from schooldays ended up in a chair after an accident playing rugby. Athletic bloke he was, good at all kinds of sport – first-class sprinter and all that. Wound up topping himself, couldn't take it. It's horses for courses, really. Some people can handle it, some can't.'

'I suppose,' Tom was overcome by a wave of sorrow.

'Right then, I'll be on my way,' said Walters.

Almost on impulse Tom asked, 'Do you think I might be allowed to see the body?'

Walters appeared surprised. 'You'll have to ask the police pathologist about that, Doctor,' he said.

'It's Charles French, isn't it?'

Walters nodded. 'He's probably on his way to the mortuary right now.'

Walters left and Tom changed his mind about going inside. Instead he walked back up the hill to the surgery to get the phone number of the forensic service. He saw by the light under her door that Julie was still there. 'Only me!' he called out, knowing that she would have heard the outside door open. 'Burning the midnight oil?'

'Paperwork,' replied Julie. 'Can't put it off any longer.'

Tom entered the room that had been her father's and found her sifting through a pile of government forms on top of the old mahogany desk. She had decided to keep everything in the room as it had been in her father's day. There was a preponderance of dark wood and leather, and an old brass microscope sat on the windowsill, ornamental rather than practical. 'Where the hell is G49?' she complained.

Tom remained silent and Julie looked up. 'Everything all right?' she asked. Her voice trailed off as she saw that it wasn't. 'What's wrong?'

'The police have found Anne-Marie Palmer. She's dead and John Palmer has confessed to her murder.'

'Oh my God, how awful.'

'Unbelievable,' said Tom, shaking his head. 'I just came in to get the number of the police forensic lab. I want to see the body.'

Julie was surprised. 'Why?' she asked.

Tom had difficulty finding an answer. He felt suddenly desolate. 'It might help me come to terms with what's happened. At the moment it all sounds like some . . . horrible mistake. I won't be able to believe the little lassie is dead until I see her with my own eyes.'

'Did they say how he did it?'

'They don't know yet. I think if he had taken her in his arms and gently smothered her while crying his eyes out, I might be able to accept it, but even then . . . As for anything else? Not John Palmer, no way.'

Julie looked thoughtful for a moment before saying, 'I've got the number here.' She opened a desk drawer and took out a well-thumbed indexed notebook before writing the number down on a Post-it note and handing it to Tom. 'Is there anything else I can do?' she asked.

'You get on with your paperchase and I'll call this number, see if I can view the body and then I'll go over to Bangor and check on Lucy Palmer. She could probably do with some help in the way of more sedation and maybe even a shoulder to cry on.'

'Something tells me there will be a lot of talking and crying in Feli tonight when word gets around,' sighed Julie.

'No more sleepy backwater,' said Tom with a resigned shrug. 'No more the place where nothing ever happens.'

'Do you think the press will have heard by now?'

'If not, they soon will have. It'll be on everyone's breakfast-table come tomorrow morning.'

Julie looked sad. She said, 'This is the kind of story that causes emotions to run riot. Everyone's going to have an opinion.'

'A lot'll depend on how they treat it. If they take a sympathetic line towards the parents we should be okay. If they go for sensation we could be in for a rough ride.'

'"Close-knit community stunned by baby murder",' intoned Julie. '"Baby's death rocks sleepy village". "Father slays crippled child".'

'And, there's not a damn thing we can do about it,' muttered Tom. They parted company and he walked through to his room to call the police forensic service. After saying who he was, he enquired about the whereabouts of Anne-Marie Palmer's body.

'She's lying in Ysbyty Gwynedd in Bangor, Doctor. Dr French is carrying out the post mortem this evening.'

'D'you know when exactly?'

'About now, I should think.'

Tom set the phone to re-route calls to his mobile number and left the surgery to drive the five miles or so to the Ysbyty Gwynedd Hospital in Bangor. The hospital sat high on a hill overlooking the main east-west carriageway across North Wales. There were two police vehicles sitting in the car park so he wasn't surprised when he found several police officers in conversation outside the Pathology Department.

'Has Dr French started?' he asked.

'About five minutes ago.'

Tom went on through to the post mortem suite, knocked and entered without waiting. French looked up from the table, knife in hand. The two plain-clothes officers standing nearby did likewise. 'I'm Tom Gordon, the Palmers' GP in Felinbach. I hoped you wouldn't mind?'

'I suppose not,' said French, although he didn't sound too enthusiastic.

'I think we've met a couple of times before at regional seminars?' prompted Tom.

'Really?' French replied indifferently.

Tom nodded to the other two men in the room. One was Chief Inspector Davies, the other was introduced to him as DI Lawrence.

Tom nodded and said, 'A sad business.'

The policemen grunted without committing themselves. French remained intent on what he was doing. Tom moved closer to the table and couldn't prevent himself from uttering a slight sound of disgust. He immediately felt embarrassed at being so unprofessional.

'She *is* a bit of a mess,' said French coldly.

'What a bastard,' murmured Davies. 'What the hell did he have to do that to her for?'

'I must be missing something,' said Tom. 'She couldn't have decomposed this much in three days.'

'He doused her in acid,' said French. 'Hydrochloric acid, if I'm not mistaken. You can still smell it.'

Tom moved closer to the blackened little body on the table and could smell the acid. 'Right,' he said, wrinkling his nose at the burning sensation in his nostrils. 'Is this going to make it difficult to establish exact cause of death?'

'Well-nigh impossible in the circumstances,' said French. 'Just as well he confessed. Look at her. What a bloody mess.'

'He must have tried to dispose of her using acid and then changed his mind and decided to bury her after all,' said

Davies, his voice suffused with distaste. 'His own kid, for Christ's sake.'

'John Palmer didn't do this,' said Tom, still staring at the body. 'I know the man. He just couldn't do anything like this.'

'If I had a pound for every time I've heard that, I'd be a very rich man,' said Davies.

'But hydrochloric acid . . .'

'He's a science teacher. It wouldn't exactly be difficult for him to get hold of it,' Davies grunted. 'The old marble chips experiment, if I remember rightly.'

French stood back from the table and said, 'Frankly, I don't think I'm going to be able to do too much more with this one, Alan. She's been too badly damaged by the acid.'

'Jesus,' the Chief Inspector said in a low whisper. 'Not to worry. Maybe the bastard'll be kind enough to tell us how he topped her in the first place.'

'If he did . . .' added French.

Tom thought for a fleeting moment that French might have had some reason for doubting Palmer's guilt but then he realised with horror that he meant something else entirely.

Davies picked up on it. 'You're not suggesting that the acid was the *cause* of death, are you, Doctor?'

French held up his palms. 'I was just being pedantic as befits my profession,' he said. 'But as we don't actually *know* the cause of death then, as it stands . . .'

'For Christ's sake, there is no way on earth that John Palmer would immerse his own child in acid under any circumstances, and certainly not while she was alive!' Tom said angrily.

Davies and Lawrence didn't respond but their silence was distressingly eloquent.

~ *Four* ~

Dr Tom Gordon left the PM room, drawing in deep breaths of fresh air to rid himself of the smell of death and formalin fixative: he felt totally confused. Although there was still no way he could bring himself to believe that John Palmer had murdered Anne-Marie, despite his confession, he did face the enormous stumbling block of trying to imagine just who had. If he ruled out Lucy Palmer – and he did – he was left with a scenario where the baby had been kidnapped by a stranger, murdered by that stranger and then returned to the Palmers' own back garden for burial, and this after an abortive attempt to dissolve her remains in acid. It just didn't make any sense but he could at least understand why the police had difficulty in considering it as a realistic possibility. He got into the Land Rover and drove over to see Lucy.

Lucy Palmer's sister lived in a small terraced house in Sackville Street, a narrow street tucked away behind the University of North Wales's main science library in Bangor. Parking was difficult round there so he decided to take a chance and use the university car park, despite dire warnings to non-permit-holders displayed at the entrance. It was after all, Saturday evening and he couldn't imagine there being too many academics around.

His firm knock on the bottle-green door was answered by

an attractive woman in her mid-thirties with a tea towel thrown casually over one shoulder.

'If it's double glazing we're not interested,' she said briskly.

'I'm Tom Gordon, Lucy's GP. I thought I might be able to help,' said Tom.

'Oh, I am sorry,' said the woman, apologising with a smile. 'It's good of you to come. I'm Gina Melford, Lucy's sister.'

Tom was ushered into a room facing the back of the house where he found Lucy sitting on a couch with her shoulders hunched and her arms folded tightly. A box of Kleenex tissues sat at her side and an untouched cup of tea lay on the table in front of her. She was staring at it distantly rather than drinking it. She looked up when she heard him come in and he saw the pain in her red-rimmed eyes.

'Lucy, I can't begin to tell you how sorry I am,' said Tom. 'This is an absolute nightmare.'

'The whole world's gone mad, Tom,' said Lucy in a low voice. 'I just don't know what's happening any more. One moment we were building a snowman in the garden and the next our life was in ruins.'

The doctor was alarmed at how frail Lucy appeared. Her normal air of self-confidence had disappeared and her body language of crossed arms and bowed head suggested defeat. Her blonde hair hung limply about her face and her cheeks seemed pale and drawn. He sat down beside her; placing his bag at his feet and putting his arm round her shoulders. 'Quite unbelievable,' he said.

'John didn't kill Anne-Marie, you must know that,' she whispered.

'Of course I know that,' said Tom, 'but for whatever reason, he's made a confession and that complicates things. I just don't understand it. Have you any idea why he did it?'

Lucy leaned forward and looked resolutely at the floor, still cradling her head with both hands. She had difficulty getting the words out, but in the end she mumbled, 'He must think I did it.'

Tom let a few moments go by before asking softly, 'Why should he think that, Lucy?'

'Sometimes I get low; I get depressed. I try to be positive like John but it's not always easy. I'm not as strong as he is. He's a natural optimist and I'm not. I see the black side of things all too clearly. I hadn't been feeling very well the day before it happened; I was very low. John must think I killed Anne-Marie while he was out in the garden working on the snowman.'

'But you didn't?'

'No, of course not!' said Lucy decisively. 'As I said, I *do* get depressed and I *did* have moments of despair when I couldn't see a future for her and thought – maybe even said, that she'd be better off dead – but I never really meant it. I loved her; I loved her very much. You have to believe that! Oh Tom, what kind of a person would do something like this?'

He shook his head. 'I don't know, Lucy. That's what we, or rather the police, have to find out.'

'Have you seen John?'

'They wouldn't let me. They're holding him at Caernarfon: he'll appear in court on Monday morning.'

'I want to be there,' said Lucy, becoming animated. 'I have to tell them that he's lying; that he's just trying to protect me. John couldn't kill anyone. He even opens the windows to let out flies.'

'I don't think going up to court's a very good idea,' said Tom. 'That would be the wrong way to go about things.

It's really the police we have to convince in the first instance and then, when John realises that you had nothing to do with Anne-Marie's death, he can retract his confession and the police can begin a proper investigation. Just as a matter of interest, what *were* you doing while John was outside building the snowman?'

'I put Anne-Marie down for a sleep and than I went to look through the wardrobes for clothes for Captain Mainwaring.'

'Who?'

'Captain Mainwaring – the snowman John built.'

'How long did that take you?'

'Half an hour or so.'

'Why so long?'

'I got side-tracked,' said Lucy. 'I'd been having a good old rake and found things in the wardrobe that I hadn't seen for years. I tried some of them on just to see if I could still get into them. John was happy in the garden – I could hear him whistling and Anne-Marie was sleeping, so . . . it was fun. A trip down Memory Lane, if you like.'

Lucy construed Tom's ensuing silence as an accusation. He was in fact wondering how the police would view the thirty-minute period she was in the house alone with the baby while John was out in the garden.

'I didn't do it,' insisted Lucy. 'Oh God, this is all just too awful to bear.' She broke down in tears and Gina did her best to soothe her.

'I believe you, Lucy,' said Tom. 'But we have to be honest with each other. I have to know everything if I'm to be able to help. That's why I have to ask you if you were still having one of your low spells on the day Anne-Marie disappeared. *Were* you depressed on that day?'

'No,' insisted Lucy. 'Like I told you, I'd been a bit down the day before, but I was definitely coming out of it and John was cheering me up with talk of the fun we were going to have when the weather got better. We were going to take Anne-Marie to the beach, the zoo . . . all sorts of things.' Tears were trickling down her face.

Tom nodded then opened up his bag. 'I'm going to give you something to help you sleep,' he said. 'You must get some rest. You'll be no good to John or anyone if you're completely exhausted.'

He gave Lucy a sedative and watched her take it before Gina escorted her off to bed.

'Tea?' asked Gina when she came back.

'Please.'

'What's going to happen?' Gina asked as she returned from the kitchen with a tea tray and laid it down on the coffee-table.

Tom looked at her and saw that her expression had become troubled. She'd been masking it well in Lucy's presence but now the worry was all too evident.

'I'm not sure,' he replied honestly. 'The real problem is the confession. It's stopping the police from even looking for anyone else and frankly, I think they'll be quite happy about that because if John and Lucy didn't do it, it's not easy to imagine who did. And what was their motive in taking the body back to bury it in the garden?'

'That's more or less what my husband was saying,' confided Gina uneasily. 'I think he thinks . . .' Her voice trailed off.

'What does he think?' prompted Tom quietly.

'That Lucy did it,' said Gina. She got the words out quickly as if they were unpleasant medicine she didn't want to have in her mouth.

'What makes him think that?'

'Like you say, the fact that he simply couldn't imagine who else would have done it, and also because he remembers what Lucy was like just after Anne-Marie was born, when she didn't want to know about the baby's problems and insisted the nurses take her away. Men don't understand post-natal depression: I had it myself after Luke was born. It's an illness but you can't explain that to outsiders. They think that's the way you really are but you're not, it's the illness talking. Lucy recovered from it just like I did. True, she got a bit down from time to time — who wouldn't in the circumstances — but she loved Anne-Marie. We all did.'

'Good, you obviously don't believe she's capable of having killed her either,' said Tom.

'No,' Gina said. '*Nothing* would make her do something like that.'

'But that still leaves the problem of who did and why?' said Tom.

Tom managed to get a meeting with Chief Inspector Davies at ten the following morning. When he told him his thoughts about the Palmers, to his surprise and annoyance, Davies seemed singularly unimpressed. He listened throughout with a cynical smile playing round the corners of his mouth. It was almost as if he'd heard it all before. When Tom had finished he asked, 'In the great scheme of things, Doctor, does it really matter?'

'Matter?' Tom was unsure of Davies's meaning.

'Which one of them did it,' the policeman explained.

'But neither of them did it!' Tom burst out.

Davies shrugged in polite incredulity. 'Now *that*,' he said, 'I find impossible to believe.'

'The Palmers loved their child.' Tom felt as though he had encountered a brick wall. 'They couldn't have murdered her.'

'Murder is such an emotive word,' said the Chief Inspector, leaning back in his chair like a don about to lecture a student. 'Maybe it's the wrong one to use in this instance. Mercy killing? Euthanasia? Cruel to be kind? Take your pick. I can even accept that their motives were honourable if misguided, but in my book they still killed that child and it will be up to the lawyers to decide what they want to call it. After that, it will be a matter for the courts as to how much sympathy and understanding they care to dispense.'

'They didn't do it,' insisted Tom.

Davies began to lose patience. 'May I just remind you that one of them has already confessed to the crime!' he rasped. 'And if he didn't really do it, then it's only because he believes his wife *did*! You must be the only person in the world who thinks that neither of them had anything to do with it! If you can come up with one single reason why anyone should break into the Palmers' house, steal their deformed child, kill it and then come back and bury it in their back garden, let me know. In the meantime I've got work to do.'

'Can I see John Palmer?'

'No.'

Tom Gordon left the police station feeling frustrated and angry, all the more so because he could understand the police point of view. It was the common-sense one. It was the one most people were going to go for.

John Palmer was due to appear in court first thing on Thursday morning. Tom was naïve enough to believe that he could drive up to Caernarfon and attend the preliminary hearing, and later on get the chance to have a quick word with John and assure him that Lucy had not killed Anne-Marie. He told Julie Rees of his plan and found her less than enthusiastic.

'Don't you think you're taking concern for John Palmer a little far?' she asked. 'I'm sure the police and the lawyers are the best people to sort everything out. We really shouldn't be seen to be taking sides.'

'They're friends of mine but it's not a question of taking sides,' insisted Tom. 'I just want to see justice done and I have the feeling that the police are more interested in securing a quick conviction than in investigating any alternative possibility.'

'John Palmer confessed to the crime of his own volition,' Julie pointed out. 'You can hardly accuse the police of fitting him up or even of exerting undue pressure on the guy.'

'People confess to things for a whole variety of reasons,' said Tom. 'Not all of them connected with guilt.' It sounded weak and he knew it. He could see that Julie was far from convinced.

'I don't think you should go,' she said.

'I'll be as quick as I can,' said Tom.

As it turned out, he couldn't get anywhere near the court when he arrived in Caernarfon. The narrow street leading down the side of the castle to the court building was full of angry people. He made a left turn the other way and parked by the harbour on the far side of the castle. When he hurried back up the hill, he discovered that it was John Palmer they were angry about.

'Murdering bastard!' shouted one man to cries of encouragement from a group of women nearby.

'They should bring back hanging, poor mite!'

'Hanging's too good for the bastard!'

A white police van escorted by two motorcycle outriders edged its way slowly through the throng. Fists pounded at its sides and more obscenities were shouted. Tom could only look on in horror. Who were these people? Where had they come from? Surely they weren't local? They looked like a mob borrowed from a film set of the French Revolution, a bloodthirsty rabble egging each other on. Their cries even competed with those of the seagulls as they wheeled round the towers of the castle, waiting to swoop down on the litter they knew a crowd must leave.

Feeling queasy, Tom Gordon turned his back on the awful scene and went in search of a newsagent. He didn't actually have to buy a paper to discover the fuel that had fired the crowd. An advertising board outside the shop announced: *Father slays three-month-old baby. Police in grisly find.* He went in and bought a selection of papers to take back to his car down by the harbour.

The clunk of the car door reduced the noise of the crowd but the scream of the headlines was almost as disturbing. *Teacher slays crippled child . . . Police find baby in shallow grave . . . Father confesses at child's graveside.*

Tom had to concede that he had little or no chance of getting into the courtroom so he drove slowly back to Felinbach, still haunted by the faces he'd seen in the crowd, their features distorted by hatred, their mouths bawling threats. Why? he wondered. There couldn't have been a personal element to it, so where had all that hatred come from? These people knew nothing of the circumstances of the case, only what they'd read in the morning papers, yet that had been enough for them to make a snap judgement and parade their second-hand emotion outside the courtroom. As he reached the outskirts of the village he concluded that the whys and wherefores must lie in the province of the psychiatrist, but he wasn't sure he wanted to know any more.

Tom thought he detected a coolness among several patients attending morning surgery. It couldn't be construed as rudeness, more a change from friendliness to distant politeness. He mentioned this to Julie when they had coffee together after surgery was over.

'It's this Palmer baby thing,' she said immediately.

'What about it?'

'I tried to warn you earlier; the villagers have got it into their heads that you are sympathetic to the Palmers. That you're on their side.'

'I am,' said Tom forcibly.

'Exactly,' said Julie. 'Everyone else thinks they're guilty.'

'Including you?'

She shrugged, aware that the Palmer affair was starting to drive a wedge between them. 'I suppose I think the evidence and the fact that one of them has confessed, tends to point that way,' she said, narrowly avoiding a note of sarcasm. 'I also can't begin to understand why anyone else would have done it.'

Tom let out a long sigh. 'I don't either, but that doesn't mean to say that the Palmers are guilty. It just means that we don't know who or why at the moment.'

'But he confessed,' protested Julie. 'You seem to keep ignoring that.'

Tom rubbed his forehead in frustration. 'I'm *not* ignoring it,' he said in a tightly controlled way. 'But after talking to Lucy and giving the matter a lot of thought, I'm sure John confessed to protect his wife.'

'You mean *she* did it?'

'No, no!' Tom was becoming agitated. 'But he *thinks* she did. It's all a misunderstanding. Neither of them did it.'

'That's what you think,' said Julie. She made it sound like an accusation.

'It is what I believe, yes,' he agreed.

Julie looked at him long and hard. 'You will have to accept that if one of the Palmers actually thinks that the other one did it, the villagers can be excused for thinking much the same thing. I don't suppose they care too much which one of them it was but they are convinced it was them.'

'Well, it wasn't,' said Tom strongly. 'Now they're being told what to think by the tabloid press. Have you seen this stuff?' He picked up the papers he'd brought in with him. 'They were a loving family, for Christ's sake! John Palmer is one of the kindest, gentlest people I know, and this lot are suggesting he's Dr bloody Mengele!'

'I saw some of it earlier,' said Julie. 'The confession is the problem. It's given them free rein to go for the jugular.' She sighed. 'If you'll take my advice, you'll stand back from it a little. You've made a lot of friends since you came here, Tom. I'd hate to see you lose them over this.'

'Thanks for the warning.'

There was a short uncomfortable silence in the room while both of them reflected that they were not going to agree about this.

~ *Five* ~

The funeral parlour of J. Prosser & Son had stood in Mould Street, Caernarfon for more than seventy-five years, its black-painted frontage and discreet gold lettering boasting its credentials for *Care and Concern in Times of Bereavement*. It was the sort of place where local people tended to hush their voices in passing, intimidated by the open Bible lying in the window on a cushion of maroon velvet in front of matching, heavy curtains. Young children might ask what lay behind the curtains but were seldom graced with an answer. If they were, they were told that it didn't concern them; it was nothing for them to worry their little heads over.

It was therefore something quite out of the ordinary when John Prosser was woken up in the flat above the parlour at seven in the morning by someone hammering on the front door and demanding that he open up shop.

Wrapping his plaid dressing gown around him and hastily perching his half-moon specs on his nose, he hurried downstairs to tiptoe through the cold gloom of a March morning and open the door. A thickset man in his late twenties with dark curly hair and an anguished expression stood there. His breath smelt of whisky and the bags under his eyes spoke of a lack of sleep.

'Martin Griffiths?' exclaimed Prosser. 'What are you doing here, man?'

'You're burying my girl today, Prosser,' said Griffiths, his speech a little slurred but his gaze steady enough.

'And right sorry I am too,' replied Prosser.

'I want her to have my mother's ring in the box with her, see.' Griffiths brought out a small, scuffed, blue leather ring-box from his jacket pocket and waved it in front of Prosser's face.

Prosser frowned then said kindly, 'It's a bit late for that, man, the casket's been closed. We're all ready for the funeral this morning. Look, you're upset and who wouldn't be after losing their baby? Come in, man, we'll have some tea and I'll call your wife and tell her you're here.'

'Don't want no tea,' insisted Griffiths, shrugging off Prosser's attempt to take his arm. 'I want my baby to have this ring with her. I need her to know I cared. I wasn't there when she died, see. I was on the Cornwall run — away for three days, I was.'

Prosser nodded. He knew Griffiths was a long-distance lorry driver and that he'd been away when his baby daughter had fallen victim to cot death syndrome.

'Christ, if only I'd been there,' continued Griffiths, his voice breaking. 'I might have heard her cry out in the night. I could have picked her up and cuddled her . . . told her her daddy was there and there was nothing to worry about. But I wasn't, was I? I was hundreds of miles away and she just slipped away in the night, crept out of our house, she did, out of our lives.'

Prosser felt a lump come to his throat. He'd seen a lot of grief in his time and become hardened to it behind a sombre professional front, but there was something raw and undiluted about Griffiths's pain that got to him. 'Come inside anyway,' he said gruffly. 'It's cold.'

Prosser led the way through the partitioned interior of the parlour to a small dark office, equipped with only a desk and three chairs. This was where he consulted the newly bereaved over their choice of funeral 'accessories'. A large, spiral-bound book lay on the desk with illustrations of coffins and their furnishings. Prosser pushed it to one side with the palm of his hand and rested both arms on the desk. 'Look, man,' he said. 'I know you mean to do what's for the best but you're so full of grief that you're not thinking straight.'

Griffiths put the ring-box on the desk and opened it clumsily with thick callused fingers to reveal an old engagement ring: it was an emerald mounted in a cluster of small diamonds. 'It was my grandmother's and then my mother's: she told me to give it to my lass when she got married but she's not getting married, not now, not ever, so if you'll just open up the box I'll give it to her now.'

Prosser moved uncomfortably in his chair. 'I don't think you should do this, Martin,' he said. 'It's better you should remember your little lass as she was, not as . . .' Prosser's voice trailed off.

Griffiths frowned. 'What the hell are you on about?' he demanded.

Prosser wrung his hands in discomfort. 'People working in medical science have to find out just how and why awful things like Megan's death happen,' he began. 'If the doctors are to have any hope of stopping other people going through what you're going through, they have to investigate things . . . thoroughly.'

'What are you trying to say, Prosser?' demanded Griffiths, now becoming suspicious about the undertaker's obvious agitation.

Prosser wriggled in his seat again before saying, 'The

pathologists at the hospital had to carry out certain examinations on Megan . . .'

Griffiths's eyes opened wide. 'Are you telling me they damaged my Megan?' he asked in a low, harsh whisper.

'A post-mortem examination has to be done in such cases,' replied Prosser quietly. 'It's the law, see, and a certain amount of . . . damage, as you put it, is inevitable.' In truth he wasn't sure what the case was with Megan Griffiths. He hadn't collected the body personally so he hadn't seen it. It was usual for the people at the hospital to make the body as presentable as possible after PM examination but on the other hand, viewing of the body was usually carried out at the hospital chapel, aided by suitable drapings and a glass partition screen.

'I want her to have my mother's ring,' said Griffiths, digging in his heels.

Prosser could see that further argument would be pointless. Griffiths had clearly made up his mind and his overwhelming sense of grief and guilt was preventing him from hearing any rational argument. 'All right,' he said resignedly. 'If that's what you really want, she's lying downstairs.'

Still in his dressing gown and slippers, Prosser led the way through to the back of the premises, a cold room with a large barred window letting in the early morning light above a big, crazed porcelain sink where a velvet cloth lay steeping in stagnant water. He clicked on a light switch to the right of the one, dark-panelled door in the room before opening it up to reveal an archway leading to cellar stairs. Prosser descended in slippered silence; Griffiths's heavy shoes clattered slowly and irregularly behind him on the wooden treads.

The small white coffin containing Megan Griffiths's body lay on a wooden bench with a white record card carrying her name and funeral details temporarily Sello-taped to the lid.

'I urge you to change your mind, man,' said Prosser, making a last attempt at trying to dissuade Griffiths. 'You and your wife are young. There will be other babies.'

'Open it.'

Prosser shrugged and took down a red-handled ratchet screwdriver from its clip on the wall above the bench. He started undoing the lid. The tortured noise of the screws turning seemed unnaturally loud in the early morning quiet. It was easy for Prosser to construe this as a kind of protest. He lingered over the last one, still hoping that Griffiths might change his mind at the last moment, but the bereaved father said nothing, his features set like granite. Prosser removed the last screw and placed it in line with the others before sliding off the lid and deliberately angling his body so that he was standing between Griffiths and the open coffin. He hoped this might give him the chance to take a quick look inside and perhaps even make a slight cosmetic adjustment if required before Griffiths had his turn.

There was an interval of less than five seconds before Prosser staggered backwards and dropped the lid on the floor with a clatter, his face filled with shock and horror. He let out a whispered, involuntary expletive and half-turned to the side as if unwilling to accept the sight that had met his eyes.

Bemused by Prosser's reaction, Griffiths looked first at the undertaker and then at the coffin before stepping forward in trepidation to look inside for himself. 'Sweet Jesus fucking Christ!' he exclaimed, before gagging twice and throwing up on the floor. He sought the support of the cellar wall with his outstretched right arm.

Prosser recovered his composure first, although still badly

shaken and having difficulty getting his breathing pattern to settle. The smell of Griffiths's whisky-tainted vomit on the floor wasn't helping. 'There's been some terrible mistake,' he said, his voice hoarse and rapid. 'I'll get on to the hospital right away.'

Griffiths, wearing the expression of a man who'd just been afforded a vision of hell, looked at him distantly. 'That's right, boyo,' he murmured. 'A terrible mistake. You get on to that fucking hospital.'

By nine a.m., Prosser had established that the coffin had already been closed and screwed down when his driver had gone to collect it from the hospital so he had not seen the contents. Next to deny any knowledge of the problem was the mortuary technician at the hospital, who told Prosser that he personally had not been on duty the previous day and that the man who had was off today. By nine-fifteen Prosser had succeeded in getting through to hospital management and finally had the ear of a man who realised just how serious the complaint was and what the repercussions might be.

'What exactly did you say was in the coffin?' asked Ronald Harcourt, Hospital Manager at Caernarfon General.

'Bits,' replied Prosser, acknowledging the inadequacy of his description but failing to come up with an alternative.

'What d'you mean, bits?'

'Dismembered remains.'

'Are you telling me that the child's body had been dismembered?' asked Harcourt, his voice rising with incredulity.

'No, no . . . there *was* no child's body,' spluttered Prosser angrily. 'Just bits, assorted human bits – lungs, kidneys, a heart maybe, and I saw a finger among the mess.'

'Bloody hell,' exclaimed Harcourt, suddenly getting the picture. 'Have you spoken to anyone in Pathology yet?'

'Just a mortuary technician; said he wasn't on duty yesterday. No one else was in when I called.'

'I'll get on to them right away and get back to you. Give me your number.'

Prosser gave him the number and added, 'The child's funeral is at eleven. We need the body.'

'Do the parents know about this?'

'The father was present when I opened the box.'

'Oh my God, worse and worse,' gasped Harcourt. 'Something tells me we're in big trouble over this one.'

'You speak for yourself,' said Prosser. 'It's nothing to do with me. My driver collected the coffin in good faith, and remember . . . the funeral's at eleven.'

A frantic search of the mortuary fridge failed to come up with the body of Megan Griffiths. Harcourt stood beside Consultant Pathologist Peter Sepp, becoming more and more agitated as he watched the proceedings. 'What the hell am I going to tell the parents?' he demanded in an angry whisper.

Sepp's expression was cast in stone. 'There's only one explanation,' he said, as the head technician closed the fridge doors and gave a final shake of the head. 'The child's body must have got mixed up with the biological waste bag.'

Harcourt looked at him as if he couldn't believe his ears. 'The biological waste bag?' he repeated slowly.

'The bits we don't need when we're finished with them,' said Sepp. 'They go into a biological waste bag for disposal along with clinical refuse from the theatres.'

Harcourt gave himself a few moments to let nightmare images dissipate before asking, 'Can't you recover the child from the bag then?'

Sepp shook his head and looked at Harcourt directly. 'I'm afraid not,' he said. 'It gets taken to the incinerator every night.'

Harcourt felt himself go weak at the knees, as the full implication of what he was hearing became apparent. 'Let me get this straight,' he said. 'You're telling me that pathological . . . offal was put into Megan Griffiths's coffin while her body was sent to the hospital incinerator in a biological waste bag?'

'That's what it looks like,' agreed Sepp reluctantly.

'Jesus Christ! How in God's name could something like that happen?' demanded Harcourt in a barely controlled whisper in deference to the fact that several of Sepp's technical staff were still within earshot.

A shake of the head from Sepp. 'I really don't know,' he said.

'Christ, the lawyers will be gathering like hyenas round a dead mammoth when they hear this,' said Harcourt. 'Find out who's responsible. Blame has to be apportioned and *seen* to be apportioned, otherwise we'll all be tarred with the same brush.'

'You'll tell the parents?' asked Sepp.

'I can't imagine a queue forming to compete for the privilege,' said Harcourt sourly.

Just then, his pager went off and he picked up the phone mounted on the tiled mortuary wall. His expression suggested he wasn't hearing good news. 'Tell them we'll issue a statement in due course,' he snapped before slamming the phone back on its hook. 'It's started,' he complained. 'The father must have been on to the papers already. The *Bangor Times* wants to know if the rumours are true: have we really lost a baby's body? God, it'll be TV and the nationals by lunchtime and something tells me they're going to think losing the body would actually have been preferable to the truth when they find out.'

'They'll lap it up,' said Sepp. 'They'll see it as a good human-interest story and milk it for all it's worth. Tears make good television.'

'We'd better have a meeting and agree on what we're going to say,' said Harcourt. 'Damage limitation is the name of the game.'

'I'll call my staff together and see if I can find out what really happened.'

'We need names,' insisted Harcourt. 'We must identify the culprit or culprits and be seen to act firmly and decisively. Those responsible must be sacked without delay.'

'But it must have been a genuine mistake,' insisted Sepp. 'No one would want something like this to happen. The guilty party will be just as devastated as the parents, I'm sure.'

'Won't do,' snapped Harcourt. 'The press will need a human sacrifice, nothing less will do. They must be sacked.'

'And their heads mounted on the hospital gates,' added Sepp sarcastically.

'And as it's your department . . .' continued Harcourt icily.

The pathologist's expression changed. 'You think I should offer my resignation?'

'In the circumstances, I think it might be the honourable thing to do, don't you?'

'Honourable?' mused Sepp. 'Where's the honour in feeding a media circus? They wouldn't know honour, or even common decency come to that, if it kicked them up the arse.'

'That's as may be,' said Harcourt, 'but we have to play

the game over this one, present a solid front. The hospital's good name is at stake. I want to be able to tell the Hospital Trust exactly what happened and what's been done about it. That means finding out who's responsible and getting rid of them whatever the extenuating circumstances.'

'And me?'

'Offer your resignation for the benefit of the press and we'll decline it when the flak dies down.'

Sepp looked at his watch and said, 'Time's getting on. You'd better tell the parents there isn't going to be a funeral.'

'I'll phone them from my office,' said Harcourt, making to leave.

'Maybe not such a good idea,' said Sepp thoughtfully.

'What d'you mean?'

'If we're into playing the media game, a phone call might be seen as callous. You wouldn't want that.'

'Maybe you're right,' agreed Harcourt. 'I'll drive over there myself and tell them personally. I'll get the address from Prosser.'

Pathology Department 1 p.m.

'So that's it?' rasped Harcourt. 'A monumental fuck-up and no one's to blame? Just what do I tell the Medical Superintendent and the Hospital Trust, and what do I tell the tabloid scavengers baying at the gates? "Just one of those things, folks"?'

Sepp shrugged his shoulders uncomfortably. 'I've talked to all my staff and none of them can throw any light on this. I'm sorry but that's the way it is at the moment.'

'Then somebody's lying,' Harcourt said in exasperation. 'What about the mortuary technician who's off today?'

'I called him at home; he doesn't know anything either.'

Harcourt sighed in frustration. 'Somebody must know

something. Have you gone through everything in chrono-logical order from the time of the post mortem on the missing child?'

'Of course.'

'And?'

'And nothing. No one admits to having put the child's body — or what he *thought* was the child's body — in the coffin.'

Harcourt shook his head. 'Who took the waste over to the incinerator then?' he asked.

'No one admits to that either. A thought that B had done it while B thought that A had done it and it turns out that neither of them did.'

'Jesus! You do realise that the press are going to crucify us over a Pathology Department where nobody knows what anyone else is doing. It's clear that someone on your staff knows more about this than he or she's letting on.'

Sepp bristled. 'Or maybe it wasn't someone on my staff at all,' he snapped.

'What d'you mean?'

'I'm simply pointing out that we don't know for sure that one of my people was responsible.'

Harcourt looked openly incredulous. 'You're surely not suggesting that someone walked in off the street and did it for a laugh, are you?'

Sepp tried manfully to keep his anger in check. He spoke more slowly. 'The fact of the matter is,' he asserted, 'that people are in and out of the Path Department all day long. You must know that. I'm simply saying that it is not inconceivable that someone other than a member of my staff caused the mix-up.'

'You've no security?'

'It's a mortuary not a bloody bank,' snapped Sepp, finally losing patience with Harcourt's aggressiveness.

'All right, all right,' said Harcourt, suddenly realising he was pushing Sepp too far. He made an open-palmed gesture with his hands. 'Let's not start fighting among ourselves, but if it *was* someone from outside your own staff, that would surely imply malicious intent rather than an innocent mix-up, wouldn't it?'

'I suppose it might,' agreed Sepp.

'Hard to believe.'

Medical Superintendent's Office 2 p.m.

'I suppose the parents took it badly?' said James Trool, Medical Superintendent of the hospital as he poured chilled water from a carafe into the crystal glass on the table in front of him. He was an undistinguished-looking man, large but with coarse features and a penchant for wearing light-coloured suits and brightly coloured ties – a trait that had only surfaced when he'd married his second wife, Sonia, some two years before. It was a marriage that had surprised many because Sonia, an American, was almost twenty years younger than he was, beautiful and very wealthy in her own right. They had met when her daughter was admitted to the hospital after a bad car crash, the same crash that had killed her first husband.

'You could say,' replied Harcourt, fiddling with his cuff links and severely editing his answer. 'The father called me an oily little bastard and assured me we wouldn't be getting away with it, as he put it. He promised we'd be hearing from his lawyers.'

'Par for the course,' said Trool, with a hint of bitterness in his voice. He leaned forward and put his elbows on the table. 'You know, I can remember a time when people faced up to the slings and arrows of outrageous fortune without the need for *counselling*, or whatever they call it, and large injections of *compensation*.' He endowed the words with extreme distaste.

'I wouldn't mention that to the press if I were you,' said Harcourt.

'Of course not,' said Trool. 'Our deepest sympathy will be extended to the family. Our hearts will go out to them . . . in an effort to minimise the damage their bloody lawyers are about to do to us.'

'With respect, Dr Trool, I think you're being a bit harsh. It was a terrible thing to have happen to them.' The speaker was a slight woman in her late thirties: she was Inga Love, Director of Nursing Services.

'Indeed it was, Miss Love, but it was an *accident*. No one meant it to happen. To use it as the basis for screwing money out of the hospital is damn nearly criminal in my book.'

'Something tells me the Griffiths are not going to see it that way,' said Harcourt.

'Of course they're not,' snapped Trool. '"*We have been to hell and back*",' he mimicked. '"*We don't want anyone to go through what we have experienced. It's not the money that's important, it's the principle.*" Yuugh! Makes me want to throw up.'

'It can't be easy to have something that awful happen to your child, Dr Trool,' lectured Inga Love.

Trool grunted.

'If I can just remind you,' interrupted Harcourt, 'I have to brief the press in fifteen minutes. Perhaps we could agree on our approach.'

'The usual,' said Trool. 'Damage limitation. Thoughts with the family at this time, all our sympathy goes out to them. Tragic error, no excuses, a momentary lapse in a busy department, full investigation under way. Steps have been taken to ensure it never happens again, that sort of thing.'

~ Six ~

Any difficulty Tom Gordon and Julie Rees were having in making conversation was resolved on Saturday morning when they both arrived at the surgery carrying copies of the local morning paper.

'Have you seen it?' asked Julie.

'I could hardly miss it,' replied Tom, opening his paper to reveal the headline *Hospital Loses Baby's Body! My Agony by Grief-stricken Mother*.

'It was the cot-death baby in Caernarfon,' said Julie. 'What a thing to happen to the parents on top of everything else.'

'Whose patient?' asked Tom.

'Jenkins,' replied Julie, giving the name of a Caernarfon GP.

'I got the impression that they still hadn't managed to find the baby's body when this went to press,' said Tom.

'I didn't pick up on that,' said Julie, 'but surely they did. I mean, you can't actually lose a body in a hospital.'

'You'd think not.'

Julie came through to Tom's room after morning surgery was over. He could tell by the expression on her face that something was seriously wrong.

'You were right about them not having found the baby,' she said. 'I've just had a phone call from James

Trool, the Medical Superintendent at Caernarfon General. They think the missing baby was sent to the hospital incinerator by mistake: they managed to keep that bit out of the papers.'

'God Almighty.' Tom was aghast. 'How could that happen?'

'Some screw-up in Pathology. The baby must have got mixed up with a biological waste bag.'

'Jesus,' said Tom. 'Someone'll pick up their jotters for that.'

Julie smiled at the young man, who was suddenly sounding very Scottish. 'They still don't know the full facts yet,' she said. 'The discovery was made when an undertaker opened up the coffin for some reason. If it hadn't been for that, no one would have been any the wiser.'

'Makes you wonder if that might not have been better, given the circumstances,' said Tom.

'Absolutely,' Julie agreed. 'But it gets worse. The baby's father was present when the coffin was opened.'

Tom rolled his eyes and let out his breath in a long low whistle. 'What a nightmare.'

'Trool says that an immediate internal enquiry has failed to uncover the reason for the mix-up so he wants to set up an informal *ad hoc* external enquiry as quickly as possible. He was wondering if one of us would serve on it.'

'Informal?' said Tom. 'Sounds like a PR move to me. If an internal investigation didn't come up with anything, what reason is there to believe that a bunch of strangers would do any better?'

'I think they're desperate to show that they're doing everything possible to find out what happened,' said Julie.

'I'm not surprised,' said Tom. 'This is exactly the kind of story that the press are going to make a meal of.'

'Another one,' Julie added meaningfully. Tom knew she

was referring to the Palmer baby but he let it go for the moment.

'They'll whip up public opinion against the hospital until the truth of the affair no longer matters to anyone,' he said, making it clear with a look that the latter part of his comment was meant for her.

In turn, Julie let that go. 'Would you be prepared to sit on the enquiry?' she asked.

'If you like,' said Tom. 'What do I have to do?'

'They're going to hold a preliminary meeting at the hospital tonight if everyone concerned agrees; it's to be at seven-thirty. James Trool will give a background talk and establish terms of reference for the committee.'

'I'll be there,' Tom promised.

'Thanks,' said Julie. 'I'd go myself but it's Owen's tenth birthday and I promised I'd take him out.'

'No problem,' Tom told her. 'But I'd like to take Monday afternoon off. I've got an appointment to see John Palmer's lawyer in Bangor. I'll be back for evening surgery.'

'Of course,' said Julie without further comment, but the coldness in her voice was evident. She looked at her watch. 'Time we were out and about or they'll think we've stopped doing house calls altogether.'

'I wish.'

Tom went out on his rounds, calling last at Lucy's sister's house in Bangor to see how she was bearing up. 'How is she?' he asked when Gina opened the door to him.

Gina shrugged her shoulders and said quietly so that she wouldn't be overheard, 'I thought she was much better this morning so we went shopping. Some stupid woman made a comment in the check-out queue at the supermarket and that was that. We had to come straight back.'

'I think there might be quite a lot of that, judging by what I saw in Caernarfon,' said Tom.

'I saw pictures on the news,' said Gina. 'Lucy was devastated. She'd been thinking about going back home.'

Tom screwed up his face and said, 'It would do her more good to get away from here completely for a little while. Do you have any other relatives who might put her up for the time being?'

'She wouldn't go.' Gina shook her head. 'She wants to be near John.'

'What exactly did the woman in the supermarket say?'

'She said to her friend, "That's the murdering bastard's wife".'

Apart from Dr Tom Gordon, the independent enquiry team was to comprise two staff doctors from Ysbyty Gwynedd in Bangor, Caernarfon's Director of Public Health, Dr Liam Swanson, Lady Arabella Paget, patron of the Anglesey-based medical charity Med-Menai, and Christine Williams, a JP from Bangor. They were welcomed individually by James Trool as they arrived and offered coffee.

'Thank you for coming,' said Trool, raising his voice to be heard above the general chatter. 'We appear to be one short, but time's getting on and I feel I should begin . . .'

He had hardly said the words when the door opened and an attractive woman in her early thirties entered. She smiled and apologised for her lateness before saying, 'I'm Dr Mary Hallam from A&E at Ysbyty Gwynedd.'

'Good of you to come, Doctor,' said Trool. 'Anyone working in A&E need offer no further explanation.'

Mary gave a half-smile and sat down. It struck Tom as being just the right response. She clearly didn't see any need to milk the sympathy usually on offer to those working in frontline medicine, and the smile suggested that she didn't take herself too seriously — a fault common enough in people at the cutting edges in many professions. She sat almost opposite Tom Gordon in the semi-circle that had formed round Trool so he was able to look at her from time to time without appearing rude. Her dark hair and olive skin made her an extremely attractive woman but it was her eyes that really caught his attention. They seemed to say so much about her. She was confident, intelligent and analytical but not, he sensed, without humour. For some reason he couldn't quite fathom he felt that he wanted to see her smile properly, without inhibition, but their current circumstances made that event seem a little unlikely.

Trool cleared his throat and continued his welcome, assuring them that they would be given every assistance by the hospital staff in their enquiry, just as if they were conducting an official investigation. 'You may go where you like and interview anyone you wish.' Trool held up a slim blue folder. 'An information file has been prepared for you and individual copies are available. Unfortunately our own internal enquiry has not been successful—'

'Why not?' interrupted Liam Swanson, surprising Trool and disrupting the smooth flow of his delivery.

'I'm sorry?' he said.

'Why was it unsuccessful?'

Trool gave an uneasy smile. 'I think we reached an *impasse* when it was widely rumoured that, once found, the people responsible would be sacked on the spot.'

'Rumour or fact?' asked Swanson.

'Fact,' admitted Trool.

'So you were met with a wall of silence?'

'More a wall of strident denial,' said Trool.

'Presumably we'll meet the same wall?'

'That is entirely possible,' agreed Trool.

Tom suspected that Swanson was thinking along the

same lines as he himself. The unofficial independent enquiry was not really expected to get anywhere: it was simply a PR exercise.

'Well, we can but try,' said Swanson, letting Trool off the hook.

The Medical Superintendent recovered his composure. 'I've asked Dr Peter Sepp, our Consultant Pathologist and the man in charge of the department from which Megan's body was taken, to say a few words to you; he's waiting outside. Is there anything else you'd like to ask me before I invite him in?'

'Does Dr Sepp accept responsibility for what's happened?' asked Lady Arabella.

She spoke with an incredibly cut-glass accent that made Tom put his hand to his mouth to cover a slight smile. He caught Mary Hallam's eye and saw that she was thinking the same thing. They had to divert their eyes to avoid making matters worse.

'Dr Sepp offered his resignation as soon as the mix-up was exposed,' said Trool smoothly. 'The Trust, however, has seen fit to decline it. I'll ask him to come in.'

Tom hadn't met Sepp before. His first impression was that he was like every other middle-aged pathologist he'd met. It wasn't so much a matter of appearance, more a case of demeanour. They invariably seemed to be people for whom life had lost interest. Sepp outlined the course of the internal enquiry in his department in a dull monotone, the bottom line being that no one admitted to knowing anything about the mix-up.

'Would anyone like to ask me anything?' he concluded.

Mary Hallam asked about the biological waste-disposal system.

'The Path Lab is the central collection point for all such waste,' explained Sepp. 'Waste tissue from the theatres is brought here first by the porters and then taken together with our own waste to the boiler-house incinerator in the evening.'

'Every day?'

'Usually — except of course when there isn't any.'

'How often would that be?'

'Maybe one day a week — depends on the surgical lists and what sort of operations they're doing.'

'So for four days out of the working five, biological waste is taken to the incinerator?'

'Yes,' replied Sepp, appearing vaguely puzzled at the line of questioning.

Mary said softly but quite clearly, 'Then surely such a regular requirement merits an organised staff rota so that you'd actually know who was responsible on any given day?'

'With hindsight, yes,' agreed Sepp, deflecting her implied criticism with the unspoken suggestion that everyone sees clearly with the benefit of hindsight. 'It just so happens that my people have always worked well together without the need for such bureaucracy. I don't believe in unnecessary tiers of administration.'

Tom and Mary exchanged another glance. He reflected on the fact that nothing was as secure as the stable door the day after the horse had bolted. The impression that Sepp ran a sloppy department was building inside him.

There was a slight lull in the questions before Christine Williams, looking vaguely uneasy and beginning by apologising for her lack of medical or scientific expertise, said, 'I'm not quite clear about the child's coffin.'

People waited for her to elaborate but she didn't. Eventually Sepp said, 'What exactly is it that you don't understand?'

'Why was the child's coffin lying about in your department in the first place?'

Good point, thought Tom. The others seemed interested too.

'This happens from time to time,' said Sepp, 'usually when there has been some sort of delay, as was the case with the PM on Megan Griffiths. In the normal course of events, the undertakers liase with the mortuary attendants about the arrangements for uplift of a body. They then bring the coffin along, load it and take it away.'

'So the undertakers are the ones responsible for putting the body in the coffin?'

'Yes.'

'But not in this instance, apparently?'

'No. Megan Griffiths' body was not ready for release when the undertakers arrived. Her PM had had to be re-scheduled at a later time for some administrative reason. I can't remember what the reason was, off-hand.'

'So they left the coffin in the mortuary?'

'That's what normally happens in such cases.'

'But surely it should still have been the job of the undertakers to put Megan's body in the coffin when they came back for it?'

'Apparently that didn't happen this time,' said Sepp. 'The child's body − or *not* the child's body as it turned out, was already in the coffin and the lid had been screwed down when Prosser's people came for it.'

'Wouldn't that have struck the undertakers as being unusual?'

'Not necessarily,' said Sepp.

'This kind of thing happens, does it?'

The pathologist moved his feet a little uneasily. 'As I explained earlier, the undertakers liase with the mortuary attendants over . . . procedural details.'

'Procedural details?' repeated Liam Swanson, sensing a vulnerability about Sepp.

'There's nothing sinister about it,' Sepp assured him. 'For instance, it's the undertakers' responsibility to come and measure a body before supplying a coffin. In practice they often reach an accommodation with the attendants.'

'You mean the attendants measure the body instead of the undertaker's men?'

'And then they phone the undertakers with the figures — yes, it saves them sending someone all the way out here with a measuring tape.'

'Presumably there's something in it for the attendants?'

'I think a small fee's involved,' agreed Sepp.

'So are you telling us then that this understanding sometimes extends to putting bodies in coffins?' asked Swanson.

'On occasion.'

'What sort of occasion?'

'If the undertakers were hardpressed, say, with several funerals on the same morning for instance, they might seek the assistance of the mortuary attendants in speeding things up.'

'You don't think it lacks . . . dignity?' asked Christine Williams.

'I don't think the corpses care too much about whether they're put into coffins by men in black suits or men in white wearing plastic aprons and Wellington boots,' replied Sepp, betraying a waspish streak. Trool gave him a warning glance.

'I presume you questioned the mortuary attendants about such an understanding in this instance?' asked Swanson.

'Of course. Neither was aware of any, and both of them denied loading the coffin.'

'And I really think that brings us to the starting point of your enquiry, ladies and gentlemen,' said Trool, interceding smoothly. 'Dr Sepp and I will now leave you to discuss details among yourselves. I've arranged with Mr Harcourt, our Hospital Manager, that this room will be kept free for you at all times.'

Trool and Sepp left the room. Swanson looked at his watch and said to the others, 'I don't see much point in our discussing things further this evening when we don't really have anything to discuss as yet. I suggest we each take our files home and acquaint ourselves with the details and then meet again.'

'When?' asked Tom.

People looked at each other. 'Thursday lunchtime?' suggested Swanson.

This suited everyone except Lady Arabella and Mary Hallam who would be on duty.

'I suspected that this might be the case,' said Swanson. 'We're all busy people; it's going to be difficult to find times that are convenient for all of us.'

'It's an informal inquiry,' Tom reminded the others. 'I suggest that we operate with a majority — or even as individuals should the occasion arise where one of us feels like pursuing a line of enquiry. We can then meet to pool our findings when we actually have something to discuss. Let those of us who can make it meet on Thursday and then we can play it by ear?'

This was agreed.

Tom started to move towards Mary Hallam as she got up to leave, intending to introduce himself, but a hand on his shoulder stopped him. It was Liam Swanson. He said, 'You must be Julie Rees's partner, Tom Gordon? I don't think we've met before.'

Tom found himself shaking hands and making small talk as, over Swanson's shoulder, he watched Mary head out of the door.

'Strange business,' commented Swanson.

'Bizarre,' agreed Tom. 'It strikes me it was a very odd mix-up to happen in the first place.'

'How so?'

'For a mix-up to have occurred between Megan Griffiths's body and the biological waste bag would require that Megan herself was in a plastic bag when she was put into her coffin. How come?'

'Good point,' nodded Swanson. 'Mind you, thinking back to my own days as a medical student, pathology departments were never places where you'd find much respect for the dead.'

~ *Seven* ~

It started to rain as Tom Gordon drove back over to Felinbach. Soothed by the sound of the wipers, he found himself thinking about Mary Hallam and wondering when he might see her again. She wasn't going to be at the meeting on Thursday and that was a pity, but there would be other times. If not, maybe he could think up some pretext for contacting her? But perhaps this was a bad idea, he reasoned. He had a lot on his plate at the moment, what with the Palmers and now the Megan Griffiths business. This was probably not the best time to look for a new relationship . . . or was he getting cold feet already? The legacy of a painful divorce was always lurking there in the back of his mind. Once bitten . . .

The rain got heavier as he reached the village and was running in a river down the cobbles of Harbour Hill as he parked the Land Rover and made a run for his front door. Tom lived in a small self-contained flat on the first floor of a converted warehouse building looking out on to the marina. The building had been renovated and converted to holiday flats back in the 1970s and sold mainly to English buyers.

Most of the flats lay empty throughout the winter months so the building was quiet at this time of year. Tom's was the exception. It was owned by a Welshman who lived down in Cardiff, who had bought it as a long-term investment and to use when he eventually retired from business. He had been happy to rent it to Tom throughout the year rather than go to the trouble of advertising it or using a holiday letting agency. The downside to this was that he had paid little or no attention to maintenance over the years and the furnishings were largely original, featuring a good deal of chrome and plastic. The flat itself comprised a small living room, with views out on to the marina, a bedroom that faced the back, a tiny kitchen with a porthole window and a long narrow bathroom with an avocado-coloured suite which had been all the rage thirty years ago.

Tom swore under his breath when he found the flat cold. The heating had failed to come on again − the third time it had done this in the past two weeks. He kept his jacket on while he played around with the timer on the wall of his tiny kitchen until it agreed to trigger the 'on' switch. The boiler sprang into life and the pump started whirring, but it would be some time before the place heated up. In the meantime he had to resort to the back-up of an electric fire in the living room. It sparked a bit when he turned it on and made a grinding noise. This was something else he'd been meaning to get fixed, but like so many things, hadn't quite got around to. He rubbed his arms against the cold and resolved to contact Pryce, the local electrician, in the morning and arrange to get repairs organised.

He looked out of the window at the rain in the harbour, speckling the still surface of the oily water and spattering off the plastic hulls of the moored yachts. There was a light in the Harbourmaster's office, suggesting that a new arrival must be imminent. He lifted the glasses he kept on the window ledge and scanned the dark Menai for any sign of approaching navigation lights but all was dark.

He shivered and closed the curtains before turning on the kettle to make tea.

As the evening wore on, Tom wondered whether or not he should check on Lucy Palmer but after some hesitation, decided against it. Sometimes too much helpful attention could delay a person's recovery; he thought he'd go round and see her after he'd met with John's lawyers. Maybe he'd have a better idea of how things were going after talking to them.

He started to read through the file he'd been given at the hospital, acquainting himself with what was already known about the mix-up. It didn't amount to much, but was useful in explaining the routines and major players in the relevant departments. At the end, it was difficult to conclude anything other than that one of the mortuary attendants had been responsible for the mix-up, but as long as both of them maintained their innocence and denied any knowledge of the affair, then it seemed likely that the *impasse* would remain.

He supposed cynically that this was what the hospital really required of the committee – the conclusion that the loss of Megan's body had been the result of a low-level mix-up, unfortunate but just one of those things.

He poured himself a whisky and turned on the television, hoping to find some distraction for a while. As he hopped through the channels, he came to an old black-and-white film about gang warfare in Chicago. The scene involved a hearse, laden with flowers dedicated to 'Bugsy'. Looking at the hearse made him think that it might be an idea to talk to the undertaker's men rather than tackle the mortuary attendants, who had already denied all knowledge of the Megan Griffiths affair and would probably continue to do so. The internal enquiry had not done that, as far as he knew – it was probably deemed to be outside their jurisdiction — but he opened up the file again to check, just in case. There was no mention of any interview with Prosser's people having taken place. In fact, there was no mention of the undertakers at all, other than to note that they had found the coffin sealed when they arrived to pick up the body.

It seemed odd to Tom that Prosser's men had arrived at the hospital mortuary to find the little coffin all closed up, and had left without expressing any surprise or even mentioning it to anyone. It might suggest that that was exactly what they had expected to find. Maybe it implied that an 'understanding' as Sepp had called it, *had* existed over the Griffiths baby. He made up his mind to call into Prosser's the next time he was up in Caernarfon; that would be on Thursday at lunchtime, just before the meeting of the enquiry team.

He put down the file and realised that he was hungry; he hadn't had time to eat before driving up to Caernarfon after evening surgery. He was also tired, too tired to cook. Cheese on toast would have to do.

On Monday afternoon, Tom jumped in the Land Rover and drove off to Bangor, to the premises of Selby, Jones & Roberts. Although located in a building just off the bustling High Street, he found it strangely quiet when the outside door clicked shut behind him on its electronic latch, and he deduced that the stone walls must be very thick. He climbed the stairs to the first floor where a glass-panelled door with black lettering on it informed him that he'd come to the right place.

The door made him think of the offices of private detectives in American films of the 1950s. He opened it and entered an outer office, half-expecting to find Mickey Spillane sitting there with his feet on the desk, loading bullets into his gun, but instead found a plump middle-aged woman typing on a computer keyboard. *Chloe Phelps*, as the plastic plate on her desk proclaimed her to be, wore a thick black cardigan over a fine-mesh, mauve sweater that emphasised the rolls of fat around her middle. She sported lipstick that clashed violently with her sweater and wore spectacles that seemed to have been glazed with the high-strength material out of which aquariums were constructed. Above her, a large wooden clock was mounted on the wall; Tom could hear it ticking when she stopped typing.

He introduced himself.

Ms Phelps took a bite from the doughnut that was on a plate beside her and said with her mouth full, 'Mr Roberts is expecting you. Just go straight in.' She used the doughnut to indicate the general direction of the door he should use.

Tom walked through to a larger office where Roberts, a slight, white-haired figure, sat in an old leather chair behind a huge oak desk surrounded on three sides by piles of cardboard files secured with red ribbon. There were even files stacked in the marble fireplace.

'Good of you to see me,' said Tom, shaking his hand.

'We're all on the same side,' replied Roberts.

Tom reckoned Roberts was in his seventies if he was a day, and reminded himself that he was actually the *junior* partner in the firm.

'What can I do for you, Doctor?'

'I tried to be in court in Caernarfon when John Palmer appeared there last week,' replied Tom. 'I couldn't get near the place. The crowd were like animals: it wasn't a pretty sight.'

'I can imagine,' the solicitor said with a sigh. 'The public on a moral high horse is never a sight to gladden the heart.'

Tom was pleased to hear that Roberts sounded far from frail. He had a firm voice which, when combined with a Welsh accent, suggested eloquence. 'It alarmed me, Mr Roberts,' Tom confided. 'I had the feeling that John Palmer was on his way to prison before he'd even appeared in court.'

'Crowds can be very frightening,' said Roberts 'but I assure you that Mr Palmer will get a fair hearing and the court will hear statements from a number of expert witnesses, presented in support of mitigation.'

Alarm bells went off in Tom's head at the word 'mitigation'. 'You're speaking as if John were guilty,' he said.

Roberts looked at him in surprise. 'Of course he's guilty,' he said. 'He's confessed to killing his daughter. You must know that?'

Tom felt himself reel. He couldn't believe he was hearing this from John Palmer's solicitor. 'But you've spoken to Lucy, haven't you?'

'Indeed,' replied Roberts.

'She must have told you that John only confessed to protect her, because he thought she might have killed their daughter when of course, she didn't.'

'She did favour me with that information,' agreed Roberts.

'Well?' demanded Tom.

'Naturally I reported what she'd said to Mr Palmer, but he dismissed it out of hand; he insisted his wife was just trying to help him out of notions of misguided loyalty. He still maintains that he did it and therefore his confession stands. The job of his defence team will largely be to put forward pleas of mitigation. We'll make sure the court is aware of the tremendous stress involved in bringing up a severely disabled child, fears for the future, feelings of hopelessness et cetera.'

Tom felt stunned. 'But he didn't do it,' he exclaimed weakly.

Roberts adopted the bemused expression of a man hearing another argue that black is white. He eventually leaned back in his chair and brought his fingertips together under his chin. 'I'm an old man, Doctor,' he said. 'I've dealt with a lot of people in my time and believe me, I've known the most unlikely people to commit the most horrendous of crimes.'

'I don't doubt it,' said Tom, 'but John Palmer did *not* kill his daughter! I'm equally convinced that the police are not bothering to investigate the circumstances of this case fully. They don't seem to have questioned his confession at all. Surely they have a duty to check?'

'Mr Palmer is a well-balanced, intelligent, rational human being,' said Roberts. 'He has confessed to killing his child. There's really no reason for the police to concern themselves any more than they have done over the case.'

'But surely they're duty-bound to check out the details of what he says?' said Tom. 'Motive, for instance.'

'Motive,' repeated Roberts.

'Why did he kill her?'

'Mr Palmer says that he feared that the quality of his daughter's life would not be good enough in the long term.'

'Rubbish,' scoffed Tom. 'John Palmer never thought that for a moment; he was always very positive.'

'It's what he said,' insisted Roberts gently.

'He obviously still thinks that Lucy did it. Have the police even bothered to pursue that line of enquiry? They must be able to pick holes in his confession if they really tried.'

Roberts looked at him as if he were a schoolmaster wondering how to go about teaching a particularly dim pupil some fundamental fact of life. 'I'm afraid I'm not privy to police thinking,' he said, 'but what I *do* know is that the Crown Prosecution Office is not disposed to being unsympathetic in this particular case.'

Tom suspected there was more to be taken from the statement than what had appeared at face value. 'What exactly are you saying, Mr Roberts?' he asked.

'Consider the facts,' the solicitor said. 'A baby has died, a severely handicapped child by all accounts with a questionable quality of life. Her father has admitted carrying out what could conceivably be deemed a mercy killing in popular parlance.'

'Not many at Caernarfon the other day were taking that view,' Tom muttered. 'They wanted to bring back hanging.'

'They were not in full possession of the facts,' said Roberts calmly. 'The press saw to that. When it suits them to change tack again, they will and then they'll sway public opinion in the opposite direction.'

Tom didn't argue; Roberts was right about that.

'It's my feeling that the court will ultimately view the case with compassion and the prosecution will not oppose such leanings . . . providing things remain as they stand at the moment.'

'But?' prompted Tom.

'If Mr Palmer were to change his mind and alter his plea to Not Guilty, then it's my belief that the police would charge both him and his wife with murder and the prosecution would push for life sentences for them both.'

'Without any hard evidence against them?'

'Frankly, I don't think they'd need any,' said Roberts with a shake of the head. 'Look at the facts: Mrs Palmer's early rejection of the child, its very severe deformity, the fact that it was found buried in the Palmers' own garden.

What jury would think anything other than that the Palmers had killed their own daughter?'

With great reluctance, Tom had to agree. 'So if John Palmer admits to a crime he did not commit, the police and the Crown Prosecution Service will go easy on him for having made life easy for *them*,' he summarised.

'I really must remind you that at no time has John Palmer even hinted at being innocent,' said Roberts.

Tom accepted defeat with a shrug. 'Who will represent him in court?' he asked.

'One of James Throgmorton's people; I've forgotten the name for the moment.'

'Not the guy who got O.J. Simpson off, then?'

'It's a lady barrister, I think,' replied Roberts, ignoring the jibe. 'Nice girl, very bright, but she only has to offer a plea of mitigation.'

'Any idea when the trial might be?'

'None at all,' replied Roberts. 'Could be weeks, could be several months.'

Tom came downstairs feeling thoroughly dejected. It was almost a relief when the main door clicked open and exposed him to the noise of the High Street as a welcome distraction. He decided to leave the car where it was in the shoppers' car park and walk round to Gina Melford's house. There was some watery sunshine to enjoy and it would give him time to think what to say to Lucy.

When he didn't get an answer after the second knock, Tom felt a strange mixture of disappointment and relief; relief because he hadn't thought of anything encouraging to say to Lucy and disappointment because her not being there just delayed the evil moment. It was not delayed long however for, as he turned to leave, he caught sight of Lucy and Gina coming round the corner into the street. He walked slowly towards them.

'Hello, Tom, this is a surprise,' said Lucy. He thought she seemed a little bit brighter.

'I came over to see John's lawyer,' said Tom. 'I thought I'd drop by afterwards and check up on you.'

'That was kind. Why were you speaking to Roberts?'

'I hoped I might be able to help in some way, offer my services in John's defence. I thought I might be useful as a character witness, being John's doctor and friend. I didn't realise that he was still pleading Guilty. That was a bit of a shock.'

'They *want* him to plead Guilty,' Lucy said passionately.

'You know this?'

'I spoke to Roberts myself earlier today. He maintains that he told John exactly what I said, but I'm not so sure,' said Lucy darkly. 'He couldn't have got the message over properly, otherwise why would John still be sticking to this stupid confession?'

Gina interrupted saying, 'Look, why don't you two have a walk together: it would be a shame to waste the sunshine. I'll have some tea ready for you when you get back.'

Tom and Lucy started walking towards the garden in front of the Cathedral. He thought that she still looked frail but not as devastated as she had the last time he'd seen her. A little composure had come back but her eyes were still sunken and full of anguish. 'How are you?' he asked gently.

Lucy gave a slight shake of the head. 'I'm as low as I can get,' she said. 'The only way left for me to go is up. I've lost my baby, my husband's in prison awaiting trial for her murder, and most people seem to think I was involved too. I keep thinking the whole thing's a bad dream and I'm going to wake up soon, but it's not and I won't. I've got to start fighting back but I just don't know where to begin.' She swallowed and looked down at her feet.

'Have they said when you can see John?' asked Tom.

Lucy gave a bitter laugh. 'John is refusing to see anyone,' she said. 'Including me.'

'But why?' Tom stammered.

'He must still believe that I did it, whatever I say.'

'Do you think he'd see me?' Tom asked.

Lucy shrugged. 'I don't know,' she said, finally raising her head to look at him. 'Might be worth a try.'

They found a bench with dappled sunshine playing on it and sat down for a few minutes. Lucy closed her eyes and held her face up to the sun, courting its warmth. Tom thought her skin had taken on a translucent appearance. After a few moments' silence she said, 'What would happen if I went to the police and told them *I* did it?' She kept her eyes closed as she waited for an answer.

'Did you?'

'Of course not.'

'Then why would you want to do that?'

'Just tell me what you think would happen,' insisted Lucy.

'Presumably the police would have to investigate your claim but it probably wouldn't take them long to show that you were lying. They'd ask you questions about Anne-Marie's death you couldn't answer.'

'They don't seem to have bothered too much about investigating John's confession,' said Lucy.

Tom had been thinking the same thing. He continued to mull it over while they enjoyed the sun in silence for a few minutes. The police really should have been able to pick holes in a false confession if they had a mind to. The fact that they hadn't, suggested that they didn't have any other kind of evidence to go on, apart from circumstantial.

'If you were to confess too, they'd probably charge you both with murder and let circumstantial evidence do the rest,' he said grimly.

'Could they do that?'

'Roberts thinks they could.'

'God, what a mess,' sighed Lucy, getting to her feet. 'Let's go.'

~ *Eight* ~

It was still quite early when Tom Gordon got back to Felinbach and found that the one-man business of Pryce Electrics had not yet been to fix his faulty central heating and electric fire. The spare key however, that he'd popped through the firm's letterbox that morning along with a note, lay inside the door. There was a brief letter attached, typed on a machine with several faulty keys, saying that 'pressure of work' would prevent 'the firm' from carrying out repairs in the foreseeable future and that it might be best if he looked elsewhere for an electrician.

Tom felt a momentary surge of anger then he shrugged and threw the note in the pedal bin. 'Glad to hear business is so good, Sparky,' he said under his breath. 'Maybe you'll be able to buy your wife a decent typewriter in the near future.' He locked up the flat again and walked up the hill to the health centre to join Julie for evening surgery. Five people were already in the waiting room when he looked round the door so he asked the first one through. The patient was a regular – a woman in her fifties who was obviously having difficulty walking. Tom waited for her at the door to his room then ushered her inside. 'Don't tell me ... it's your arm,' he joked.

The woman made a dismissive gesture with a wave of

her hand. 'It's my *veins*, Doctor. They're getting worse. They're killing me.'

Tom examined her legs and saw the knotted mess of varicose veins on the back of both her calves.

'Dai says they look like a road map of Gwynedd.'

'Sensitive soul, your Dai,' said Tom.

'Wouldn't know the meaning of the word, Doctor.'

'I think we should see about getting you an appointment at the hospital,' Tom told her. 'We'll get these veins stripped out and you'll find walking a lot easier with the circulation restored. You may have to wait a bit, though. It's not an emergency so there'll be a list . . . but I'll do my best. I'll tell them it's interfering with your international career as a ballerina.'

The woman smiled but Tom thought her reaction a bit restrained: he'd always found it easy to make her laugh in the past. She got up to limp out and he called in the next patient — this time using the buzzer. The patient, another middle-aged woman, shapeless in a long, loose raincoat that buttoned up to her chin, came in and sat down in front of his desk, placing her shopping basket on her knees.

Tom thought her vaguely familiar but didn't know her name, that was the thing about working in a fairly small community, everyone seemed familiar by sight if not by name. 'How can I help?' he asked.

The woman said something in Welsh and Tom smiled. 'I'm sorry,' he said. 'I'm a Celt but not a Welsh one.'

The woman did not smile in return but said something else in Welsh. Tom shrugged again and felt puzzled because although Welsh was spoken widely in the area he hadn't come across anyone before who didn't speak English as well: it made him suspicious. As the woman got up to leave and put her hand on the door handle he said, to test her: 'Excuse me, I think you've dropped something.' She immediately turned round and looked at the floor before slowly raising her eyes to meet his. There was no appearance of guilt about her, now that he'd exposed her, and certainly no apology forthcoming. He interpreted her expression as one of pious superiority, the pitying look of a Christian fundamentalist for a lesser being, currently being used as the devil's tool.

'My mistake,' he said.

The woman went back to the waiting room to wait for Julie Rees and Tom reflected on this latest example of his growing unpopularity in Felinbach. He saw one more patient without incident before Julie came in to declare the waiting room empty.

'It seemed unusually busy today,' she said.

Tom told her about the woman pretending she couldn't speak English in order to be seen by Julie rather than him.

Julie grimaced. 'I didn't think it had gone that far,' she said. 'But don't let that old harridan upset you; Meg Richards was born miserable. If there's a bad side to anything she'll seek it out and see it as her Christian duty to expose it. Compassion is as much a stranger to her as humour.'

Tom nodded: he didn't tell her about the electrician's note but Julie could see that things were getting to him.

'You look as if you've had a bad day,' she said.

'You could say,' he replied wearily.

'Problems?'

'John Palmer insists on continuing to plead Guilty when he's not and now he's refusing to see anyone, even his wife.'

Julie paused as if editing what she wanted to say so as not to cause offence. 'Tom . . .' she began, 'Have you even considered the possibility that John Palmer might actually *be* guilty?'

He shook his head. 'No, I haven't,' he said flatly. 'Because he isn't.' He realised immediately that his reply needed some expansion if only in the interests of harmony. 'If I'm perfectly honest,' he said, 'there was a moment when I did wonder if Lucy might not have had some kind of relapse and killed Anne-Marie in a fit of depression, but now I'm convinced she had nothing to do with it either.'

'So where does that leave you?'

'Looking for the *real* killer – something no one else is even considering, including the police.'

'No one could fault your credentials as a loyal friend,' said Julie, 'but I do wish for your sake that you'd leave the investigating to the professionals. You have neither the time nor the background to carry out a criminal investigation on your own.'

'I haven't been too impressed with what the professionals have accomplished so far,' said Tom. 'I have to do what I can.'

Julie shrugged her acceptance. 'What does that involve now?' she asked.

'I want to visit John in prison if they'll let me.'

Julie nodded, then changed the subject. 'How did the meeting at the General go on Saturday?'

'Pretty much as expected. They'd really just like us to go through the motions of an enquiry, conclude that there was nothing basically wrong and that it was all just one of those things.'

'Something tells me Mr and Mrs Griffiths won't be thinking along these lines,' said Julie.

He nodded. 'I think the hospital know that. They're resigned to having to make a pretty hefty pay-out at some point,' he said, 'but they want to limit damage to the hospital's reputation. I think they'd like it if it could be shown that neither mismanagement nor professional incompetence played any part in the proceedings and that the whole thing was just a low-level mix-up.'

'God, it must have been awful for Mr Griffiths,' sighed Julie. 'By all accounts, it was bad enough for Prosser, the undertaker. I hear he collapsed on the floor when he saw what was in the coffin. I can't imagine what it must have been like for the little girl's father.'

'How come?' said Tom suddenly.

'How come what?'

He frowned and remained deep in thought for a few moments. 'When Prosser opened the coffin,' he began hesitantly, 'he shouldn't have seen anything more sinister than a plastic bag.'

'I don't understand what you're getting at,' said Julie.

'If it was all down to a simple mix-up, as the hospital are keen to claim, it would suggest that both the child's body and the biological waste must have been in the same kind of disposal bag. Yes?'

'I suppose so,' agreed Julie. 'I hadn't really thought about it.'

'The bags must have been sealed as well otherwise they would have realised their mistake right away.'

'Yes.'

'So why would Prosser faint at the sight of a plastic bag?'

'Presumably he opened it.'

'But surely his first thought would have been to realise that there was something wrong and that he should stop Griffiths coming anywhere near it?'

'Maybe he got such an awful shock when he looked inside it,' said Julie.

'He's an undertaker,' said Tom. 'He's been in the business for years. He shouldn't shock that easily.'

'I take your point.'

'There's something not right here,' said Tom. 'I smell a rat.'

On Thursday morning Tom planned his house calls so that the one nearest to Caernarfon would be the last. It turned out to be at Plas Coch Farm, a hill farm about three miles south-east of Caernarfon. The farmer, Glyn Edwards, had taken a fall from his quad bike while out on the hills and had gashed his leg. His wife had phoned the surgery to say that he was in a lot of pain and hadn't managed any sleep for two nights.

Ellen Edwards came out into the yard to meet the doctor as he parked the Land Rover and tried to find a dry line of approach to the house. Two sheepdogs stalked him on the flanks as he tiptoed cautiously through the mud, sending hens clucking off in all directions. 'I should have put on my wellies,' he joked. 'How is he?'

'You know Glyn, Doctor, he keeps insisting I'm making a lot of fuss about nothing but I can see he's in great pain. He didn't even try to go out on the hills this morning: it's just not like him.'

Tom did his best to scrape the mud off his shoes on the metal scraper bar by the door before entering the warmth of the kitchen and following Ellen through to where Edwards lay with his bandaged leg stretched out along the couch in front of him. He grunted when he saw the young GP.

'Fell off the quad, I hear,' said Tom. 'That'll teach you to play Evel Knievel at your age.'

The comment got a grudging grin from Edwards, whose complexion after a lifetime on the hills almost matched the reddish-orange of the curtains in the living room. Tom could tell from his eyes that the man was in considerable pain.

'Let's have a look,' he said, opening up his bag and taking out scissors to cut away the old dressings. The leg felt very hot and there was an unpleasant smell coming from the bandaging. 'When exactly did this happen?' he asked.

'Three days ago,' panted Edwards. 'Didn't seem too bad at first but it's giving me merry hell now.'

Tom examined the exposed wound closely and made a face. 'It's infected,' he said. 'That's what's giving you the pain. Do you know what caused the cut?'

'Sharp stone,' said Edwards.

'You're sure no metal was involved? No rusty nails or barbed wire?'

'It was a stone, I'm sure,' said Edwards.

'Right. I'm just going to take a swab for the lab then I'll write you up for painkillers so you'll get some sleep tonight. I'll give you a strong-acting antibiotic to fight the infection. You should notice a big difference by Saturday. If you don't, give me a ring.'

'I will, Doctor,' said Ellen, 'and I'll see that he takes his medicine.'

Tom took a swab from his bag and slid off the outer tube, taking care not to touch the sterile tip against anything else before rubbing it gently along the gash to absorb a sample of the exudate. He placed it back in the tube and wrote the date and Edwards's full name and address on the outside, before dropping it back into his bag. He put a fresh dressing on the wound then stood up saying, 'There you go. You'll be right as rain by next week.'

'Thanks, Doc.'

Tom tore the prescription off his pad and handed it to Ellen. 'This should do the trick,' he said, then turning to Edwards, he added, 'Easy on those fast corners, boyo.' Tom went back to the car and checked his watch: it was a few minutes after noon. There would still be time to visit Prosser's before the meeting at one.

He parked the car in his usual place down by the

harbour in Caernarfon and walked round the outside of the castle walls to begin working his way back up through the narrow lanes to reach Mould Street and the premises of J. Prosser & Son. A bell above Prosser's door gave a solitary 'ting' as he entered and a man wearing a dark suit and black tie materialised from the back. 'How can I help?' he asked reverentially: his hands were folded in front of him and his head held slightly to one side.

'Mr Prosser?' Tom asked cheerily.

'Yes?' answered the man, uncertainty creeping into his voice.

'I'm Tom Gordon − I'm a GP in Felinbach. I've been co-opted on to the enquiry team investigating the Megan Griffiths affair.'

Prosser's manner changed in an instant. The hands fell to his sides and his shoulders sagged forwards. 'Whoever was responsible for that deserves a right old bollocking,' he said.

'I agree,' said Tom. 'I was wondering if I might ask your staff a few questions?'

Prosser looked suspicious. 'What is this?' he growled. 'If that lot think they're going to shift the blame on to me and my staff, they've got another think coming. It had nothing to do with the boys or me. The coffin was closed when we collected it from the General.'

'No, it's nothing like that,' Tom assured him. 'I'm doing this off my own bat − it's completely unofficial. I realise you're under no obligation to talk to me at all but I thought, as you've obviously got nothing to hide, that you might be willing to help?'

'If you put it that way,' said Prosser slowly. 'Ask away. The boys are out in the yard cleaning the vehicles.'

'Thanks,' Tom beamed. 'I wonder if I might ask you something first?'

Prosser led Tom into the same small office where he had talked to Martin Griffiths on that awful morning, and invited him to sit. 'What can I tell you?' he asked.

'I'd like you to describe exactly what happened when you opened up Megan Griffiths's coffin.'

Prosser swallowed before answering. 'I'll never forget it as long as I live. People keep saying I should be used to awful sights with my job, but I wasn't prepared for anything like that, to see all those bits and pieces . . . Jesus!'

'Didn't the plastic bag make you suspicious before you opened it?' asked Tom.

'What plastic bag?' asked Prosser slowly and cautiously, as if fearing it might be a trick question.

Tom felt the hairs on the back of his neck start to bristle. 'Are you telling me that the bits and pieces, as you call them, were not contained within a plastic bag? That they were visible when you opened the lid?'

'Absolutely, that's what gave me such a shock like.'

If there was no bag, there had been no mix-up: it was as simple as that. *The person who had put the waste into the coffin had known full well what they were doing.* But maybe the bag had been there and had simply burst open. He asked Prosser if this was the case.

'I didn't see no bag,' he replied.

'What happened to the contents?' asked Tom.

'The hospital sent down a van, sealed them in one of their bags . . . and took the whole lot away, coffin and all.'

So *that's* when the material went into a disposal bag, thought Tom. He thanked Prosser for his help and said, 'Maybe I could speak with your men now?'

Prosser led the way through the shop and out into the yard at the back where two hearses and a black limousine were parked. One man was hosing down the limousine while the other two sat on wooden crates, smoking and watching him. They got up when they saw Prosser, who turned and nodded in Tom's direction. 'This is Dr Gordon; he'd like to ask you some questions about the Griffiths business.' Prosser introduced the three men. 'This is my son, Paul.' Tom could see the strong family resemblance. 'This is Tyler Morse and the fellow with the hose there is Maurice Cleef. Right — I'll leave you to it.'

Tom thanked Prosser and nodded to all three men who were dressed in their mourning clothes but wearing green plastic aprons over them.

'As I understand it,' he began, 'Megan Griffiths's coffin was already closed and had the lid screwed down when you went to collect it at the hospital mortuary?'

'That's right. Weren't anything to do with us,' said Paul Prosser.

'You collected it personally, did you?' Tom asked.

'No, Maurice here did.'

Cleef, a painfully thin six-footer with a sallow complexion and sunken eyes, turned off the hose and walked over to join them. Water was running off his apron on to his Wellington boots. 'What's the problem?' he asked.

'No problem,' Tom said pleasantly, 'I'm just trying to clear up a few details. Tell me, when you went up to the hospital to collect Megan Griffiths's body, did you expect to be putting her into the coffin yourself?'

'I suppose I did,' replied Cleef.

'So what did you think when you found the coffin already closed and ready for collection?'

Cleef shrugged his shoulders. 'I thought that must have been the arrangement,' he said. 'And nobody had told me.'

'The arrangement?'

'I thought Paul here or his father had made an arrangement with the lads at the mortuary to close up the coffin, and they'd forgotten to tell me, like.'

'But that wasn't the case?'

Paul Prosser shook his head. 'We knew nothing about it.'

'If it came as a surprise to you, did you say anything about it to anyone at the hospital?' Tom asked Cleef.

Another shrug. 'Not as I recall.'

'Not even to the mortuary attendants?'

'I didn't see them, did I?'

'Did you see anyone else?'

'Not as I recall.'

'You simply walked in, picked up the coffin and walked out again?'

'Why not?' asked Cleef defensively. 'That's what I was there for.'

'No reason,' said Tom but he was intrigued by the nervous twitch that had started on Cleef's left cheek and the look in his eyes that suggested extreme unease, maybe even fear.

— *Nine* —

Tom arrived at the meeting and apologised for being a few minutes late. Dr Liam Swanson, Caernarfon's Director of Public Health, volunteered that they were actually just waiting for the two mortuary attendants to come up from Pathology. He had requested that they present themselves for questioning and Mr Harcourt was bringing them upstairs. Tom was about to tell everyone what he had discovered when a knock came at the door and Harcourt put his head round it to announce that he had mortuary technician David Meek with him. Swanson nodded and said, 'Let's at least go through the motions.'

Meek was ushered to a seat in front of the committee. He was a slight, sallow-skinned individual with greasy dark hair and a speech impediment that made understanding what he said difficult at first, but it was something that became progressively easier as ears became attuned to his voice.

Tom was surprised that the man turned out to be more resentful than nervous and displayed a marked sullenness throughout the interview. He was subjected to robust, if not openly aggressive questioning for almost fifteen minutes but maintained ignorance of anything to do with the Megan Griffiths affair. He seemed openly annoyed that he was being questioned about something he clearly felt he'd been asked too much about already.

Meek was followed by the other attendant, an older man named Henriques, who smelled strongly of pipe tobacco and had a disconcerting habit of wiping his lips with the back of his hand before and after every answer. He said much the same as Meek, his answers often matching Meek's word for word. He knew nothing at all about any mix-up and had no suggestion to make as to how it could have happened.

Swanson's disappointment was obvious when the interviews were over.

'Pretty much as we expected, I'm afraid,' he said. 'What d'you feel? Were they lying to save their jobs or were they telling the truth?'

'I believed them,' said Christine Williams.

There were resigned murmurs of agreement from the others. Once again Tom was about to say what he'd found out at Prosser's when another knock came on the door and Harcourt re-entered. 'Any luck?' he asked.

'They continued to deny all knowledge of any mix-up and I think it's fair to say we believed them,' said Swanson.

Harcourt looked sceptical. 'Personally, I think they've worked out that if they both keep mum or tell the same story, they'll hang on to their jobs and no one will be able to touch them for the mix-up. Common sense says that it *had* to be down to them.'

'It wasn't a simple mix-up,' Tom announced loudly.

'I'm sorry?' said Harcourt as the room fell silent.

Tom told them about his visit to Prosser's. He concluded by saying, 'The person who put the biological waste into Megan Griffiths's coffin knew *exactly* what they were doing. There *was* no innocent mix-up involving waste bags. The material was never actually *inside* a biological waste bag until it was put in one by the men sent over by the hospital to recover it.'

There were gasps from the others and requests for more

information. Harcourt seemed to lose colour. 'I don't think I understand,' he said. 'Are you saying that it was a deliberate, malicious act, designed to shock or discredit the hospital in some way?'

Tom shook his head. 'I hardly think so; the person responsible could not have anticipated the coffin being opened again, so if things had gone to plan, no one would ever have known about it.'

'I think Dr Trool had better hear this,' said Harcourt. He left the room, saying he'd be back shortly.

Dr Liam Swanson took Tom to one side. 'You've obviously had some time to think about this on the way over,' he said. 'Have *you* reached any conclusions?'

Tom said that he thought some kind of mix-up might still be possible, although now it would have to involve the disposal of Megan Griffiths's body at some earlier time, followed by an attempted cover-up using the contents of the biological waste bag to make up weight in the coffin.

'What sort of disposal?' asked Swanson.

'Good question.'

Harcourt returned with a grim-looking James Trool who came into the room, gasping, 'This is all I need. The papers will have a field day when they get hold of it — they'll crucify us! Are you absolutely certain?'

'The undertaker is adamant that the waste material was not held inside any kind of bag. That being the case, it could *not* have been put there by mistake,' Tom stated.

Trool shook his head. 'I thought a mix-up was bad enough,' he said, 'but the suggestion that the act was deliberate just beggars belief. This could do the hospital untold damage, and it's come at the worst possible time — just when we were looking forward to some well-deserved, positive publicity.'

'Why do you say that?' asked Swanson.

'The IVF symposium next week,' replied Trool. 'Some of the world's leading authorities on *in vitro* fertilisation are coming to Caernarfon General to pay tribute to the work of Professor Carwyn Thomas. They are holding a four-day symposium and we were anticipating some favourable press and television coverage. I need hardly point out that this sort of thing means a lot to hospitals these days, when we are all competing for funds. We have here a centre of excellence in Professor Thomas's unit – and public awareness of that fact is so important. A successful symposium could put us up there on the stage with some of the best hospitals in the country. Now it looks as though all that press attention will go to the Griffiths business.'

'It is quite a serious business,' Swanson reminded him.

Trool immediately held up his hands and adopted a pained expression. 'Please, please, don't get me wrong,' he pleaded. 'It was not my intention to minimise the awfulness of what's happened. I just care so deeply about this hospital and its reputation that it pains me to see our being pilloried for what, after all, must have been some tragic sort of mistake, however it came to pass.'

'I think we can all appreciate how you feel, Doctor,' said Swanson to nods of agreement all round.

'This is still an *unofficial* enquiry,' Tom pointed out. 'There's no requirement for us to give the press a blow-by-blow account of what's happening during the course of our investigations. In fact, we are under no obligation to tell anyone anything at all at the moment.'

'Good point,' said Swanson, seeing what Tom was getting at. The others nodded their agreement.

'I suggest we adopt a policy of saying nothing to the press until our enquiries are complete.'

No one had a problem with that.

Trool himself was obviously very relieved. 'I'm very grateful to you all,' he said. 'We'd certainly appreciate a breathing space and I reckon we are about due for a lull in press coverage. They've said as much as they can about Megan without repeating themselves. They may now be content to wait for something new to come along, or for enough time to elapse so they can start complaining about tardiness or maybe start seeking out one of the cover-ups they're so fond of.'

'There is one thing you should be prepared for however, Dr Trool,' warned Swanson. 'Unless we come up with some evidence over the next few weeks to confirm the accidental disposal of Megan Griffiths's body, we may well have to hand things over to the police.'

Trool nodded gravely. 'I understand,' he said quietly and left the room accompanied by Harcourt.

'So where do we go from here?' asked Christine Williams.

'I suggest we go away and have another look at the timing of events in the files we were given,' said Swanson. 'In the light of what Dr Gordon has come up with, we have to consider that Megan's body went astray at an earlier time than we first thought. Perhaps we can narrow it down to the period between when it came into the mortuary from the PM room and probably before the biological waste arrived from the theatres. Let's see if we can correlate that with the names of people who were seen in the Path Department around that time?'

The meeting broke up with Swanson saying that he would contact them individually by phone in due course. 'In the meantime, we say nothing at all to the press except that our enquiries are continuing.'

Tom was about to get into his car when he saw James Trool hurrying across the car park towards him; he paused, resting his arm on the open door.

'Glad I caught you,' said Trool. 'Are you in an awful hurry or can you spare a few minutes?'

'No great hurry,' said Tom. 'I was just going to pick up a sandwich for lunch.'

'Then perhaps you'd care to join us,' said Trool. 'By us I mean Professor Thomas and myself. I was telling him of your understanding attitude over our concern with the press; he's very grateful too. Have you met him?'

Tom said that he hadn't. He was concerned that having lunch with senior members of the hospital staff might be construed as being a little too cosy with the establishment he was supposed to be investigating, but dismissed the notion as being over-cautious. He hadn't agreed to cover anything up, just not to make any unnecessary statements to the papers.

'Brilliant man,' said Trool.

Tom locked up the car again and walked back to the hospital with Trool. They met up with Thomas in a small dining room on the same floor as Trool's office. There were perhaps eight tables, each seating four people and spaced at a discreet distance from each other. Tom counted ten people in the room; their clothes and confident manner suggested consultant-grade medical staff.

Trool led the way over to a table by the window where a small man with a swept-back mane of white hair rose to meet them.

'Carwyn, I'd like you to meet Tom Gordon, one of our local GPs. Tom, may I present Professor Carwyn Thomas, director of the IVF unit here at Caernarfon General.'

Tom shook hands with the Professor, noting that he'd become 'Tom' on the way up from the car park. 'A great pleasure, Professor, he said. 'I'm familiar with your work, of course. In fact, I've referred patients to you in the past.'

'With some success, I hope,' smiled Thomas.

Tom thought it prudent not to mention the Palmers at that particular moment.

'Whereabouts are you a GP?' asked Thomas.

'Felinbach and surrounding area.'

The man nodded. 'It can't be easy being a GP at a time when medicine is advancing on all fronts; there must be so much for you to keep up with.'

'A constant struggle,' agreed Tom, who joked, 'I'm never short of bedtime reading.'

He found the food passable and the conversation agreeable, if a little strained. He thought he detected a slight atmosphere between Trool and Thomas, but wasn't sure. Their politeness to each other seemed to suggest a lack of warmth. He got the impression that the conversation was being deliberately steered to topics outside the hospital and medicine in a search for neutral ground. They ended up discussing the relative merits of the five nations rugby teams in the current international season. As Trool was English, they already had three of the nations at the table.

Halfway through the main course, Trool's phone went off and he had to excuse himself from the table. Before he left, he apologised profusely to Tom about having to go and said again how grateful he was for the understanding he had shown. He would be in touch soon.

'That man lives on his nerves,' said Thomas as Trool left.

'He seems to care a great deal about the hospital. I suppose it must be a pretty stressful job,' Tom said tactfully.

'Try "marriage",' said Thomas. 'He should have listened to what Chaucer said about January and June.' He didn't volunteer any more and Tom thought it impolite to ask.

As he finished his coffee, Tom was pleased when the Professor offered to show him around the IVF unit. 'I really feel we should interact more with our colleagues outside the hospital,' the older man said as they made their way through busy corridors. 'It can only be in the patients' interest in the long run, don't you agree?'

The tour started in the Professor's own office where Tom was amused by the walls being covered with photographs of young children.

'My other family,' said Thomas proudly. 'These are all children who resulted from their parents receiving treatment here.'

'Wonderful!' Tom was full of genuine admiration. 'Not many doctors can point to such tangible proof of their impact on people's lives.'

'I get Christmas cards from nearly all of them,' said Thomas.

'Is this where you meet patients for the first time?'

The Professor replied that it was. 'I think it puts them at their ease. Breaks the ice, so to speak. You know I'm still constantly surprised at the strength of feeling involved in wanting to become parents. It's such a powerful force and they are very vulnerable people: we constantly have to be on our guard about offering false hope.'

'I know what you mean,' said Tom, thinking of the Palmers and their long quest to become parents.

There was something about the way he said it that Thomas caught on to. 'You said you'd referred patients to me in the past?' he prompted.

'John and Lucy Palmer were my patients,' said Tom quietly.

'Oh, I see.' Thomas sounded thoughtful. 'Felinbach and surrounding area — I should have realised. Such a sad case, an absolute tragedy and at a time when I felt so sure they'd both come to terms with their baby's problems and were doing so well.'

'They had and they were,' Tom said stoutly.

'How can you say that after what happened?' asked the Professor, looking puzzled.

'I believe John Palmer admitted to the crime because he mistakenly thought that Lucy might have done it after having some kind of relapse. If you remember, she suffered quite badly from post-natal depression?'

'I do. Have you mentioned this to the police?'

'I've been telling anyone who will listen,' said Tom ruefully. 'No one wants to know, least of all the police.'

'But the baby was found in the Palmers' own garden,' said Thomas.

'I know,' sighed Tom. 'But I'm still convinced he didn't do it.'

'I can see that, ' said Thomas, leaning back in his chair. 'I didn't realise there was more to this than met the eye. It needs thinking about. In the meantime, if there's anything I can do to help, you must let me know.'

'I'm hoping they'll at least let me visit John; he's not been speaking to anyone,' said Tom.

Thomas recalled: 'It was a blow to all of us here when young Anne-Marie was born the way she was. They'd been one of our most difficult cases and we were all prepared to celebrate our success when suddenly it all went terribly wrong.'

'Have you had many cases of babies being born with deformities?' asked Tom.

'It never used to be the case,' the Professor mused. 'Our problem in the past, apart from complete failure, of course, usually had to do with multiple births, but since we started using ICSI for the more difficult cases we've had quite a few serious problems. Mercifully, most of them haven't gone to term; they've spontaneously aborted. The Palmers' baby was an exception – a badly deformed foetus that did go to term and survived post-natal surgery.'

'ICSI is where you inject the sperm directly into the ovum, isn't it?' asked Tom.

The other man nodded. 'That's right. Intra-Cytoplasmic Sperm Injection, more usually called "icksee" for obvious reasons. Our chief embryologist is quite expert at it but the technique still seems to carry quite a high risk of foetal abnormality. It'll be interesting to hear the experience of others at next week's symposium. Why don't you come along?'

'To the symposium?' exclaimed Tom, taken by surprise. 'I'm a simple GP; most of it will go over my head.'

'There's no such thing as a simple GP,' the Professor said. 'Think about it – you'd be most welcome.'

'You know, I'd like that,' said Tom after a moment's thought. 'Maybe I will come along to a couple of talks if I can find the time. Thanks for asking.'

'Come on, I'll show you around the rest of the unit.'

~ *Ten* ~

Tom was taken on a tour of the state-of-the-art lab facilities that occupied most of the east wing of the hospital on the third floor. He found that the unit also had its own surgical facilities. This was true even for women requiring Caesarean section, the theatres being equipped to handle all likely obstetric emergencies. He asked about the incidence of such problems before moving on to a long narrow room without windows and with only minimal background lighting where two very sophisticated looking microscopes sat side by side on a single long bench. A tall man wearing surgical smock and trousers sat working at one of them, his fingers deftly moving the complicated micro-manipulation apparatus attached to the microscope stage.

'This is where it all happens,' said Thomas. 'Ran is our chief embryologist: maybe we shouldn't disturb him,' he added in a stage whisper.

'Not at all,' said the man at the microscope, taking his cue without averting his eyes. 'I'm just about finished here . . . there, all done.'

Thomas introduced Dr Gordon to the tall man who smiled and got up from the swivel stool on which he'd been perched. They shook hands. 'Nice to meet you. I'm Ranulph Dawes. Perhaps you'd care to take a look?' he asked.

Tom accepted enthusiastically and sat down to begin adjusting the width of the binocular eyepieces on the 'scope to suit his eyes before peering down at a green circle of light. He focused on the two darker circles in the middle, using the fine knurled knob on the side of the 'scope and said, 'I don't often get the chance to do this. What am I looking at?'

'This culture started out as a single fertilised ovum,' explained Dawes. 'You'll see there are now two cells and they're already showing early signs of mitosis so they're almost ready to become four. When they do, they'll be ready for implantation in the patient's womb. If all goes well, we'll have another happy, pregnant lady on our hands.'

'Marvellous,' said Tom, moving the fine focus control again to capture detail on the pulsating surface of the cells. 'The very cradle of life.'

'Still gives me a buzz too,' said the embryologist.

'Is this the result of icksee?' Tom enquired.

'No, this was ordinary, random collision IVF. Ova and sperm were mixed in a test tube and Mother Nature did the rest.'

'Dr Gordon probably asked about ICSI because he's Mr and Mrs Palmer's GP,' said Thomas.

'Oh, I see,' said the embryologist. 'Such a sad business.'

'Dr Gordon does not believe that John Palmer was responsible for his baby's death,' Thomas went on.

'I don't understand.'

Tom had little heart at that particular moment for arguing his case again and no doubt having it pointed out to him once more that Palmer *had* confessed to the crime and that Anne-Marie's body *had* been found in the Palmers' own back garden.

'He confessed and they found the baby in the garden, didn't they?' Dawes said.

'I just think there's more to it,' said Tom a trifle wearily.

'I'd be most interested to hear what it is,' said the embryologist. 'I liked the Palmers a lot.'

The young GP now had no option but to say what he thought about the Palmer case and was rewarded, as he'd feared, with a look of scepticism appearing on Dawes's face.

'If you'll forgive me, Doctor,' said Dawes, 'what you're actually saying is that John Palmer couldn't have done it because you think he's far too nice a person.'

The words did a pretty fair impression of sticks and stones on Tom and he had to admit reluctantly that what Dawes had said was a reasonable summation of his position. 'I do think he's incapable of having done it,' he said.

There was a slightly uncomfortable pause before Professor Thomas changed tack and directed his visitor's attention to the other microscope, saying, 'We carry out the ICSI procedure using this instrument. Ran's quite an expert.'

'Injecting a single cell sounds horrendously difficult,' said Tom.

'It's certainly not easy,' acknowledged Dawes, 'but equipment is getting better all the time so it's nowhere near as bad as it was. It's a bit like playing a computer game; the more you play, the better you get.'

'Ran's too modest,' said Thomas briskly. 'It still demands a very high level of skill whichever way you look at it.'

'Do you do a lot?' asked Tom.

'Maybe a couple a month.'

'What's the success rate?'

'Not as good as we'd like. We've had quite a few problems with miscarried foetuses.'

Tom nodded. 'Professor Thomas mentioned that it hadn't all been plain sailing.'

'It's bound to improve. The more we do, the more experienced we get, so it's important we keep trying.'

'Absolutely,' agreed Tom. Then it was time to move on and he thanked the embryologist for the demonstration, saying, 'I'm very grateful, Doctor Dawes.'

'Ran — everyone calls me Ran.'

'Thanks, Ran. It's not often we GPs get a chance to see what's going on in the hi-tech world. It's more a case of lancing boils on bums and treating recurrent bronchitis.'

'Any time,' smiled Dawes. 'You should come along to the symposium next week: you'll get a much better feel for what's going on in the field than you will from reading the journals.'

The Professor said, 'I've already suggested that.'

'Maybe I'll manage to come along at some point,' said Tom politely. 'I'd certainly like to.'

'Then make the time,' smiled the embryologist.

The tour of the department finished with Tom being shown the long-term storage tanks for embryos — huge, floor-standing, stainless-steel vessels kept cool with liquid nitrogen that swirled around like thick fog when Thomas removed one of the lids. 'Possible brothers and sisters, should they be required,' he explained.

'How long do you keep them?' Tom felt slightly awed.

'We've kept them all so far,' the Professor told him. 'Partly to avoid the moral dilemma that everyone talks about, but we're going to have to face up to it soon: we're running out of storage space.'

Tom thanked him for the tour and Carwyn Thomas reiterated that he hoped he might see him at some time during next week's symposium.

On the drive back to the surgery from Caernarfon, Tom returned to thinking about John Palmer; he was beginning to feel the strain of isolation over the affair. He was clearly the only person in the world who believed that *both* the Palmers were innocent. He could explain away John's confession, but not the fact that Anne-Marie had been found buried in the couple's own garden. This was something he'd avoided thinking too much about, perhaps because it stretched his own faith to the limit. But maybe this was exactly what he *should* be doing, he considered; he should be facing the problem head on and trying to figure out why the real killer had done something so bizarre.

It was glaringly obvious, he decided only minutes later. If the murderer had gone to all the trouble of returning the baby's body to the Palmers' garden, *he must have wanted the Palmers to get the blame for the crime.* But why, for God's sake? The killer must hold an outrageous grudge against the couple. Could it be that either or both of them had such a monstrous enemy? It was hard to believe. John and Lucy had been generally well liked by people before the event – but it was a thought worth bearing in mind.

'A new cot-death directive came in today,' said Julie by way of greeting as Tom strolled inside the Health Centre. 'I've left a copy of it on your desk: it's over twenty pages long.'

'Saying what?'

'Very little. I think the bottom line is that they still don't know what causes it,' she said, 'but they take twenty pages to say it.'

'The powers-that-be have to be seen to be doing something but God, when you think about it, the experts have had the kids lying on their backs, their fronts, their sides, with the window open, the window closed. What is it this time? Upside down from the ceiling?'

Julie could understand her partner's frustration. 'Our

profession has never been known for its willingness to employ the words "we don't know" with any great relish, has it?' she said sympathetically. 'They prefer us to work that out for ourselves . . . over twenty pages in this case.'

'I met Carwyn Thomas today,' said Tom, changing the subject. 'He invited me to attend the IVF symposium next week at the General.'

'You *are* honoured,' said Julie. 'Do you plan on going?'

'I've really got quite enough on my plate already in the way of extra-curricular activity,' said Tom.

'I'd much rather you abandoned one of the other things,' said Julie, but she softened the comment with a smile.

'Maybe I'll manage one or two of the talks.' No way did he want to be drawn into any new argument over the Palmer affair. 'Anything new?' he asked, noticing that Julie was going over their case figures for the month.

'It's really been quite quiet,' she replied. 'I think this means we've successfully come through another winter. The bronchitics are wheezing their way into spring, and colds and flu are fading away for another year. We're enjoying a bit of a lull at the moment.'

'Until the hay fever and asthma people start up again,' Tom smiled.

'Life's a circle,' said Julie.

Then Tom, who had been opening the mail that had come in while he'd been up at Caernarfon, let out a quiet expletive.

'Trouble?' Julie asked.

'It's Debbie Farningham's histology report. The lump on her breast is malignant — they want her in right away.'

'Oh, rotten luck,' sighed Julie. 'Are we talking radical surgery here?'

'From the size and position of the lump I think they

might well opt for a lumpectomy rather than anything more drastic at this stage,' replied Tom.

'I hope so. She's young.'

'We'll just have to hope for the best until they've done the scans,' said Tom. 'And please God it's the primary lesion.'

'Better call her in.'

'I'll do it now.'

Tom poured himself a large whisky when he got in around seven and slumped down in a chair. It had been a lousy day, he decided – a promising start but a hellish end. Having to tell a thirty-four-year-old woman with two small children that she'd got cancer hadn't been easy, but then, giving out that kind of news never was. It was something that he hadn't become hardened to in the job. He'd then come home to find that the heating had failed yet again and there was no hot water for the relaxing soak to which he'd been looking forward. He threw back the whisky in one big gulp and opted for a second.

How, he wondered as he sipped it, did one go about getting permission to visit a prisoner being held on remand? He pondered this for a few minutes, allowing the whisky to restore his equanimity, before deciding that he would have to seek advice on the matter. He would telephone John Palmer's solicitor, Mr Roberts, in Bangor in the morning and ask him. With that decided, he kicked off his shoes and padded through to the kitchen to open the freezer door, only to discover that he'd run out of packet meals. He'd had so much on his mind at the weekend that he'd forgotten to fit in a trip to the supermarket.

He looked at his watch; it was seven-thirty. He could go this evening, he reckoned, many of these places stayed open till late. First he would have some coffee, ignoring the rest of that second whisky, maybe read the evening paper and then drive along to the Tesco store that lay on the main road between Felinbach and Bangor. He'd fill the Land Rover with fuel at the same time and kill two birds with one stone.

He settled down with the paper in front of the electric fire and was reading an article about the problems caused by the spread of wild rhododendrons down in Beddgelert when the phone rang.

'Is that the Dr Gordon who came to Prosser's today?' asked a gruff-sounding male voice.

'It is. Who's that?'

'Maurice Cleef.'

Tom felt a frisson of excitement grip him but he did his best to keep it out of his voice. 'What can I do for you, Mr Cleef?'

'Look, I don't want to get in no trouble over this Griffiths baby business, see.'

'What sort of trouble are we talking about?' asked Tom calmly, although he felt very different inside.

'The deal is, I tell you what you want to know and let that be an end to it, see? You leave me out of everything after that. I had nothing to do with any of it. Is that understood?'

'Tell me.'

There was a pause then Tom heard Cleef say, 'Shit, I've no more change and I'm in a call box.'

'Give me the number and I'll call you back.'

'I can't see a number. Bloody thing's been vandalised. Bastards! Look, I'll be in the Harlech Arms in Caernarfon. Meet me there in half an hour.'

The line went dead and Tom replaced the receiver. His pulse was racing. He felt as if he'd just been given a role in a movie and wasn't quite sure how to play it. Presumably Cleef was going to tell him who in the Pathology Department had been responsible for putting the waste tissue into Megan Griffiths's coffin.

Maybe, he thought, he should contact one of the other members of the enquiry team — say Swanson, and get him to come along as a witness. On the other hand, you didn't have to be Albert Einstein to work out that the presence of another person would almost certainly scare Cleef out of saying anything at all. There was no alternative; he would have to go back up to Caernarfon and meet Cleef alone if he really wanted to find out the name of the culprit.

Tom had only a vague notion of where the Harlech Arms was in Caernarfon and he could still be wrong, he admitted as he turned left in the square opposite the castle and drove down the steep hill leading to the docks. He thought he'd seen a pub of that name down on the lower dock road to the west of where he usually parked his car.

The rows of dark sheds and warehouses did not seem encouraging and he was beginning to think that he'd been mistaken when a yellow pub sign loomed up out of the darkness and he read to his relief *Harlech Arms* above the door. The pub sign was a soldier wearing a red tunic, holding a musket and standing to attention, looking out over the dark Menai.

The road was too narrow to park outside so Tom crawled slowly past until he found a clear stretch of tarmac alongside the entrance to a warehouse. It seemed a reasonable bet that access would not be required until the morning so he left the Land Rover there and walked back.

He was expecting the pub to be quiet, being a bit off the beaten track, so he was surprised to find it busy. The clientèle were mainly men although there were a couple of women sitting at a table just inside the door. The pub itself was like a million others of its sort — smoky, dirty and less than welcoming to strangers. Cleef did not appear to be there.

'What'll it be?' asked a fat barman with thinning blonde hair and a smile that might have been more convincing had it featured teeth. Tom started to wonder what had happened to them, but thought it best not to continue with this line of thought. 'Half of Fosters,' he said.

He was down to the last two inches in his glass and was checking his watch for the third time when Cleef finally arrived. He looked very scared.

~ *Eleven* ~

Cleef joined him at the bar and Tom could see that the man was living on his nerves.

'What will you have?' he asked, trying to introduce a note of normality.

Cleef looked at him distantly as if drink was the last thing on his mind. 'Err . . . pint of bitter,' he said.

'Pint of bitter, please.'

'I was followed,' said Cleef in a hoarse whisper. 'That's why I'm late – I had to give him the slip.'

The doctor found this melodramatic. 'Followed? Are you sure?' he asked, handing over a five-pound note as the pint arrived.

Cleef waited until the barman had given Tom his change before saying, 'I'm sure all right. This guy was hanging about outside Prosser's at knocking off time, and there he was again, standing across the road from my house when I left to come here. I walked around the block just to test him like, and sure enough, the bastard followed me. I had to nip up a lane and take him for a tour round the docks to lose him.'

'But why would anyone want to follow you?' asked Tom.

'It's this Griffiths baby business,' said Cleef, 'I'm sure of it. I wish to Christ I'd blown the whistle at the time and been done with it.'

'Go on.'

Cleef looked nervously around him before saying, 'Look, all I did was keep my mouth shut about the coffin being closed when I arrived. I didn't know the kid wasn't in it, for Christ's sake.'

'Who asked you to keep your mouth shut?'

'Dunno.'

'You don't know?' exclaimed Tom, his voice full of disbelief.

'I'd never seen the guy before.'

'It wasn't one of the mortuary attendants, then?'

'No, nothing to do with those guys – I know *them* well enough. They weren't around when I got there. In fact, I was looking for them when this guy came up to me and asked what the problem was. I told him I was looking for someone to tell me why the Griffiths coffin was all closed up and he said it was nothing to worry about; they'd done it because they needed the space.'

'What did you say to that?'

'I told him they'd just have to open the bloody thing up again because I'd brought up the clothes the couple wanted their kid to wear for the funeral.'

Cleef paused and Tom had to prompt him to go on.

Cleef looked sheepish. 'He gave me a hundred quid to go away and keep my mouth shut – said there was no need for it to bother my conscience. The kid was dead, didn't matter what she wore.'

'You took the money?'

Cleef shrugged defiantly. ' 'Course I took the money. Humping stiffs around doesn't exactly put you at the top of the earnings league.'

'So you took the money and brought the coffin back to Prosser's without saying anything to anyone.'

Cleef nodded. 'That's it and now I wish to Christ I hadn't.'

'Can you describe this man?'

'He was wearing hospital gear like a lot of them wear. You know . . .'

'White coat or tunic and trousers?'

'Tunic and trousers. He was mid-thirties, dark hair, tall — about the same height as me, but proper spoken, like — sounded like a doctor.'

'It's really important that we identify this man. Can you think of anything else about him? Scars? Identifying marks? Anything at all that would be useful?'

Cleef shook his head. 'I wasn't with him for that long. Nothing about him made much of an impression on me.'

'Will you come up to the hospital with me and point him out?'

'No bloody way,' spluttered Cleef. 'I don't even like being here right now, talking about it with that bastard following me earlier on.'

Tom could see that there would be no point in trying to persuade Cleef to change his mind; he was clearly scared. He tried another tack. 'Even supposing you're right about someone following you,' he said, 'there's really nothing to suggest it has anything to do with what happened at the hospital, is there?'

'What other reason could there be?' Cleef retorted.

Tom shrugged. 'You don't owe anyone money?'

Cleef shook his head.

'You haven't been seeing someone else's lady?'

'I wish,' grunted Cleef.

Tom had to admit that Cleef was not a front runner in the matinée idol stakes, so he changed tack again. 'Maybe you're just feeling guilty about having taken the money. It's making you imagine you were being followed. Guilt can do that to people.'

Cleef became annoyed. 'I'm telling you I *was* being followed,' he snapped. 'That was no bloody Jehovah's Witness chasing me round the docks!'

'All right,' said Tom. 'Do you think it was the same man who paid you?'

'Dunno. It was dark and he was well wrapped up. It could have been.'

'Supposing I can lay my hands on some staff photos from the hospital, will you at least take a look at them and maybe point out the man?'

Cleef agreed. 'But that's as far as it goes,' he warned.

The two men left the bar and parted company, with Cleef saying that he was in the Harlech Arms on most nights; Tom should seek him out there rather than by phoning or turning up at Prosser's. Tom agreed and walked back to the car, his eyes struggling with the gloom and a damp mist that had come down after the rain.

He paused for a moment while unlocking the car door. For a moment he thought he heard someone cry out in the distance . . . but there was nothing now save for the groan of a fog horn somewhere out on the Menai. He chided himself for feeling nervous but it wasn't the nicest area to be in at night. God knows why Cleef chose this as his local. Tom shivered suddenly. There was no denying that it felt better to be inside the car and on the move again. His mind turned to thoughts of food. He'd stop off and pick up a Chinese take-away on the way home.

Next morning, in between seeing two patients, Tom phoned John Palmer's solicitor, Mr Roberts, in Bangor to ask how he should go about arranging a visit to see John. The man hummed and hawed a good deal, but finally agreed to see what he could do. 'I can make no promises,' he warned.

'Of course not,' replied Tom, adding silently inside his head, 'Lawyers never can.'

He slipped in another phone call between the next two patients, this time to ask Ronald Harcourt, the Hospital Manager at Caernarfon General, about staff photographs.

'All members of staff have their photograph attached to their personnel records, it's part of our admin procedure,' said Harcourt. 'Why do you ask?'

'I'd like to see some.'

'May I ask why?'

'I've come up with a witness, someone who may be able to help with our enquiry,' replied Tom. 'I don't think I want to say any more than that at the moment.'

'I see,' replied Harcourt. 'Perhaps it would be better if you spoke to our Human Resources Manager, Miss Edwards.'

Tom was put through to a woman whose rich, deep voice suggested she probably made a fine contralto in some chapel choir. 'If you'd like to come over to the office some time, Doctor, I'm sure we'll do our best to help,' she said.

Tom explained that that wouldn't be any good; he would have to take the photographs away, probably just for one evening. He heard the woman sigh and knew that this was obviously going to pose a problem.

'The trouble is, the photos are actually attached to the personnel files through a special bonding process and the files themselves are confidential documents. We couldn't let you take them away, I'm afraid.'

Tom accepted this and tried to think of a compromise. 'Maybe a photocopy of the photographs alone?' he suggested.

'That might be possible,' conceded Miss Edwards slowly,

in the manner of someone not overly enthusiastic about an idea. 'What type of staff are you interested in, Doctor, and how many photographs are we talking about here?' she asked.

'I'm not quite sure myself,' he confessed. 'Let's start with the staff of the Pathology Department and then maybe move on to the medical staff.'

'All of them?'

'Just the males.'

'I'll see what I can do,' said Miss Edwards, sounding definitely cooler than she had been at the outset. 'Perhaps you could leave me a number and I'll get back to you in due course.'

Tom finished morning surgery and joined Julie for coffee before starting out on his rounds. She threw him the local morning paper as he sat down. 'Want a look?'

'Nothing concerning us, I hope,' he said.

'No, thank goodness. They've found another shock-horror story to occupy themselves with — a murder by the sound of it.'

Tom sipped his coffee and glanced at the photograph on the front page; he recognised the riverside area up in Caernarfon and was suddenly filled with foreboding. The accompanying story said that a man had been pulled from the river in the early hours of the morning; police were treating the death as suspicious. Tom suddenly recalled the cry he had heard. He read on. The dead man had been named as Maurice Cleef of Pont Street in Caernarfon; he had been seen drinking in a local dockside pub earlier in the evening. Police were anxious to interview anyone who'd seen him, especially the man he had been drinking with.

'Is anything the matter?' asked Julie. 'You look as if you've just seen a ghost.'

When he had recovered sufficiently from the initial

shock, Tom said, 'It's me — *I'm* the one they're looking for. I was with Maurice Cleef last night.'

'You!' she exclaimed.

'He works . . . he worked for Prosser's.' Tom told her why he had agreed to meet him and how Cleef had thought he could identify the man who had interfered with Megan Griffiths's coffin.

Julie shook her head. 'You seem to have a talent for getting yourself mixed up in trouble, Tom. Do you want me to do your rounds for you while you sort out this mess?'

He declined. 'It'll be okay, I'll call into the police station on the way back when I've finished. I can't really tell them anything except that Cleef thought someone was following him, and I didn't believe him. I suggested it was his imagination. Wasn't that just brilliant?'

'I'm sure I would have said much the same thing,' said Julie comfortingly. 'Being followed? It sounds like something from an episode of *Inspector Morse*. It's all quite bizarre.'

'That's more or less what I told Cleef, but it looks as if he was right all along, poor sod.'

'So what *did* happen to the Griffiths baby exactly?' asked Julie.

'That's still a very good question. The only thing I'm sure about is that it wasn't just a simple mix-up.' Tom said it calmly but his insides were turning over at the thought of Cleef's murder. It had been a very long time since he'd felt this afraid. The last time had been when he'd slipped on a narrow ridge high up on a mountain and had just managed to save himself from falling. Now the feeling in his stomach was just the same.

'Are you all right?' asked Julie, noticing his sudden preoccupation.

'I'm okay. I'd better start my rounds.'

* * *

Tom found the interview with Chief Inspector Davies difficult. It was quite clear the man regarded him as a pest because of his earlier refusal to accept John Palmer's guilt. 'I might have known,' he said rudely when Tom announced that he'd been the man in the pub with Cleef. 'What in God's name were you doing in a dump like the Harlech?'

Tom chose to tell the policeman as little as he possibly could, not out of a desire to obstruct or out of any feeling of animosity, but simply because he didn't want a new scandal story to break which would affect the hospital adversely. He therefore didn't tell him the details about Cleef's involvement in the Griffiths baby affair, just that he thought he might have had some information that would have helped with the independent enquiry.

'What sort of information?' Davies persisted.

'He wanted to assure me that neither of the two mortuary attendants were involved in the mix-up.' There was an element of truth to this, even if it was not the whole story.

Davies took down details of the meeting, noting the time they'd met and the time they'd parted, also the fact that Cleef had felt he was being followed but that he had not said by whom nor had he been able to suggest a reason.

'But you say he was scared?' the policeman concluded.

'Very,' said Tom.

'That fits in with what they said in the pub,' said Davies. '"Not like his old self at all",' they commented. 'They thought it must have had something to do with the stranger he was with last night . . . *you*, Doctor.'

Tom insisted that Cleef's unease had had nothing to do with him.

'Ah yes, it would have been down to the man who was

following him,' said Davies, deliberately introducing a note of sarcasm into his voice.

It annoyed Tom. 'I presume you *are* going to look for this man, Chief Inspector?' he said. 'Or are you going to sit on your backside just like you've been doing in the Palmer baby case?'

'I'm sure we're all very grateful for your input into police matters, Doctor,' said Davies calmly. 'In return, may I suggest that any time you need medical advice, you just give us a call.'

Tom regretted losing his temper for now he'd also lost the bout with Davies on a technical knockout. He tried bridge building. 'I don't suppose there's a chance that Cleef fell into the river on his own?'

'Possibly he did,' replied Davies evenly. 'Right after somebody caved his head in with a heavy metal object.'

Tom drove back over to Felinbach, harbouring a mixture of feelings inside him, none of them good. Cleef had definitely been murdered, and if he'd been right about the reason for his being followed, then it raised several unpleasant questions concerning his own safety. Cleef's attacker had obviously been lying in wait for him when he'd come out of the Harlech last night. Where did that leave Tom, if the murderer knew he'd been with Cleef all evening? Unless the killer was confident that Cleef hadn't actually known him by name or what his function was at the hospital, he himself could well be next on the killer's list. Telling Chief Inspector Davies that wasn't going to elicit much sympathy, he reckoned. Davies might even find it amusing.

Maybe he was getting this whole thing out of proportion. There was still a chance that Cleef had been killed for a reason he knew nothing at all about. Just because the man had denied having any money or women problems didn't automatically mean that that was so, nor that there hadn't been a whole lot of other bad things going on in his life. When it came right down to it, he knew nothing at all about Maurice Cleef. And this was North Wales, for God's sake, not gangland Chicago.

It didn't work. His gut instinct was telling him that things were going to get a whole lot worse before they got better. It was telling him that Maurice Cleef had been murdered to stop him identifying the man at the hospital, the dark-haired, well-spoken man — possibly a doctor — who had packed pathological waste into Megan Griffiths's coffin in place of her body. But *why* had he done that? There had to be more to this affair than just a clumsy attempt at covering up a mistake. It suggested that Megan Griffiths's body had been stolen. It had been taken for a reason.

This was the first time Tom had articulated this possibility. Although the idea had surfaced before, he had dismissed it in favour of a less dramatic explanation. Now he was faced with a sudden rise in the stakes, a move up from incompetence to crime, and a change from accidental mix-up to deliberate body snatching and murder. He couldn't begin to imagine why anyone would want to steal the body of a cot-death baby, but someone had — and was prepared to resort to bribery and murder in order to conceal their identity and motive.

— Twelve —

Roberts phoned back at four-thirty to tell Tom that he had arranged for him to visit John Palmer in prison at three o'clock on Saturday afternoon. Roberts urged him to 'embrace pragmatism' and not say or do anything to upset what might be best for Palmer in the long run. Tom assured the man that he had John's best interests at heart, without adding that his ideas on what that might be were probably very different from his solicitor's.

Although he was pleased at the prospect of seeing John again and getting the chance to talk some sense into him, Tom was still haunted by the spectre of Cleef's killer, tormented by thoughts of what he might be planning. He'd given up trying not to worry. Maybe it was his Scottish upbringing, but he believed in the adage 'expect the worst and you won't be disappointed'.

In his worst imaginings, Cleef's killer was out there, biding his time — maybe even watching the surgery, waiting for a chance to kill him too, just to make doubly sure that his secret was safe. Tom looked out of the window into the darkness and shivered.

'Is everything all right?' asked Julie behind him.

Tom nearly jumped out of his skin.

Julie looked at him quizzically, surprised at the strength of his reaction. 'I'm sorry, I didn't mean to startle you.'

He recovered quickly. 'Sorry – I was away in a dream. I didn't hear you come in.'

Julie wasn't convinced. 'What's wrong?' she asked.

Tom slumped back down into his chair. 'Let's call it a reaction to Cleef's death. I must have been the last person he saw or spoke to. It's an unnerving thought.'

'Apart from his killer, of course,' said Julie.

'I suppose.'

Julie, who still suspected that the younger doctor wasn't telling her everything, suddenly saw what he might be concealing and was alarmed. 'You don't think this man's death had anything to do with the business at the hospital, do you?' she asked, as if afraid of the answer.

Tom said in a low voice: 'Cleef was sure that was why he was being followed.'

'Good God, it never even occurred to me that there was a connection! But this is awful. Have you told the police?' And when he shook his head, 'Why ever not?' she demanded.

'Any suggestion of a link between Cleef's death and the Griffiths baby scandal would explode all over the papers and eclipse any coverage of Caernarfon General's IVF symposium. It's important to them. They've put a lot of effort into it and they deserve a break.'

'Oh my God,' sighed Julie, sinking down into the chair usually occupied by patients in Tom's room. 'It's just one thing after another.' She sat there mulling things over in her mind for a few moments before a new thought occurred to her. 'But you must be in danger too!'

'The thought had crossed my mind,' Tom said with a half-hearted smile.

'What did this man Cleef tell you exactly?'

Tom related it all.

'That's not much, is it?' said Julie. 'Unfortunately, I don't suppose the killer knows that.'

'That's precisely the problem.'

They lapsed into a worried silence then Tom had a more encouraging thought. 'The Harlech was Cleef's local,' he said, as if this were a sudden revelation to him.

'So?'

'Cleef told me that he was there most evenings. If I needed to get in touch with him I should go there rather than phone him or go to Prosser's place.'

'That's not going to be much good now,' Julie joked grimly.

'That's not the point,' said Tom. 'Maybe the killer doesn't know about me at all!'

'Explain.'

'Cleef knew he was being followed when he left home last night so he took evasive action and gave the man the slip before coming to the Harlech. If the killer *knew* that the Harlech was Cleef's local, he might just have set up camp outside and waited for Cleef to either arrive or emerge. He wouldn't necessarily know that Cleef had arranged to meet anyone there!'

'I suppose not,' agreed Julie.

Tom warmed to the idea. 'Even if the killer saw me come out of the pub with Cleef, I could just have been someone leaving at the same time. We parted company almost immediately and what's more, we went off in different directions!'

'Unless of course, the killer recognised you as a doctor and wondered what you were doing in a dive like the Harlech Arms in the first place,' said Julie.

This took the edge off Tom's euphoria: Julie had a point. He left the surgery and stepped apprehensively out into the darkness to walk down the hill to his flat. The night in Felinbach suddenly seemed threatening. The houses on the way to the harbour, which in the past had always assumed the friendly silhouette of a fairy-tale village, were now huddled together in cold indifference. Every nook and cranny on Harbour Hill concealed a hidden threat. Even the small boats, riding at anchor in the marina, eyed him suspiciously.

It was a relief to close the door of the flat behind him and lean his back on it for a few seconds; the flat might be cold but at least it felt safe. He put the snib up on the lock and went into the kitchen to do battle with the heating controller yet again. He was just delivering a second thump to the pump when he remembered that he *still* hadn't been to the supermarket so there was nothing in the freezer.

Cursing, he started opening cupboards in a search for something to eat and so avoid going out again. The one above the sink yielded up a tin of sardines so he made himself sardines on toast and put his feet up to watch some TV before having an early night.

Tom slept badly. His mind was too full of thoughts that transmuted themselves easily into the stuff of nightmares. Black goblins rose from muddy graves to pursue him across a barren wasteland, herding him, like a stricken animal, towards a deep moat in front of a dark forbidding castle. The drawbridge was up and there was nowhere to go. The choice lay between the deep, dark water and the razor-sharp teeth of the goblins. As he fell backwards into the water he woke up with a start to find himself covered in sweat. He attributed this to the terror of the dream until he realised that it really was very warm in the flat. For once, the heating had jammed in the 'on' position, and when he got up to look, the temperature in the room was well over thirty degrees. It was a little after 5 a.m. so he decided to have a long bath before going out for a walk to blow away the cobwebs of the night.

He ended up walking for much longer than he'd anticipated due to the fact that, for once, there was a clear sky
and it was good to watch the sun come up while on the
beach. It reminded him of happier times in his life, and as
he walked towards Bangor, watching the sun's rays light
up the structural details of the old Telford Bridge spanning
the Menai, he reflected on the fabled, age-old battle between
the forces of light and darkness. The warmth of the sun on
his face did much to wipe out the lingering aftermath of
the nightmare.

Julie called out to him as soon as he walked into the
surgery. 'There was a call for you; you've just missed her.
Ellen Edwards at Plas Coch Farm says Glyn isn't getting
any better. She said you asked her to phone if there was
no improvement by Saturday.'

Tom felt the blood drain from his face as all the good
the walk had done him was wiped out in an instant. He
sat down in front of Julie like an automaton.

'What on earth's the matter?' she asked, alarmed at the
sudden change in his appearance.

'I forgot.'

'Forgot what?'

'I forgot to take Glyn's swab over to the lab in Bangor:
it's still in my bag.'

'I see,' said Julie, her manner changing, reproach entering
her voice.

'It went clean out of my head.'

'So what's the damage?'

'I gave him chlor-tetracycline for the infection, but I
took a swab for the lab so they could identify the infection
and do sensitivity tests on the bug just in case it proved
necessary. The tet's clearly not working. If I'd taken the
swab to the lab on Thursday as I intended, I would have
had the sensitivity report this morning and I could have

changed him to another drug I knew would work. As it is, I'll have to guess again. God, this is awful.'

'As you say, you'll just have to guess again,' said Julie.

'Christ, I'm so sorry.'

'It's Glyn Edwards you should be apologising to.'

'I'll get right over there. I don't know what came over me.'

'I do,' said Julie. 'You've just taken on far too much. Your work is beginning to suffer.'

'Maybe you'd like my resignation?' said Tom. He was serious.

Julie looked at him for a moment before her expression relaxed. 'No, of course I don't want your resignation,' she said. 'We all make mistakes, it's just that when *we* make them, other people tend to suffer. It's partly my fault anyway; I passed over the Griffiths baby business to you instead of dealing with it myself. I had no idea what it was going to turn into.'

'I'm really sorry about this: I feel terrible.'

'Look,' said Julie, 'get over to Plas Coch and prescribe a different broad-spectrum antibiotic for Glyn. You can't be that unlucky twice in a row. If it works, and I'm sure it will, then no time's been lost and no real harm's been done.'

'On my way,' Tom said.

Julie stopped his rush to the door. 'Look, Tom,' she said, 'you haven't had a holiday in over a year. Why don't you take a couple of weeks off, starting now – sort out what's on your mind and then come back refreshed?'

'What about the surgery?' he asked.

'I'll manage,' she said. 'Just like you managed when I went away for a few days last autumn.'

Tom was hesitant.

'Go on, off with you.'

* * *

John Palmer was being held at HM Prison Cardiff, which presented Tom with a problem. Should he drive down through the Welsh mountains, or should he head over to join the M6 and circle round using the motorway network? As he was a bit late in setting off due to his unscheduled trip out to Plas Coch Farm, he opted for the motorway: it was a longer journey but it would take less time in the end.

The journey down to Cardiff proved uneventful and Tom found the prison without any trouble. He parked the Land Rover and approached the gates on foot. He had never actually been inside a prison before, but a lifetime's exposure to films and television made it seem almost familiar, right down to the echoing metallic sounds and the stale smell of boiled cabbage. He reflected that if atmosphere had colour, the prison's would be grey. It was a place where despair had a clear head-start over optimism.

Two hefty prison officers escorted John Palmer into the room and Tom stood up to meet him. He had to make a conscious effort to hide the shock he felt at his appearance, for Palmer seemed to have aged twenty years in the past two weeks. His face was much thinner and the stubble on his cheeks looked grey if not white. His eyes were sunk in dark hollows and he had an air of detachment about him as if he'd been heavily sedated.

'Hello, John. Good to see you.'

'Tom,' said Palmer weakly. 'Thanks for coming.'

The prison officers stepped back, one leaving the room, the other taking up a stance by the door, not quite out of earshot for ordinary levels of speech.

'This isn't just a social visit,' said Tom in an urgent whisper. 'You do know why I'm here?'

'Roberts said something,' said Palmer.

Tom leaned forward on the table that separated them.

'You didn't do it!' he said. 'I know you didn't, Lucy knows you didn't, so why in God's name are you persisting with this ridiculous confession?'

'I did do it,' said Palmer calmly. 'I appreciate your concern but I've made a full confession and that's an end to it.'

Tom stared at him and Palmer held his gaze, obviously quite resolute in what he said.

'Nonsense!' exclaimed Tom, attracting a glance from the guard on the door, which made him lower his voice again. 'It doesn't make any sense! I know you're lying. You couldn't possibly have done anything like that and Lucy certainly didn't do it either, so why on earth are you persisting with this?'

Palmer seemed to relax a little. There was almost a hint of amusement in his eyes at seeing his friend so upset. 'Tom, what do you imagine would happen if Lucy and I were to maintain that we were both innocent and knew nothing at all about our baby's death?' he asked.

'It would simply be the truth.'

'What would happen?' Palmer insisted.

Tom felt suddenly uncomfortable because he knew the answer but didn't want to say it.

'Well?'

'The police would be forced to look for the real killer,' said Tom, finally coming up with something positive to say.

Palmer looked at him accusingly. 'Want to try again?' he said.

'All right, I think you and Lucy would both be charged with her murder, but you'd get a fair trial and the truth would be bound to come out. The police would find the real killer once they put some effort into it.'

'We would be convicted,' said Palmer flatly. 'Now, tell me to my face that I'm wrong.'

'You can't just give up like that,' said Tom but it sounded weak and in his heart he knew that Palmer was right; they would be convicted by overwhelming circumstantial evidence. It suddenly made him realise the enormity of Palmer's action: it wasn't anything to do with him believing that Lucy had done it. He knew full well that his wife was innocent! He had actually decided to confess so that he alone would take the blame in a battle against overwhelming odds.

Tom was forced to look at his friend through new eyes. 'Do you really love Lucy that much?' he asked.

Palmer smiled distantly and gave just the hint of a nod.

'You do realise that you'll be branded a child-killer for life, and that the real killer will get away with it because no one will ever bother to look for him now? No one will ever know that you were completely innocent except you and Lucy . . . and me.'

Palmer sat up straight and said in a louder voice for the benefit of the prison officer, 'Like I said, I'm guilty.'

— *Thirteen* —

As he turned off the M6, heading back to the North Wales coast, Tom felt angry and frustrated. If only he could think of a plausible motive for Anne-Marie's murder, something other than a pathological desire to frame the Palmers and see their lives ruined. He'd actually asked John at one point about the possibility of any such enemy and had been met with a simple, 'Don't be ridiculous.'

But if sheer malice had to be ruled out, it didn't leave much else. There again, Tom considered as his mind strayed, who would want to steal the body of a cot-death baby and fill her coffin with human offal instead? Both crimes defied analysis, using either logic or common sense. Both seemed absolutely pointless and . . . unless these two bizarre happenings were actually connected in some way?

If Maurice Cleef had been right and a doctor *had* been involved in the Griffiths baby affair, might not he have stolen the body for some scientific or experimental reason? Maybe he needed tissue or some organ from it? If that were the case, then surely it was just conceivable that the same motive had applied to the Palmer baby, only he had had to kill in order to get it.

Tom knew that he was probing the outer reaches of plausibility with this idea, but at least it was a new line of thought and therefore worth pursuing. Could it be that some kind of research project was involved? Something that required the bodies of two baby girls? Something that the researcher thought was so important he was prepared to kill for it?

He couldn't examine Megan Griffiths's body, but there was a chance that Anne-Marie Palmer's remains were still in the custody of the forensic service. He wanted to examine them. Although acid had been used extensively, it might yet be possible to detect evidence of some surgical procedure having been carried out on her before she'd been killed. Some portion of an internal organ might even be missing.

He didn't suppose this sort of thing was exactly what Julie had in mind when she'd suggested he take some time off, but it was something he had to pursue. He would get in touch with the police pathologist Charles French as soon as he got back, even if it meant calling him at home on a Saturday evening. The thought was still uppermost in his mind when he noticed the Tesco supermarket sign and remembered just in time to turn into the car park and go in search of food to see him through the week ahead.

'She's still in the fridge at Ysbyty Gwynedd,' said French. 'Why do you ask?'

'I'd like to take a look at her if it's all right with you,' said Tom, politely but matter of factly.

'It's very much *not* all right with me,' French responded tartly. 'Any unauthorised access to the body could prejudice the Crown case. That body is evidence; I can't allow anyone to interfere with it.'

'Sorry, I didn't think about it that way,' said a chastened Tom who hadn't even considered this aspect of it at all.

French said, 'May I ask why you wanted to examine her anyway? It's a pretty unlikely request for a GP to make.'

Tom ignored what he thought might be an intended

insult and said, 'I wanted to see if there was any sign of recent surgical intervention before her death.' Without thinking, he'd created a rod for his own back.

'Surgical intervention?' repeated French slowly. 'Something that I *missed*, you mean? Like the cause of death?'

'No, no, I didn't mean to imply that for a moment,' exclaimed Tom, embarrassed at his own thoughtlessness. 'Really, I was thinking of something entirely different, something possibly very trivial, some tiny thing you might not even have noticed because it had no relevance . . .'

'Nothing is too trivial for a forensic pathologist, Dr Gordon, that's the nature of the job. They pay me to look for everything!'

'Of course,' conceded Tom, berating himself silently.

'The only sign of surgical activity on the baby's body was in her lower extremities where her birth defect had been dealt with surgically shortly after she was born. Evidence of this was still clearly visible despite the acid damage to the tissue.'

'Is it possible then that the acid may have obscured other such evidence?' suggested Tom.

'Anything's possible in the imagination. What sort of surgery did you have in mind?'

'I'm not sure,' Tom replied.

'Are you feeling all right, Doctor?'

Tom decided to stop pursuing a lost cause. 'I'm sorry to have bothered you, Doctor, please forgive the intrusion.'

He put the phone down and stood still for a moment, feeling absolutely stupid. He cringed with embarrassment as he thought through his conversation with French again. Maybe Julie was right about his state of mind. Maybe he *did* need a holiday before people started to question his sanity. But it was too late to consider that option seriously. He'd end up taking all that was going on inside his head with him wherever he went: there would be no escape. He would however, he decided, have a day out in the hills tomorrow to get things into perspective.

Tom could tell by Ellen Edwards's expression when she came out to meet him in the farmyard the next morning that things were better. She was smiling and the worry had gone from her eyes. She stood, drying her hands on her apron, until Tom reached the door. 'I wasn't expecting to see you this morning,' she said pleasantly.

'I'm off to the hills for the day so I thought I'd pop in on my way past,' lied Tom; it had always been his intention to visit Glyn. 'How is he?'

'A lot better, thank you, Doctor, he's much more like his old self this morning. I had a bit of a fight to keep him indoors when he saw the sun, but I'm glad to say he saw sense and is staying put for the time being.'

Tom felt pleased and relieved. In the final analysis, his mistake had not caused any delay in Glyn's treatment. He had prescribed the new drug on Saturday morning and he couldn't have done it any quicker had a lab report been available – although he could have been more sure of its efficacy. But as he listened to Ellen, Tom knew that if he had not told her to call the surgery on Saturday if Glyn was not getting any better, several more days might have elapsed. Glyn might even have ended up losing his leg. He declined Ellen's offer of tea but popped in to have a quick word with her husband before setting off for the mountains.

Julie had been right about him having too much on his plate and his work suffering because of it. He couldn't afford to make any more mistakes like the one over Glyn Edwards, not if he wanted to continue working in the practice. He was taking some time off, which he'd use to pursue his investigation of the Palmer case, but if he didn't start making progress soon, he would have to call a halt to his investigations and think again.

He could even resign his partnership. To his own amazement, he found himself actually considering this as an option, so great was his sense of injustice over what was happening to the Palmers. As he turned the Land Rover into the mountain car park, he made an effort to concentrate on the more immediate future and put all other thoughts to one side.

Halfway up the Llanberis path on Snowdon, he decided that he would drive up to Caernarfon General on Monday morning. There lay the answer to the Megan Griffiths riddle and possibly the connection, if there was one, with the Palmer baby's death. Happily, he had a tailor-made excuse for going there in Carwyn Thomas's invitation to attend the IVF symposium. If he turned up at the opening session he might just manage to have a word with Thomas himself and ask about research projects in general in the hospital. That would be a start. He might even spot a project that could conceivably involve the corpses of two young baby girls.

It was worth a try and certainly better than doing nothing. With this plan in mind, he continued with the climb, knowing that the exertion involved would do him good and help relieve the stress that had been building up inside him all week.

Carwyn Thomas was a good speaker and his audience warmed to him quickly. This was especially so when he put up a first slide of happy-looking children, announcing that they were, 'The end product of our science.'

Thomas gave an overview of IVF treatment from the time of its inception to the present day, when it was now, as he put it, 'just another everyday run of the mill sort of service'. He recalled that in the early days he had once been called the 'Son of Satan' by one of the tabloid newspapers, which had accused him of playing God by attempting to create life in the laboratory and had orchestrated a petition against him to have the work stopped. Several years later, the same paper sponsored triplets, born as a result of IVF treatment here in Caernarfon.

'We've always had to struggle,' continued Thomas. 'These days people will argue that our funding be cut in order to finance what they see as the more pressing needs of medicine. We must resist them. Children are our future, our fulfilment; there is no more pressing need in medicine than that of a woman who wants to conceive but cannot. We can make it happen and we must be allowed to continue to make it happen.'

The Professor sat down to warm applause, his place at the lectern being taken by a tall distinguished-looking man with close-cropped grey hair and silver-framed spectacles. Tom thought that he looked American and was proved right when the speaker was introduced as Professor Richard Meyer from the University of California at Los Angeles.

'Carwyn has spoken eloquently of the past,' began Meyer. 'It's my job to say a little about the future of IVF. We've come a long way from the time when we mixed ova and sperm, injected the mixture and hoped for the best. The technique has become more and more refined, multiple births are no longer as prevalent as they used to be, and the specificity of ICSI is becoming almost commonplace in many labs. The use of helper cells has increased our success rate and we are able to treat more and more difficult cases with an ever-growing confidence in our ability. But there is one challenge on our horizon, ladies and gentlemen, and one we will all have to face up to sooner or later. This is the challenge of human cloning. The public's imagination has been captured by this subject and the technological advances we are making in the lab are bringing us ever closer to making it possible in the foreseeable future. There will undoubtedly be a demand for it. We must think about our response.'

A murmur ran round the room and Meyer looked over his spectacles at his audience.

'You speak as if human cloning is inevitable,' said a German voice from among the delegates.

'I believe it is,' replied Meyer bluntly. 'I've always found the maxim, "if it can be done, it will be done", to be a safe bet in science.'

'Surely it needn't be, if there's a will to stop it,' said an Englishwoman who announced herself as Dr Linda Moore from Cambridge.

Meyer shook his head. 'Even then, someone somewhere will do it. Be sure of that.'

'Isn't this all rather academic anyway?' said someone else. 'We can't do it yet: the technology doesn't exist.'

'We're not that far off,' said Meyer, 'so it's as well to be prepared, don't you think? Our development of ICSI technology will be very relevant to human cloning. You could say we're becoming expert in the required techniques without even realising it.'

'But why? What's the point of it all?' asked a man in the front row. 'We'll never be able to clone a person in the true sense of the word, in terms of character and personality; the best we can ever hope to do is produce a baby with a clean sheet for a mind, just like any other baby. The child may grow up to look exactly like the person he or she was cloned from, but its mind will comprise its own ideas and experiences, not anyone else's.'

'But the potential is there,' said the Swedish woman Dr Linnstrom. 'Clone a genius and you'll get a genius.'

'I think Dr Linnstrom has just put her finger on it,' said Meyer with a smile. 'Applied selectively, human cloning could enrich society by ensuring that our finest minds remain with us always.'

'Well, I'm against it. It wouldn't stop there and we all know it. Most people will consider themselves unique in some way or other, and no doubt worthy of preserving. We'll be inundated with requests if we don't do something to regulate it now.'

There was a general murmur of agreement before a woman in the row in front of Tom stood up and identified herself as Dr Maisie Land from Trinity College Dublin. She said, 'But aren't we all forgetting that human cloning technology could make a tremendous impact in transplant surgery?'

'So I keep hearing,' said Meyer testily. 'Perhaps you'd care to explain how, Doctor?'

A hush fell over the room, caused by the American's change of tone. Everyone looked to the woman who had attracted his aggression; she herself was obviously embarrassed and bemused. 'Surely it's obvious, Professor, that organs taken from a clone of an individual would be a perfect match for that individual.'

'Of course, but how do you clone an organ, Doctor?'

Maisie Land became even more embarrassed: Tom was close enough to see her hands tremble. 'Well, it's not exactly my field,' she said, 'but I imagine some sort of cell culture might be . . .'

The American started shaking his head long before she had finished her sentence. 'Can't be done,' he said. 'To obtain a living kidney, liver, heart or whatever, you need a living human being. That means you start out with a cloned healthy baby, so are you telling me that you would consider cutting up live babies to provide spare parts, Doctor? I think not. Human cloning when it starts, will give you human babies, ladies and gentlemen, nothing else — no supermarket shelves with livers and kidneys, just bonny, bouncing babies.'

'Food for thought,' said Carwyn Thomas, getting to his feet again, obviously pleased that the general level of interest in the opening session boded well for a lively symposium.

~ *Fourteen* ~

Professor Thomas noticed Tom's presence for the first time during the buffet lunch and looked surprised. 'Dr Gordon! You decided to come after all. I'm delighted.'

'I've taken a few days off,' Tom told him, 'so I thought I'd take you up on your kind invitation. It seems to have got off to a cracking start.'

'You can say that again,' smiled Thomas. 'Anything to do with human cloning always arouses strong emotions in people.'

'How about you?' asked Tom as he quickly put a few pieces of salad on a plate and joined the old man as he moved away from the table to stand by a window.

'Oh, me too,' Thomas confirmed.

'For or against?'

'For, in the long run,' he said thoughtfully. 'But then it's always pointless to stand in the way of progress. I think one has to accept that it's going to happen, whether one likes it or not. We must simply do our best to see that it's well controlled and regulated when it does. But, as Meyer pointed out, a successful cloning at the moment can only result in the birth of a baby, with all the moral and ethical issues that that would raise.'

'You said "at the moment". Does that mean things might change in the future?'

'Almost certainly, once we understand the true nature of cell differentiation – by that I mean what makes cells decide to become a liver or a lung or whatever. The idea of being able to grow human organs from single cells is a very attractive one. It could solve so many problems, not least the continual search for suitable donor organs.'

'How close are we to being able to do that?'

'Quite a long way off, but there's a lot of research being carried out on it, so who knows? Someone may make the breakthrough.'

'Is this an area of research that you're personally involved in?' asked Tom.

The Professor shook his head. 'No,' he said, 'I'm just a simple obstetrician at heart; I dabble at being a scientist.'

Tom pointed out that in no way could the Professor's research achievements be described as 'dabbling'.

Thomas smiled modestly.

'Actually, I'd be interested to hear what sort of research *is* going on at Caernarfon General?' Tom remarked in what he hoped was a matter-of-fact way.

'Very little,' shrugged Thomas. 'NHS funding tends not to accommodate research budgets; that sort of thing is best left to the research councils and they're not big spenders in Welsh hospitals. I think it would be fair to say that my unit is the only one engaged in active clinical research to any degree.'

'I see,' said Tom thoughtfully. Then, changing the subject, he said, 'I went to see John Palmer on Saturday.'

'Really? How is he?'

'Nothing's changed.'

'He still believes his wife did it?'

'Not exactly . . .'

Thomas looked at the young GP out of the corner of his eye but did not press the question. He took a forkful of his salad and corrected the bend forming in his paper plate through his quiche being too near the edge. 'Why did you ask about research at Caernarfon General?' he asked, looking Tom straight in the eye.

Tom was disconcerted: he cleared his throat, trying to gain time and get his thoughts in order. He wasn't sure how much he wanted to confide in Thomas; he was still smarting over having made a fool of himself in his dealings with Charles French. 'I was . . . just curious.'

'You were just curious,' repeated Thomas in a manner that invited further comment and suggested that he didn't believe it for a moment.

'Yes,' replied Tom innocently.

The Professor gave him an appraising look and Tom thought he detected a flicker of uncertainty in his eyes and then everything changed. He smiled broadly at someone he knew before moving away in the manner of the practised party-goer.

Tom was about to move on himself when he saw James Trool approaching.

'I thought I'd come over and apologise for having to leave so abruptly the other day at lunch.'

'Not at all,' said Tom. 'I quite understand.'

'Look, why don't you come over to supper this evening and meet Sonia. We'd love to see you and I really am most grateful for you giving the hospital this breathing space.'

'I really didn't do anything,' Tom told him.

'You'll come?' insisted Trool.

'Thank you, I'd like that very much.'

'We live over on Anglesey,' said Trool. 'I'll give you directions.'

Tom made a few notes on how to get to the house and agreed to be there at seven-thirty.

Trool moved away and Tom wandered over to the French

windows to look out at the rain on the grass while he considered what his morning had yielded. His objective had been to discover what kind of research was going on at Caernarfon General and the answer appeared to be very little, apart from what was happening in Thomas's own unit. In the light of his theory, that automatically invited Tom to consider that the mysterious doctor who'd taken Megan's body was on the staff of the IVF unit.

A cot-death child and a murdered baby — what possible relevance could they have to any aspect of IVF research? he wondered. Then he remembered that the Palmer baby had been an IVF child. He'd almost forgotten that. He supposed it might be worth his while checking to see if the same applied to Megan Griffiths. In the meantime, lunch was over and people were drifting back to the lecture hall.

The afternoon session of the symposium was taken up with talks on the value of the ICSI technique, its limitations and the problems associated with it. Apart from the actual technology of being able to inject single sperm into ova, Tom found most of the session too technical to be interesting. He did, however, take an interest near the end when it became apparent from slides put up on the screen that the American lab, where the speaker had come from, had apparently had much more success with the technique than the IVF unit at Caernarfon General. A chart of normal versus abnormal births resulting from ICSI pregnancies made Caernarfon's results seem very poor, so much so that Carwyn Thomas seemed compelled to acknowledge the fact and ask the speaker why he thought this might be so.

The speaker, an American physician from a private IVF clinic in Seattle, fat, bald and avuncular, shrugged his shoulders diplomatically and said, 'Hard to say, Professor. Perhaps we should get together and compare technical notes?'

'Let's do that,' responded Thomas, getting up on to the platform, much to the speaker's surprise. He hadn't meant immediately and the suggestion had largely been light-hearted but Thomas had taken over. 'Ran, perhaps you'd care to come down here?' he said into the microphone.

Ranulph Dawes, the embryologist who had demonstrated cell manipulation to Tom, walked down the aisle, putting his jacket back on as he did so and straightening his tie. He climbed up to join the speaker and Carwyn Thomas on the platform. Thomas responded by sitting down on a chair at the side of the stage while the speaker and Dawes were left to compare technical notes publicly about ICSI technology in their respective laboratories, ranging in subject from needle gauge to incubation times.

After a few minutes, Tom saw that this had been a good 'show-business' move on Thomas's part. Embryologists in the audience were joining in and the whole session had become lively and productively interactive. At the end of the exchange however, the bottom line seemed to be that both Caernarfon and the American clinic were using exactly the same technique.

Dawes left the platform to return to his seat and the American turned to the side to address Thomas. He said, 'I guess the difference must lie in the type of patients we treat, Professor. As I understand it, you reserve ICSI for your difficult cases whereas we carry it out on anyone who's prepared to pay for it!'

There was general laughter and an appreciation of the American's willingness to poke fun at himself but Tom noted that the Professor appeared not to join in. He remained seated at the edge of the platform, looking down at the floor for quite a long time before finally raising his head and smiling politely as if suddenly realising he should be seen to be sharing the joke. He looked along the rows of the audience, nodding slightly but stopped when he appeared to be looking generally in Tom's direction. Tom couldn't say for certain that the man was looking directly at *him* – he was slightly too far away to be sure, but he saw the smile fade to become the look of a very worried man.

Tom was puzzled. The explanation offered by the American for Caernarfon's ICSI patients not doing as well as his own seemed perfectly reasonable to him. Many of the American patients didn't actually need the sophisticated treatment, whereas all Thomas's patients did, as there was really no other alternative for them: it was their last chance. The American success rate was bound to have been better.

Almost on impulse, Tom wrote down the figures from the slide still showing on the screen, planning to have a think about them later just to see if he could spot what was bothering Carwyn Thomas. In the meantime he thought he would give the next session a miss and nip upstairs to get a copy of the pamphlet put out by the IVF clinic for the benefit of prospective patients. He remembered seeing them lying on the front desk in the clinic's reception area when he was being given the guided tour. He felt he could do this in his capacity as a local GP, but his real interest lay in the hope that the pamphlets might include a list of the clinic's staff.

Rather than return to the symposium after that, Tom decided to drive over to Bangor to see how Lucy was, and find out how she was bearing up under the strain of knowing that John was still intent on pleading Guilty. Still in limbo, but managing to cope, seemed to be his conclusion, as they left the house to go for a short walk.

'I'm going to move back home,' Lucy announced suddenly.

'Do you think that's wise?' Tom was more than a little alarmed at the idea.

Lucy shrugged and said, 'I'm not sure if wisdom comes into it. My sister's been a gem but there are limits to how long I can keep imposing on her and her husband; they have a life of their own to be getting on with. Apart from that, I miss my home. It's never going to be the same – it couldn't possibly be without our Anne-Marie – but it's still my home, John's home too.'

Tom saw Lucy's eyes become moist; she was fighting back the tears. He said gently, 'He loves you very much, you know.'

'Then why won't he see me? He must still think in his heart of hearts that I did it.'

'No, that's not the reason. John knows that the circumstantial evidence against you both is so damning that you'd *both* end up going to prison for a very long time if he pleaded Not Guilty. He wants to take the blame alone so that only one of you need go to jail and probably for a shorter time, if what Roberts says is true. He loves you that much, Lucy.'

At that she broke down in floods of tears. Tom wrapped his arm round her shoulders, holding and shushing her until she regained control. 'I'm sorry,' she gulped.

'No need.'

'I can't allow him to do this,' said Lucy. 'It's not fair and it's not right. We didn't do it! We didn't kill our baby! Oh God, I miss her so much, Tom. I keep thinking of her in the cold ground, and I feel I may go mad. Poor Anne-Marie. Poor, poor baby. She didn't stand a chance.' Lucy sobbed into her handkerchief.

Tom held her close until she wept herself to a standstill. 'For justice to prevail,' he said gently. 'We'll have to catch the person who *did* kill Anne-Marie.'

'And just how are we going to do that?' asked Lucy. 'The police won't listen to anyone or anything except John's stupid confession.'

'There are a couple of things to go on,' Tom told her.

'Are you serious?' asked Lucy. She obviously wanted to believe what she was hearing, but remained cautious.

He nodded. 'I don't want to raise your hopes too much but with a bit of luck, I may have some information to give the police in the next few days. I won't say any more than that for the moment but believe me, whatever happens, I'm not going to stop trying.'

'Tom, I can't begin to thank you enough for what you've done and what you're doing. You've been a real friend.'

The Trools lived in a mansion house, obviously built in Victorian times, with lawns stretching down to the water's edge. They had their own boathouse and landing-stage. As he drew to a halt in front of the main entrance, Tom had the feeling that his aged Land Rover might look more at home round the back or down by the stable block. Nevertheless he parked it on the gravel drive outside the front door.

'Good to see you, Tom. In you come and meet Sonia,' said James Trool as he opened the door and made Tom welcome.

Tom had heard that Trool's wife was extremely good-looking, and various references had been made to the fact that she was considerably younger than Trool, but he was still unprepared for what he saw when Sonia Trool walked into the room. She looked as if she had just stepped out from the pages of *Vogue* or had taken a wrong turning off the catwalk in Milan. She was stunning.

'And this is Charlotte,' said Trool, sweeping a toddler up into his arms from the floor where she had been playing with a white furry rabbit, decked out in blue ribbon with little bells attached to its neck. Charlotte giggled as her father tickled her and said, 'Time for bed, little one.'

The smile on Tom's lips faltered a little when Trool

turned and he could see that Charlotte was blind. Her face had clearly suffered some major trauma in the past although it was not badly disfigured now. He thought he remembered some mention of a car accident having featured in the Trools' meeting.

'Hello, Charlotte,' said Tom, and gently stroked the back of her hand, but the child was more interested in arguing about going to bed.

'Just a little while longer,' she wheedled.

'No, it's bedtime, honey,' said Sonia firmly, then turning to Tom she added, 'Charlotte has more stamina and energy than James and me put together.'

'It's a wonderful house to be a child in,' said Tom, his eyes alluding to the sheer size of the place.

'You know, that's exactly what I thought when I first saw it,' Trool admitted. 'It's just the place for the Famous Five or the Secret Seven to have their adventures.'

Sonia smiled and said, 'Why don't you put Charlotte to bed, darling, and I'll show Tom around.'

Trool took Charlotte upstairs and Sonia started to show Tom the house. 'I don't know if James told you about the accident?' she said.

Tom said not.

'That's really how James and I came to meet. Don — my first husband — and I were over in Britain with Charlotte on vacation, doing the tourist thing. We were on our way to visit Caernarfon Castle when we were involved in a car accident on the dual carriageway. Teenage joyriders lost control of the car they'd stolen and it crossed the central reservation right into our path. We were all brought into Caernarfon General but Don was already dead and Charlotte was badly hurt. I got away with a ruptured spleen and some fractured ribs from which I made a full recovery, but my daughter was left blind.'

'I'm sorry,' said Tom.

'James oversaw our treatment throughout our rather lengthy stay at the General. He was wonderful with Charlotte, seeing that she got nothing but the best of treatment. To cut a long story short, we ended up getting married and I never went back to the States.'

Tom smiled and nodded politely, but he wondered about the foundations for such a marriage. It was a common enough thing for patients to fall in love with their physicians and an understandable one too, in situations where trust and dependency were involved. But such feelings usually faded with the help of gentle discouragement from the doctor or simply with the returning self-confidence of the patient as part of the recovery process. He was tempted to consider that Trool, who was clearly old enough to be Sonia's father, might have abused the situation and exploited his patient's vulnerability but, from what little he'd seen of them together so far, it was Sonia who seemed to have the dominant personality. Whatever the circumstances, he reminded himself that it was really none of his business.

The tour of the house ended in the huge, iron-framed Victorian conservatory which commanded uninterrupted views over the Menai. Although it was dark and these views were restricted to lights twinkling on the other side of the water, Tom realised that, in the daytime, it would be possible to see the mountains of Snowdonia.

'Why don't we sit here a while,' suggested Sonia. 'James will join us soon and we can have a drink before we eat.'

Tom sat down in one of the cane armchairs among the potted plants, enjoying the smell of leaves and earth indoors. 'You know,' said Sonia, 'James really is grateful to you for back-pedalling on the Megan Griffiths thing. I am, too . . .'

For a moment, the American woman seemed to look directly at Tom as if adding a silent, sexual emphasis to what she'd said. 'It wasn't a case of back-pedalling,' he said, feeling a bit flustered. 'There was just no reason to say anything to the press right now.'

'Nonetheless, we're *very* grateful,' Sonia said huskily. 'James really cares about the hospital's reputation, you know — he takes it all so personally. He's an old sweetie.'

Tom thought there might just be a suggestion of that look again when she'd used the word 'old', but he couldn't be sure. He did, however, feel more comfortable when James Trool entered the room, rubbing his hands and asking what everyone wanted to drink.

'About time too, honey,' said Sonia. 'We're dying of thirst down here.'

A pleasant evening followed, one which ended with Tom leaving just after eleven, thanking his hosts and now more than ever convinced that Sonia was the dominant partner in that marriage.

It was impossible for him not to wonder about Sonia Trool on the drive back to the mainland. Had she really been making eyes at him? Or was it all his imagination? Perhaps she had just been backing up her husband's bid to keep the Megan Griffiths enquiry as low-key as possible. He suspected that Sonia was a very spoiled individual, used to having her own way over everything.

When he got in, Tom made some coffee and settled down to take a look at the notes he'd written down at the symposium. He was still puzzled by the Professor's obvious concern over the difference in success-rates between his own ICSI patients and those of the American clinic. Of the forty American cases, thirty had been successful, four had failed at the implant stage, five had failed through early miscarriage and one was a stillbirth — the stillborn baby had been found to have a lung problem. The Caernarfon data listed thirty-six ICSI patients, of whom twenty had been successful and sixteen had failed. Three had failed at the implant stage, five had been ascribed to early miscarriage and eight had been stillborn. The stillborn foetuses had shown a wide range of deformities. One of the live births had resulted in a child with severe deformity. Her name was Anne-Marie Palmer.

Tom stared at the figures and summarised them in Biro at the edge of the paper. The Americans had succeeded in thirty successes out of forty, Thomas's unit in twenty out of thirty-six — a disparity easily explained through the difference in patient selection. The implant failure rate was similar, as was the number of early miscarriages. The big difference lay in the number of stillbirths: eight in Caernarfon, only one in Seattle. All the Welsh cases had shown marked deformity while the American baby had simply failed to thrive.

Tom wondered if that was what had concerned the Professor so much: eight deformed babies dead at birth and one live one . . . *subsequently murdered.*

~ *Fifteen* ~

It occurred to Tom in the morning that he should really take a look at the Palmer house if Lucy was seriously thinking about returning. He decided to drive up there on his way to Caernarfon, ostensibly to check that it was wind- and water-tight, but what was really on his mind were fears about the back garden. He wondered if the police, or whoever was responsible for that sort of thing, had restored it after the nightmare excavations.

The thought that Lucy might find an open grave on her return was just too awful to contemplate. In fact, the more he thought about what had taken place there, the more he felt it was a bad idea that she should come back at all, but of course, he had to recognise that she might have no real alternative. In Bangor he'd had the distinct impression that Gina's husband hadn't been too keen on Lucy being there at all. He'd probably only agreed to it after pressure from his wife. Maybe that factor was beginning to make itself felt and Lucy had sensed that it was time to move out.

Lucy, or rather her sister speaking for her, had ruled out any notion of her going to stay with relatives up north, where she would be too far away from John, so what did that leave? It wasn't as if she and John could go away somewhere together to get over the death of Anne-Marie and start a new life. In her current circumstances, she was painfully alone. She might need the comfort of familiar things around her, and although the garden of the house had been the grave of her daughter, the house itself had been the focus of her life with John for the past six years.

All such considerations ceased as Tom rounded the corner into the street where the Palmers lived and saw what spray-paint vandals had done to the house. His heart sank as he read the messages, ranging from *Murdering bastards* to a Biblical text, '*Suffer the little children to come unto Me.*' The paint had run in several areas, giving the unintentional impression of dripping blood, and there was a change of colour from red to blue between *little* and *children* where the 'artist' had run out of paint and changed cans.

Tom swore under his breath as he got out of the car and walked slowly up the path, appraising the extent of the damage and taking what comfort he could from the fact that the windows were still intact. As he made his way round to the back of the house, watching his footing on the cracked paving slabs, he wondered if the vandals had been encouraged by the fact that the house was empty. Would they have risked doing this if Lucy had been living there? he wondered. It was her safety he was worried about, but it was difficult for him to gauge the depth of feeling among the locals in Feli at the moment as he himself was no longer privy to their confidences. If not exactly subjected to downright hostility, he was regarded with something less than open affection. The state of the Palmers' walls made the feeling mutual.

He was relieved to find that the back garden had been levelled after the digger had done its job. Capability Brown had clearly not carried out the restoration but at least the garden was tidy and daffodils were encroaching on the edge of the excavation site to herald the coming of another spring.

He would have to do something about the mess on the front walls though; he couldn't let Lucy come home to that.

If his recent experience with the electrician was anything to go by, Tom knew he wouldn't have much joy in finding local help so he decided to cut the Gordian knot immediately and do the clean-up himself. He drove back down into Feli and arrived just as Lillian Evans was opening up her hardware store. He bought brushes and solvent without saying why to Lillian, a particularly gossipy woman who had seen two husbands into an early grave and reaped a substantial insurance harvest on both occasions.

He was, however, obliged to confirm what they were *not* for as she mounted an interrogation under the guise of friendly conversation. She tried in succession, 'A bit of work at the surgery then, Doctor?' followed by, 'Giving the flat a bit of a face-lift then?' As she handed him his change she looked pointedly at him, as if deserving of an explanation. 'Not exactly, Mrs Evans,' was all Tom said.

In all, it took him two and a half hours and a great deal of sweat, blood and almost tears when he persistently caught his knuckles on the rendering, to remove the worst of the graffiti from the walls. He finished up by giving them a good hose down. Finding the hose reel on the wall of the garage and still connected to the mains supply had been a major bonus. When he'd finished, he walked down to the front gate and turned to have a look at his handiwork. He stood with one foot on the garden wall and reflected that not one neighbour had come out to pass the time of day with him or even offer a cup of tea. Resentment or shame? he wondered. It hadn't occurred to him before but he supposed some of them might even have been involved in defacing the walls. He had the feeling that he knew a lot less about human nature than he had previously imagined.

As he was preparing to leave he started to worry that

the perpetrators might redo their graffiti tonight: it was a depressing thought. In an effort to stop it happening, he decided to phone the local police at Caernarfon on his mobile phone and request that they keep an eye on the house for the next couple of days.

'Which house is that, sir?' asked the duty officer.

'The Palmer house in Menai View, number seven.'

There was a pause before the policeman said slowly, 'Oh yes, I know it. Actually, we're a bit stretched at the moment.'

Doing what? North Wales wasn't exactly a hotbed of crime. Maybe there had been an outbreak of lost dogs or cats up trees or a determined raid by a five-year-old on the sweetie counter at the local newsagent's. Tom sighed. Getting into a slanging match with the police wasn't going to help matters. 'Do what you can,' he said and stuck the phone back in his pocket.

Back at his flat, he took a look at the IVF clinic handout he'd picked up yesterday. The core staff of the unit, excepting Carwyn Thomas as its Clinical Director, comprised four medical staff, two clinical scientists, four lab technicians and a nursing staff of eight. Various other consultant staff at the hospital were affiliated to the unit through either part-time or honorary consultancy posts. These positions were exclusively the province of either surgeons or obstetricians.

He brought out the file that Trool had supplied to members of the investigating committee and looked down the list of names extracted from the Pathology Department's records as those who had visited the department on the day that Megan's body had disappeared. Two people appeared on both the handout and this list: one was Michael Deans, a senior technician in the IVF unit and the other was Professor Carwyn Thomas himself. Tom tapped the thumbnail of his right hand slowly against his teeth as he digested this piece of information: Only Thomas and one of his technicians . . . what price his theory now?

He quickly decided that no idea, even the most ridiculous at first sight, should be dismissed out of hand. Everything had to be considered and appraised coldly on the facts. The idea of a man like Carwyn Thomas stealing bodies from the Pathology Department in his own hospital might seem patently ludicrous, but then the idea of *anyone* stealing babies' bodies was going to appear ludicrous until a reason for it could be established.

Thinking about the type of research that Thomas was engaged in, reminded Tom that he had been meaning to find out if the Griffiths baby had been a product of the IVF unit. He was wondering just how he might go about doing this when he remembered that Julie had mentioned at one point that the cot-death baby had been on 'Jenkins's list' up in Caernarfon. He didn't know the Caernarfon GP that well, but they had met on occasion at seminars and area meetings. He looked up the telephone number and dialled it.

'What can I do for you, Doctor?' asked Jenkins when Tom had said who he was.

Tom was pleased to hear that he sounded a friendly sort of man. 'I'm part of the investigation team looking into what happened to Megan Griffiths's body at Caernarfon General,' he explained. 'I understand Megan was your patient?'

'She was indeed, poor mite.'

'This is going to sound an odd question, Doctor, but was Megan conceived with the help of IVF, by any chance?'

'No, she certainly was not,' replied Jenkins, with a chuckle. 'I distinctly remember Gwen Griffiths telling me at the time that Megan had been conceived on a package tour to Majorca. Sangria may have been involved but definitely not IVF. Why do you ask?'

'I'm just trying to gather together as many facts as I can,' replied Tom vaguely. 'Thanks for your help.'

'Are you any nearer finding out what happened to the child's body?'

'Not yet, I'm afraid.'

Tom put down the phone; he was disappointed but none too surprised that his notion that Megan and Anne-Marie might both be IVF babies was wrong. He still had nothing to connect them and no indicator as to what kind of research might be involved either — if any. He had to concede that his idea was beginning to look decidedly frail but he would, however, ask both Carwyn Thomas and the technician, Michael Deans, about their logged visits to the Pathology Department on the day Megan disappeared.

On his way up to Caernarfon, Tom circled round by the Palmer house again to have a look at his morning's handiwork with the eyes of someone just driving into the street. He congratulated himself on the job he'd done and hoped the house would stay that way until Lucy got back.

One of the neighbours looked out to see who was sitting there. Tom recognised him as a retired accountant — he couldn't recall the name, but he did remember that the man had come to see him at the surgery a few months ago about an allergy. Their eyes met but no sign of recognition appeared on the man's part, just stony indifference. 'Have a nice day,' murmured Tom.

Several top microscope manufacturers had laid on a trade exhibition in the foyer outside the main lecture hall. It was here that Tom found Ran Dawes and Carwyn Thomas discussing the finer points of micromanipulation with the man from Leitz. Tom listened in at a discreet distance and was impressed with Thomas's contribution to the discussion. He seemed to know a great deal about the advantages and disadvantages of the various systems on the market. Tom remarked on this to Ran Dawes when Thomas had moved on.

Dawes smiled and said, 'Carwyn likes to keep his hand in; he still has his own lab attached to his office. Technically he's still one of the best there is.'

'Really,' said Tom politely. He was wondering why Thomas hadn't mentioned this when he'd shown him around his unit.

'Come on, have a try,' said Dawes, leading him by the arm to where a microscope was set up with micromanipulators in place. This was part of the Zeiss company's interactive equipment display. 'See if you can thread the needle.'

Tom looked down the eyepieces and saw what had to be done. A tiny needle with a bore smaller than the diameter of a human hair had to be moved with the right-hand controls through a small loop whose movement was controlled by those on the left. A video screen above the microscope relayed progress of the attempt to those standing watching. Tom's first touch sent the needle whizzing across the screen and he had to hunt around to find it again, but he quickly became accustomed to the sensitivity of the controls and managed at his fourth attempt to put the needle cleanly through the loop. Dawes applauded, as did three other bystanders who were keen to have a go themselves.

The good-humoured commotion and sporadic applause attracted more people until there were about twenty in all watching the proceedings. Someone said loudly, 'Come on, Ran, let's see what a real professional can do.'

Dawes was cheered as he sat down on the stool and played to the crowd by flexing his fingers like a concert pianist before lightly gripping the delicate stage controls.

The needle went smoothly across the screen and through the loop without faltering. Tom joined in the applause but his smile faded when he caught sight of Carwyn Thomas standing in the second row of the crowd. Thomas was not applauding; in fact he looked a long way from being impressed by what he was seeing. His eyes were hard above a stone-like expression.

Tom wondered if the Professor could be jealous of the younger man — envious of his prowess and his popularity? Surely he couldn't be that petty! But when all was said and done, Thomas was a showman himself — a man who, like many top researchers, enjoyed the limelight. The approval and applause of their peers became like a drug to them, often causing them to pressurise their research groups into ever-greater efforts so that their leader might continually have something new to announce to the world as 'his' research.

Tom kept watching Thomas out of the corner of his eye as Dawes did an encore, again threading the needle in one smooth movement. This time, aware of the scrutiny of others, Thomas did applaud, but his eyes remained flinty.

People began making their way to the lecture hall for the start of the afternoon session. As they did so, they passed by a series of trade posters, showing good-looking people in white coats, wreathed in smiles as they used the advertisers' equipment to great effect in their quest for knowledge and success.

Tom sat at the back of the hall in deference to the fact that he deemed himself an observer rather than a participant, and was surprised to find himself sitting next to Ran Dawes.

'I don't think I'm going to stay for all of this,' confided Dawes. 'I've heard this talk given at just about every meeting in the last five years.'

Tom checked his programme and read that the first talk was to be given by Dr Shirley Spencer-Freeman, an American from Colorado: it was to be about her ongoing comparison of IVF children with a peer group of conventionally conceived children.

'The bottom line is that there *is* no difference,' whispered Dawes, 'but she can't see it. She prefers to concentrate on supposed discrepancies in IQ and academic achievement when all she's looking at are statistical blips, well within the normal range of experimental error.'

'Hasn't anyone pointed this out to her?' asked Tom.

'Many people on many occasions,' grinned Dawes, 'but there's no thicker skin than that of a scientist with a bee in his or her bonnet.'

After fifteen minutes, Tom began to appreciate what Dawes had said. The woman's talk was an exercise in what statistics could do with nothing of substance.

'Fancy some coffee?' whispered Dawes.

Tom nodded and the pair of them slipped out at an appropriate moment when Spencer-Freeman turned her back to look up at the screen and highlight some data with her pointer.

'They can't all be gems,' said Dawes with a smile as they started off along the corridor to the hospital coffee-shop.

'I suppose scientific presentation is an art form in its own way,' Tom remarked.

'But it helps if you have something to say in the first place,' said Dawes. 'Sometimes I think there's an awfully strong correlation between having nothing to say and wanting to say it at great length. The bottom line is simply that some people just like to hear the sound of their own voice.'

'It's much the same in all walks of life,' Tom said as they entered the coffee-shop where Dawes opted for cappuccino and Tom an espresso.

'Carwyn told me you'd been to visit John Palmer in prison,' said Dawes.

'At the weekend,' agreed Tom.

'How's he bearing up?'

'Not that well. He looked dreadful, as if he hadn't slept for a month, and he's lost a lot of weight. Worst of all, he's still determined to plead Guilty to something he didn't do.'

'You'll have to forgive me if I harbour some doubts about that,' said Dawes quietly. 'Stress can push people into doing some pretty awful things.'

'We'll agree to differ,' said Tom.

Dawes nodded thoughtfully and sipped his coffee. He changed the subject. 'I understand that you're one of the people investigating the Megan Griffiths business?'

'That's right.'

'Have you figured out what happened yet?'

'We know it wasn't an accidental switch, if that's what you mean,' said Tom. 'Someone knew exactly what they were putting in the coffin in place of her body.'

'You're kidding!' Dawes looked disbelieving.

'Unfortunately not.'

'But why would anyone do a thing like that?'

'That's something we'll know if and when we find out what happened to Megan's body,' said Tom grimly.

'I understood it had gone to the incinerator by mistake?'

'That's still a possibility,' said Tom, finishing off his coffee.

Dawes made a face. 'Only a possibility?' he said. 'You mean there's some doubt about it?'

'Until we know for sure that's what happened, there has to be,' said Tom.

'You're making it all sound very sinister. I thought

body-snatching went out last century with Burke and Hare. Damned if I can remember why they did it though.'

'They stole bodies to supply the needs of the medical profession,' said Tom with a wry smile. 'The medical school needed them for their anatomy work.'

'Of course!' exclaimed Dawes. 'I remember now. Still, digging up the odd body wasn't such a terrible crime in the great scheme of things. They came from your neck of the woods, didn't they? Edinburgh, I believe?'

Tom nodded. 'The trouble was, demand started to exceed supply so they started a second production line, based on murder.'

'Thankfully it was all a very long time ago,' said Dawes.

'Well . . . there were a couple of convictions last year for the theft of the bodies of stillborn children,' Tom reminded him. 'They were used to supply a pharmaceutical company's need for foetal tissue.'

'So it still goes on,' said Dawes thoughtfully. 'But surely you're not suggesting that Megan's body was used for something like that?'

'I'm not suggesting anything,' countered Tom. 'I'm just trying to cover all possibilities. How well do you know Carwyn Thomas?'

Dawes seemed surprised at the sudden swerve of the question. He made a vague hand gesture. 'Pretty well, I suppose. I mean, we're not bosom buddies but we get on. I'm a bit in awe of him really; he's achieved so much in his career.'

'Thinking about what you said earlier, about him keeping his hand in, do you reckon he still sees himself as a front-line researcher?'

Dawes thought for a moment before saying, 'I suppose he does. Research isn't something you ever really retire from, if you know what I mean. If you happen to get an idea then I suppose, whatever age you are, you'd want to follow it through to its conclusion.'

'To get the glory,' said Tom.

'We're all human.'

— *Sixteen* —

Dawes left Tom alone in the coffee-shop, saying that he wanted to catch the second talk. It was going to be on the option of sex determination in IVF cases, an increasingly likely possibility in the near future. Carwyn was chairing the session and Dawes thought he might be asked for his views at some point. Tom decided not to join him, saying that he'd heard most of the moral arguments, both for and against the choice of sex in pregnancy, and didn't wish to add to his technical knowledge of the techniques involved. He opted instead for more coffee and a doughnut.

The fact that both Thomas and Dawes were going to be away from the IVF unit for the next hour was uppermost in his mind as he sipped his coffee. He was intrigued by the notion of Thomas having his own private lab and there was no doubt that the easiest way to find out what he might be up to in it would be to take a look while he wasn't there. He wasn't sure if he had the courage to do such a thing or if he should even be contemplating it . . . but it was a tempting thought. While he was debating the pros and cons, he noticed that his second cup of coffee tasted different from the first and glanced back at the counter. It had come from the same flask. It wasn't the coffee that had changed but his taste buds: they were reacting to the mixture of fear and excitement building up inside him as he made his decision.

He left the coffee-shop and walked back along the main corridor, feeling that everyone he passed knew exactly what he was planning. A casual glance from a porter seemed rife with accusation; the laughter of two nurses suggested they knew more than they should. He felt his pulse rate rise as he mounted the stairs leading up to the IVF unit and rehearsed his excuse should he be challenged. He would say that he needed some more leaflets about the IVF service for the surgery; he had underestimated the demand for them.

He reached the head of the stairs and looked in through the glass panel on the door. There was no one about so he opened the door, just far enough to slip inside, then paused for a moment to listen. He could hear the hum of lab equipment but little else until he caught the sound of laughter coming from a room along the corridor on the left. He remembered, from his conducted tour, that this was where the staff common room was. He glanced at his watch and saw that it was coming up to three o'clock; they were probably having coffee. It was a bit of luck for him that they were all in the one place for the time being, but things could change at any second.

He moved swiftly along to where Thomas's room was situated — three doors short of the staff room and on the same side. He did so on tiptoe, holding his breath as he came to the door and tried the handle. There was no resistance; the lever went right down and the door opened quietly without any noise from the hinges. He gave silent thanks and slipped inside, steeling himself to close the door slowly again behind him.

As the door closed fully and the handle reached the top of its travel, he relaxed and leaned his forehead against the wood for a moment, letting out his breath and taking a moment to allow his nerves to calm down. There was sweat on his forehead and he was aware of the blood pounding in his ears. He turned round to see the photographs of children that he'd admired on his first visit here. This time the smiles of their parents made him feel dishonest.

He looked at the dark blue door at the window end of the wall. He had noticed it last time, but had assumed that it was a cupboard or a toilet, not the laboratory that Dawes had alerted him to. The Venetian blinds on the main window of the office were half tilted, making the room slightly gloomy, but not dark enough to warrant turning on the lights. He walked over to the blue door and tried it: it was locked.

He closed his eyes and swore softly as it started to look as if he'd taken a big risk for nothing but then it occurred to him that the key might be somewhere in the room. He looked in the various receptacles on Thomas's desk and felt along the flat surfaces of the bookshelves before conceding the possibility that the man kept it on his person, but then again . . .

With a growing sense of wrongdoing, he sat down in Thomas's swivel chair to pull open the top drawer of the desk and start sifting through the contents. For a moment he thought he'd been successful as his fingers came across two metal keys on a small ring but he quickly realised that they were too small to be what he was looking for: the lab had a Yale lock, these were for something like a filing cabinet. The bottom drawer held a series of files in a corrugated cardboard holder. They contained patients' notes, about ten sets in all. Tom guessed that these would be the current patients in the clinic. He pushed them back to see if a key could be lying on the bottom of the drawer but stopped suddenly when he heard voices outside in the corridor.

'Is the Professor back yet?' asked a male voice with a strong Welsh accent.

'He's at a meeting; just go in and leave them on his desk,' replied a softer female voice.

Tom, who had frozen at the sound of voices, was galvanised into action. He crouched down and crawled into the kneehole of the desk, prepared to remain stock-still and hold his breath for as long as was necessary. He heard the door open and feet move across the carpet. There was a plop, as mail was dropped on to the desk above his head, then nothing. For the next few moments there was no sound at all. The unseen man was standing perfectly still in front of the desk.

Tom's nerves were stretched to breaking point as he imagined the man's suspicions had been aroused, but then he realised with immense relief that he was probably looking at the baby pictures on the wall. Another few moments and the feet moved away. The door closed and Tom could let out his breath. He was about to crawl out from his hiding place when his head brushed against something on the underside of the desk. He reached up and felt a round metal block there. There was something stuck to it but it moved without losing adhesion to the surface. The block was a magnet and there was a key stuck to it! He'd found what he was looking for.

Thomas's lab was quite small but obviously well-equipped, the centrepiece being an island bench with a Zeiss microscope and revolving test-tube holder on it. Half a dozen tubes were on its rollers. They contained a red fluid that Tom remembered being told on his tour, was cell-culture fluid. The fluid would bathe the cells sticking to the glass as the rollers turned the tubes and keep them supplied with nutriment. There was a fridge, a chest freezer, two incubators and a piece of apparatus that looked as if it was designed for delivering electric current at varying voltage. A large sink was equipped with arm-operated tap levers with a liquid soap dispenser mounted above it and a pedal bin below. Surgical gloves were available from a box at the side.

Tom became frustratingly aware of his own limitations in laboratory medicine. He had succeeded in getting into the Professor's lab, but how could he tell what was going on there if he had no idea what the test tubes and incubators contained? The numbers on the tubes meant nothing to him and he had no idea what half the chemicals in the fridge were for. He needed to find some kind of written indication of what was going on, a notebook or scientific protocol.

There were a number of photocopied scientific papers sitting beside the microscope. He leafed through them and felt a tingle at the back of his neck as he found a common factor: they were all concerned with some aspect of human cloning. Was that it? he wondered. Was Thomas actually dabbling in human cloning? Such a venture would undoubtedly be dangerous and definitely illegal, but it was not unknown for very bright people to consider that rules and regulations were meant for everyone else but themselves. But how would this fit in with what had happened to Anne-Marie Palmer, or Megan Griffiths for that matter?

He searched through all the under-bench drawers of the lab, looking for more substantial evidence. Lying under a pile of chemical company catalogues, he found one cardboard envelope file. It was a patient's notes file and the white name tag on the front was dirty but the writing itself was decipherable. It read: *Anne-Marie Palmer.*

Tom felt his throat tighten as he sat down on a stool by the microscope to open the file and start reading. He quickly realised that this was the full medical record file for Anne-Marie, running from the time of Lucy Palmer's first appointment at the IVF clinic up until Anne-Marie's birth. He turned to the end to look at the most recent entries, hoping to find anything that would suggest a connection between Thomas's research and the baby's death, but there appeared to be nothing like that. The file ended with Anne-Marie's death simply being recorded as 'violent'.

Tom felt a giant pang of disappointment as he concluded that there was nothing to indicate why hers was the only file that Thomas had been keeping in his lab. He felt there had to be a reason; there had to be a clue around somewhere. He flicked through the pages two or three times more until his eye was caught by a series of highlighted text markings. Three groups of numbers had been highlighted in blue. The first was the date of the ICSI procedure carried out on Lucy Palmer's ova, the second was the date of implantation of a fertilised tetrad into her womb and the third was a reference number. A comment in pencil beside the number said, 'no siblings!' Tom noted the exclamation mark then wrote the numbers down on one of the Post-it notes lying beside the microscope. He folded it and slipped it into his inside pocket while he continued a search of the drawers. He found nothing else.

Tom glanced at his watch and decided that it was time to leave: he'd been here longer than he'd intended but he thought he'd just take a quick look in the cupboards before he left, in case he had missed something. He really didn't have that much to go on in terms of hard evidence. The cupboards contained various pieces of scientific apparatus but little else. Almost as a last gesture, he raised the lid of the chest freezer and froze with horror. The faces of three foetuses stared up at him through clear but misty plastic bags.

'Jesus Christ,' muttered Tom. What were they? *Who* were they? He lifted up one of the bags and looked for labelling on it. There was a number written on the back in black grease pencil. He noticed that it had the same number of digits in it as the reference number he'd copied down from Anne-Marie's file. He made a note of the numbers of all three then laid the little bundles back down in their icy lair and closed the lid. He rested his hands on it for a moment to recover his composure for they were shaking slightly: it was definitely time he was out of this place.

He clicked the lab door shut and replaced the key on its holder under Thomas's desk. His nerves were beginning to settle and anxiety was being replaced by almost a sense of elation. He put his ear to the outside door, listening for any sounds in the corridor. To his dismay he heard the sound of raised voices, both male and they were getting louder. What was worse, he recognised one as belonging to Carwyn Thomas. The talk must have finished early. He was going to be caught red-handed!

Tom took a deep breath and decided that there was no alternative but to brass it out. Hiding under the desk was not going to be an option this time. Hoping to disguise the fact that the door to the office had been closed, Tom opened it wide and backed out into the corridor, holding the door handle and hoping to give the impression that he had just looked into the room to see if anyone was there. He turned to face the men coming towards him who had seen him and stopped talking. He could now see that Carwyn Thomas had been arguing with James Trool.

'Ah, there you are, Professor,' said Tom, hoping his smile wasn't going to fracture like that of an anxious beauty contestant held too long on camera. His heart rate was topping 140.

Trool smiled and said, 'Hello there.'

'What can I do for you, Doctor?' asked Thomas, looking distinctly puzzled.

'I know you're very busy, Professor, but I hoped I might

catch you here between symposium sessions. I wanted to have a private word with you. It'll only take a couple of minutes.'

'What about?'

Tom noted that the man appeared to have lost his usual charm. He seemed preoccupied with something, presumably what he and Trool had been arguing about. 'The Megan Griffiths business,' said Tom.

Carwyn Thomas looked at him blankly for a moment before turning to Trool and saying, 'I'll get back to you. We'll talk further.'

'As you wish,' said Trool coldly and walked off.

Tom decided not to say anything about having come at a 'bad time'. He followed Thomas into his office and sat down as invited.

'I'm wearing a different hat this afternoon, Professor. I think you know that I'm a member of the unofficial investigation team into what happened to Megan Griffiths's body,' said Tom pleasantly. 'I'm talking to everyone who was listed as visiting the Pathology Department on the day in question.'

'So?'

'You were listed,' Tom said.

The Professor looked at him as if his mind were still elsewhere. 'Was I?' he murmured.

'You signed in at two-fifteen along with one of your technicians − a Michael Deans.'

'Oh yes, I remember,' said Thomas quietly, still sounding heavily preoccupied. 'I went down to see Sepp.'

'Was Dr Sepp there?'

Thomas snapped out of his preoccupation. 'Of course he was. I had an appointment to see him.'

'And Deans?'

'I thought he might be needed.'

Tom let his silence prompt the other man into saying more.

'I thought we might have some tissue samples to deal with, that's why I asked Deans to come along.'

'Tissue samples?'

'I hoped Sepp might still have path specimens from some patients I was interested in.'

'Dead patients?'

'Yes.'

'Your patients? Babies?'

'Yes.'

'Why?'

'I don't think that need concern you,' said Thomas.

'As you wish,' said Tom evenly.

Thomas suddenly seemed uncomfortable with what he'd said. 'All right, I'll tell you,' he said heavily. 'I wanted to know if Sepp still had samples of tissue taken from the stillbirth babies at the unit. I wanted to carry out further tests on them to see if I could find some clue as to what had gone wrong.'

'I see,' said Tom, immediately thinking that he'd been right about what had been upsetting Thomas at the American's seminar. But now, in the light of what he'd seen in the Professor's lab, he could imagine an alternative reason for Thomas wanting to get his hands on the specimens. It was possible that he had planned to get rid of them to make sure that there was no damning evidence lying around in the Pathology Department. If Thomas really *had* been experimenting with human cloning, and that was the reason for the increase in stillbirths in the clinic, he'd want to make sure his tracks were covered if people started asking questions.

With the symposium coming up, the high failure-rate of ICSI babies in his unit might well come to light when

Caernarfon's figures were compared with those of other labs. This was exactly what had happened during the American physician's talk. The only thing that didn't fit was that Thomas himself had seemed the one most keen to investigate the problem. The double bluff of a clever man? Tom wondered. He smiled politely and said, 'Thank you for your time, Professor. I'll take my leave now and let you get on.'

There were two messages on the answering machine when Tom got back to Feli, the first from Liam Swanson, the Director of Public Health in Caernarfon, asking that he get in touch and the second from Lucy, saying that she was moving back home today. She wondered if he'd care to join her for supper tonight around seven? If he couldn't manage it, he wasn't to worry. It was very short notice and she'd quite understand.

Tom immediately rang Lucy's number to tell her machine that he would be there at seven. He called Swanson next.

'I thought we might have a meeting when this symposium thing is over,' said Swanson.

'If you like.'

'Between us, we've talked to most of the people recorded in the Path. Department's book apart from Professor Thomas. He's been tied up with the symposium.'

'I spoke to him today,' said Tom. 'I knew he was on the list and as I've been attending the symposium, it seemed too good a chance to miss.'

'No joy, I suppose?' said Swanson.

'Afraid not. I didn't speak to his technician Deans, though.'

'I did, yesterday,' said Swanson. 'He'd been asked to accompany Thomas to collect some tissue samples from the Path. Department.'

'That's my understanding too,' said Tom.

'I suspect we're not going to get anywhere with this,' said Swanson. 'We'd be as well handing it over to the police.'

'The question is, will they?' said Tom.

'Maybe not,' agreed Swanson. 'But I've been ringing round some of the others and there's a general feeling that we're not making progress and won't, however many times we question the staff. There's not a lot more we can do, really.'

'I'd like one more week before doing as you suggest,' announced Tom.

'You have an idea then?'

'Maybe.'

～ *Seventeen* ～

T om arrived at Lucy's house carrying a bottle of wine he'd bought at the supermarket on the Bangor Road and some flowers from the stand outside the filling station: there simply hadn't been enough time to go back into town. He knew Lucy would understand.

As he walked up the path to the front door, he thought how good it was to see lights on in the windows again; it reminded him of how happy the house had been at Christmas and please God, it was the harbinger of better times to come. Lucy heard his feet on the gravel and looked out of the window to smile and wave before coming to open the door.

'Good to see you home,' smiled Tom.

'It's been a while,' said Lucy.

He had been apprehensive about how Lucy might feel once she was actually back in the house, knowing that this would be a difficult psychological step to take, but there was no outward sign of a problem. 'How are you?' he asked, as he was ushered into the living room where a fire had been lit and table lamps created a cosy atmosphere, although for some reason, maybe the obvious one, it all seemed a little unreal.

'I'm fine,' said Lucy, adding, 'really I am,' when Tom looked at her to see if she was telling the truth. 'I suppose it's you I have to thank for cleaning the mess off the walls?'

Tom had hoped that Lucy might not notice the occasional small smudge of spray paint remaining from his clean-up operation – at least, not right away, but he should have known better. Now he didn't quite know what to say; he hoped she wouldn't ask about the words. In the event, his obvious discomfort told Lucy all that she needed to know and she smiled affectionately. 'I'm grateful, Tom,' she said, adding, 'again.'

He nodded.

'Well, there weren't too many yellow ribbons in evidence when I got back and the good folks of Felinbach haven't exactly been rushing round to say, "Welcome home, Lucy", but it's still good to be back,' she said. 'In spite of everything.'

'I'm glad you feel that way.'

Lucy folded her arms and looked serious for a moment. She said with cold determination in her voice, 'The way I see it is, the bastard who did this to John and me took away my baby, and my husband, too. He's not taking away my home as well.'

'Good for you,' said Tom.

Lucy went through to the kitchen but kept talking. 'This is not exactly going to be a culinary extravaganza, I'm afraid, but I did want to see you and thank you for all you've been doing. I can't imagine how I would have coped without you.'

'That's what friends are for,' said Tom.

'Seriously,' said Lucy, returning to stand in the doorway, 'I'll never be able to thank you enough.'

Tom who suddenly felt embarrassed. He said, 'Shush, I'll open the wine, shall I?'

The Palmers' dining room was one of two bay-windowed

rooms that looked out on the front garden, one on either side of the front door. Lucy had set up the table by the window and Tom looked out over it down to the lights on the Menai while he waited. He felt he knew the wall beneath that particular window intimately: it was the area that had given him most trouble during the clean-up, the spot where the paint had run in rivulets down the rendering. Unconsciously, he rubbed the knuckles of his right hand. The skin there was still raw in places.

Just before she brought the food in, Lucy came through and lit two candles on the table. They were of odd sizes and stood in different holders, a tall white one in a silver stick and a small coloured one in the middle of a plastercast Beatrix Potter scene.

'This one is for John,' said Lucy as she lit the white one. 'And this one is for Anne-Marie; John bought it on the day we got her home for the first time and we lit it that night. The next time was going to be on her first birthday . . . but it hasn't quite worked out that way.' There was a short silence before Lucy stood back and said, 'Bless them both.'

'Bless them both,' echoed Tom, raising his glass.

The food was simple but good. Lucy had made pasta with a deliciously spicy sauce and followed it up with lemon cheesecake and strong espresso coffee.

'Last time we spoke you seemed to think you were on to something?' said Lucy. The hope in her voice was muted but unmistakable.

'I'm still working on it,' Tom replied, wondering just what to tell her. He was pretty sure that Thomas's unit was involved in something underhand, possibly illegal, but the only thing to tie Anne-Marie Palmer into the scheme of things was the fact that the Professor had her medical file in his lab.

'There's some kind of experimental work going on up at Caernarfon General,' he said. 'At the moment I don't quite know what it is, but I think there's a chance that Anne-Marie's death is tied up in it in some way.'

'What kind of research?' asked Lucy.

'Genetic manipulation.'

'What?' exclaimed Lucy as if it was the last thing in the world she expected to hear.

'There's something going on in Professor Thomas's unit, involving children who were born there.'

'But what could such experiments possibly have to do with Anne-Marie?' Lucy sounded far from convinced. 'It doesn't make sense.'

'I know, but there's a link somewhere and that's what I have to find out,' said Tom.

Lucy tried to cover up her obvious disappointment at not having been given more encouraging news by changing tack and offering to top up Tom's glass. He pushed it across the table but just at that moment, something came hurtling in through the window and hit the glass, which burst into fragments. He shut his eyes and flung up his hands as flying glass peppered his face and Lucy's screams filled his ears.

Almost immediately he felt blood running down his cheeks and he found that he couldn't open his eyes properly to see what was going on. As soon as he tried, he felt a burning pain that made him fear that his sight had been damaged. It was a nightmare thought that induced its own panic. He tried to see again, wiping away the blood, and managed to make out a blur that he thought might be Lucy's face. He saw it only briefly before she toppled backwards off her chair.

Tom felt the tablecloth go with her and heard plates and glasses crash all around his feet as he was forced to close his eyes again to get some respite. Suddenly there was a terrible smell of burning in his nostrils. A yellow blur flared up in front of his eyelids and a sudden blast of heat made him recoil. The toppling candles had set light to Lucy's dress and she was now screaming in pain and fright as she writhed on the floor, fighting to free herself of the toppled chair and the general mess around her.

Tom was aware of the bright glare of the flames but not much more as he struggled to find the tablecloth at his feet and get a grip on it. He needed something to smother the flames with and this was it. He found a corner of it, recognising it by its thickness, and tugged at it ferociously until he had it in his hands and could make an attempt to extinguish the flames that were now engulfing Lucy. He fell on top of the brightly glowing bundle, using his own body in addition to the cloth to snuff out the bright blur, but paid the price as the fire found his own skin to add to his pain.

Lucy had stopped screaming but she wasn't unconscious; she was whimpering and gasping, obviously now in shock. Tom was pretty sure that the flames had been smothered because there was no more heat, only the sickening smell of charred flesh and burnt fabric. The smoke and fumes caught in his throat as he staggered to his feet and started to feel his way to the door, knocking over a succession of unseen and now unimportant objects on his journey.

Incredibly, the street outside seemed devoid of people. But they must have heard the glass break, Tom thought angrily. What the fuck were they all doing? Watching? Hiding behind the curtains? Pretending nothing was amiss? His temper soared out of control as he yelled out, 'Get a fucking ambulance, you bunch of mindless cretins!' He continued his half-blind stagger down the path, trying to get a response from someone, anyone, his only vision a mess of blurred colours. Yelling out brought on a paroxysm of coughing that hurt his throat and he sank to his knees, retching and spitting and suddenly filled with a deep loathing of the world or more correctly, its inhabitants.

He recoiled when he felt a hand on his shoulders. 'Who's that?'

'I'm from next door. An ambulance is on its way, won't be long. What the devil happened here?'

'Some bastard threw a brick through the dining-room window. We were sitting there . . .'

'I suppose they didn't realise that,' said the voice evenly.

Tom could hardly believe his ears as he knelt on the ground, his hands flat on the path in front of him, blood dripping from his face. 'And that makes it fucking all right, does it?' he exploded. 'What kind of people are you?'

'No need to be like that,' retorted the man, obviously aggrieved at Tom's language and tone.

Tom struggled to regain his composure. Finally, he said, 'See if you can help Lucy, will you, she's badly burned.'

Tom was aware that the man hadn't moved. 'Do it, for Christ's sake!' he snapped.

'That's probably best left to them who know about these things,' came the uncomfortable reply. 'The ambulance will be here shortly.'

'Give me bloody strength!' cried Tom; 'Get the fuck out of my way!' He got to his feet unsteadily, feeling his way back to the house, his progress fuelled by anger and adrenaline, following the kerb on the path and calling out Lucy's name. He found the doorway and dropped to all fours to crawl through to the dining room where Lucy was still lying where he'd left her on the floor. She was unconscious. He felt for a pulse in her neck and, at the second attempt, found a small beat in his fingertips. Somewhere, far off in the distance, a siren started to make beautiful music.

*   *   *

Tom came round with the smell of antiseptic in his nostrils, and a soft pillow under his head. He felt warm and comfortable and a bit drowsy, but this only lasted until he realised that either the room was in total darkness or he couldn't see! His fingers flew to his eyes and were stopped by heavy bandaging. Panic was replaced by relief but only briefly. 'Nurse!' he called out. He was on his third chorus when a voice said, 'So you're back with us then.'

'Who's that?'

'Student Nurse Gwen Richards, and before you ask, you're in Ysbyty Gwynedd.'

'My eyes . . . Lucy, where is she? What happened to her?'

'Take it easy,' soothed the nurse. 'I'll tell the doctor, you've come round and she'll deal with all your questions. Won't be long.'

A few moments passed before Tom became aware of someone near him; it was a woman — he could smell her perfume. He almost recognised it but couldn't quite find the name in the whirl of his subconscious. It was the one that smelled like the American Cream Soda.

'And they told me that a GP's life was pretty dull,' said a voice that he immediately recognised with a tingle of pleasure.

'You're Mary,' he said. 'Mary Hallam.'

'That's right, and you are the Scottish GP from Felinbach. I'm surprised you remembered me. I don't think we got round to introductions at the meeting.'

'Of course I remember,' said Tom, stopping himself from going on to say that he'd thought about her a good deal since the meeting at Caernarfon General.

'What's wrong with my eyes?' he asked.

'Glass fragments perforated your lids. Damage is minimal, I'm glad to say, although there has been a little scratching to your right cornea. We've removed all the fragments and cleaned you up. We'll take off the dressings tomorrow after you've had a chance to rest, and then we'll have a reappraisal. You've got various small cuts from flying glass, nothing serious and your forearms have minor burns on them – again, nothing too serious.'

Tom felt relief flood through him like a wonderfully powerful analgesic but the moment quickly passed and he asked, 'What about Lucy?'

'Mrs Palmer has not been so lucky,' said Mary. 'She has a couple of deep cuts from flying glass, one on her left cheek and one on her neck, but it's her burns that are giving us most cause for concern.'

'She's in danger?'

'Her life is not in danger . . .' said Mary.

He heard the hesitation in the reply and read the worst into it. 'She's going to be disfigured?'

'She'll need plastic surgery but . . .'

'Her face?' interrupted Tom.

'Thankfully no, although the left side of her neck sustained some tissue damage. Her torso took the brunt of it. Her dress melted and fused with her skin in places.'

'God Almighty,' sighed Tom. 'Poor Lucy.'

'Lots of people have been ringing up about you,' said Mary.

'Who?'

'The newspapers, for a start. I'd be careful there, if I were you.'

'What d'you mean?'

'I took one of the calls. They wanted to know if it was true that John Palmer's wife had been having a cosy candlelit dinner with her GP while her husband was "banged up inside", to use their expression.'

'Jesus!' exclaimed Tom angrily. It really hadn't occurred to him that anyone would look at it like that.

'I think these people make up their own rules,' said Mary.

'They're the cause of so much of this in the first place,' said Tom bitterly. 'The Palmers never had a chance after the way the papers turned public opinion against them.'

'But John Palmer confessed, didn't he?' said Mary.

Tom said nothing.

'The police want to see you as well.'

'For all the good *that* will do,' Tom snorted. 'They couldn't find their arse in their trousers. Sorry, I was thinking out loud.'

'Don't apologise. I prefer people to say what they're thinking. Inscrutability is best left to the Chinese in my book.'

'And you? English or Welsh, I can't make up my mind.'

'Welsh and proud of it. From Beaumaris.'

'Almost a local girl,' said Tom.

'While I remember, your practice partner Dr Rees asked to be informed when you were able to have visitors.'

Tom nodded. Julie was getting more than she'd bargained for over this.

'Get some rest now,' said Mary. 'Everything else can wait.'

'What's the time?'

'Three-fifteen.'

'In the afternoon?'

'In the morning.'

Tom heard Mary leave and he smiled. He'd wanted to meet up with her again and Fate had decreed that it happen; only the circumstances were not quite what he would have wanted. Silence returned to the room to accompany the complete blackness imposed on him by the bandaging, but the lingering scent of Mary's perfume took away any threatening edge and kept the smile on his lips.

It wasn't often that he had experienced total darkness, he reflected. Waking up in the middle of the night was nothing like this. Little reference points of light from some source or other were always there to aid orientation. The bandages afforded him nothing like that, just an endless dark infinity where there was nothing to do but think.

As he lay there, unable to sleep, his thoughts returned to Carwyn Thomas and what evidence there was for his involvement in human cloning. There were, of course, the bad figures for ICSI treatment when compared to those of other labs using the same techniques. Although these could be explained away by other reasons, there was no doubt that an increase in failure-rate would be expected if human cloning was being attempted under the guise of IVF treatment. Cloning experiments with animals had shown that this would certainly be the case.

The more he thought about it, the more Tom began to appreciate that an IVF unit would be the perfect cover for carrying out cloning experiments. Once the technical problems had been sorted out, it would be a case of obtaining eggs from women patients in the usual way, but then removing the nuclei from them and injecting them with DNA from the subjects being cloned instead of sperm from the prospective fathers. Yes, the perfect cover.

He shivered at the thought but also saw the problems that would arise if such a secret cloning were to be successful. A baby would be born after an apparently normal pregnancy but it would not be the one the parents were expecting. They, of course, wouldn't know that. In reality, the mother would have acted as a surrogate for an entirely foreign child but she'd be none the wiser.

And then what?

~ *Eighteen* ~

T om considered what the implications of a *successful* human cloning might be.

Until now, he'd been assuming that all such experiments would end in abortion or stillbirth. Now he found himself forced to consider the problems and repercussions of success. In the event of that happening, what *would* the cloner tell the mother? That the child she'd just given birth to wasn't really hers? That the little bundle she was cradling in her arms was the result of a secret experiment and had absolutely nothing to do with her and her husband at all? That he had conned her and her husband into believing they were having the child they'd always longed for, when in reality they weren't?

He supposed not, but also felt uncomfortable with the alternative of the perpetrator staying quiet and saying nothing about what he'd done. Would he really allow his 'experiment' to grow up as the son or daughter of a family that was totally alien to them in terms of blood relationship, a bizarre situation where the *parents* didn't know that their offspring was adopted. He wondered if simply knowing that the experiment had succeeded would be satisfaction enough for a researcher. Again, he thought not. Surely the point of carrying out such an experiment in the first place would be to add to his scientific achievements?

There could be no peer acclaim if the outcome remained a secret, no international awards, medals or prizes to be modestly accepted. On the other hand, the whole thing would be so grossly illegal that none of that would be possible anyway. So the puzzle remained. Why do it? Curiosity? Vanity? The desire for scientific knowledge? Or some other reason altogether?

Supposing it *wasn't* just an experiment. Supposing there had been a *reason* for the cloning and that the cloned child was not just any child but the result of a DNA cloning of a specific individual. Thomas was involved in cloning *somebody*! A deliberate choice suddenly seemed to be a more realistic option, but who had the donor been? Could Thomas be cloning himself? Surely the ultimate ego trip for any scientist! But if the cloned child were to be left with its 'adoptive' family and neither he nor they were to know anything about his true origins . . . would that make any sense?

Tom wrestled unsuccessfully with this notion. Common sense dictated that if anyone were to risk their reputation and career in a bid to clone a specific individual, then surely there had to be more to it than simply wanting to know if it could be done. The cloner would want access to the child, however difficult it might be to achieve, and it certainly would. It might even be the highest hurdle of them all. Just how *would* he manage it? he wondered.

The child would be the most treasured possession of a couple who believed that IVF treatment had finally paid off for them: they would be the least likely parents on earth to give up their child under any circumstances, so it would be necessary to *take* it from them. That would mean kidnapping it − not exactly a minor crime in any society, and not one that either the public or the police were going to take lightly. Kidnapping was something that very few

people ever got away with, so it was out of the question
. . . or was it?

Tom felt his skin tingle with excitement as he realised
that that was exactly what had happened to one of the IVF
babies from Thomas's unit. Anne-Marie Palmer had been
kidnapped! Tom, John and Lucy might be the only people
on earth who believed that, but it was true nevertheless.
Tom's excitement foundered almost immediately on the fact
that Anne-Marie had subsequently been murdered within
days of her abduction. This didn't fit in with what he was
considering . . . unless of course, she had been regarded as a
failed cloning because of the severity of her disability. Was
it possible that she had been disposed of as an untidy loose
end, maybe to prevent anyone ever finding out the true facts
of her origin?

Tom moved his head restlessly on the pillow as he saw
that there would have been no need to murder Anne-Marie
to keep her origins secret, because it was just so unlikely
that the truth would ever have come to light. DNA
fingerprinting of both Anne-Marie and her parents would
have been required to reveal the secret, and the possibility
of that ever happening for any reason seemed very remote.
On the other hand, Tom suddenly saw that . . . it could
still be done!

Anne-Marie's remains were still being kept in refrigerated
limbo by the police forensic service. She was lying in
the mortuary of this very hospital *at this very moment*.
Anne-Marie could be DNA tested and her profile compared
with that of her parents! If it didn't match, it would be
conclusive proof that she had not been the natural child
of the Palmers, and go a long way towards suggesting that
she had been instead the outcome of a human cloning
experiment. It would certainly provide justifiable grounds
for a police investigation into the IVF unit!

'Yes!' he murmured as, at last, he realised that he had come up with a way of obtaining hard evidence.

His slight exclamation was loud enough to attract the attention of a passing nurse.

'Everything all right, Dr Gordon?' she asked.

'Yes, fine,' he replied feeling slightly embarrassed. 'Bit of a bad dream.'

The nurse came in and gave the bedclothes a cosmetic tuck in and turned his pillow. 'There now, you get some rest.'

Tom made appropriate sleepy noises but he was already considering how he would go about getting material from Anne-Marie Palmer's body for DNA fingerprinting. Nothing to it, he mused wryly. All he had to do was break into the mortuary at Ysbyty Gwynedd and take a sample of Anne-Marie's tissue – after having been expressly forbidden to go near the body by the forensic pathologist in charge of the case. Tom felt a chill run down his spine at the thought but he'd cross that bridge when he came to it. A wave of tiredness swept over him. Sleep was almost upon him with its sweet promise of forgetfulness. Under the bandages, he closed his eyes and wished Lucy well before drifting off into merciful oblivion.

Lucy was the first thing on Tom's mind when he awoke at eight, suddenly aware of the hustle and bustle of morning in the wards of a large hospital.

'We knew you'd ask,' said the nurse, 'so I phoned the ward less than fifteen minutes ago. Mrs Palmer has had a comfortable night and Mr Paxton will be coming in to see her later this morning: he's the consultant plastic surgeon.'

'Can I see her?' Tom started to ask, then: 'Can I see anything?' he corrected himself, touching his bandages.

The nurse smiled. 'Dr Hallam will be in to see you around ten. She'll be able to tell you more. In the meantime, how about some breakfast?'

Tom accepted the offer of tea and toast and fidgeted away the time until Mary Hallam arrived to examine him. The nurse accompanying her removed the bandages from his eyes gently; he could smell antiseptic soap on her skin as her hands moved skilfully and intermittently across his face as she unwound the long ribbon. He felt strangely naked and vulnerable when they'd all gone.

'Just keep your lids closed for a moment,' said Mary before the last of the dressings — two gauze pads — were about to be taken away. 'Now open your left eye slowly.'

Tom did as he was told and was unprepared for the immediate flood of brightness and colour. He had to blink several times until he could see clearly and then he was looking at Mary Hallam. 'You're absolutely beautiful,' he said. It had come out spontaneously.

'All my blind patients say that,' said Hallam. 'Now, your right.'

Tom opened his right eye and found he could see out of that one too, although there was a fair amount of pain associated with it and he closed it again to get relief.

'Just take your time.'

Tom let his fingers rest lightly on the right lid for a moment before trying again with more success. 'It's okay,' he said.

'Want to give the card a go?' asked Mary.

Tom agreed with a grunt and she propped up a vision test card on the other side of the room. 'Now then, when you're ready.'

Tom found he was a lot more interested in looking at Mary than the test card; he knew within himself that his sight was basically okay so reading the card was just a case of going through the motions.

'When you're ready, Doctor,' repeated Mary, acutely aware that Tom was looking at her rather than the card. 'I'll give you a clue, the big one at the top is "Z".'

He started reading.

'Second line,' commanded Mary.

Tom passed the test. His sight was perfectly all right. 'Any chance of seeing Lucy this morning?' he asked.

'Don't see why not – I'll check with the ward if you like. Her husband confessed to killing their daughter, didn't he?'

'He didn't do it,' Tom said tightly.

Mary saw that she had touched on a raw nerve and was slightly taken aback at the strength of his reaction. 'Give me a minute,' she said. 'I'll go and ring the ward.' She left the room but returned shortly to say, 'It's all right with them. She's upstairs in the side room attached to Princess Anne Ward. Turn left at the top of the stairs and go straight along. You can't miss it.'

'Thanks,' said Tom. 'Sorry I snapped your head off.'

Lucy was lying on her back staring up at the ceiling when Tom entered the room. At first he wasn't sure whether or not she was awake because the room was shaded but she moved her head slightly when she heard the door click shut behind him. 'May I come in?' he whispered.

'Tom, you're all right,' said Lucy, turning her head. She sounded weak. 'I'm so glad.'

'I'm fine,' he said quietly. 'You've been through a bit of a rough time, though.'

'Fate seems to have it in for John and me,' Lucy said. 'I'm beginning to think that the odds are just too heavily stacked against us.'

'You mustn't give up,' Tom urged. 'It's got to bottom out somewhere. I've a feeling this is it.'

Lucy smiled weakly and put her hand on his.

'Are you in much pain?' he asked.

'The doctors gave me something; my head's full of cotton wool.'

'People pay good money for that,' joked Tom. It brought the suggestion of a smile to Lucy's lips.

'Was there much damage to the house?' she asked anxiously.

'Don't worry about that just now: I'll check it out later – make it secure and do what needs doing. It'll be back to normal by the time you get home.'

Lucy suddenly gripped his hand tightly, her fingers like talons. 'And I *am* coming back,' she said. 'Make no mistake about it. They are *not* going to take my home away from me.'

'That's it!' Tom was delighted. 'Hang in there.'

'What's going to happen to me?' asked Lucy. It wasn't a casual enquiry. She looked Tom directly in the eye and he knew that she expected the whole truth.

'You'll be transferred to another hospital for skin grafts. I think probably Manchester.'

'Will I be scarred?'

'Your face wasn't injured,' said Tom.

'But the rest of me?'

'There will be some marking.'

'Thanks, Tom.'

Soon afterwards, Tom left Lucy and came back downstairs to get his things together. He was on the point of leaving, having thanked and said goodbye to the nurses, when Julie Rees arrived. She seemed surprised to see him up and about.

'I thought things were more serious,' she said.

'They are for Lucy Palmer,' Tom told her. 'She's going to need plastic surgery.'

'I'm sorry to hear that. What's your damage?'

Tom held out his arms and said, 'Some minor burns to the forearms and a sore eye; that's about the strength of it. I was lucky — as people in my position feel compelled to say whatever's happened to them short of death.'

'Stops someone else saying it,' smiled Julie.

He sensed her unease. 'It was nice of you to come,' he said. It sounded awkward and made him realise that he and Julie had never had anything more than a strictly working relationship. They had never become real friends. They were colleagues who never invaded each other's personal space without feeling uncomfortable. He didn't know why and it had never mattered until now, when he suddenly felt as if he were talking to a stranger.

'I thought maybe we could have a word and then I'll give you a lift home, if you like.'

Tom thought Julie's tone sounded ominous, a view reinforced when she made a point of closing the room door. As they sat down and faced each other, she began, 'Tom, I know how strongly you feel about the Palmers and the raw deal you think they've been getting . . .'

'But?'

'But frankly it's beginning to damage the practice. People are starting to transfer to GPs in Bangor and Caernarfon as a mark of protest.'

'I saw one of their protests come in through the window last night,' Tom said bitterly.

'People do stupid things when they get emotionally upset,' said Julie, 'and the death of a child is something that does cause a great deal of strong feeling around the village.'

'It's secondhand emotion, Julie,' Tom protested. 'They're using Anne-Marie's death to parade their self-righteousness before each other. The truth is, they didn't give a shit about Anne-Marie when she was alive and they don't really give a shit about her now that she's dead. She's just a convenient vehicle for self-promotion.'

'That may well be true,' conceded Julie. 'But these are our patients you are talking about. We have to get along with them.'

'I don't have a problem with that,' said Tom. 'But if that means turning my back on my friends when I know they're innocent, the answer is no.'

There was a long silence before Julie said, 'We really can't go on like this.'

'No,' Tom agreed. 'What is it that you want me to do?'

Julie hesitated before saying, 'I think it might be best if I brought in a locum for the time being, at least until the Palmer business blows over.'

'Blows over?' he questioned.

'Well, until the trial is over and things settle down again.'

Tom let out his breath in a long sigh. 'You mean until John is convicted and gets sent down. Maybe you're right,' he said. 'But I have to tell you, I've no intention of leaving Felinbach.'

'Understood,' said Julie. 'I'm not sure what our financial state is exactly, but we'll work something out when I've done the figures.'

'Sure,' said Tom.

'Want that lift?'

'Maybe not,' said Tom. 'I've got one or two things to do in Bangor before I go back.'

'Okay . . . well, see you around.'

'See you.'

Julie left and Tom remained seated on the bed for a few

moments. He felt numb. Mary Hallam looked in and saw him sitting there. 'I thought you'd left without saying goodbye,' she said. 'What's the matter?'

'I think I just got the sack,' he said.

She looked at him for a few moments in silence before saying, 'In that case, the least I can do is offer to buy an unemployed colleague some brunch. You can tell me all about it and while you're at it, you can also tell me why you think John Palmer is innocent. I'm off duty in five minutes. Deal?'

'Deal,' said Tom.

They drove down into the town in Mary's car, a Honda Civic with more than 90,000 miles on the clock. 'Never let me down yet,' replied Mary when Tom commented on it.

'How long have you had it?'

'Three weeks.'

Tom found himself chuckling when it was the very last thing in the world he felt like doing. Mary was not only attractive; she was extremely easy to like.

They stopped at a pub near the pier in Bangor that Mary said she liked, and ordered bacon and eggs from their table by a bay window overlooking the Menai.

'Right – I'm all ears,' Mary announced as they waited for their food.

At first, Tom tried to be guarded about what he said, a bit unsure of Mary's motives in bringing him here, but he had taken such an intuitive liking to her that he found himself telling her everything. It was positively therapeutic, and made him realise that he'd had no one to confide in for a very long time.

'Well?' he said, when he'd ended by telling her about taking a surreptitious look round Thomas's private lab. 'What d'you think?'

'I think you're mad,' said Mary.

— Nineteen —

Tom saw that Mary was serious and immediately regretted having been so forthcoming. He now felt embarrassed.

'You can't possibly believe that a man like Carwyn Thomas is mixed up in something like that,' she said. 'He's a national institution — people round here regard him as a saint.'

'So he has a pretty formidable reputation and he's at the show-business end of medicine,' countered Tom. 'That doesn't mean he's any different from the rest of us when it comes to self-interest and ambition — quite the reverse, I would have said. Successful people tend to be ruthlessly ambitious; that's largely why they get to be successful in the first place.'

'There's a big difference between being ambitious and being some kind of criminal,' protested Mary. 'I think you're letting your imagination run away with you. In fact, if you don't mind me saying so, don't you think you're being just a little obsessive about this whole Palmer thing?' She accented the words 'just a little' to make them sound like 'a whole lot'.

Tom rubbed his forehead, betraying growing feelings of vulnerability. The incident involving Lucy and the at-least temporary parting of the ways with Julie had brought him close to nervous exhaustion. It was a gesture that reached Mary.

'Look,' she said softly, 'I appreciate that you are absolutely convinced that your friend is innocent and I understand your desire to help him, but making wild accusations about respected figures in the medical profession isn't going to get you anywhere. Apart from anything else, the profession itself will crucify you. You'll end up practising in Greenland!'

Tom smiled ruefully and nodded. Mary put a reassuring hand on his. It was a gesture that made his skin tingle and made him realise how much he missed human contact. He looked at her, hoping that nothing of what he was thinking would show on his face. 'I really haven't been making wild accusations, you know,' he said. 'You're the first person I've confided in.'

Mary looked puzzled. 'Why me?' she asked quietly.

Tom shook his head. 'I don't know,' he prevaricated. 'Sympathetic stranger and all that,' he continued. 'Maybe the time was right: I needed to tell someone.'

'I can understand that,' said Mary. 'You certainly seem to be all on your own when it comes to the Palmer case, and swimming against the tide is never easy. You must have been under a lot of strain over the past few weeks.'

'Maybe, but it hasn't coloured the way I feel about things.' Tom sounded almost defiant.

Mary smiled at what she saw as the streak of obstinacy in him. She didn't think it unattractive. 'You really *do* believe that the IVF unit is trying to clone a human being, don't you?' she said.

'How else would you interpret what I found in Thomas's lab?' Tom countered.

Mary looked thoughtful. 'I suppose I would expect a man in Professor Thomas's position to keep up to date with the research literature in his field, so I wouldn't think it odd at all to discover he'd been reading up on factors relevant to human cloning.'

'What about Caernarfon's poorer-than-average success figures for the birth of ICSI babies?'

'I don't know,' confessed Mary. 'But that doesn't automatically mean that someone is putting donor DNA into patients' ova instead of sperm. The failure rate could be down to a lot of things; you said so yourself.'

'I did,' he agreed. 'And I'm not suggesting for one moment that, taken on its own, it proves anything one way or the other, but when everything is taken into consideration, I'm convinced that something illegal has been going on in Thomas's unit. He did have Anne-Marie Palmer's notes in his lab, remember? Just hers, no other patient's.'

'That's harder to explain, I agree,' conceded Mary.

'The disappearance of Megan's body fits into it somewhere too,' Tom said. 'It's just that I can't see where at the moment.'

'Liam Swanson wants to hand that over to the police,' said Mary.

Tom nodded but added, 'Not just yet.'

Mary saw the steely determination in his eyes and found it slightly unnerving. This seemed to convey itself to Tom, who felt obliged to explain. 'I'm really not mad, Mary. I'm just someone who got caught up in something he hadn't bargained for. I was quite content as a country GP, but all this just happened out of the blue and now I'm determined to see it through to the bitter end. I have to.'

His last comment and the look in his eyes triggered off the same reaction in Mary, as had his earlier gesture of rubbing his forehead. She nodded and asked, 'So what do you do next?'

'I need to get a sample of Anne-Marie's tissue for DNA fingerprinting,' he said.

'What?' exclaimed Mary. 'Why on earth do you want to do that?'

Tom told her why and volunteered the information that Anne-Marie's body was still being held in the mortuary at Ysbyty Gwynedd. He planned to get in there somehow.

'But security has been tightened in Pathology after what happened over in Caernarfon with Megan Griffiths,' protested Mary.

'I'll find a way,' said Tom. 'All I need are a few cells from her body. If I can just show that Anne-Marie could not possibly have been the natural child of John and Lucy Palmer, then I think the dam will burst and the whole truth will come out. The police will have to investigate then.'

Mary looked apprehensive. 'You're already on the brink of losing your job. Breaking into the hospital mortuary and interfering with forensic evidence could lose you your license. You could end up in jail *with* John Palmer instead of helping him!'

'There must be a way,' said Tom, refusing to see anything other than his objective.

Mary watched him rack his brain for a few moments then she said with an air of resignation, 'I'll do it. I'll get it for you.'

Tom stared at her, almost unable to believe what he'd just heard.

'I do at least work at the hospital. I can sign myself into Pathology on some perfectly reasonable pretext and get your sample for you while I'm there.'

'But why?' asked an astonished Tom.

'I don't know,' she confessed, echoing Tom's earlier reply.

'That would be absolutely wonderful,' he said.

'But you must promise me one thing,' Mary declared. 'If it should turn out that Anne-Marie Palmer *was* the natural child of the Palmers, you'll stop all this and get your life back together again. It strikes me that Julie Rees will take you back if you mend your ways, eat a slice of humble pie and come up with a few well-chosen words. What d'you say?'

'Agreed,' grinned Tom. 'When d'you think you'll do it?'

'I'll try when I go back on duty tonight. There'll be fewer people around in the evening anyway. Give me your number and I'll call you when I have the sample.'

'I can't tell you how grateful I am,' Tom said.

'I haven't got it yet,' said Mary, picking up her handbag and getting out her purse. Tom protested but she insisted on paying. 'I invited *you*, remember? And a deal is a deal. You won't forget that, will you?'

He took her meaning. 'No,' he assured her. 'I won't.'

They left the pub and found that the wind had got up. It was whipping in from the north, across the open waters of the Menai, carrying with it the suggestion of rain as they buttoned up their coats and stood talking on the pavement for a few moments.

'Can I give you a lift back to Felinbach?' Mary offered.

Tom wouldn't hear of it. 'I've already kept you out of bed long enough,' he said. 'You get some rest; I'll catch the bus.'

Mary nodded. 'I'll call you later,' she said, beginning to yawn.

'Please, don't take any unnecessary risks,' said Tom. 'This is my cross to bear, not yours.'

She nodded. There was an awkward moment when they didn't seem sure how to part. In the end they did so with a smile and a handshake. Tom watched Mary drive off, wishing he could have put his arms around her and held her tight, then he walked slowly up into the town. He thought he'd have a look for a plumber and make arrangements to have his heating fixed before catching the bus home.

The phone rang at 9 p.m. and Tom let it ring twice before answering to disguise the fact that he'd been sitting there, waiting anxiously for the call.

'Tom? It's Mary. I've been down to the mortuary.'

'How d'you get on?' he asked nervously.

'No joy, I'm afraid. She's not there.'

This wasn't what Tom had expected to hear. 'But she's been there since they did the post mortem!' he exclaimed.

'She's been moved.'

'Where?'

'To Caernarfon General. The duty technician was quite talkative, a natural gossip if truth be told. She told me that Anne-Marie Palmer had been transferred to Caernarfon at the request of one Professor Carwyn Thomas.'

'Thomas!' Tom breathed.

'Exactly,' said Mary. 'She was quite surprised too, but apparently the police pathologist agreed to this because Anne-Marie had been one of the unit's patients and Thomas wanted to carry out some tests of his own. Being who he is, the pathologist gave it the okay. Apparently he and Thomas are in the same golf club.'

'It's against the law to interfere with forensic evidence,' said Tom. 'A certain police pathologist told me that,' he added sourly.

'That's more or less what the technician said too,' said Mary. 'But apparently Professor Thomas could be trusted because of who and what he was.'

'Carry out tests, my foot,' Tom snorted. 'He's going to destroy the evidence!'

'Surely he couldn't do that,' said Mary. 'Caernarfon can't afford to have another body go missing.'

'It's the only reason I can think of, for him wanting the body there. Do you know when she was transferred?'

'The technician said earlier today.'

'Then there's a chance I can still get to it,' Tom said grimly. 'I'm going up there.'

'You'll be taking a terrible risk,' protested Mary.

'Providing her body's still there, this actually suits me better. Being on the enquiry team into Megan's disappearance gives me the right of access to anywhere I want at Caernarfon General. That's what Trool said, remember? Getting into the mortuary should present no problem.'

'Don't do anything stupid,' said Mary.

'I won't,' Tom assured her. 'And I'm still very grateful to you for what you tried to do this evening.'

'Let me know how you get on.'

It was just after ten-fifteen when Tom drove into the car park at Caernarfon General. His earlier confidence about gaining access to the mortuary was beginning to waver as he considered the practicalities of actually doing it. The Pathology Department would be locked at that time of night so he would have to seek assistance from the staff in the hospital's front office. They in turn would have to check that he had the proper authority, so that would mean informing the powers-that-be that he was there, and even then it might mean calling out the duty technician or Sepp himself to unlock the door.

Although he would be under no obligation to explain why he wanted access to the mortuary, he could hardly request that he be left alone on the premises. And he would not be able to work on Anne-Marie's body while someone stood there watching. He was musing that nothing was ever easy when another car drew up in the car park and the driver got out. It was Carwyn Thomas.

Tom felt his pulse rate rise as Thomas looked across the tarmac and recognised him. Tom saw him frown and look puzzled as he locked his car door and came towards him.

'Well, Doctor,' said Thomas with what looked like a forced grin, 'What brings *you* here at this time of night?'

'I might ask you the same question, Professor,' Tom replied steadily. 'Bit late for a clinic, is it not?'

Thomas seemed to take this as a challenge. He stared at Tom without blinking for a few moments. Tom suspected this was a technique the man used for intimidating nurses and junior doctors when something had displeased him. He returned the stare and Thomas blinked first.

'I had to spend the day in London. Another of these damned Research Council meetings. I thought I'd pop in to see that everything was all right.'

Tom was delighted to hear that the Professor had been away all day. It meant that he hadn't had a chance to do anything about Anne-Marie's body. 'I'm here to check up on a few things to do with the Megan Griffiths business,' he volunteered.

'At this time of night?'

'Never put off until tomorrow what you can do today,' Tom joked. It didn't get much of a smile. They walked together towards the main door in silence but just before they reached it, Thomas stopped beside a dark green Jaguar car and looked puzzled.

'Something the matter?' Tom asked.

The other man appeared not to hear him at first, then realised he had been spoken to. 'I'm sorry?'

'I asked if something was wrong,' repeated Tom.

'No, nothing.'

'Good. Perhaps you can help me? I need to gain access to

the Pathology Department. There are one or two procedural things I need to check on.'

'Surely that sort of thing is best done when the staff are actually there?' said Thomas.

'Maybe, but I'd just like to have a look around on my own and get a feel for a few things that have been bothering me,' said Tom.

'I don't think I understand,' the Professor said.

'I have the same sort of feeling,' said Tom. 'I don't think I understand why you requested that Anne-Marie Palmer's body be brought here to Caernarfon.'

Thomas was taken aback. 'What has that got to do with you? Who told you that?'

'No matter,' replied Tom. 'It's true, isn't it?'

'I wanted to carry out a few tests. Dr French was kind enough to give me permission.'

'As to whether it's in Dr French's power to grant you such permission is another matter,' said Tom evenly. 'Personally, I find it odd. He seemed quite a stickler for the rules when I asked if I could do much the same thing.'

'Of course!' nodded Thomas, suddenly remembering Tom's interest in the case. 'Your belief in John Palmer's innocence! You are meddling in something you don't understand here, Doctor. If you'll take my advice, you'll leave things as they are.'

This for Tom was a seminal moment. It confirmed that there was something to 'meddle' in. 'Thanks for the advice, Professor, but what I really need to know right now is how I get into Pathology?'

For a few seconds it seemed that Thomas might lose his temper; his mouth twitched and his eyes flashed but he kept control. Finally, he simply said, 'I'll accompany you to the office and they'll give you a key.'

Things had worked out better than Tom could have

hoped. The fact that he was being given a key meant that he *would* be alone in Pathology. Getting a tissue sample from Anne-Marie was going to be a much simpler business all round.

The elderly man on the desk rose from his chair as the Professor entered. He was short, tubby and wore red braces over a green striped shirt; they held the waistband of his trousers somewhere between his navel and his nipples. He had been watching a small portable television and his eyes still seemed reluctant to leave it for more than a few seconds. He kept glancing back at the screen as Thomas made his request, taking sideways looks at it as he collected a key from a row of keys hanging up along the back wall of the office. He slapped it down on the desk and brought out a grubby hardcover notebook from under the desk. He opened it where a pen had been inserted as a marker. 'Sign here,' he said, sliding the book around through 180 degrees and pushing it across to them. The Professor indicated that Tom do the signing and he did so. He took possession of the key and the man returned to his television programme, never really having ever been away.

'Remember to take the key back when you're finished,' said Thomas when it came to the parting of the ways. Tom assured him that he would and wished him goodnight. The other man grunted in reply and walked off, leaving Tom to go downstairs to Pathology.

The bottom corridor was badly lit and totally deserted. Tom unlocked the door to Pathology and stood for a moment in the darkness before switching on the lights and listening to the stutter of the fluorescent tubes as they struggled up to full brightness. It was about time he had a bit of luck, he thought, and so far this was proving a doddle. He would take what he'd come for and be on his way within minutes.

He walked through the labs and into the post-mortem suite where he looked for and found a couple of sterile specimen containers and some surgical gloves. It was important that he did not contaminate the sample with any other source of DNA. For this reason he planned to take a cell sample from Anne-Marie's internal tissue rather than surface material that could conceivably have been tainted with foreign material during earlier examinations. He selected a scalpel and fitted it with a new sterile blade before replacing it temporarily in its foil sheath while he opened up the clasp bolts on the fridge door.

There were four bodies inside; Anne-Marie's remains were on the lower left shelf. He engaged the hooks on the transporter trolley and slid out the body, deciding that there would be no need to transfer it to an examination table. He'd simply open up the body bag and carry out the procedure while it lay on the trolley. He recoiled slightly at the smell when he unzipped the bag then steeled himself to continue.

He cleaned up an area on the outer aspect of Anne-Marie's upper arm and made an incision with the scalpel before inserting a pipette and withdrawing some material, being careful to avoid touching the edges of the cut. Almost as an afterthought, he decided to take a second sample from a different site just to make sure. Two matching DNA fingerprints from different sites should rule out any suggestion of cross-contamination at a later stage.

He was just about to expel the contents of the second pipette into a specimen container when he sensed that he was no longer alone. He hadn't heard anything; he just felt a presence. His mouth went dry and he imagined that it had suddenly turned colder. He was just about to turn round when the inside of his head exploded in white stars of pain and he was sent hurtling into oblivion.

~ Twenty ~

T om could not believe the pain inside his head when he finally came round. The pressure behind his eyes was such that it seemed his skull must explode. He was suffering so much that he almost wished it would. The pain took up so much of his attention that it was some time before he got round to considering other factors, like what had happened to him and just where the hell was he now?

It didn't take a rocket scientist to work out that someone had crept up behind him in the mortuary – someone who had taken great exception to him being there – and hit him over the head very hard. He was currently in complete darkness and there was something over his mouth . . . God, there was something *in* his mouth too, he realised – a piece of rough cloth. Someone who didn't believe in half measures had gagged him securely. He couldn't make the tiniest sound.

This thought was immediately replaced by one that suggested he might actually choke on the cloth should it move too far back. He flung his head to the side, knowing that he would have to avoid lying on his back at all costs. His next discovery was that his arms and legs were tightly bound, something that did little to improve morale and much to encourage a growing feeling of despair. He lay absolutely still for a few moments, sweat trickling down his face, fear causing his stomach muscles to cramp as he tried to work out what was likely to happen next. Whatever it was, it seemed there was very little he could do about it. Not a happy thought.

It must have been Thomas, he decided. Thomas knew that he'd been in the hospital and had known exactly where he was going to be. He'd probably also figured out what he was about to do. He must have followed him down to the mortuary and waited his chance. If Thomas had gone this far, he concluded with a hollow stab of fear, he couldn't afford to stop now. He would have to go all the way and kill him.

Tom had put the fact that he was sweating profusely down to the effects of fear, but he suddenly realised that it *was* unbearably hot. There was something else bothering him too, something about the quality of the air . . . it was bad. He was in a confined space and the air was thin. It was the sort of air you'd expect to find in submarines trapped on the seabed, coal mines after a roof collapse . . . escape tunnels dug without ventilation shafts. Such thoughts added claustrophobia to the equation and put even more pressure on the panic button inside his aching head. On top of everything else there was an unpleasant smell, too – a sickly-sweet odour that seemed to swirl in counterpoint to the pain. It made a hellish cocktail, one that threatened ever-increasing waves of nausea. God, no! He mustn't be sick! If he did that, he would surely die. Being securely gagged, his lungs would fill and he would drown in his own vomit like some hapless drunk in a dark alley.

Tom fought against the urge to panic as best he could, disciplining himself to stay calm against all the odds and think rationally. He needed to know as much as he could about his situation and surroundings. Knowledge was power and right now he was without any; he knew absolutely nothing. He started by moving his hands behind his back, feeling the surface he was lying on. It was metallic, he concluded. That was worth knowing; it meant that it was unlikely to be a floor. He tried stretching out his legs and found something soft, maybe a cushion or a pillow, and beyond that, an obstruction only a matter of inches from his feet. He pushed against it and discovered that it wasn't solid. The amount of give in it suggested that it was almost certainly metal too. A metal base and a metal wall?

He tried moving the other way, wriggling his hips slowly and pushing himself up with his shoulder. His head came into contact with something solid and the pain soared again to nausea-inducing levels. He lay very still, scarcely daring to breathe until it had subsided a little and he could think again. Now he was sure his surroundings were metal because of the noise the obstacle had made when his head had hit it.

The pain swirled in waves of red mist but it was lessening. A box? Was he in some kind of metal box? He moved cautiously from side to side and made much the same discovery – metal walls on all four sides of him. The word 'coffin' made a bid to replace 'box' in his mind and conjured up images of iron mort-safes in old churchyards where relatives had protected the bodies of their loved ones from the grave-robbers of long ago. The image thankfully faded when he tried to move into a more comfortable position and felt the whole structure shift. He shimmied his hips once more and got the same sensation. The box was mobile! He was lying on a trolley! The metal base must be the shelf of a hospital trolley, possibly the one he'd used to support Anne-Marie's body? But what about the metal ends and the fact that the air was bad? This trolley was enclosed; it had some kind of cover over it. There were no covers on the mortuary body transporters. The only trolley he knew to have a cover . . .

Tom's eyes opened wide inside his black prison as the truth came to him on wings of terror. He was lying on the biological waste transporter; that's why it smelled so bad. God Almighty! The soft object near his feet must be the source of the smell. He tried a hesitant examination with his bound feet before suddenly realising what the bundle must be. It was Anne-Marie Palmer's body. His attacker had taken the chance to kill two birds with one stone, do away with him and destroy the only remaining evidence at the same time. And the heat? Christ! He was already in the incinerator room. He was waiting to be cremated along with Anne-Marie!

The circumstances of his situation were pushing him to the very edge of insanity. He had never been so afraid in all his life. His lungs wanted to explode in screams of terror but the gag kept him agonisingly mute. He lay, wide-eyed in the darkness, wondering if suffocation might not be a better option than being burned alive. Maybe he should actually try to swallow the gag and thus block his airway. Wouldn't it be better to be already dead when the transporter tipped his body into the flames?

But even on the verge of blind panic and undreamed-of terror, he refused to give in completely. Suicide was not for him. He wanted to fight, if only he knew how, but he was bound hand and foot and in complete darkness, only one wrong turn away from choking to death and about to be consigned to the flames of the incinerator.

He remembered from an earlier inspection visit to the incinerator room at the outset of the Megan Griffiths enquiry that the disposal process was entirely automatic. Once the transporter was locked in position and the timer set, no human hand was required. His killer could be sitting at home having a quiet drink when the electric motor whirred into action, the fire door opened, the trolley was lifted and angled and its load slid down the entry chute into the flames.

No one really knows how he or she will behave in a life-threatening crisis until it actually happens. In times of peace, most people can live their entire life without ever having to face such a challenge. Until that moment, Tom might have decided that he had failed the test of courage because he felt so afraid, but now, to his amazement he actually found anger taking over from fear. It seemed to flow through his veins like extra adrenaline, making him strain at his bindings like a man possessed.

It didn't take long for him to conclude that he was not going to be able to snap the surgical tape that held his hands and feet. It would have to be cut, and the chances of him finding something sharp in his current predicament seemed remote – not that it stopped him from examining the edge of the trolley. As he feared, it was smooth and rounded but he still tried rubbing the tape against the lip, hoping to generate enough friction to cut it, but in his heart he suspected it was going to take much longer than he had left. How long that actually was, was anyone's guess except the bastard who had set the timer. It was, however, a reasonable assumption that his murderer wouldn't want him lying around any longer than necessary.

There was one outside chance – or at least Tom convinced himself there was. Maybe it was entirely imaginary, but he saw it as a straw to cling to and at that particular moment, straws seemed pretty substantial elements. He seemed to recall that the fire door was quite wide but not actually very deep. If he had been unconscious, his body would simply slide through it without a problem but if he were to lie on his back and raise his knees, there was a chance that his body might jam in the open doorway. As to what he could do then . . . he couldn't think that far ahead and he couldn't remember if there was enough room for him to roll off to the side. In the meantime, and in the absence of any other idea, he would take the risk of moving on to his back and raising his knees in preparation.

He shifted slowly, trying to keep his head facing the side so that the gag wouldn't move backwards, but he still felt it resting dangerously near the area that would induce a gag response. But at least he was doing *something*. It might all be to no avail and he still might sail through the entry hatch to the fire, but at least he was not giving up without a fight – and for some strange unfathomable reason this was important to him. His test had come and he had passed it, whatever happened now.

What happened now was that an electric motor whirred into life with a jolt and the transporter started to move. Tom felt the angle of the trolley base change and his head start to rise, forcing him to seek as much purchase as he could find on the tray to avoid sliding down. He spread his hands flat behind his back and stretched his fingers as far as they would go, pressing them hard against the metal. He did the same with his feet as the incline went on increasing. Outside, he heard a loud metallic clang and there was a sudden increase in temperature; the fire door had opened.

The tray reached an angle of nearly sixty degrees and all at once the end cover flew open. Tom lost all adhesion to the base. He slid down the metal chute, out into blinding brightness and almost unbearable heat in what he recognised might be the last few seconds of his life. His desire to seek forgiveness from some higher power was cut short when his raised kneecaps made contact with the top of the iron fire door and sent a new dimension in pain to his brain. But he had stopped moving; he was jammed in the open hatch and was currently being barbecued by the blast of heat emanating from the furnace. The heat was such that he could smell his clothes start to smoulder but he had become oblivious to pain in the realisation that there was still a chance he could come out of this nightmare alive. Sheer adrenaline was now running the show.

To his left he could see that the tilting mechanism blocked any chance of getting out that way, but to the right there was a space. He was only able to take a quick look before closing his eyes again against the fierce heat, but he knew that this would be his only chance. The notion that the automatic mechanism might return the transporter to the horizontal was a non-starter. It obviously depended on the fire door closing and that wasn't going to happen while his body was jammed in the entrance.

Tom prepared himself for one huge effort. He was failing so fast in the heat that he doubted there would be time for a second attempt. He needed to push explosively hard with his legs so that his body would fall off the transporter to the right where he would drop down to the floor. The fact that the floor of the boiler-house would probably be stone was not a consideration at present.

Tom braced himself, wriggling down a little to get maximum spring potential into his legs. He pressed his feet against the side of the fire door and could feel the searing heat through the soles of his shoes as he pushed hard with all his might. There was a brief feeling of euphoria as he felt himself tumble off the transporter, but this ended abruptly when he met the unforgiving floor in a three-point landing on elbow, knee and ankle. Above him, the fire door slid shut and the transporter slowly returned to its level position.

With the heat shield in place, the temperature in the room dropped and Tom watched the uncaring wheels and cogs come to a halt, unwilling to accept that this was an entirely inanimate object and not his deadly enemy. Gingerly, he tried moving the limbs that had come into hard contact with the floor in case there had been a breakage. He was in so much generalised pain that it was hard to tell, but after a few moments, he thought not.

His priority now was to free himself of his gag and bindings to get rid of the constant threat of asphyxiation. The prospects looked good; there seemed to be plenty of rough metal edges around in the boiler-house and his bindings were of tape, not rope. He moved across the floor like a sidewinder snake to where a number of boiler-house tools were propped up in a corner and found a fire rake with a rough edge that was just what he was looking for. He got into a sitting position with his back to it and started to work the tape against the top edge of the rake, rejoicing in the feel of every rough serration on its edge.

It took less than a minute to work through the tape that held his hands, and he was free to rip off his gag and pull the cloth out of his mouth with a gasp. He sat still for a few moments, running through every swearword he could think of, his head bowed, taking deep breaths and generally calming himself. His limbs started to fill with lead as the effects of the adrenaline began to wear off.

As he started to undo the tape round his ankles he had difficulty with limb co-ordination. It was as if he were wearing thick, weighted gloves but he knew exactly what was wrong. There was a price to be paid for his body's prolonged fight and flight response; all that adrenaline had to be accounted for, and complete exhaustion for him was going to be the bottom line.

As he finally managed to free his feet, he wasn't quite sure if he still had enough energy to stand up. He tried and staggered about for a few moments like a wild animal fighting the effects of a tranquilliser dart, his hands reaching out to seek support wherever they could find it. Finally, having managed to reach an upright position, he took a few more moments to compose himself before setting off on an expedition across the floor of the boiler-house to where he could see a large porcelain sink. He managed it in the precarious gait of a toddler's first unaided walk in the park and was glad to have the support of the heavy old sink as he turned on the water and sluiced it up into his face and over his head.

The cold water had a revitalising effect on him, cooling him, cleaning him and slaking his thirst. He let it drip from his face into the crazed bottom of the old sink when he finally turned off the tap and remained leaning on the edge, thinking about where he should go from here. Thoughts of Thomas now occupied his entire attention as an unrelenting anger was born in him. It was too strong to be subject to rational thought and decision. To hell with the police, this was personal. He wanted to see the Professor's face when he realised that Tom wasn't dead after all. More than that, he wanted to see Thomas's face just after he'd hit it with every ounce of strength he could muster. Maybe when he'd done that he would think about calling the police.

Tom had no idea what the time was as he cautiously opened the door of the boiler-house and found himself in the cool of what he thought was the night but could conceivably have been early morning. His watch had not survived the rigours of the night and he had to consider that he might have been unconscious for some time before coming round in the transporter. Alternatively, he suspected that if that had been the case, he would have been consigned to the flames without ever having come round. Thomas would not have introduced any unnecessary delay into the proceedings.

There was a chance that the man might still be here in the hospital; Tom would check out the IVF unit before he did anything else.

He was about to set off along the corridor when he realised what he must look like. There were unlikely to be many people around, but if anyone should see him in his current state, his presence would almost certainly be reported. His hair and face were soaking wet, and his clothes were absolutely filthy. He looked like an escaped convict who'd been living rough for several days. Walking round the outside of the building would be a better option.

As he started out, it occurred to him that the really bright thing to do would be to check the car park to see if Thomas's car was still there. Three minutes later, he could see that it was. He stood motionless for a few moments, staring at it, fists bunching at the prospect of confronting the man who'd given him the worst experience of his life, then he looked across to his own car and knew that the right thing to do would be to get into it and drive away from here. He should let the police sort it all out, but something inside him wouldn't go along with that so he turned his back on the car park and started out towards the main building, courting as much in the way of shadow as he could find.

Light was spilling out from the main doors, creating a no-go area as far as he was concerned but he managed to get a view of the reception desk, using a small conifer for cover. There were two people there, a receptionist and maybe a porter, Tom thought. They were chatting and looked as if they might be doing so for some time to come. Even if the porter were to move on, he reckoned, it would still be almost impossible to get through the swing doors without attracting the attention of the receptionist. He looked along the wall to the right of the front door and saw an open window.

It was a small, single, frosted-glass window that was almost certainly a toilet, he thought. If he could get himself in through it, he could by-pass the reception area entirely and get out into the corridor to head straight for the IVF unit. The trouble was that the window was not in shadow; it was clearly visible to anyone approaching the building from the front. He would have to choose his moment well. He looked about him nervously, seeing no one but still feeling anxious. A final glance over his shoulder and he scurried across to the window and pushed it up.

To his great relief it moved without difficulty. With another quick look back over his shoulder, he started to clamber in through the narrow opening head first, stifling a series of curses, as he seemed to hit every earlier bruise and knock on his body on the frame on the way in. He supported himself with his arms on the toilet cistern as he pulled his legs through and struggled in the narrow space to gain an upright position. When he'd finally achieved it, he turned and looked out to the right and left outside before re-closing the window and preparing himself for the next phase. He listened for a moment, although this was not too effective as the cistern in the lavatory was faulty and water was running noisily down the overflow. He decided that he'd have to take a chance and drew in a deep breath before opening the door and stepping out into the brightness of the corridor. It was deserted.

As he moved along it, the silence was suddenly fractured by the sound of male voices, so many that Tom couldn't quite make up his mind at first where they were coming from. He looked around him anxiously before deciding that returning to the toilet was the only available option. He turned on his heel and hurried back to the door as the voices got suddenly louder.

He stepped quickly inside the toilet and put his back against the door. Had they seen him? he wondered anxiously. There was a chance they had . . . he couldn't risk waiting to find out – he'd better get out of here. He tugged at the window again and pushed it up as far as it would go, managing to get both feet out before the toilet door burst open and the loud voices arrived. He wasn't sure what to think when he saw that they belonged to policemen. He dropped back from the window only to fall into the arms of two more policemen who'd come round the outside.

'Got you!' snarled one, as he brought Tom to the ground and held him there while his colleague handcuffed his wrists together. Tom felt his cheek scrape along the ground as one of the policemen put pressure on the side of his head to make sure he remained immobile. He lay completely still as the officer spoke into his radio. 'Intruder apprehended; he was trying to escape through a ground-floor toilet window.'

For Tom, this was the final straw. A nightmare end to a nightmare day, he concluded, as events around him started to swirl into a nebulous mist of nothingness.

⁓ Twenty-One ⁓

'I tell you, I was trying to get *in* to the bloody place, not running away!' insisted Tom for what seemed the fifth time at least. He was back in Ysbyty Gwynedd, he noted, recognising the room he'd had before. 'What the hell am I supposed to have done, anyway?' He let his head slump back on the pillow in exasperation, as Chief Inspector Davies stood over him, red-faced and angry.

'Christ, I've got to hand it to you, Gordon. When it comes to insulting my intelligence, you're in a class of your own. First it was some fantasy killer planting Palmer's kid in his own garden, and now when you're caught climbing out of a hospital window late at night in suspicious circumstances, you insist you were climbing *in*!'

Tom jerked his head round to stare at Davies. 'What suspicious circumstances?' he asked. 'What are you talking about?'

'Author, author,' murmured Davies. 'There must be a BAFTA award in here somewhere.'

'Cut the crap, Davies,' said Tom angrily. 'What are you talking about? What's happened?'

Davies looked down at Tom for fully thirty seconds before sighing and saying, 'All right, we'll play it your way, sunshine. Professor Carwyn Thomas was found dead in his office this evening. He was discovered by one of the night porters who'd gone up to tell him he'd left his car lights on.'

Tom felt as if he'd been struck by a train. He could only stare at Davies, speechless with shock. 'Thomas is *dead*?'

'The hospital medics say it was a heart attack, but then who do we find emerging from a ground-floor window?'

Tom was still too shocked to say anything.

'Now, when I question you about it, you behave as if it was the most natural thing in the world to be climbing out of a lavatory window at Caernarfon General Hospital in the middle of the night, and your alibi is that you were actually climbing *into* the place. If nothing else, you should have the jury in stitches. Of course, the prosecution might go and ruin everything by venturing to suggest that there was a perfectly good front door not twenty metres from the toilet window, and that it's open twenty-four hours a day, but I feel confident you'll come up with some suitable explanation.'

Tom was too distracted to defend himself. His mind was reeling with the implications of Thomas's death, for it was the last thing in the world he expected and, coming on top of everything else, it seemed like the cruellest blow that Fate could have delivered at that particular moment. Now he just couldn't see how he could possibly link Thomas's research to the Palmer baby's death. Gradually he became aware of what Davies was saying.

'Forensic haven't done their stuff yet, but I'm going to make sure they do a thorough job, seeing as how you popped up at the scene. You've got a lot of explaining to do, and right now, you're not doing a very good line in "stricken by grief" if I may say so.'

'You wouldn't understand,' said Tom wearily.

Davies pursed his lips and looked as if his exasperation level was getting perilously high. 'Oh, wouldn't I?'

he exclaimed. 'Just why were you running away, Gordon? What was your contribution to the Professor having a heart attack? Come to that, my officers said you looked as if you'd gone three rounds with Mike Tyson when they picked you up. And your clothes stank as if you'd crawled out of a sewer. Just what the hell has been going on?'

'I wasn't running away,' insisted Tom. 'I climbed in; I heard voices in the corridor; I climbed back out again.'

'All right, why you were climbing in?'

'I didn't want to be seen.'

'You didn't want to be seen,' the other man repeated sarcastically. 'Apart from the state of your clothes, why didn't you want to be seen – or would that question be considered an intrusion into your own personal Disneyworld?'

'I wanted to get to Thomas without anyone stopping me or warning him I was coming.'

'Go on.'

Tom took a long, shuddering breath.

'Earlier this evening . . . he tried to kill me.'

Davies shook his head and looked up at the ceiling as if seeking guidance from above. 'You know, I've never been the greatest fan of the medical profession, Gordon, but I thought it was only psychiatrists who were as loony as their patients. He tried to kill you?'

'You don't understand,' said Tom once more.

'Well, I'm not all that bright, see,' said Davies, pressing the loud pedal on the Welsh accent. 'But I do like a good story.' He pulled up a chair and sat down beside Tom's bed. 'On you go, boyo. Enthrall me.'

By the time Tom had finished telling him what had happened, Davies was looking openly bemused. He shook his head in bewilderment as he repeated some of the key words. 'Kidnapping? Human cloning? Attempted murder?

And you're suggesting that the most distinguished man in Welsh medicine was mixed up in all this?'

'I think so,' said Tom. 'He knew I was going down to the mortuary and probably suspected that I was going to take samples from Anne-Marie Palmer. Things were obviously getting a bit too hot for him.'

'Sounds like they were getting even hotter for you, if what you told me checks out,' said the Chief Inspector. 'So, you confronted him after you'd managed to escape and he had a heart attack?'

'No! Like I say, I never got to him. Your men intervened,' said Tom. He was beginning to feel dizzy again.

'Well, we'll see what the PM comes up with. If what you tell me is true, it's understandable that you went up there and frightened him into having a heart attack. In the circumstances, I think I might have felt like putting his lights out myself.'

'*No*,' Tom insisted. 'I never got to him.'

Davies looked doubtful. He was about to say something when Mary Hallam put her head round the door and said, 'Your five minutes is up, Chief Inspector. You promised.'

Davies nodded and got to his feet. 'Well, it's been hugely entertaining as always, Dr Gordon,' he said. 'I dare say we'll be talking again quite soon. In fact, just to make sure I'm not disappointed, I'm going to leave a man outside your door to keep you company.'

'Oh, come on, Davies — you can't seriously believe that I had anything to do with Thomas's death?' Tom exclaimed.

'I think I'm going to keep an open mind on that for the moment, Doctor,' said Davies, turning the door handle to leave and holding it open for a few seconds. 'You don't know a good cure for piles, do you? Mine are killing me.' With that, he left.

'An open mind about what?' asked Mary Hallam who came in as soon as Davies had gone.

Tom sighed and looked up at the ceiling. 'Open, as in vast, empty, windswept and uninhabited by anything remotely resembling brains. I think a frontal lobotomy is a prerequisite for the police entrance exam round here. Carwyn Thomas has been found dead. Apparently he had a heart attack and Davies thinks *I* might have had something to do with it.'

Mary's mouth fell open. 'Professor Thomas is dead?' she exclaimed. 'My God, how awful. When did this happen?'

'Late last night. They found him in his office at Caernarfon General.'

'But that's where you went when you left me,' said Mary.

'I met him in the car park when I got there,' Tom told her. 'He'd been in London all day. We talked and I challenged him about having Anne-Marie's body moved. I think he probably realised why I was there and what I was going to do. He must have followed me down to the mortuary later.' He touched his head wound and grimaced.

Mary shook her head in bewilderment. 'Professor Thomas did this to you?' she exclaimed. 'God, this is unbelievable!'

'Don't you start.'

'Tell me everything.'

He did so, covering everything that had happened to him since he'd spoken to her last.

'Did you tell the police this?' Mary asked, her eyes wide with astonishment.

'I tried to, but I don't think Davies wanted to hear it. All he seemed interested in was implicating me in some way in Thomas's death.'

You aren't, are you?' asked Mary, looking as if she didn't know what to believe any more.

'Of course not – but I might have been, had I got to him.'

'Just thought I'd check,' said Mary distantly.

'I'm sorry,' said Tom with a weak attempt at a smile. 'I know it must all sound absolutely bizarre, but that's the way it happened.'

'Did you actually see Thomas before he hit you?' asked Mary.

Tom confessed that he hadn't.

'So you don't know for sure that it was him. I mean, it could have been anyone when you think about it.'

Tom gave her a look.

'I'm just saying that you don't know for sure,' Mary reiterated.

Tom was too shattered to argue the point. 'If you say so,' he conceded. He let out his breath in a long sigh and closed his eyes for a few moments. Mary smiled and sat down on the edge of the bed. 'You look out for the count,' she said, tousling his hair gently.

'God, that's nice,' murmured Tom, as his eyelids grew heavy. He reached up and found Mary's hand. He held it against his cheek for a moment before slipping off into a deep sleep. His last happy thought was that she hadn't taken it away.

Tom's first *depressing* thought on waking up at 7.30 a.m. was that he had failed to get a sample of tissue from Anne-Marie Palmer's body and it was now too late: her remains had been destroyed. He swore and sat up, until his head wound reminded him that this was a bad idea. He sank slowly back down on the pillow and lay still while he wondered if his last chance to get any real evidence had gone. He wasn't at all sure what he would do now, but a first step would be trying to get out of bed.

The effects of the painkillers he'd been given the previous night had now completely worn off, leaving him aching in places he hadn't realised he'd got. He sat up and swung his legs round, but with the slowness and difficulty of a man forty years his senior. He was just about to try standing up when Chief Inspector Davies arrived.

'Not a bloody thing,' announced Davies by way of greeting.

Tom looked at him, hoping for an explanation but felt apprehensive about the look of self-satisfaction on the man's face.

'Not a bloody thing, Tom.'

'Do we go on like this or are you going to tell me what you're talking about?' asked Tom sourly.

'We didn't find one single thing to corroborate your story about being tied up in the boiler-house last night,' said Davies. 'Not one little thing.'

'But you must have found bits of tape? And that rag he stuffed in my mouth? I threw it on the floor,' protested Tom.

'Not a dickie bird.'

'Blood on the transporter from my head? There must be something!'

Davies shook his head slowly. 'No, nothing.'

'Well, maybe the boiler-house man cleaned up. Did you ask him?'

'Of course we did,' said Davies. 'He came on duty at eight, just before I came over here. That was the first sign of him: there is no night shift.'

'Well . . .' began Tom before failing to find any words to follow it up with. He waved his hands helplessly as he tried to think of an explanation.

'Don't tell me,' said Davies with a humourless smile. 'Carwyn Thomas came back from the dead to clean up the boiler-house and spoil your alibi.'

'Don't be ridiculous,' snapped Tom.

'You think *I'm* being ridiculous?' Davies pantomimed astonishment.

'What about the mortuary?' Tom put his hand gingerly to his bandaged head wound. 'There must have been blood on the floor after he hit me.'

'If there was, he cleaned that up too,' said Davies.

'Anne-Marie's body!' exclaimed Tom. 'It's not there any more, is it!'

'It *is* missing,' the policeman said.

'At last we are agreed on something.' Tom slumped back on the pillow. 'You can't really believe that I had a hand in Thomas's death?' he pleaded.

'Let's wait and see what the pathologist says. In the meantime you can tell me about this secret research you say Professor Thomas was involved in.'

In his present condition, Tom had little heart for it, but he sat on the edge of the bed and supported his head in his hands while he got his thoughts in order.

'I don't think Anne-Marie Palmer was really Anne-Marie Palmer,' he began. It was a bad start as far as the policeman was concerned: he rolled his eyes. 'I think she was the result of a human cloning procedure performed in Thomas's IVF unit.'

'Human cloning procedure? You mean like in creating a copy of a living person?'

Tom nodded.

'Can you prove this?'

'That's what I was trying to do last night when I got knocked unconscious and sent to an early cremation. I found out through a friend that Anne-Marie Palmer's body had been transferred to Caernarfon General at Thomas's request. I wanted to get a tissue sample for DNA fingerprinting before he'd had a chance to destroy the evidence. Unfortunately I met him in the car park when I arrived and I think he suspected that was why I was there. Now it's too late to get the proof I was after. Anne-Marie went into the incinerator.'

'Of course, *you* could have put Anne-Marie Palmer's body into the fire, couldn't you?' said Davies.

'Why the hell would I do that?' exploded Tom, his exasperation boiling over. 'My whole reason for being there was to prove that she wasn't the natural child of the Palmers. Her body was evidence, as far as I was concerned. Why would I want to destroy it? What possible motive could I have had?'

'Maybe you discovered that Anne-Marie *was* in fact the Palmers' natural child so *you* wanted to get rid of the evidence before you made a complete prat of yourself — yet again! Professor Thomas might have caught you in the act and had a heart attack all because of you and your loony ideas.'

'What a fine mind you have, Davies,' said Tom caustically.

'You're in deep enough shit as it is, man,' growled Davies. 'Don't make things worse for yourself.'

Tom ignored the warning. 'Who's carrying out the pathology on Thomas?' he asked.

'Dr Charles French.'

'The same man who agreed to transfer Anne-Marie's remains to Caernarfon at Thomas's request.'

'What are you trying to say?'

'I'm not *trying* to say anything. I'm just pointing out that the body, despite being subject to Crown Prosecution Service regulations, was moved here at the request of Carwyn

Thomas, I think so that he could destroy it, but I don't know what he told French. I understand they were in the same golf club, so instead of making up stories about me, why not ask French about it and find out why he agreed to do something so grossly illegal.'

'You're not exactly making yourself popular round here, are you, Doctor?' sighed Davies.

'I don't think I'd like to be popular round here,' replied Tom with plain meaning.

Davies left and Mary came in. 'Can I take it that you two haven't exactly become firm friends yet?' she commented, looking after the departing Chief Inspector.

'You could say that,' Tom replied wearily. He was still sitting on the edge of the bed.

'You've decided to leave us, then?'

'I feel okay,' he yawned.

'You'll have to sign the form,' said Mary, suspecting that any argument would be useless. She was referring to the liability waiver that had to be signed when a patient wanted to leave before an official discharge was granted.

'No problem.'

'I'll be off duty soon. Coffee?'

'Yes, please.' Tom got his clothes out from the bedside locker. The act of bending down brought on a severe headache and he sat back down on the edge of the bed for a moment.

'Sure you won't change your mind?' asked Mary.

'Quite sure.'

— Twenty-Two —

'I suppose Professor Thomas's death changes everything?' said Mary, as they took coffee in the hospital cafeteria.

'It's certainly not going to help John Palmer,' said Tom, feeling low. 'Thomas was probably the only person in the world who could have told me why Anne-Marie Palmer was murdered. It might be academic now, but I can't even follow up on my suspicion that she wasn't really the Palmers' child. The evidence went into the incinerator.'

'It's still so hard to believe the Professor was involved in something like that,' said Mary. 'I didn't know him well, but you get a feeling about people. He always seemed such a genuine man.'

'It did seem out of character, I'll grant you,' Tom agreed.

'Maybe none of us is all that we seem,' said Mary ruefully.

Tom nodded. 'It's the age of the image.'

'What will you do now?'

'I'm not at all sure,' said Tom, with a shrug of the shoulders. 'I think my only chance lies in finding something that Thomas left in writing. I keep thinking he must have made notes about his experiments or kept some kind of records: he couldn't possibly have stored everything in his head. Scientists don't do that.'

'I hope you're right.'

'He was pretty thorough, by all accounts. It would be out of character for him not to.'

'Where will you start?'

'Maybe I'll take another look at his lab. I might have more success when I'm not so nervous, and I didn't have long enough to look properly last time.'

'Won't the police have sealed it off?'

'No reason to. The medical staff on the spot seemed satisfied that it was death by natural causes despite what Davies was proposing about my involvement. Anyway, the PM results should be out today.'

'Do you really have to do this all on your own?' asked Mary. 'Surely there must be someone in Thomas's unit who could help you look through his files and records? Isn't it possible that some of the people there might even have suspected that something odd was going on?'

Tom knew that he should have thought of this himself. 'You're absolutely right. I could have a word with Dawes. He's the chief cytologist in the IVF unit; to all intents he was Thomas's right-hand man. If anyone was in a position to smell a rat, he was. I'll talk to him.'

Mary was glad to see that the cloud of depression had lifted a little from Tom. 'I'm off to bed now,' she announced, 'but I'm not on duty tonight. Why don't you come round this evening? I'll cook for us.'

Tom smiled broadly and said, 'That sounds good to me. I'll look forward to it. Tell me where you live.'

Mary wrote her address on a page of a small, spiral-bound notebook she took out of her handbag, and tore it off to give to Tom. He said that he knew it.

'About eight,' said Mary. 'Your car's still at Caernarfon?'

Tom said that it was. It was still in the car park at the hospital.

'I'll run you up.'

He protested but Mary insisted, saying that she was in no great hurry to get to bed as she wouldn't be on duty that evening and it was always difficult to sleep on shift change-over nights. It was just coming up to nine-thirty when she dropped him off in the car park at Caernarfon General and he waved goodbye. The prospect of dinner with Mary had already done much to raise his spirits. He found it hard to keep the smile off his face as he walked up to the hospital.

The staff in the IVF unit were talking in little huddles as Tom passed through on his way to find Ran Dawes. The snatches of conversation he picked up suggested that they were still in a state of shock at the news. They were also concerned about what might happen to their jobs, should the hospital decide not to continue with the unit. He found Ran Dawes sitting at one of his microscopes. Dawes turned round when Tom asked, 'Can we talk?'

'Of course,' replied the other man. 'I'm on autopilot: I'm just going through the motions this morning. I still can't believe it.'

Tom nodded. 'Actually, it's a bit delicate,' he said, half glancing over his shoulder.

Dawes looked intrigued. 'We can talk in my office,' he said, indicating the door at the end of the micros-copy lab.

The room was small and cluttered but, unlike the main cytology lab, it had a window in it. Dawes cleared away a pile of scientific journals from the chair in front of his desk and invited Tom to sit. He himself sat down on a swivel chair behind the desk and leaned forward to rest his elbows on it. 'How can I help?' he asked.

Tom saw no easy way of approaching the subject so he took the plunge. 'I think Professor Thomas was involved in some illegal experimentation,' he said. 'I think he was dabbling in human cloning.'

Dawes looked shocked. 'You can't be serious!' he exclaimed.

Tom affirmed that he was. 'I think that's why the unit's figures for ICSI were worse than other labs. Donor DNA was being injected into patients' ova instead of their husbands' sperm. The high failure rate from these implants was skewing the figures.'

'God Almighty.' Dawes had turned pale. 'I don't rightly know what to say.'

'You didn't suspect anything?' Tom was disappointed that Dawes' reaction already suggested that was the case.

Dawes shrugged and said not. 'It never even occurred to me. What put you on to this?'

'It's where my interest in Anne-Marie Palmer's death has led me,' replied Tom. 'I think Anne-Marie herself was the result of a cloning experiment: I don't think she was the natural child of the Palmers at all and this fact had a bearing on her death.'

'My God,' whispered Dawes. 'But I suppose that might well explain her deformity.'

'Last night I met Professor Thomas in the car park when I came up to the hospital. He helped me gain access to the mortuary where it was my intention to take a tissue sample from Anne-Marie: I wanted her DNA fingerprinted to get conclusive proof that she'd been cloned, but it didn't quite work out that way.' He told Dawes what had happened.

'You think Carwyn tried to kill you?' exclaimed Dawes, his voice now strained. 'This is absolutely incredible.'

'I was destined for the incinerator along with Anne-Marie Palmer's body,' said Tom. 'I survived but her remains didn't, so I can't prove what Thomas was up to. That's where I'd like you come in.'

'Me?'

'I need your help,' said Tom. 'He must have written something down about what he was doing; he couldn't have kept it all in his head. I have to find these notes or records to have any chance at all of convincing the police that there was more to the death of Anne-Marie Palmer than meets the eye.'

'So who do you think did kill her?' asked Dawes.

'I don't know,' Tom admitted. 'But I am convinced that her death was linked to what's been going on here in the unit. I found her file in Thomas's lab along with a lot of stuff on human cloning.'

'You searched the Professor's lab?'

Tom nodded.

'Now you come to mention it,' said Dawes thoughtfully, 'Carwyn *had* become rather secretive about what he was doing on his own account.'

'Did you normally share the lab work?'

'Between three of us.'

'Will you help me?' asked Tom.

'I'll certainly do what I can,' agreed Dawes. 'Where would you like to start?'

'I think we should make a thorough search of his lab and office and see what we come up with.'

Dawes nodded but said, 'I think I'll have to leave you to do that on your own while I explain to the symposium delegates just what's happened. I'll suggest that we suspend proceedings as a mark of respect. We've only got one more day to go anyway, but I suspect the press will be swarming all over the hospital by lunchtime.'

'Probably,' said Tom. 'Maybe you could mention to the rest of the IVF unit staff that I'll be around for a bit?'

Dawes nodded and said that he would. 'I'll be back by lunchtime,' he promised. 'You can tell me how you've got on, and we can talk about what you'd like to do next.'

Tom arranged to meet Dawes outside in the car park rather than inside the hospital. 'It'll stop the staff wondering what we're up to.'

Dawes accompanied Tom along to Thomas's office where they found the door locked. 'Damn,' said Dawes. 'I'll ask Rita.' He left Tom alone for a few moments before returning with a key and saying, 'His secretary had a spare.' He unlocked the door, handed the key to Tom and said, 'I'll leave you now. Hope you find what you're looking for. See you later.'

Tom entered the Professor's office and closed the door behind him. This time there was a feeling of anticlimax and sadness. The pictures on the wall seemed to be a poignant reminder of a brilliant career that had taken a fatal wrong turning, but it wouldn't be the first, he mused. He walked across to the lab door and paused to look out of the window through the slats of the Venetian blinds as he'd done last time. He saw Ran Dawes hurrying across the yard but then saw him stop as if someone had called out to him.

James Trool came into view and the two men stood talking for a few moments. Tom drew back involuntarily when both men looked up at the window. He supposed that they were discussing the tragedy that had befallen Thomas, but he wondered if Dawes might be telling Trool about his presence. He wasn't sure how he felt about that.

Thomas's lab looked pretty much as it had on the last occasion. The man hadn't had much occasion to use it again, Tom thought, what with the symposium taking up so much of his time, although he did notice that the articles on cloning were no longer sitting by the microscope. There was a layer of dust on its plastic cover.

He pulled out the drawer where he'd found Anne-Marie

Palmer's medical file last time: it was empty. He stood for a moment, transfixed by the empty space, wondering if he'd made a mistake, although quite sure in his own mind that he hadn't. He pulled out several other drawers in quick succession but the file wasn't there either. They were all completely empty.

Tom cursed and faced the fact that the file had gone the same way as the articles on cloning. The lab had been cleared out. 'Shit!' he exclaimed, resting both hands on the bench, then he had another thought. The freezer! What about the bloody freezer? He hurried over to the chest freezer and pushed up the lid. As he'd feared, the frozen foetuses had gone too. Only test tubes and chemical bottles remained.

Tom cursed again. His chances of proving anything now seemed more remote than ever. The Professor must have been panicked into destroying everything – maybe that was why he'd had a heart attack. Then Tom remembered that he'd also had a lot of cleaning-up work to do before that, down in the mortuary and in the incinerator room too. It struck him as odd that Thomas had done all that clearing up . . . then he'd destroyed everything in his lab that could possibly implicate him in cloning experiments . . . and then he'd had a heart attack and died. It all suddenly seemed just too tidy to be true.

As he prepared to leave, he felt troubled. He closed all the drawers and cupboards he'd opened, but when it came to closing the last drawer – something he did with his knee – he heard a noise as the drawer slid in. The drawer still appeared to be empty when he pulled it out again to take another look, but when he slid it backwards and forwards on its runners the sound of crinkling paper was coming from somewhere.

Tom pulled the drawer completely out and looked into

the space to see that something had fallen down the back. He reached in and tugged free a single, folded sheet of paper. It was a carbon copy of a hospital lab requisition for supplies and services that had been submitted to Dr Leonard Fairbrother, School of Biological Sciences, University of Wales at Bangor. There was an official order number along with a date, but no other details. Tom refolded it and put it in his pocket. It was the only document he found in an extensive search of the lab and office.

He returned the key to the secretary and asked her to give his apologies to Dawes for not having waited. He left the unit to walk out into watery sunshine and a stiff breeze. There seemed to be little point in hanging around now.

He was just about to start up the Land Rover when he noticed a worried-looking James Trool leave the front door of the hospital and get into his car. Tom noted that it was the Jaguar that Carwyn Thomas had been surprised to see in the car park last night. Tom mused that he didn't envy the man his job in trying to defend the hospital's image at a time when scandal and shock seemed hell-bent on damaging it from all angles. He watched him drive off before he himself followed suit and set out on the road back to Felinbach.

When he got home, he made coffee and sat down to re-read the piece of paper he'd found in Thomas's lab. 'Well, Leonard Fairbrother,' he murmured, 'just who the hell are you?' Feeling that he had nothing to lose, he grabbed at the phone directory and looked up the number for the University of Wales. He was going to go for the direct approach. 'I'd like to speak to Dr Fairbrother in the Department of Biological Sciences,' he told the operator.

'Trying to connect you . . .'

'Fairbrother.'

'Dr Fairbrother, my name is Tom Gordon; I'm a GP in

Felinbach. I was wondering if I might come over and talk to you — some time today if possible?'

'What about?'

'I'd rather leave that until I saw you, Doctor.'

'Intriguing,' said Fairbrother. 'Let's see . . . Would twelve noon be any good?'

'Ideal,' replied Tom. He hadn't meant to sound cryptic but establishing contact with Fairbrother had been so easy and so rapid that he hadn't had time to think about what he wanted to say. By the time he was dodging traffic to cross the main road outside the Biological Sciences building, he had a better idea.

Fairbrother had ivy growing on the wall outside his office, but the room itself was located in a dirty brick building fronting a busy main thoroughfare. The ivy was its only claim to cloistered charm. An ambulance went wailing by outside as Fairbrother invited Tom to sit. 'What can I do for you, Doctor?'

Fairbrother turned out to be much younger than Tom had imagined from his voice on the telephone. He'd pictured a middle-aged man in sports jacket and flannels, but here was a fresh-faced young fellow, dressed in sweatshirt and jeans who looked more like a member of a rock band than a don.

'I believe you know Professor Carwyn Thomas at Caernarfon General,' began Tom.

'I do — or rather, I did,' agreed Fairbrother. 'I couldn't believe it when I heard the news. What a tragedy!'

'How did you come to know Professor Thomas?'

'I only met him for the first time recently,' said Fairbrother. 'He asked me to help him out with something. Why do you ask?'

'It's what he asked you to do for him that I'm interested in,' said Tom.

Fairbrother gave a little laugh that suggested the discomfort of a person about to be rude when it really wasn't in their nature. 'Frankly, you have me at a disadvantage, Doctor,' he said. 'I don't quite see how what I was doing for Professor Thomas has anything to do with you.'

'I've reason to believe that illegal experiments were being carried out in Professor Thomas's unit,' said Tom, hoping for shock value in the blunt statement. 'I'm helping the police with their enquiries by piecing together what the Professor was doing scientifically before he died. It's not easy for people outside the profession to carry out that kind of investigation.'

'Of course not,' agreed Fairbrother. 'Very well — Professor Thomas asked me to do some DNA fingerprinting for him.'

'DNA fingerprinting?' exclaimed Tom, failing to mask his excitement at Fairbrother's reply. The words almost stuck in his throat when he asked, 'What sort of work, exactly?'

'He hoped to establish the true identity of a child he had some doubts about. He wanted me to DNA test a tissue sample — discreetly.'

'Were you able to do what he wanted?' asked Tom.

'Yes, I think so. He seemed satisfied with the results — looked shocked, surprised and then pleased, I'd say, if I'm any judge of reaction. It was as if he'd just solved some puzzle that had been bothering him.'

'What were these results?' asked Tom calmly, his mouth going dry at seeing only one more hurdle to cross.

'I can't rightly say,' confessed Fairbrother, appearing embarrassed at his own answer.

Tom felt himself fall at the final hurdle and come crashing to the ground. Surely Fate couldn't be this cruel. 'You can't rightly say?' he repeated.

'I was working blind, you see, with numbered samples. Professor Thomas didn't want me to have the names of those involved. I just know that the child I was fingerprinting was definitely *not* the child of samples one and two but was in fact the child of samples three and four.'

Tom put a hand to his forehead in anguish. 'No names,' he said. 'Just numbers! Jesus!'

'Actually, Professor Thomas did mention a name at one point. He seemed to be taken so much by surprise that he sort of blurted it out,' said Fairbrother.

'Can you remember it?'

'Give me a moment . . . there was something familiar about it. It was a girl's name, I remember that much.'

'Anne-Marie Palmer?' prompted Tom, prepared to bet money that he was right.

'No, it wasn't that,' said Fairbrother. 'Ah yes, I remember now. It was Megan Griffiths.'

~ Twenty-Three ~

'Are you all right?' asked Fairbrother.

Tom looked at him blankly, taking fully ten seconds for the question to register. 'Yes, I'm fine,' he murmured. 'Are you absolutely sure about that?' he asked.

'Positive,' said Fairbrother. 'At the time I thought that the name seemed vaguely familiar, then I remembered it was the name of the little girl whose body disappeared from the hospital up in Caernarfon. Her name was Megan Griffiths, wasn't it?'

Tom nodded. 'Yes, it was. Did Professor Thomas say anything apart from her name?'

'I don't think so,' said Fairbrother. 'I assumed that his investigation had something to do with that sorry business so I didn't ask too much. They haven't got to the bottom of it yet, have they?'

Tom said not and thanked Fairbrother for seeing him at such short notice.

He stood outside on the pavement for a few moments, oblivious to the heavy traffic rumbling by as he tried to make some sense out of this latest piece of information. It seemed bitterly ironic that a link to Megan Griffiths – the one he'd been racking his brains to find – should suddenly appear at a time when his whole investigation had hit the wall with Thomas's death. But what was the link? he wondered. Just what kind of sample had Thomas been DNA-sequencing, and where had it come from? Could this mean that Megan's body hadn't been destroyed?

Almost without realising it, Tom found that he had walked as far as the pier. After a moment's hesitation, he strode out on the boardwalk, pulling his collar up against the strong March wind and feeling occasional gusts of sea spray on his cheek. It was a good quarter of a mile to the end where he turned his back to the wind and leaned over the leeward rail to look down at the rough waters of the Menai. As he did so, a thought struck him. Fairbrother had said that Thomas had sought his help in establishing *identity*. This meant that Thomas had been unsure of the origin of the sample he'd given to Fairbrother. It also implied that he had been conducting an *investigation*.

When viewed along with the fact that the Professor's lab had been thoroughly cleared out, Tom was forced to consider for the first time, and not without some embarrassment, that the man might actually have been an innocent party in this whole affair. It made the wind feel all the colder.

'Of course he was innocent,' said Mary, when Tom posed the question. 'His suspicions must have been aroused too, and probably at a much earlier stage. I daresay he was trying to find out what was going on, just like you were. It's a great pity he didn't confide in you.'

Tom was sitting in Mary's small but comfortable living room on the second floor of a modern block of flats, about a mile from Ysbyty Gwynedd: they had just eaten and had moved away from the table to have coffee in front of the fire.

'The heart attack was therefore most unfortunate,' said Tom thoughtfully.

'But awfully convenient for someone, when you think about it,' said Mary.

He nodded slowly. 'I may have been doing the Professor a grave injustice. Your gut feeling was right about him. He was probably a good guy all along. He knew something wasn't quite right in the unit so he was looking into it, but on his own because his pride wouldn't let him confide in anyone else where the reputation of his clinic was at stake.'

'Just supposing it wasn't a heart attack,' said Mary.

'You mean it could have been murder?' Tom had been thinking along the same lines.'

'It would make a lot of sense.'

'They'll be doing the PM today so we shouldn't have too long to wait to find out,' he said.

'But if it should turn out that he was murdered,' said Mary slowly, 'and he didn't do the cloning . . . *who did*?'

'Ranulph Dawes,' replied Tom without hesitation.

'The cytologist? The man you asked to help you?'

'Thanks for reminding me,' said Tom wryly. 'Look — if it wasn't Thomas, it *must* have been Dawes. Everything points to that now, and suddenly a lot of things become clearer. Thomas knew something strange was going on in the clinic, but he didn't know exactly what until he saw the ICSI figures from the American lab. Coming just after the heated discussion on human cloning, he must have put two and two together and realised what Dawes had been up to. That's why he looked the way he did when he watched Dawes demonstrate his skills at the microscope. Not many people have the necessary expertise to even attempt a cloning, but Dawes had.'

'You must tell the police this,' Mary advised.

'Let's wait for the PM result first. If French says it was natural causes then we're back to square one. Even if it turns out to be murder, there's still going to be a problem getting proof. Anne-Marie's body and the suspect foetuses that Thomas had in his freezer have all been destroyed. Dawes has had time to clean up absolutely everything.'

Unconsciously, Tom put a hand up to feel the lump on the back of his head. It prompted Mary to ask, 'Painful?'

'Not really, just a dull ache.'

She moved closer and Tom bent forward to let her fingers probe the area gently. 'The swelling's gone down quite a bit,' she said. 'But if it's troubling you . . .'

Tom was acutely aware of Mary's closeness. Her perfume filled his senses and her touch was awakening feelings in him that he'd almost forgotten. He raised his head slowly and turned to face her. 'It's fine,' he said softly, and kissed her gently on the lips, tracing his fingers slowly down her right cheek. There was only the slightest hesitation before Mary responded and they embraced hungrily.

'God, I've wanted to do that since the first moment I saw you,' breathed Tom.

'I bet you say that to all the girls,' murmured Mary as Tom kissed her neck.

He looked at her and saw the smile he'd wanted to see from the time of their first encounter. Any lingering doubts he had about his feelings for her and whether it was a good idea or not, disappeared like snow in summer. 'I want you,' he said. 'God, how I want you!'

Mary put a finger up to his lips and held it there. 'I need a little more time,' she said softly. 'Just a little more. Is that all right?'

Tom smiled and nodded, feeling quite relaxed and happy about it.

'But don't feel discouraged . . .' Mary smiled broadly and they both laughed.

When Tom reached home, he found a message on his

answering machine from Charles French, asking him to call back. 'Well, well,' muttered Tom, wondering why on earth French would be calling him. He dialled the number.

'Dr Gordon? Thank you for returning my call.'

Tom recognised the sound of someone trying to be 'nice' even if it was a struggle. 'What can I do for you, Doctor?' he asked, feeling intrigued.

'Look, I appreciate that you and Chief Inspector Davies don't exactly see eye to eye over a lot of things,' began French. 'But I don't think that should be allowed to sour *our* relationship, do you?'

'Quite honestly, I didn't think we had one,' said Tom.

'Well, no, I suppose I meant that, as two medical men, we naturally have a strong professional bond . . .'

'What are you getting at, Dr French?' asked Tom bluntly.

'This business with the Palmer child's body,' said French awkwardly. 'I know what I did was technically wrong, a gross error of judgement on my part, but my intentions were good and in no way did I imagine it was going to lead to the destruction of Crown evidence. You do accept that, don't you?'

'What I accept or don't accept has no relevance in this case, Doctor,' said Tom. 'I really don't see why you're telling me this.'

'I wanted to know if the Palmer defence team are planning to make a big thing out of it,' confessed French.

'I really couldn't say.'

'Does that mean that they're not actually aware of what has happened as yet?' asked French, a hopeful note creeping into his voice.

So that was it, thought Tom. French was trying to minimise the fall-out as far as he was concerned from the destruction of Anne-Marie's body. 'Not from me,' he said.

French gave a small but audible sigh of relief before continuing, 'Are you planning to tell them?'

'They have a right to know,' said Tom, stalling for time. He hadn't fully thought this through, although now that French had brought up the subject, he supposed that John Palmer's defence team could make trouble over the unavailability of the body for any further examination.

'I understand from Chief Inspector Davies that you yourself admit to being in the mortuary at Caernarfon General with the express purpose of carrying out an illegal procedure on the body?' said French, more haughtily now.

Tom smiled to himself as the threat entered the negotiations.

'After I had refused you access . . .' continued French.

'. . . Presumably because I'm not a member of the same golf club as you and Carwyn Thomas,' Tom put in smoothly.

'That is outrageous!' spluttered French.

'I agree,' Tom said calmly, 'What you're suggesting, Doctor, is that if you go down for screwing around with Crown evidence, you're going to make sure that I go down with you. There, that didn't take long to say, did it?'

'There was absolutely no criminal intent in what I did,' protested French.

'Me neither,' said Tom, matter-of-factly. 'I simply wanted a small tissue sample for DNA fingerprinting.'

'Fingerprinting?'

'I had doubts over the true identity of the child.'

After a short pause, French said, 'You don't need much in the way of biological material for DNA fingerprinting.'

'Very little,' agreed Tom, immediately wondering why French had said something like that.

'Then it would still be possible.'

'What do you mean?'

'I could let you have a pathological specimen taken from Anne-Marie Palmer at post mortem,' said French. 'I still have a range of lab specimens taken from her. If it would help mend fences between us, I am prepared to let you have access to what you need without asking too much.'

Tom was excited at the prospect but not so excited that he couldn't see that he and French would now be colluding. His concern was quickly overruled by deciding that he'd be doing what was right. If there was the remotest chance of obtaining sound scientific evidence relevant to the case, it had to be taken. Medical facts were definitely preferable in court to John Palmer's lawyers introducing legal arguments over technicalities. Apart from that, John's luck was so bad that the judge at his trial would probably turn out to be a member of the same golf club as French and Thomas.

'Perhaps I could pick up a sample in the morning?'

'Of course, and if by any chance you should be able to get the information that you want from the sample . . .'

'I can't make any promises, Doctor, but I have no wish to see you get into trouble for the sake of it.' Tom decided that this would be an opportune moment to ask French about the post mortem on Carwyn Thomas.

'I'm satisfied it was a heart attack.'

Fuck, thought Tom.

'I've still to get the toxicology results but I don't think DCI Davies will be giving you any more hassle over it. Natural causes, as far as I'm concerned.'

Tom put the phone down. He was disappointed that Thomas's death had proved to be natural after all, but he felt pleased that DNA fingerprinting Anne-Marie had become a possibility again. It seemed to signal that maybe not all the fates were against him. He poured himself a large whisky and wondered if Fairbrother at the University would be willing to carry out the tests. He'd call and ask him in the morning, but he suddenly realised that sequencing Anne-Marie's DNA would not be enough on its own; he would also need DNA samples from John and Lucy Palmer with which to compare the profile. This was clearly going to be his next problem, but he now had an appetite for it. He would find a way. He'd been given a second chance, and nothing was going to stop him following his theory through to the end.

He could see no possibility of getting a blood or tissue sample from John Palmer, but material from Lucy alone would do. She must have had various specimens taken from her when she was admitted to Ysbyty Gwynedd after the fire incident, so it should be possible to lay hands on one of these, but that would involve giving reasons to lab staff, going through channels and risking possible refusal. If the worst came to the worst, he could always approach Lucy directly in the Manchester hospital where she'd been transferred for plastic surgery. He'd been keeping in touch by telephone and planned to go over there in a couple of days' time anyway, now that she'd settled in. But this in many ways would be the least attractive course of action. He really didn't want to say anything at all about this to Lucy while there was still a chance he might be wrong. If that were the case and Anne-Marie should be shown to be the Palmers' natural child, it would be unforgivable to have caused her all that angst on top of everything else. He wanted to be absolutely sure of his facts before he said anything at all to either John or Lucy. That meant obtaining samples without their knowing.

The house! Lucy's house! thought Tom. He had arranged for it to be made secure, but that had just involved having the broken window boarded up. As yet, he hadn't been back there to tidy up the mess. Lucy had lost a lot of blood on the floor on that hellish night. He would be able to get the sample he needed from there.

There was a drawback in that some of the bloodstains would almost certainly be his own so he'd ask Fairbrother to fingerprint a number of samples from the floor and also provide him with a fresh sample of his own blood for elimination purposes. He looked at his watch; it was just after midnight. The question now was, should he leave it until morning or should he do this right now? There was no way he could sleep; he'd go now.

As he drew up outside the house, it struck Tom that number 7, Menai View looked as if it had been unoccupied for years instead of only a few short weeks. This was an impression largely created by the boarded-up window and the fact that it was night-time: modern streetlights seemed to exaggerate any sign of disrepair. Sunlight did the opposite. No further graffiti had appeared on the walls, but he did notice that moss was starting to creep over the path through lack of use and weeds were popping up in the cracks.

He took a few specimen containers from the medical case he kept in the Land Rover along with a pair of surgical gloves and a packet of sterile scalpel blades. It was important that he didn't contaminate any of the samples he collected, either with each other or through contact with his own skin.

A bedroom curtain moved in the neighbouring house when he slammed the car door but he didn't look up. Instead, he walked briskly up the path and opened the door with the key Lucy had given him at the hospital. Clicking on the hall light brought back memories of the fire and stopped him in his tracks for a moment. He felt his throat tighten. The house still smelt of burning and in his mind he could hear Lucy screaming again.

He made a conscious effort to put such thoughts behind him before beginning a search of the floor where Lucy had fallen. He identified four separate bloodstains, far enough apart to suggest that cross contamination had not taken place. Using a separate sterile scalpel blade for each, he scraped samples up into each of four specimen containers and secured the caps. He'd got exactly what he'd come for and would now call a halt. He couldn't face doing any tidying up right now; he'd come back another time. He checked that the rooms at the back of the house were secure before locking up at the front and returning to the car.

The wind that had been the main feature of the weather over the last few days died away during the night to leave a still, calm morning when Tom awoke at seven and looked out at the harbour. The downside to this was that the temperature had fallen, a feature that was apparent in the flat where the heating had failed to come on again. There was a frost in evidence on the rigging and mooring ropes of the resident yachts in the basin, making them look like decorations on a wedding cake. He could see that he'd be scraping ice off the Land Rover's windscreen before he went anywhere this morning.

He rubbed his hands and swung his arms across his chest several times before spending a few minutes coaxing the heating into turning on. Despite having arranged to have it repaired by a firm in Bangor, there had been a misunderstanding about the time they were due to come. They had in fact turned up when he had been out and as yet, no alternative arrangement had been made.

He got back into bed and switched on the radio to catch up on the news while the water heated up and the chill was taken off the air. There would be no point in trying to phone Fairbrother at the University before nine, he reckoned. If the man agreed to do the DNA fingerprinting – and it was still a big 'if' – he'd collect a sample of Anne-Marie's tissue from French's lab in Bangor and take it over to him, along with the samples he'd collected from Lucy's house. It was ten past nine when Tom managed to reach Fairbrother at his third attempt.

'Dr Fairbrother? It's Tom Gordon here. You were kind enough to speak with me yesterday.'

'Of course. What can I do for you?'

'Frankly, I need your help again – pretty much in the same way that Professor Thomas did and for pretty much the same reason. I need to have some samples DNA fingerprinted.'

'You folks are going to finish up with a DNA database for everyone in Bangor by the time you're finished,' said Fairbrother, but he didn't sound annoyed.

'I'd really be very grateful for your help,' said Tom.

'How many samples are we talking about?'

'Six, but there is a slight problem. Only two are conventional samples; four are scrapings from bloodstains.' Tom bit his lip as he waited for Fairbrother's response.

'Are you sure this isn't a job best done through the police forensic service?'

'I'd prefer if it was done by a reliable independent agent if at all possible,' stated Tom.

'All right,' said Fairbrother. 'Bring 'em over; I'll see what I can do.'

Tom let out a long sigh of relief as he put down the phone. Everything was in place. All he had to do now was pick up the sample from French and the ball would start rolling.

~ Twenty-Four ~

F rench wasn't in the police lab when Tom arrived to pick up the promised sample of Anne-Marie's tissue. A colleague said that he had been called away suddenly, after 'some shit had really hit the fan', but had left a package for him. Tom opened up the small Jiffy bag to check that it contained the right thing and he pulled out a small, clear plastic container with a one cubic centimetre sample of tissue in it. An adhesive label on one side of it had Anne-Marie's name inscribed on it in black marker pen.

Tom drove over to the University and handed it in with the other samples to Fairbrother, who took down details and labelled them meticulously, using his own system. He said he'd get them done as quickly as possible. Tom was back in Feli by ten-thirty, where he found a dark grey saloon car waiting outside his flat: the three aerials on the roof suggested that it was a police car. As he got out of the Land Rover, DCI Davies and his Sergeant got out of the other car to stand in front of the door, blocking his way. Both wore blank expressions.

'Problems?' said Tom, feeling decidedly apprehensive.

'Thomas Gordon, I'm arresting you for the murder of Professor Carwyn Arthur Thomas . . .'

The words dissolved into a hollow echo inside Tom's head. His jaw dropped in disbelief.

'You are not obliged to say anything, but . . .'

Tom didn't know whether to laugh or cry. The desire to pour scorn on Davies and the shock of being arrested was offset by the realisation that Thomas actually *had* been murdered. He ended up by simply saying, 'That makes much more sense.'

Davies looked at him as if he were mad. Sergeant Walters wrote it down in his notebook.

'You're admitting it?' asked Davies.

'Don't be ridiculous,' replied Tom.

'Get in the car.'

The drive up to Caernarfon was completed in absolute silence, with Tom feeling as if he were sandwiched between two silent robots. He declined the opportunity to call a solicitor, opting instead to phone Mary to tell her what had happened.

She too asked if she should contact a lawyer on his behalf.

'I haven't done anything,' he replied.

Davies switched on the recorder in the interview room, related who was present and permitted himself a small smirk as he faced Tom across the table.

'I would strongly suggest, Dr Gordon, that you make a clean breast of it all and tell us everything.'

'What's to tell? I'm completely in the dark. I was under the impression that the Professor had died of natural causes – at least that's what Dr French told me last night.'

'You spoke to French?'

Tom didn't think a confirmation was necessary.

Davies said sarkily, 'All doctors together, is it? You scratch my back and I'll scratch yours? Well, let me tell you this, my son, you might have been clever enough to fool your fellow medics but you didn't fool the forensic toxicology boys for one moment. Amyl nitrate ring a bell?'

'Should it?'

'That's what they found in the Professor's samples. He'd been given a large amount of the stuff. It makes the heart race, but then you'd know that, being a doctor, wouldn't you?' Davies leaned over the table till his face was very close to Tom's. 'And because *you* administered it!'

'So that's how he did it,' Tom said calmly.

'Who?' asked Davies, sounding more annoyed than inquisitive.

'The man who killed Professor Thomas and probably Maurice Cleef too, maybe even Anne-Marie Palmer.'

Davies did not break into fits of sarcastic laughter. Instead he sat back in his chair again, looking at Tom Gordon as if he were an exhibit in a zoo. He turned his pen, end over end on the surface of the table several times, then he said, 'What is this shit?'

'I was wrong about Thomas experimenting with human cloning,' said Tom. 'It wasn't him — it was a member of his staff, an embryologist named Ranulph Dawes. Thomas must have latched on to what he was up to and started to investigate on his own.'

'And what brought you to that conclusion?'

Tom calmly told Davies all that he'd worked out and was relieved to see that the policeman was — or appeared to be — taking what he said seriously.

'That's quite a story,' said Davies when he'd finished. 'But is that all it is, or can you prove any of it?'

Tom was honest. 'It's going to be difficult,' he admitted. 'I stupidly tried to enlist Dawes's help when I thought Thomas was the guilty party, so he's had time to get rid of all the evidence. I did, however, take down some reference numbers from the frozen foetuses I found in Thomas's freezer, and there's the all-important tissue sample taken from Anne-Marie Palmer's body that French came up with.

I took it up to the University labs this morning; they're going to DNA fingerprint it. I'm sure it's going to show that she wasn't the natural child of the Palmers.'

'The University labs?' asked Davies, latching on to the last bit.

'I asked the same scientist that Professor Thomas used when he started to become suspicious. An entirely independent expert on the technique.'

Davies looked at Tom like an owl contemplating its supper but decided against any more confrontation at this juncture. 'And if this should confirm what you claim, what then? How does it help?'

'The IVF unit must have records of who actually carried out the actual lab work for each patient. If it was Dawes who carried out the IVF procedure in the case of Lucy Palmer, and it should turn out that her baby was not her biological child, then he obviously has some explaining to do. With a bit of luck he'll see that the game's up and fill in the missing details himself.'

'And maybe Bangor will win the European Cup next year,' said Davies, but that was as far as the sarcasm went. He turned and said to Walters, 'We'd better check this out.' Turning back to Tom, he asked, 'Will this Dawes character be at the hospital right now?'

'I should think so,' said Tom. 'He's still under the impression that I think Thomas was the guilty man. He also still thinks that the Professor's death has been put down to natural causes, unless you've told anyone it was murder?'

'It's not common knowledge but I did inform Dr Trool that Thomas had been murdered,' said Davies. 'He's been phoning up every five minutes, worried about possible scandal and the bloody hospital's reputation. He just about had a heart attack himself when I told him what the toxicology report on Thomas said.'

'Did you ask him to keep it to himself?'

'He was hardly likely to go blurting it out to all and sundry, was he?' retorted Davies.

'If Dawes hears about that report, chances are he'll be off like a scalded cat. If not, he probably believes he's in the clear and possibly even in a good position to take over the unit if the hospital decides to continue with it.'

'We'd better get over there and you'd better come with us.'

'Does that mean I'm no longer under arrest?'

'For the moment. Do you have these reference numbers you spoke of?'

'They're in my wallet.'

Tom and Davies sat together in the back of the unmarked police car that took them up to the hospital. DS Walters sat in the front with the uniformed driver. They didn't talk much on the way: the uneasy truce between Davies and Tom Gordon did not as yet extend to small talk.

The IVF unit seemed deserted when Tom, leading the way, entered and started looking into rooms as they came to them. They found a group of four female technicians sitting in the staff room, drinking coffee and talking in hushed tones. They stopped when they saw Gordon.

'Is Dr Dawes around?' he asked.

'I haven't seen him today,' said a fair-haired girl.

'Are you expecting him?'

The girl shrugged. 'He didn't say he wasn't coming in,' she said. 'But no one seems to know who's doing what or what's going on.'

Tom nodded. He glanced over his shoulder and said, 'These gentlemen are policemen. We'd like to take a look round, if that's okay with you?'

'Of course. Let us know if you need help with anything. Is it true that Professor Thomas was murdered?'

Tom stopped in his tracks. 'Where did you hear that?' he asked.

'One of the secretaries heard a rumour,' said the girl.

Tom turned and looked at Davies who shrugged and said, 'Bush telegraph, faster than satellite technology.'

A man wearing thick black-rimmed glasses and a black polo shirt under his white lab coat came into the room and the girls stiffened. They got up from the table and queued to wash out their coffee mugs at the sink.

'I'm Michael Deans, the chief technician. Can I help you?'

Again, Davies let Tom do the talking, hoping to keep an air of informality about their presence for the moment. Tom explained who they were and that they had hoped to have a word with Dawes. 'I understand he's not been in today?'

'Not yet anyway. I'm afraid everything's in a state of flux at the moment. We're all in shock, you could say.'

'Quite understandable,' sympathised Tom, hoping the man might be useful to them. 'Perhaps you can help us,' he said. 'I've got a series of reference numbers here that Professor Thomas gave me. Would it be possible for you to find out for us which patients they relate to and who carried out the actual IVF lab work on them?'

'Possible, yes . . .' Deans hesitated. 'But I'd need authorisation.'

Davies held out his warrant card. 'This is all the authority you need.'

The technician took a deep breath as if giving himself time to decide whether it was worth digging in his heels or not. In the end he took the numbers from Tom and said, 'Follow me.'

They trooped in single file through to the unit office where the technician asked one of two secretaries for, 'The blue book'.

The woman looked up from her desk at the three men waiting there but did not say anything. She just opened up her desk drawer and took out a blue covered notebook that she handed over without question.

'Police,' said the technician by way of explanation before leading the others out into the main lab area. There was a small, glass-panelled office at the far end where he put the book down on a desk and flipped it open to start tracing the numbers Tom had given him. He found the page he was looking for and ran his index finger down the left-hand side before stopping about a third of the way down. '275643 . . . Maitland baby, malformed foetus, aborted 14 July, 1998. Parents, Iris and Glyn Maitland, 14, Ryder Close, Caernarfon.'

The man paused while DS Walters finished writing the details down.

'Next,' said Davies.

'275809 . . . Bannister baby, malformed foetus, aborted 23 August, 1998. Parents, Robert and Beatrice Bannister, 7/14, Fford Glyder, Felinheli. 275882 . . . Griffiths-Williams baby, malformed foetus, aborted 3 November, 1998. Parents, Trevor and Ann Griffiths-Williams, Moonstone Cottage, Beddgelert.'

'One final one,' said Tom. He handed over another number and the technician looked it up.

'275933 . . . Anne-Marie Palmer, born 14 December, 1998 to John and Lucy Palmer, Menai View, Aberton, Felinbach. Severe deformity to lower limbs, survived and went home after corrective surgery.'

'What now?' Davies asked Tom.

'Who did the lab work on these four cases?'

'All done by Dr Dawes,' replied Deans, without having to refer to the book again.

'Would you expect there to be siblings in cold storage for these reference numbers?'

'It's normal practice.'

'Would you check, please.'

Tom and the two policemen stood by while Deans came out of the office and into the main lab where he walked over to the storage freezers. He took down a pair of long gauntlets that hung from a hook on the wall and put them on before undoing the clasp on one of the freezers, releasing as he did so, a cloud of nitrogen vapour into the air. He reached in and brought out a stack of ice-encrusted racks, clearing the front of it with his gloved hand so that he could read the labels. He found the one he was looking for and traced the correct row and number with his gloved forefinger.

'Missing,' he said.

Tom and Davies exchanged a glance before Deans went on to check for vials corresponding to the other numbers. All were missing.

'No siblings for any of them,' said Deans.

Tom steered Davies to a corner of the lab. 'That's what Thomas discovered,' he said. 'He wrote *no siblings* on Anne-Marie Palmer's notes.'

'But that in itself doesn't prove anything,' said Davies. 'Does it?'

'No, but it put Thomas on the right track. Normally after IVF, more than one egg would be fertilised so they'd store the ones they weren't using for possible future use if the couple wanted more children. This wouldn't be the case in a cloning. That's what made him suspect that these four pregnancies were attempts at human cloning. And that's why he got the three foetuses back from Pathology. Only one resulted in a live birth — Anne-Marie Palmer. The DNA profile on her tissue will show that she wasn't really the Palmers' daughter.'

As they walked back over to join Deans, Tom remembered that he had been the technician who had accompanied the Professor to the Path. Department on the day that Megan Griffiths's body went missing. He asked him about it.

'There's not much to tell,' Deans shrugged. 'As I told your colleagues when they questioned me, Professor Thomas was a bit secretive about why he wanted the foetuses. I thought he and Dr Sepp were going to have a right old set-to about it when he made the request. I reckon Dr Sepp thought his competence was being questioned but he relented in the end, although I'm sure the argument continued when I left to bring them back up here.'

'You didn't come back with Professor Thomas?'

'No, it seemed like they were going to be at it all afternoon. Professor Thomas was already late for an important meeting when I left. I met Ran Dawes coming down to remind him.'

'Ran Dawes was on his way to Pathology?' asked Tom, surprise showing in his voice. 'There was no record of him being there.'

'Like I say, he was just going there to remind Professor Thomas that he was due at a meeting.'

'Did you know about this meeting, or was that something that Ran Dawes told you when you met him?' asked Tom.

'Something he told me.'

'Did Ran Dawes return to the unit with Professor Thomas?'

Deans thought for a moment before saying, 'No, he didn't, come to think of it. I remember seeing Professor Thomas come back a good bit later: I remember because he was in a bad mood, but Ran wasn't with him.'

'Maybe you could ask the secretaries about Thomas's meeting on that day. Get them to check the diary. Find out what time it was at and who it was with.'

'Okay.'

'I think we should go and talk to Dr Dawes at home,' said Davies heavily. He turned to Deans. 'Do you have an address for him, sir?'

'The office will. I'll get it.'

Deans returned a few minutes later, saying, 'Here you are. He stays over in Aberlyn: he rents a house there.' He handed the address to Davies.

The policeman looked thoughtful for a moment then he said, 'It might be an idea if you were to phone him first.'

'What d'you want me to say?'

'Ask him if he intends coming in today. Make up your own reasons for asking.'

'I'll call from the office,' said Deans.

Davies nodded to Walters who took this as a directive to accompany Deans.

'What d'you reckon?' Davies asked Tom when they were alone.

'Wouldn't surprise me if he's done a runner,' said Tom. 'If he heard the rumour about you treating Thomas's death as murder.'

'Maybe that's for the best,' said Davies thoughtfully.

Tom looked at him.

'If he runs, it's as good as an admission of guilt and it means he's scared. He'll be more inclined to come clean when we catch him — and we will. If he stays cool and brasses it out then we could be hard pushed to pin anything at all on him.'

'But if the DNA test on Anne-Marie proves she wasn't the Palmers' child?'

'He could simply plead a mix-up in the lab. He'd claim that Lucy Palmer was implanted with the wrong egg.'

Tom saw Davies's point. 'And you could hardly DNA test everybody in the country to find out just exactly who it was he cloned,' he added.

'Precisely.'

'God, you don't think he could still get away with it, do you?'

'A few suspicious reference numbers and a dodgy DNA fingerprint from a dead baby — what do you think?'

'Damn,' said Tom. 'Let's hope he talks.'

'Amen to that.'

Deans returned and said, 'No answer.'

'And the secretaries say that Professor Thomas didn't have a meeting at all on the afternoon in question,' added Walters. 'Dawes must have made it up.'

'Let's hope he's shitting himself in some service station motel on the M6,' grunted Davies. 'The more scared he is, the better.' Then Davies said they should be going and Deans made to show them out.

As they left the main lab, one of the female technicians they'd seen earlier was entering. Deans stopped her and said, 'Top up storage tank three with liquid nitrogen, will you, Karen? I had to open it: it's lost a bit.'

'Will do,' replied the girl.

Davies turned to Deans as they reached the front door and said, 'I'd rather you didn't spread any of this around.'

'Understood,' said Deans. 'What if Dr Dawes should turn up?'

'Let us know immed—'

Davies was interrupted by the sound of a muffled scream coming from the main lab. All three men turned to see the girl called Karen standing in the doorway. She was wearing long gloves and a plastic full-face visor. Her hands were by her sides and she seemed unsteady on her feet.

'Karen! What is it?' exclaimed Deans. 'What's the matter?'

The girl looked at him, her face white inside the mask. Suddenly her body heaved and she vomited over the inside of her visor. Deans rushed forward to offer her support while Davies and Tom Gordon hurried past into the main lab. At first they couldn't see anything amiss, but wisps of white vapour alerted Tom to the fact that the heavy door to the liquid nitrogen store was ajar. He pointed this out to Davies and they approached cautiously. Tom pulled the clasp and a cloud of vapour enveloped them like sea mist for a moment. When it cleared they could see the frozen body of a man lying there. Despite the crusting of ice on his face and in his hair, Tom could see that it was Ran Dawes. 'It's him.'

'Christ,' said Davies. 'Where does this leave us?'

Tom was lost for words.

— *Twenty-Five* —

'Oh, thank God!' exclaimed Mary when Tom phoned her. 'Does this mean they've let you go?'

'Well, I managed to convince them that I didn't murder Carwyn Thomas,' Tom told her.

'But he *was* murdered?'

'He was injected with amyl nitrate. Apparently he did have a slight heart condition, so the chemical over-stimulated it and provoked a genuine cardiac arrest. Pretty clever, huh? Damn nearly the perfect crime. The forensic people were really on the ball to pick up on it. The murderer must have used a bit too much nitrate.'

'Have they arrested Dawes?'

Tom paused. 'You're not going to believe this,' he said, his voice betraying the confusion he felt. 'Dawes is dead.'

'You're right — I don't believe it,' murmured Mary.

'We found his body in the liquid nitrogen store in the lab. We'll have to wait for the PM to establish the exact cause of death, but at the moment it looks like someone locked him in there and he froze to death.'

'God, this just goes from bad to worse.'

'Tell me about it,' sighed Tom. 'What's the time?'

'Just after three, a bit late for lunch. Have you eaten?'

Tom said not.

'Why don't we pick up some sandwiches and go for a

walk somewhere. You sound as if a bit of fresh air will do you good and we can talk.'

Tom drove over to Mary's place and they changed to her car. She had already bought sandwiches from a local baker while she'd been waiting. 'Let's go to Bodnant,' she said. 'Do you know it?'

He shook his head.

'It's my favourite garden in the world,' said Mary. 'I go there when I have things to think about. It's in the Conwy Valley, just about eight miles south of Llandudno and it's just reopened after the winter break. This will be my first trip this year. Maybe the rhododendrons will be out.'

It turned out to be a bit early for the rhododendrons, but Tom had to admit that the garden was something special. The fact that Mary was beside him made it even more so, and he could not fail to sense the magic he'd been promised. He turned and smiled at her without saying anything, and she nodded in reply, knowing that they both felt the same.

The lack of visitors this early in the season only added to the pleasure of being able to wander along quiet paths without hindrance. It seemed the most natural thing in the world for them to have their arms around each other. They had been walking and talking for about twenty minutes, although time seemed to have stood still, when they came to a striking stone building. Tom walked over to it, feeling strangely drawn. He touched the stone lightly with his fingertips and turned to ask Mary what it was.

'It's called *The Poem*,' she answered quietly. 'It's a mausoleum.'

Tom shrugged. 'I can't escape death, even here.' He rejoined Mary and they continued walking. 'I thought I had it all worked out,' he said. 'The truth is, I was wrong about almost everything.'

'Does that include John Palmer's innocence?' asked Mary, with a sideways glance.

'No, he's innocent all right and I still believe Anne-Marie's death was connected with what was going on in the IVF clinic, but as for everything else . . .'

'You're being too hard on yourself,' she said, rubbing the back of his hand.

Tom shook his head. 'I was so sure that Thomas was guilty because of what I saw in his lab, but we both know I read it all wrong. The man was completely innocent all along. That was unforgivable.'

'You're not a professional detective,' said Mary, 'but your heart's in the right place. You were doing what you thought was right. If nothing else, you've goaded the police into getting off their backsides at last. Even they must recognise now after two murders that things in the IVF unit are not all above board. Try to look on the positive side.'

Tom gave Mary's shoulders a grateful squeeze as they continued walking.

'What's bugging you most right now?' she asked.

'Dawes's death,' replied Tom. 'I thought I'd definitely got it right this time. Dawes was the guilty man — and then we find him dead, just like Thomas.'

'But that doesn't mean to say he was innocent like Thomas,' said Mary.

'True,' conceded Tom.

'Everything you said about Dawes still fits, doesn't it?'

'I suppose.'

'If he was murdered too, it just means there's another level to this affair. Dawes wasn't the prime mover after all: there must be someone else involved. Dawes must have panicked when he heard that the police were treating Thomas's death as murder so he had to be silenced. It might help if we go through it step by step.'

Tom smiled at Mary's determination to introduce order and logic to a situation he had been seeing as chaotic. There was a pause in the conversation while they crossed a small wooden bridge over a tumbling waterfall. When the noise of the water had died away Mary continued, 'Dawes makes several attempts at human cloning at the IVF clinic. They all fail apart from one – that was Anne-Marie Palmer – but she wasn't a complete success; she was born deformed. Somewhere along the line, Professor Thomas begins to suspect what's going on and carries out his own investigation. He gets killed for his trouble. By Dawes, d'you think?'

'Probably, but we can't rule out the person who killed Dawes himself.'

'Is there anything to connect Dawes to Megan Griffiths?' asked Mary.

'There is,' said Tom. 'Dawes was seen going down to Pathology by the chief technician in the IVF unit, on the day in question. He made something up about going there to warn Thomas about being late for a meeting, but it turns out that there was no such meeting. Dawes also fits Maurice Cleef's description of the man he'd spoken to about Megan's body.'

'So it seems to me that Dawes was up to his neck in everything that was going on,' said Mary. 'What we don't know is who he was trying to clone or why.'

'And where Megan Griffiths fits into all this.'

'Still no thoughts?'

Tom shook his head.

'A cloned baby and a normal baby. Could somebody have wanted to compare something about them?' asked Mary.

Tom shrugged. 'I just don't know.'

They had completed a circle of the garden and were sitting on a bench seat in the upper rose terrace, looking out to the hills of Snowdonia. Mary snuggled up close to Tom as a cold wind sprang up and let them know that winter hadn't quite finished yet. 'I wish the spring would come properly,' she said. 'I hate this time when we're between seasons. One day it's spring then it's back to winter with a frost, then it's back to spring again. You never know where you are.'

'Know the feeling,' said Tom.

'Let's go and get some coffee.'

At Mary's suggestion, they drove on down to Betws-y-Coed where they had coffee and scones in the conservatory of the George Hotel while rain pattered gently down on the roof. It didn't seem to matter: they were oblivious to it. They were just happy in each other's company.

'Can I ask what you're going to do now?' said Mary.

'I'm going to wait for the DNA result on Anne-Marie so at least there will be one solid piece of evidence. Chief Inspector Davies said he'd let me know about the PM on Ran Dawes so we'll take it from there.'

'So you two are on speaking terms then?'

'At the moment.'

'You know, logic tells me that the unknown third person was actually running the show,' said Mary slowly.

'How so?'

'I suspect, from what's happened and what you've told me, that Dawes was just someone hired to carry out the cloning.'

'Hired?' exclaimed Tom, sounding surprised.

'You said yourself that he was in the ideal position to do that sort of work and he did have the expertise. I think someone paid him – probably a great deal of money – to carry out a designer cloning, if you like.'

'You know, that's a good thought,' said Tom. 'Maybe I'll

ask Davies to check Dawes's bank account to see if there were any large payments made into it.'

'It's getting dark; we should be going.'

They left the hotel and opted to take the mountain road through the Llanberis Pass back to Bangor, thereby completing a big circle. Mary accepted Tom's offer to drive, admitting that she really didn't like driving on narrow mountain roads at night.

'Let's just take our time,' said Tom. 'Unless you have to be back for anything?'

'Nothing,' said Mary. 'You don't really have a social life when you work in A&E.' She slipped a cassette into the player on the dash and Mozart drifted out from the speakers. 'All right?' asked Mary.

'Just perfect.'

Mary fell asleep after five miles and her head came to rest on Tom's shoulder for the remainder of the drive home. She woke with a start as they drew up in the car park outside her home. 'Oh, I'm so sorry,' she mumbled, taking a moment to get her bearings. 'I must have been more tired than I thought.'

'Don't apologise,' said Tom, taking her hand in his. 'I've enjoyed this afternoon more than anything I can remember in a very long time.'

'Me too,' she agreed. 'You must come and see Bodnant with me when the spring is really here.'

'I'd like nothing better,' said Tom. 'Are you back on duty tomorrow night?'

''Fraid so, but you will let me know if you hear anything?'

'Of course.' Tom leaned over and kissed her gently. Mary smiled when he pulled back. 'Was that a goodnight kiss?' she asked softly.

'Only if you want it to be,' he replied.

'Maybe . . . you'd like to come up for coffee?'

'Very much.'

The fact that his flat was cold for the usual reason did not detract from Tom Gordon's feelings of euphoria one iota when he got home just after nine-thirty in the morning. He hummed Mozart as he fiddled with the timer and gave the pump its customary kick. He turned on the electric fire and the kettle before checking the answer machine – there were no messages. He might have lost his job and made a fool of himself over Thomas's involvement, but not *everything* in his world was going badly.

Davies phoned at 11 a.m. to say that Dawes had undoubtedly been murdered. He'd been hit on the back of the head before being locked in the liquid nitrogen store. Tom said that he appreciated being told, but sensed that Davies wanted to say more.

The policeman cleared his throat a couple of times before beginning: 'I know we got off on the wrong foot, but frankly I'd appreciate your input in this case, Doctor. It's not exactly your run-of-the-mill murder.'

Tom was also in the mood for reconciliation. He said, 'I know I've been making a bit of a nuisance of myself to the police in the last few weeks. I apologise for that. I'll be happy to help in any way I can.'

'Good. Now we've been trying to establish who was the last person to see Ranulph Dawes alive. Apparently, Dawes was still in the IVF unit at eight o'clock last night. One of the secretaries was there – she was using her word processor to type up her son's degree thesis. Dawes told her he was hoping to see the hospital's Medical Superintendent to discuss what implications Thomas's death might have for the unit. He was still trying to track him down when the secretary left. We haven't yet managed to ask Dr Trool if he made contact.'

'I'm just waiting for the DNA result on Anne-Marie,' said Tom. 'It'll probably be another day at least. I'll call you when I have it.'

When he'd put down the phone, Tom decided to walk up to the village and get a few things from the local shops. It had been a while since he'd run the gauntlet and he wondered if anything had changed. He was aware of groups of women whispering behind his back in Main Street but no one he came across was overtly rude. He said good morning to a few of them and got a civil reply. That, he decided, was probably as good as it got. He bought a morning paper at the newsagent and some bread rolls from the bakers before walking back along the street to the steps leading down to the harbour. He'd almost reached them when a double-decker bus pulled up at the stop next to them and Ida Marsh, the woman he'd treated for fume inhalation, got off. She seemed a bit anxious and upset.

'Good morning, Mrs Marsh. He's not been stripping furniture again, I hope?' said Tom politely.

'Oh, good morning, Doctor, I didn't see you there. No, it's worse than that. God bless 'im, the poor man's dead. He was found dead at his work, apparently.'

'How awful,' said Tom. 'What happened?'

'The police aren't saying. It was his neighbour who told me. Poor Mr Dawis, such a gentleman, he was.'

'Dawis,' repeated Tom, bells ringing in his head. The woman had pronounced the name da-wis, but the fact that he had died at work and the police were involved suggested suddenly that the name was, in fact, Dawes.

'Did your Mr Dawis work in Caernarfon, Mrs Marsh?'

'Yes,' replied the woman. 'Why?'

'At the hospital?'

'I don't rightly know what he did,' Ida Marsh told him. 'I don't think he ever said. We never spoke much — he was always out when I arrived, see. He just used to leave the money for me on the hall table. I think the last time I saw him was when I had to complain about the fumes. Remember?'

'I do indeed,' said Tom. He was thinking that he couldn't see Ranulph Dawes as the furniture-stripping type and the bells inside his head were still ringing. 'You must have your own key for the place,' he said.

'Yes, agreed the woman cautiously.

'Could I have it?'

Ida Marsh's eyes opened wide. 'I don't rightly know about that.'

'I'll see that the police get it, I promise,' said Tom. 'They'll know what to do with it.'

'Well, that would save me having to do it, I suppose. I don't mind telling you, the news gave me quite a turn.'

'You could do with a cup of tea,' said Tom solicitously. 'I'll walk you over to your house.'

Brushing aside Mrs Marsh's protestations, which were weak enough to suggest that she was secretly pleased at the offer, Tom accompanied her the few streets to her home where her husband came out to see what the matter was. 'She's had a bit of a shock,' Tom explained. 'I think strong sweet tea is called for.'

Then, feeling that he'd done his good deed for the day, Tom walked back to Main Street, the fingers of his right hand playing with the keys to Dawes's house in his jacket pocket. Just what was it that Dawes had been doing that involved fuming chemicals? he wondered. Apart from that, he had been living in furnished, rented accommodation. The furniture wasn't his to play around with, even if he had been into DIY. The intriguing question was, could he have been carrying out some kind of experimental work at home? Something to do with the cloning business, something that he couldn't do openly at the IVF unit?

Tom supposed that the police would get round to looking the place over but, at the moment, they were more interested in making enquiries about Dawes's movements. He toyed with the idea of taking a look for himself as he descended the harbour steps. He knew that it was something that he shouldn't even be contemplating – Davies would probably go ballistic – but the temptation was just too great. He started up the Land Rover and set out for Aberlyn.

It was only four miles from Felinbach to Aberlyn, but Tom had seldom had occasion to visit it. It was a small village, much like Feli itself, sitting on the shores of the Menai, looking out towards Anglesey, but access to it was by a single-lane road that led down from the main road. You didn't drive through Aberlyn on the way to anywhere else.

Tom was unlucky enough to meet a tractor coming towards him about a mile from the edge of the village. He had to back up nearly 300 metres before he found a suitable cutting to move into. The tractor driver drove by without any gesture of thanks. 'Sod you, too,' murmured Tom.

He made it into the village without meeting any other vehicles and parked the Land Rover well away from the houses on a patch of shingle leading down to the shore. In North Wales Land Rovers are so common that they are practically invisible. They are the standard form of transport for the sheepfarming community and also much in evidence for mountain training and rescue organisations, not to mention the Coastguard Service and the Electricity Board. Tom Gordon's car would not attract any undue attention.

The tag on the keyring said *13, Beach Road*. It suggested

to Tom a cottage in one of the narrow streets fronting the water but, as it turned out, Beach Road stretched a good bit inland and the houses on the outlying part of it were really quite large. Number 13 turned out to be a sandstone, Victorian family house. It had clearly seen better times; its gardens were unkempt and its roof looked as if it could have done with some attention but all the same, Tom was impressed by it. It had character.

At first, he walked past the house, wondering if he was being observed from the neighbouring house — pedestrians would not be too common on this road. Noting that there was a side door to the garden of number 13 — on the blind side of the neighbouring house — he decided to try for entry there. One of the three keys on the ring must fit the back door, which again, would be sheltered from view.

He was lucky: the side door to the garden opened after a turn of the iron ring handle and a hefty push with his shoulder to clear beech leaves and other debris piled up behind it. He stood for a few moments after closing the door in the wall behind him and took in the broody silence of the place. He wasn't sure if the unpleasant atmosphere he sensed was associated with knowing that Dawes had lived here, or was down to the house in its own right, but he certainly didn't like it. He walked round the back and found that the long key on the ring fitted the kitchen door. It opened with a slight shudder due to an imperfect fit in the frame and Tom stepped inside to a smell of dampness and old carpets.

He saw immediately that Mrs Marsh had not stayed to carry out her cleaning duties today. Breakfast dishes from the previous day still lay in the sink and a packet of cereal stood on the draining board, the back of which advertised subsidised air fares to Paris through the collection of tokens on packet lids. 'Guess not, Ran,' Tom muttered, as he started a tour of the ground floor rooms, not entirely sure what he was looking for but alert to everything.

— Twenty-Six —

It was clear that Dawes had only made use of three rooms on the ground floor — the kitchen, a large bay-windowed room he'd used as a sitting room, evidenced by a portable television and various books and magazines left lying around, and a small study. There were three other rooms on this level, including a dining room, but the lack of any personal objects in them suggested that Dawes hadn't used them. In fact, a general absence of personal possessions made Tom wonder why Dawes had needed or wanted such a large house in the first place. It must have been like living in a Victorian museum. It even had a stuffed owl in a glass case sitting on top of an old upright piano.

One thing he realised as he neared the end of his tour was that he had seen no evidence of any recently stripped or revarnished furniture in any of the rooms, but then he hadn't expected to. Such an activity would have been out of character for the man, especially as he had so little in the way of worldly goods.

Tom returned to the study and sat down behind the desk. The desk itself was an old oak twin-pedestal model with an apple tree carved on the front panel and with two deep, brass-handled drawers on either side of the kneehole. He pulled each out in turn, reluctant to touch anything unnecessarily, just as he had been with Thomas's personal things at the hospital, but this time he reminded himself that it really didn't matter. Dawes was dead.

Noticing a letter bearing a Barclays Bank logo, he recalled what Mary had said about Dawes being a hired hand rather than the prime mover in the cloning affair. He pulled it out: it was a bank statement for February in the name of Ranulph Joseph Dawes and gave details of a cheque account with a current balance of £740.16. Tom glanced down the list of entries for the past month and saw nothing untoward. The largest figure paid in over the period had been £1511.34 – presumably Dawes's last salary cheque – and the largest single outgoing had been £500, paid by standing order to the woman in Felinbach from whom he was renting the house. It was quite a lot for one person to pay, but a reasonable rent for such a big place, he thought.

Tom returned the statement to the drawer but, again bearing in mind what Mary had suggested, he started looking for anything else connected with Dawes's financial affairs. He found a current Visa bill and scanned through the entries. Nothing exciting, he concluded; petrol, off-license, petrol, Interflora, petrol, a shop in Llandudno. The total came to £137.27. He was about to put the bill back in the drawer when the figures at the top of the page caught his attention. The previous balance had been £2725.14, but a credit payment for that amount had been received on the seventeenth of the month. Dawes had paid off the entire sum owing on his credit card last month. That was more interesting, he thought, and continued his search with renewed vigour. Dawes had clearly not paid the bill from funds in his cheque account – at least not the one he'd found details of, so maybe he had another account? Maybe he had several?

Tom carried out an exhaustive search of all the drawers

but found nothing else to do with money save for an electricity bill and a plastic wallet containing mobile phone bills. Thinking back to the hiding place where he'd found the key to Thomas's lab, Tom took a look underneath the desktop but found he wasn't going to be that lucky twice. But Dawes *had* lived here alone and was out at work all day; it was certainly conceivable that he might have felt the need to hide away secret or valuable items. It was just a question of where.

Tom had seen no signs of a safe on his tour but it was possible that the safe itself might be hidden, not that finding one would do him much good if he didn't have access to the key or combination. He could look behind the pictures on the walls, like they did in films, but first he thought he'd try some of the more obvious and mundane hiding places — under things, on top of things, behind things.

The house had central heating and was equipped with old-fashioned iron radiators and large-bore piping. Tom looked behind the two radiators in the study, thinking that this might be a possible place to hide something, but found nothing. However, he did notice that a piece of rag had been stuffed into what seemed to be a hole in the floor near the valve of the radiator below the window.

He felt a twinge of excitement as he bent down to pull out the rag. The hole was large enough to get his hand into so he reached down inside, spreading his fingers out to make contact with anything that might be lying there. He was disappointed when it really seemed to be just a hole, not a secret hiding place after all.

Withdrawing his hand, he crouched down close to the floor to see if he could see into the hole by finding the right angle for the light. He was almost directly on top of it when he suddenly had to recoil as he breathed in a lungful of fumes that made him feel as if his chest was on fire. He rolled away, coughing and spluttering, his eyes watering as he stumbled his way to the back door and staggered outside to gulp in fresh air.

When he'd finished cursing and had calmed down sufficiently to think clearly again, he realised that he must have come across the fumes that had made Mrs Marsh so ill. He recognised the smell, not least because he'd come across it in the recent past. It had been present in the PM room at Ysbyty Gwynedd when he'd been watching French perform the PM examination on Anne-Marie Palmer. The smell was hydrochloric acid.

Tom went back into the house and returned to Dawes's study. He replaced the rag in the hole in the floor, keeping his face well away from it and then opened a window to help disperse the lingering smell – or at least replace it with that of moss and wet earth from the garden. He slumped back down in the desk chair for a few moments, thinking about what he had to do now.

He was quite sure about the smell. It was the acid that had been used on Anne-Marie's body and it was coming from a cellar below. In the course of her cleaning, Ida Marsh must have removed the rag from the hole in the floor and breathed in the fumes just as he had done. He would have to go down there and investigate.

The door to the cellar, as Tom found after a brief search, was located in a small pantry leading off the kitchen and it was no great surprise to find it locked. Nor was it any great surprise to find that the key was nowhere to be seen. There was a hook in the wall by the door, but no key. The door itself did not seem all that substantial and moved quite a bit in the frame when Tom pushed and pulled the handle, so he reckoned that he had three choices. He could search for the key; he could stop now and suggest to the police that it might be a good idea to take a look at the house, or he could simply put his shoulder to the door. Choice number three won by a clear margin. The door parted company with its lock at the third attempt and swung back to judder off the stone cellar wall.

Tom found an old-fashioned, brass light switch on the wall and clicked it on before pausing at the head of the stairs for a moment. He could smell acid in the air but it was nowhere near as strong as it had been by the hole in the floor. He went down slowly, giving his eyes time to get accustomed to the gloom, as there was only one light bulb to illuminate a pretty big cellar. Although it was unshaded, he doubted if it were more than forty watts.

The smell of dampness, evident upstairs, was much stronger down here and was mixed with the smell of old wood from the stairs and of course, acid fumes. He took out some paper tissues from his pocket and held them over his nose as a precaution as he made his way over to the area he reckoned would be directly below the radiator upstairs. It was dark there because it was a good way away from the light bulb, but when he got closer, Tom could see that there was a workbench there with two modern Anglepoise lamps sitting on it. He clicked them on to illuminate the rough bench like an island in the darkness.

At the side of the bench was a heavy porcelain sink mounted on a frame constructed of thick wooden stilts. It had a loose polystyrene cover on it but it was quite clear to Tom that this was what held the acid. He took the tissues away from his face for a moment, gingerly testing the air at this location and found to his surprise that the fumes still weren't as strong as he'd anticipated. The lid, albeit light, seemed to contain them quite well. This posed the question of why they had been so strong upstairs.

Tom was pondering this when the question answered itself, thanks to a gust of wind outside. There was a wall ventilator mounted in the stonework below the acid bath — a simple iron grid leading to the outside. Every so often the wind would gust through it, sending an up-draught that caught the polystyrene lid and raised it a little. Fumes would escape and be wafted directly upwards to where the hole in the floor was located. It was a very localised concentration of the fumes. Both he and Ida Marsh had just been unlucky to be near the hole when the wind had blown.

There was no evidence of any furniture-stripping activity in the cellar although Tom could see that there were some tools hanging up above the bench. Had he misjudged Dawes after all? he wondered. Many professional men did find relaxation in carpentry. He redirected the light from one of the Anglepoise lamps upwards to the rack, but his blood ran cold as he saw that they were not woodworkers' tools at all but pathology instruments comprising several knives and a bone saw. He noted with added horror that the saw bore evidence of tissue trapped in its teeth.

His mind rebelled against the images this invoked, but it looked to him as if this was the place where the attempt had been made to dissolve Anne-Marie Palmer's body in acid. Ranulph Dawes had been the guilty party. 'Oh Christ,' he muttered, as the horror of such a scene fired his imagination. He pressed the tissues to his mouth, this time more in an effort to head off the urge to vomit than shut out the fumes, as he continued to take in everything around him. Next to the acid bath a heavy apron hung on the wall, the one Dawes must have worn while he was doing the job, thought Tom. 'Bastard!'

He backed away from the area and sat down on the cellar steps for a moment, glancing upwards for the reassurance of daylight at the head of the stairs where he'd left the door open — maybe a subconscious admission of unease. There was a conflict going on inside his head. On the one hand, he was recoiling in horror at the images this place conjured up, on the other, his brain was telling him that there was something wrong with what he concluding.

He tried to home in on what it was until finally, he thought he could see it. Dawes was a professional scientist, not some bumbling criminal playing around with acids without knowing anything about their properties. If Dawes had really wanted to destroy Anne-Marie's body by dissolving it in acid, he could have and *would* have done just that: he would not have failed and been forced to resort to something else. If it came to that, he would not have used hydrochloric acid in the first place; there were many more efficient acids available for the purpose . . . and what were the surgical instruments all about? No attempt had been made to cut Anne-Marie's body into pieces.

There were just too many unanswered questions floating about for Tom's liking. The pieces seemed to fit but the final picture was flawed. Something was terribly wrong with his reading of the situation. He went back over to the bench and stood there, looking first at the instruments and then at the acid bath. Once again, he held the paper tissues over his nose and mouth as he slid back the lid, feeling apprehensive as he looked down into the gently fuming liquid. He blinked quickly to keep his eyes moist, knowing that he should be wearing goggles or a face visor but not having access to either.

He was relieved to see that the acid seemed clear enough and wondered if it had been changed after or during the 'failed' attempt. He was about to replace the lid when something lying in the foot of the bath caught his eye; it looked like a short white stick but instinctively, he knew it must be a bone. At first he thought that it must have been missed, but then he had to wonder what bone it could possibly be. Anne-Marie's body had suffered tissue damage from the acid but no skeletal destruction.

Tom looked to both sides of the bath and underneath, and finally found what he was looking for, lying on the frame cross members – a pair of long-handled tongs. His proximity to the uncovered bath was exposing him to too much in the way of fumes from the acid. He backed off for a few moments to take in some deep breaths before returning to his task.

Holding the tissues to his face with one hand while fishing with the tongs held in the other proved successful, but only after half a dozen frustrating attempts with watering eyes and lungs bursting through holding his breath as long as possible. He finally extracted the bone to bring it over to a conventional sink, mounted on the wall to his right, to rinse away the acid and take it in his hand. He decided that he would examine it upstairs in daylight, maybe even outside in the garden: he felt the desperate need for fresh air and for more than one reason.

As he stood outside the kitchen door, running his fingers lightly along the smooth white bone, he found no difficulty at all in identifying it, but this in itself posed a new problem – and one that utterly confused him. What he was holding in his hands was a leg bone – the tibia of a small child. The trouble was, it was a bone that Anne-Marie Palmer *did not have*; it could not possibly have come from her.

Tom started to walk round the garden, his head bowed as he tried to think through this latest twist. He had the distinct feeling that he was playing three-dimensional chess with God but yet . . . he felt excited, not dejected. He knew he was getting closer to the truth. He had the right pieces: they were just being played in the wrong order. If the child in the acid bath had had leg bones, then the child was not Anne-Marie Palmer . . . Oh, sweet Jesus Christ! It was Megan Griffiths!

It suddenly became clear to him what had happened. It had been Megan in the bath, not Anne-Marie. Megan's dead body had been altered to make it look as if she was Anne-Marie Palmer! Her legs had been removed with the saw on the wall and then tissue damage inflicted, particularly on her lower extremities with acid in order to disguise the recent surgery. The whole exercise had been undertaken to create a corpse that would be accepted as that of Anne-Marie Palmer.

Why? Because 'finding' Anne-Marie's body would stop people looking for her! He'd already considered the difficulties involved in stealing a cloned child from doting 'parents'. Kidnapping had appeared to be a major stumbling block and one that he had not managed to see a way around. Dawes, or whoever he'd been in league with, had come up with a solution. Anne-Marie Palmer *had* been abducted, but in order to stop a police hunt for the kidnapped child, the body of an already dead child had been made to look like her and was then buried in the Palmers' garden. The police, seeing no conceivable motive for the kidnap of a handicapped child, had followed their instincts, as the kidnappers must have reckoned they would, and this had led them to suspect the parents. They had found what they expected to find when they dug up the Palmers' garden — a small legless corpse. Case closed. The child's father even confessed to the crime. What a bonus that must have been, thought Tom. Either way, it meant the police hunt for Anne-Marie was off. The cloners had got clean away with their child.

In the same way that pain can be described as 'exquisite', Tom found an almost mesmerising beauty about the whole horrific scheme. Whoever had dreamed up the scam was both brilliant and evil in equal measure. As everything started to fit, he wondered if thought had even been given to the type of acid used on the child's body. Had they deliberately chosen hydrochloric over a more appropriate one because they knew that John Palmer would have had access to hydrochloric in his school science lab, and the police would latch on to that fact?

Tom returned to the cellar for a last look around. The tissue from the teeth of the saw would be subjected to forensic study, and there was no doubt in his mind as to what the outcome would be. The tissue would match that of the body found in the Palmers' garden but neither would match the DNA profile of the Palmers — not because she wasn't their biological child, but because she wasn't even Anne-Marie!

Carwyn Thomas must have worked this out for himself when Fairbrother had given him his DNA fingerprinting results. The fact that he'd blurted out Megan Griffiths's name at the time suggested that he'd made the connection and realised the motive for the theft of the cot-death baby's body.

Tom sat down again behind Dawes's desk to figure out where all this was leading him. There were two very important questions he still had to answer. Who had been cloned to produce Anne-Marie Palmer? And perhaps, most important of all, why? He was wrestling with this when he suddenly realised with a jolt that there was more to all this than an intellectual puzzle. There was something that had to be considered urgently. *Anne-Marie Palmer could still be alive!*

~ Twenty-Seven ~

Tom had the feeling that he was trapped in the plot
of an Ancient Greek play, with events becoming so
bizarre that they demanded the appearance of a *deus ex
machina* to sort everything out. He regretted the fact that
he couldn't finally feel good about having paved the way
for John Palmer's release against what had been tremendous
odds by any standards; the things that were coming to
light were eclipsing any such feelings of joy with dark
foreboding.

He had not been looking forward to telling Lucy and
John that Anne-Marie had not actually been their daughter
in strictly biological terms, although they had obviously
loved her as if she had been. Now he was faced with the
possibility that Anne-Marie might not even be dead . . . but
there again, she still might be. It all depended on why she
had been cloned in the first place. He was reminded again
of the words of the American scientist at the symposium.
A successful cloning, *done for whatever reason*, will result
in a baby being born. If Anne-Marie had been cloned to
provide spare parts, then she might well already be dead.
How would anyone who had loved her cope with that
kind of revelation? he wondered. For Lucy it might prove
the final straw — a nightmare from which she might never
recover.

The motives behind the cloning seemed to depend entirely on finding out who had commissioned it in the first place. His best chance of doing that still seemed to rest with the investigation of Dawes's finances. If he had been paid to do it, the money had to be somewhere — recorded on paper or hidden in cash. Tom decided to have one more thorough search of every room in the house before he called the police.

Apart from the bathroom, Dawes had only used one room upstairs — a large bedroom with pale green walls and a window that looked out on to the Menai. The bed, an old-fashioned double with a walnut headboard, remained unmade and the grey light coming in through the window did nothing to make the room seem attractive. Tom looked through all the drawers in the room and in both wardrobes as outside, the skies seemed to grow darker by the minute. The bedside cabinet was the only thing to reveal contents other than clothes. It contained bedtime reading material, a number of catalogues and magazines, mainly to do with cars but there were several holiday brochures too. Tom was about to dismiss them as irrelevant when he had second thoughts and flicked through them. His interest was rewarded when he saw that certain pages had been marked with Biro. From what he could deduce, Dawes had had an interest in the new Jaguar S-type and also in holidays in the Caribbean — not tastes easily satisfied by a National Health Service salary. Unfortunately, there did not seem to be any information about how he intended to pay for them.

There was an interesting bookmark in one of the holiday brochures — a leaflet advertising a private medical clinic in Paris. Tom wondered if Dawes had been offered a job there. He slipped the leaflet into his pocket just in case.

Finally he took a look at the bathroom — the only room

he hadn't yet searched. The dark skies outside had decided to break open, and rain battered against the large frosted window above the bath as he checked the cabinet over the mirror and then the cupboard under the basin, both without success. Lifting its lid, he peered into the old dirty linen basket. Empty. The bath itself was a Victorian iron monster with peeling paint on the outside and feet fashioned as seashells. There was no panelling round it so Tom knelt down and felt round underneath it as far as he could reach; he found only more peeling paint and cobwebs.

When he stood up, he pulled the lavatory chain, for no other reason than the fact that you didn't often see a high cistern these days and they sounded different from modern ones. Thinking about cisterns caused him to recall that he'd seen them used in films as classic hiding places, guns and drugs usually. He looked up at the one with *Gates Pat. Pending* etched into its iron front and thought that he had nothing to lose by taking a look.

Dragging the heavy linen basket over, he climbed up on it. He still wasn't high enough to be able to look into the cistern, but he could reach in and feel around the inside with his fingers. The inner wall felt cold, wet and rough, like the surface of a rock on the seashore just after high tide has receded. The ball cock made a grinding noise when he moved the operating lever but, apart from that, everything seemed normal.

Halfway along the back wall of the cistern, however, his fingers came into contact with a plastic bag. He gave it a strong tug and brought out what looked to be a plastic-covered passbook wrapped inside a freezer storage bag. Fate for once had been kind.

Tom stood down and paused to dry his hands before opening the bag. Inside was a Nationwide Building Society passbook, the record of an account in Dawes's name, and it currently contained £197,000 exactly. There were only three entries in it – a deposit of £50,000 made on a date in December last, and another of £150,000 made some four weeks ago. One withdrawal was listed: the sum of £3000 had been taken out a week after the last deposit. Tom guessed at the Visa bill payment. He could also guess that the first payment had been made on the birth of Anne-Marie and the second when she had been abducted. It was definitely time to inform the police. They would have ways of finding out where the deposited money had come from.

As Tom came downstairs he was feeling pleased with himself, but the feeling did not last long, for, as he reached the last three steps, he found himself staring into the twin barrels of a shotgun.

A thin, sullen-faced man with a stoop, who looked as if he hadn't smiled much in the last thirty years, held the gun. He was wearing a dark, waxed-cotton jacket and had a gamekeeper's satchel slung over his shoulder. A collie dog sat at his feet, anxious to be doing something but restrained by training and discipline.

Tom smiled, hoping to convey the impression that he was no threat, and put his hands up slowly, eager to defuse the situation before accident or misunderstanding led to his chest being opened up like a volcanic crater. 'I didn't hear you come in,' he ventured.

The man gestured that he move away from the foot of the stairs and back into the kitchen. Tom complied, saying, 'I don't think we've met before. I'm Dr Tom Gordon from Felinbach.'

'My arse you are,' growled the man. 'Thievin' bastard.'

'Really I am,' insisted Tom.

'So how's the patient?' sneered the man.

'Dr Dawes is dead,' Tom replied, thinking it sounded stupid in the circumstances.

'Bloody right he is, and he didn't die here! Poor bugger's not even cold in his grave before bastards like you start sniffin' round like bloody hyenas.'

'Look, I really am a doctor. I'm not here to rob anyone,' said Tom. He was beginning to get fed up.

'What's that in your hand then?' the man demanded. 'Your prescription pad? Give it here!'

Tom handed over the passbook and the man snatched it quickly from him with his left hand while still keeping the gun trained on him in his right. He swore when he read out the cover. 'Nationwide Building Society. Didn't come here to rob, did you – on no!' He put the passbook down on the table and returned to holding the gun in both hands.

Tom could see that the man was becoming dangerously angry. 'Look,' he said, 'why don't you call the police and we can sort the whole thing out. I was just about to do that myself.'

'Police? Judges? Courts? Bunch of tossers. It's about time we returned to making our own justice round here. Leave it to that lot and the likes of you'll end up getting off with a poxy fine, couple of weeks' community service and not so much as a kick up the arse.'

'Just call the police, will you?' said Tom, becoming increasingly anxious.

The man moved a little closer and leered at him. 'You'd like that, wouldn't you? The whole system's designed for criminals these days, and bugger the victims. Well, boyo, you fucked up this time!' With that, the man swung the stock of his gun round to stab it with both hands into Tom's face, knocking him clean out.

When Tom opened his eyes, the first thing he saw was

Mary's face and she seemed angry. 'I do not believe it, Tom,' she ground out. '*You* make Inspector Clouseau seem like the consummate professional! What is it about you that makes you do these things?'

He struggled to find a reply but his jaw hurt, and before he could get anything out, a voice on the other side of the bed that he recognised with a sinking feeling as belonging to Chief Inspector Davies boomed, 'Frankly, I've given up on you, Gordon. I've decided that there must be a limit to how much your head can take in the way of punishment, so I'm going to let you reach that limit and maybe that'll convince you not to play the Lone bloody Ranger all the time.'

Tom closed his eyes again, wishing he were somewhere else.

Mary continued, 'We're thinking of keeping a special bed just for you because you're here so often. What on earth possessed you to break into Dawes's house?'

'All right, all right, give me a chance, will you?' said Tom, holding up his hands in self-defence. He insisted that he hadn't broken in; he'd been given a key and had just gone to take a look around when some madman had attacked him.

'Clem Morgan,' interrupted Davies. 'Slightly to the right of Saddam Hussain is old Clem. His sister's place was done over by yobs two or three months ago. Duffed her up bad, they did. Clem didn't take it too well. I think he sees himself as Charles Bronson in that film *Death Wish*? He says you attacked him and he had to hit you in self-defence. Is that right?'

'What d'you think?' said Tom sourly.

'Do you want to press charges?'

Tom shook his head. 'First things first,' he said wearily. 'I found out so much in that house today. Did you get the passbook?'

'Clem presented it as evidence of your intention to rob. He was quite disappointed to find out you really were a doctor. Surprises me too, sometimes.'

'And me,' agreed Mary.

'You've *got* to find out where that money came from,' Tom fretted. 'It's the key to the whole thing. Listen to me! There's a chance that Anne-Marie Palmer might still be alive.'

Davies and Mary gave each other a look that suggested that Tom might really have gone too far this time, and they should be perhaps sectioning him under the auspices of the Mental Health Act.

'I'm serious. Just listen, will you?' Tom told them both what he'd discovered at the house in Aberlyn and finally felt he was getting somewhere in the credibility stakes when he saw the look of horror on both their faces as he described the cellar and what had gone on there. 'So you see, it wasn't Anne-Marie Palmer that you found in the garden, it was Megan Griffiths made to look like Anne-Marie.'

'My God, that's sick,' Mary muttered.

'But it worked,' Tom said. 'They took Anne-Marie and nobody bothered to look for her. The perfect kidnap.'

'So the big question is, what did they intend doing with her?' said Davies.

Tom nodded and went through the possibilities.

'Well, what d'you reckon?' asked Davies.

'I think they wanted some or all of her organs,' confessed Tom. 'If they'd wanted a cloned child, the fact that Anne-Marie was so badly disabled might have persuaded them to try the cloning again rather than kidnap her. I hope I'm wrong but . . .'

'Makes sense,' conceded Davies quietly.

'I agree,' said Mary, sounding very subdued. 'But how could they do such a thing?'

'Maybe they *haven't* yet,' Tom stated. 'Maybe Anne-Marie is still alive.'

'Do you really think there's a chance?' asked Mary.

'It's a slim one, considering the amount of time that's elapsed,' Tom said thoughtfully, 'but while we don't know for sure, we've got to try and find her — and the key to doing that lies in that damned passbook!'

The Chief Inspector was galvanised into action. 'Right,' he said, 'I'll get on to the Nationwide straight away — see what they can tell us. Mind you, if Dawes walked into their office with cash in a brown paper bag, we're all up Shit Creek.'

Davies left, and Tom was alone with Mary. 'How's the jaw?' she asked.

He rubbed it cautiously. 'Okay,' he said.

Mary smiled affectionately. I've never met anyone like you before. You're either the bravest, most noble man I'm ever likely to come across, or you're a complete and utter pillock.'

'Plenty of room for manoeuvre there,' said Tom comfortably. 'I'd happily settle for somewhere in the middle.'

'We'll see,' grinned Mary.

'I suppose you know what happens next by now,' said Tom, swinging his legs round and off the bed.

She looked at him and said: 'You ask me for your clothes, I say you shouldn't go yet, and then you sign yourself out?'

'Correct.'

'Look — are you sure you won't stay in overnight this time. You *were* knocked unconscious and damn it, you should know better than to play the John Wayne thing.'

'A man's gotta do . . .'

'What exactly, in your case?' interrupted Mary.

He sighed and looked down at the floor for a moment

in silence. 'I do have my pride, you know,' he said, finally looking up at her. 'I'm aware of people giggling in the corridor as I turn up yet again in A&E as a patient when I'm supposed to be a bloody doctor!'

Mary stifled a giggle behind her hand.

'I just want to be out of here. I never want to see the place again, if truth be told!' Then he looked at her lovely face and said craftily: 'Of course, if you were to kiss me long and hard I might be able to convince that lot out there that I keep getting my head bashed in just so I can come and see you . . .'

'Oh well, if it's a question of saving your street cred, Doctor, that would seem to be the very least I could do.'

They were kissing when a domestic assistant came in to remove a tray. They were still kissing when she left.

'That should do it,' sighed Tom happily.

'Did it for me,' beamed Mary.

Tom made to kiss her again but she put her hands on his chest. 'I'm on duty, and you are going to go straight home to bed.'

'If I get knocked out again, can I come back for more?'

'Don't even dream it!' said Mary. 'I'll get your clothes.'

'Shit, my car's over in Aberlyn,' said Tom.

'No, it isn't,' said Mary. 'The police brought it here. It's in the car park. I think they regard you as one of their own these days . . . or something like that.'

'The bone!' exclaimed Tom. 'The saw! They'll need those as evidence. I didn't tell Davies where they were exactly. I'd better get over to Aberlyn and—'

'*No!*' insisted Mary. 'You told Chief Inspector Davies about these things. His men are perfectly capable of finding them without your help. YOU are going home. Understood?'

'Understood,' said Tom weakly.

'Promise?'

'Promise.'

Tom drove back over to Felinbach, wondering how Davies was getting on with the Nationwide. It was now eight in the evening. Someone must have been dragged from his or her home to open up the office in Caernarfon where the account was registered; he wondered idly if they would see this as a nuisance or something to brighten the humdrum existence of working in a building society. Either way, please God, they'd come up with something useful.

When Davies rang at nine-thirty. Tom snatched the receiver off its cradle.

'We've got the source,' the Chief Inspector announced. 'Both payments were in the form of personal cheques signed by one Sonia Trool.'

'*Sonia Trool?*' exclaimed Tom. 'Bloody hell.'

'Make any sense?'

'Her daughter!' breathed Tom, light dawning. 'Her daughter Charlotte was blinded in a car accident. It was through the accident that Sonia met James Trool. The little girl's eyes were too badly damaged for a corneal transplant to be of any use, but the optic nerve was undamaged – so if more material were available and it was a perfect match . . .' Tom paused.

'Jesus Christ, are you telling me they cloned a kid to steal her eyes?'

'That's what it looks like.'

~ Twenty-Eight ~

'I take it you're on your way to pick up the Trools?'
said Tom.

'It's not as easy as that,' said Davies's voice over the
phone line. 'According to a neighbour, they're not at home.
They left last night, saying they'd be away for a few
days. The neighbour doesn't know where they've gone and
neither does Trool's secretary. Apparently, he told her that
he felt physically and mentally drained after all the strain
of the past few weeks so he'd decided to take some time
off. He and his wife were going to go away somewhere
together.'

'What about their daughter?' asked Tom.

'No, the daughter was to stay here,' said Davies. 'The
neighbour told us that her mother had taken her into some
clinic or other a few days ago for some minor treatment. The
clinic would be looking after her until they got back.'

'Something doesn't sound right to me,' said Tom suspiciously. 'Their daughter goes into hospital and they prance
off on holiday? No way! They're up to something. Chances
are, if the kid has gone into a clinic, it's for the main event.
God, we're *that* close!'

'We've put out an alert for them but it could take some
time,' said Davies.

'Anne-Marie doesn't have much of that.'

'I'll keep you posted,' the policeman promised.

Tom felt a tremendous sense of frustration and anti-climax. There was nothing worse than just having to sit and wait, but there was no alternative. They simply didn't have a clue where the Trools had gone. With the benefit of hindsight, he thought he should have suspected Trool's involvement at an earlier stage. He remembered Thomas's surprise – discomfort even – at finding Trool's green Jaguar in the car park on the night Tom had gone back to get a tissue sample from Anne-Marie. It now seemed highly probable that it had been Trool who had tried to kill him that night and had later gone on to murder Thomas in his office. Come to think of it, he had even heard Thomas arguing with Trool, on an earlier occasion when he'd come close to being caught searching Thomas's lab. Thomas may have confided his fears to Trool about what Dawes was up to, possibly asking him to take some kind of action in his capacity as Medical Superintendent of the hospital. He couldn't have suspected that Trool had actually been the instigator of the whole affair – or maybe he *had* and that was why Trool killed him.

God, what a mess, thought Tom. It occurred to him now that maybe some Faustian bargain had been struck between Sonia and James Trool over what could be done for her daughter in the long term. Their marriage had puzzled a great many people, including Tom himself. Perhaps the beautiful Sonia had agreed to marry James Trool on the understanding that he would restore her daughter's eyesight? It made some kind of hellish sense . . . suddenly it seemed a very long time since he had last had a proper sleep. He was getting into bed when the phone rang. Thinking it might be Davies with more news, he snatched it up.

'Just checking,' said Mary's voice.

'I'm just on my way to bed, honest.'

'Good. Any word from the police?'

Tom told her about Sonia being the source of the payments to Dawes but swore her to secrecy for the moment. There was nothing they could do until the police found out where the Trools had gone.

'So it's possible that Anne-Marie *is* still alive?' asked Mary.

'Just. But it's going to be a pretty close-run thing. If Charlotte Trool has been in a clinic for a few days . . . the chances are, frankly, not good.'

'What kind of people are they?' exclaimed Mary. 'How can they see a child as a bag of spare parts? Trool's a doctor, for God's sake! He took the Hippocratic oath just like we did. Medicine is supposed to be about helping people, all people, not about the survival of the fittest or the richest.'

'It is,' Tom assured her. 'Helping people is what you're doing, isn't it?'

'What — stitching up the heads of three drunks who had a fight after a football match and extracting an aniseed ball from the nose of a teenager, who "did it for a laugh"? If you say so,' replied Mary, summarising her most recent activities.

'Of course it is. It means you're one of the good guys,' said Tom warmly. 'And thank God there are still a lot more goodies than baddies in the game.'

'Sometimes I wonder,' said Mary.

'Just a few bad apples.'

'Get some sleep, Tom.'

Mary had a point, thought Tom sleepily as his head hit the pillow. People expected such a lot of certain professions, doctors, policemen, nurses. Bad apples could do an untold amount of damage in these particular barrels.

*   *   *

Tom was woken at seven by a call from the police in Caernarfon. It didn't come from Davies personally – he was off duty – but he had left instructions that Tom should be informed if there were any developments during the night.

'We've heard from Manchester Airport that Dr and Mrs Trool and their daughter were on a BA flight to Paris two nights ago.'

'Paris?' repeated Tom flatly, not knowing what to make of the news, then it registered that the officer had said their daughter was with them. 'Are you sure about that?' he asked.

'That's what it says here.'

'So what's happening?'

'We've asked the French police for urgent assistance in finding them.'

Tom put down the phone but it rang again almost immediately. This time it was Davies himself. 'You've heard?'

Tom said that he had. 'They've gone to Paris, and their daughter is with them.'

'Don't understand that,' Davies grunted. 'Their neigh-bour was adamant that the child had gone into the clinic a few days ago and that the Trools were alone when they left.'

'Must have picked her up somewhere along the way,' said Tom.

'So what the hell are they doing?' asked the Chief Inspector.

'I'm not sure,' Tom said slowly. 'But they're definitely up to something.'

'If the kid's already had the operation, maybe they've taken her away to recuperate?' suggested Davies. 'I mean, Paris doesn't have to be their final destination, does it?

The South of France can be very nice at this time of year.'

'Then why not fly there directly,' queried Tom.

'Maybe flights were difficult. It doesn't take that long on the TGV from Paris.'

'Hmm.' Tom was unconvinced.

'Look, if they've booked into a hotel in Paris, the French police will find them,' said Davies.

'And if they haven't booked into a hotel?' Tom's anxiety levels were rising.

'Then it could take a bit longer,' conceded Davies. 'But if the operation has already taken place, then I don't see . . .'

'What the hurry is,' said Tom, completing his sentence. 'You're right. If they've done it, Anne-Marie will be dead already. But we don't know that for sure. We have to keep trying.'

'Understood,' said Davies.

Tom put the phone down, within seconds it rang again. This time it was Mary. 'I thought I'd see how you were this morning,' she said. 'If you are feeling okay, shall we meet up when I come off duty in half an hour? I've got the next three days off, thank God.'

'I'm fine. See you later then.'

Mary was aware of Tom's preoccupation as they sat talking and drinking coffee in a small café near Bangor Cathedral. Although polite and apparently attentive to what she was saying, she noticed his gaze drift off and the tight muscles in his cheeks were a dead giveaway.

'What's wrong?' she asked.

'It's the prospect of yet more waiting. I keep thinking there must be something I can do.'

'Not if you don't know where they are,' said Mary. 'It's really up to the French police now.'

'The airport!' Tom said. 'Maybe they said something about what their plans were to someone at the airport. I'm going over there!'

Mary looked at him with a slightly anguished expression on her face. 'You're doing it again,' she said.

'It's worth a try,' he insisted. 'What harm can it do? And it's better than sitting here doing nothing.'

'All right,' conceded Mary. 'But I'm coming with you.'

'Hang on — you've been working all night.' Tom felt guilty.

'I'm coming,' she repeated. 'If only to stand behind you and make sure that no one hits you over the head again!'

There was a moment when Tom didn't know whether to take offence or laugh. In the end, he did the latter and agreed to her coming along. 'All right,' he said. 'We'll take the Land Rover. You can sleep on the way. Let's go.'

Manchester Airport was unpleasantly crowded. Early-morning fog had persisted until well after ten, causing a number of delays to both inbound and outbound traffic.

'Where do we start?' asked Mary, as they came to a halt in the crowds.

'The police said they took a British Airways flight, so let's try the BA information desk.'

It took them some five minutes to find it and another ten waiting in the queue before they got close enough to see that the desk was staffed by two women in smart navy-blue uniforms who were fending off complaints and dealing with enquiries with stock replies and auto-pilot smiles. 'Sorry, sir, your flight will be leaving as soon as possible . . . Of course, madam, just ask the flight attendant when you board . . . Your baggage will be checked right through to Warsaw, sir. No need to worry.'

Tom reached the head of the queue and addressed the

one whose name-badge read *Angela*. 'I'd like to speak to someone about passengers on your Paris flight last Tuesday evening.'

Angela's brittle smile was extinguished as suddenly as if a fuse had blown. 'I'm sorry?'

Tom repeated his request.

'We don't actually give out that kind of information,' the woman said smoothly.

'It's very important,' pleaded Tom.

Mary intervened. 'We're doctors,' she said. 'These passengers are our patients. It's extremely urgent that we trace them.'

'I see,' said Angela thoughtfully. 'I'll have to call my supervisor.' She picked up a house phone and after a slight pause, spoke to someone she addressed as Mrs Roberts. When she'd finished she asked Tom and Mary to wait to one side. A few minutes later, Mrs Roberts, a woman in her early forties, wearing the same uniform as Angela, appeared and asked them to accompany her to her office. This turned out to be a small room with no windows on the first floor.

Tom noted that Mrs Roberts appeared quite unfazed when he explained to her what he wanted to know. Such neutrality was obviously part and parcel of dealing with the public. 'We were hoping that the Trools might have said something to one of your staff about their plans?'

'Angela tells me that you are both doctors?'

'Yes.'

'I'm afraid I'll have to ask you for some proof. I'm sure you understand.'

Mary showed her hospital staff card, while Tom displayed a range of ID from his wallet.

'Fine,' said Mrs Roberts. 'Do you have the exact details of the flight your patients were on?'

Tom said not, and apologised for the fact.

'No matter. I'll check the staff rota for the Tuesday flights and we'll take it from there. Just bear with me.'

The couple sat in nervous silence while the supervisor checked lists and made several calls on the internal phone network, all apparently without success. They were becoming depressed when a more positive-sounding conversation seemed to be taking place. 'You were on the desk on Tuesday evening, weren't you, Lisa? Good . . . the Paris flight, that's right. Do you happen to remember a family named Trool boarding the aircraft? . . . You do? Excellent! Could you come upstairs when your current boarding is finished?'

Mrs Roberts turned to them and smiled. 'Lisa remembers them,' she said. 'She'll be up as soon as they've finished boarding the Zurich flight.'

A fresh-faced blonde girl appeared some ten minutes later, carrying a clipboard under one arm and a bag slung over her other shoulder. Mrs Roberts did the introductions and added, 'These two people are doctors, Lisa. They're trying to trace the Trool family. I understand it's quite important.'

'I'm not sure I can help really,' said Lisa diffidently. 'I remember them because I got their name wrong and called them "Troll". We made some jokes about Norwegian fairy folk and had a bit of a laugh, but that's about it.'

'Who was carrying the child?' asked Tom urgently.

'Mrs Trool was,' replied Lisa.

'Were her eyes bandaged?'

The air hostess looked at Tom in surprise. 'No,' she replied, sounding puzzled.

Tom let out a sigh of relief and smiled at Mary. 'They couldn't have done it yet.' He turned back to Lisa and said, 'But you did notice that their daughter was blind?'

'No,' replied Lisa, sounding even more puzzled.

'Did she say anything to you about where she was going?'

'Their daughter? Of course not! She couldn't have been any more than three or four months old,' exclaimed Lisa.

'But Charlotte Trool is three or four *years* old!' said Tom. He looked at Mary and asked, 'What on earth is going on?'

'The child couldn't have been their daughter. That's the only explanation.'

Tom turned to Lisa again and asked, 'Can you tell us anything else about the baby?'

'Not really. She giggled when I tickled her tummy. I remember thinking she was a little short in the body, but I'm not sure why I'm saying that.'

Mary suddenly paled and said, 'It was because she had no legs.'

Tom made a pyramid with his two hands and tapped his fingertips rapidly against his chin while he thought through the implications. 'So where's their daughter?' he murmured.

'The neighbour said she went into a clinic,' Mary reminded him.

'But not here!' exclaimed Tom. He turned to the patiently waiting women and asked Mrs Roberts: 'Could you check to see if Mrs Trool made another trip to Paris a few days ago with her daughter?'

'I suppose . . .'

'Please. I promise you — it's *very* important.'

As Mrs Roberts turned to her computer screen and started her search, Tom murmured to Mary, 'They've gone to Paris to have the operation done there — I'm sure of it.'

'But we still don't know where!' whispered Mary. 'Maybe you should get in touch with Inspector Davies and tell him that Anne-Marie is still alive. It might make a difference if he can tell the French police that.'

Tom nodded his agreement.

At the same moment, Mrs Roberts announced, 'Yes, here it is, five days ago. Mrs Trool flew to Paris with her daughter, but without her husband on that occasion.'

'Thank you, Mrs Roberts, and you too, Lisa. You've been most helpful.'

Tom and Mary left the office and returned to the main concourse. 'I should have realised earlier that there was no way the operation could have been carried out in such a short space of time. Davies's idea of recuperation in France was really a non-starter. The Trools just came up with a clever way of getting Anne-Marie out the country; they pretended she was their daughter.'

'They seem to have thought of everything,' said Mary.

'God, I wish I knew where they'd gone!' exclaimed Tom.

'The sooner you phone Davies the better. Make sure the French police are checking the Paris hospitals and clinics,' said Mary.

'Clinics!' Tom struck his forehead. 'Of course! God, I'm slow. Dawes's clinic!'

'You're not making any sense,' said Mary, watching Tom search frantically through all his pockets as if he were on fire

'When I was at Dawes's house in Aberlyn,' said Tom, 'I found a leaflet about a French clinic. It was being used as a bookmark. I didn't think too much about it at the time but now I see it has to be the place. Anything else would just be too much of a coincidence.'

With a cry of relief, Tom found what he was looking for and unfolded it. 'See!' he said, showing it to Mary.

'Phone Davies and tell him right now!' she urged.

Tom made the call on his mobile phone after finding a quiet corner behind a row of cleaning trolleys. Mary waited nearby. 'Did you get him all right?' she asked when he rejoined her.

Tom nodded. 'He's going to contact the French police right away.'

'Good,' said Mary, her shoulders sagging in relief. 'I only hope they get there on time to stop it. Meanwhile, I suppose we're back to playing the waiting game.'

'Wait?' echoed Tom. 'Us? Oh no. *We're* off to Paris!'

~ *Twenty-Nine* ~

'You're not serious,' groaned Mary, although more in hope than expectation.

'We can do more good there than we can here,' Tom told her. 'Here, we're just waiting around like spare parts at a wedding.'

'But surely the French police will—'

'Think about it! The French police can't possibly have a real understanding of what's going on, solely on the basis of a couple of phone calls from the North Wales Constabulary. It would be much better if they actually had someone there on the ground to answer questions and give advice.'

Mary took a moment to consider Tom's claim. Then: 'We don't have passports with us,' she reminded him.

'Shit!' exclaimed Tom. He stood there like a statue for a few moments before he took hold of Mary's arm and started leading her through the crowds.

Mary's protests were lost as he led her towards the airport shops to start scanning the shelves of a book and souvenir stall. He soon found what he was looking for — leather passport covers which resembled the old style of British passport, issued before the EEC ones took over.

'We could chance it with these,' he said. 'Passport control between European countries is notoriously lax.'

When Mary hesitated, he added, 'I really think there's a good chance that Anne-Marie is still alive.'

At that, Mary gave in and shook her head, saying, 'What the hell! In for a penny . . .'

Tom paid for two covers and slipped them into his inside pocket. On the Departures screen they read that an Air France flight was scheduled to leave for Paris in forty-five minutes. Another struggle through the crowds and Tom was attempting to persuade the staff at the Air France counter to let them fly on it. 'I know, I know,' he countered their objections with raised palms and smiles. 'I understand, but it really is vitally important that we get to Paris as quickly as possible. Please make an exception . . . just this once?'

Finally the two staff members smiled and gave in. Tom paid for the tickets with his credit card and accepted the two boarding cards.

'You must go straight to the gate,' they were told.

'Of course,' Tom beamed.

As they headed for the International Departure hall, he turned to Mary and murmured, 'Now for the big test. Are you okay?'

'I feel sick,' she replied.

They could see the Passport Control desk up ahead. Tom hissed, 'Keep talking. Say anything you like, but keep talking.'

Mary started to chatter, using a series of medical statistics as her chosen subject. The nearer they got to the desk, the faster she seemed to speak. They were almost on it when Tom, still looking at Mary as if totally wrapped up in what she was saying, took out the two covers from his inside pocket and waved them in the general direction of the desk while interrupting Mary. 'No, no, no,' he exclaimed, without breaking stride. 'You simply *can't* start that kind of patient on chemotherapy at that point. It's much better to wait until . . .'

At no time did either of them look directly at the man on the desk. They walked straight past, both fearing a call to halt but it never came. Ever so gradually, relief replaced fear.

'I'd better sit down before I fall down,' whispered Mary shakily. 'I'm not cut out for this kind of thing.'

'To be perfectly honest, neither am I,' confessed Tom. 'I hated every second of it.'

Mary looked at him sideways and smiled. 'You were brilliant! You should change your name to Bond.'

'Be a change from Mud,' he said wryly, and she laughed.

The flight was only three minutes late in taking off. Tom and Mary lapsed into silence and communed with their own thoughts until the aircraft reached cruising height and the flight attendants started a round with the drinks trolley.

'This is where we have to decide whether we should have a drink or keep our reflexes perfectly honed,' said Tom, tongue in cheek.

Mary gave him a look that sufficed as a reply.

'Two gin and tonics, please.'

Mary let out a long sigh of appreciation. 'I don't think I've ever needed a drink so much in all my life,' she said, putting her head back on the rest.

'I'll drink to that,' he agreed.

They both sat with their eyes closed for a few minutes, savouring the calming effect of the alcohol before Tom took out the French clinic's blurb and started to read it. The St Pierre boasted the finest facilities currently available for the discerning client and was equipped for procedures varying from minor to major surgery, it claimed. Prospective patients could avail themselves of the in-house medical teams or appoint their own physicians and surgeons as they saw fit.

'Do you know Paris?' asked Mary.

'Not well. You?'

'Hardly at all.'

'There's a little map on the back,' said Tom. 'This place is in the Rue de Bagneux in Montrouge, just outside the Périphérique ring road on the south side.'

Mary took a look at the map and added, 'It says that you take the exit at Porte d'Orléans. But how do we get there?'

'Do you have your driving licence with you?'

Mary shook her head.

'Me neither,' said Tom. 'So renting a car is out. Let's get whatever seems fastest into Paris — bus, train, taxi, you name it — and then play it by ear.'

'Assuming we get into the country in the first place,' Mary reminded him. 'There's the time factor to consider too,' she said, looking at her watch. 'It's going to be the evening rush hour if and when we do get there.'

'All we need,' Tom sighed.

The flight landed at Charles De Gaulle Airport with a large bump due to a crosswind catching the aircraft at the last moment in its approach. Many of the passengers started to talk about it but Mary and Tom didn't say a word: they were too focused on other things.

'I wonder what French jails are like,' whispered Mary.

Tom squeezed her hand and tried to assure her that it wouldn't come to that. He said they should attempt to go through Passport Control with the biggest group of people they could find. This meant being neither the first to get off the plane nor the last. Fortunately, they had very little in the way of hand baggage to deal with and no luggage to collect from the carousel at all, so they could afford to be flexible in their timing.

As soon as he saw the Passport Control booths, Tom knew that everything was going to be all right. The bored-looking officials were just waving people on through with a lazy wave of the hand as passengers held up their passports to them. Tom held up the two covers, pretending to struggle to open them up as they passed, and suddenly they were into France.

There was a tourist information desk directly opposite as they emerged through Customs, again unchallenged. As there was no queue at it, Tom took the opportunity to ask the quickest way into Paris. The man pointed through the glass doors and said, 'There's an express bus leaving in three minutes. It will save you waiting for anything else.'

Tom took Mary's hand and they rushed over to the Bureau de Change to change a handful of money before running out through the doors and reaching the steps of the bus just as the doors closed with a hydraulic hiss. To their relief, the driver saw them and opened them up again. They climbed aboard, thanking him, and sat down one row behind him on the other side as the bus moved off.

'That was a bit of luck,' gasped Mary.

'Something tells me we're going to need a whole lot more,' said Tom, but she was right. Presumably a taxi or train might have been faster had all things been equal but they hadn't, and there was no telling how long they would have had to wait for either of these other options.

'How's your French?' Tom asked.

'Quite good,' replied Mary.

'Good enough to ask the driver the quickest way to Montrouge at this time of day?' he asked.

'Piece of *gâteau*,' Mary joked and, still sitting in her seat, she leaned forward and said across the aisle, 'Monsieur?'

Tom was impressed as Mary held a fluent conversation with the driver, ending in smiles and thanks. 'Thank God you came,' he whispered.

Mary said, 'He reckons the Metro would be quickest at this time of day without a doubt. He told me which line we want and the nearest station to where the bus stops. More than that, he used to be a cab driver, so he told me how we get to Rue De Bagneux from our station.'

'What a star!' said Tom.

As they left the bus at Gare de L'Est and stepped out on to the pavement into the darkness of early evening, Tom looked about him. 'There!' he said, pointing to the steps with the Paris Metro sign above them. They hurried down them, with Tom joking, 'It's a smell you don't forget.'

'Like no other,' agreed Mary.

They had to queue at the ticket booth but not for long. Most passengers seemed to have season tickets. 'Where do we want to go?' asked Tom.

'Porte D'Orléans.'

The train was crowded so they had to stand. By the time it had cleared Montparnasse Bienvenue, there were seats to be had. After Denfert Rochereau, it was more than half-empty. 'Two more stations and then it's ours,' said Mary. 'Porte D'Orléans – the end of the line.'

The train emptied and the pair made their way to the station exit, pausing to look for street signs in order to get their bearings. While Tom examined his small map, Mary said, 'This should be Boulevard Brun, according to the bus driver.'

'It is and we should cross it.'

They took the pedestrian underpass and surfaced on the other side, happy to be going under the heavy rush-hour traffic instead of having to dodge through it.

Mary pointed to a sign on the wall of a building to their right. It said, *Rue de Bagneux*.

The clinic itself was three blocks down the Rue de Bagneux, standing on the corner at a road junction and overlooking a cemetery. Neither of them commented on the fact; both were too nervous.

The door to the clinic was locked. In fact, the only outward sign that the building might be either a hospital or clinic was an ambulance standing outside. There was an entryphone mounted on the wall. Tom pressed the button and waited.

'*Oui?*'

Tom looked at Mary, took a deep breath then said firmly in English who they were, adding, 'We've just arrived from the UK and we need to speak to someone urgently about one of your patients — a child named Trool.'

'*Un moment.*'

'Tom made a face as they waited for a reply.

'That was fine,' said Mary encouragingly. 'The police will have been here by now, so the clinic staff will know that something is amiss with the Trool child.'

The door lock clicked open and they were admitted to a short, brightly lit hall leading to a flight of marble stairs. The air inside was warm and there was a smell of antiseptic. A woman dressed in a smart lilac suit and white blouse met them at the head of the stairs; she introduced herself as Antoinette Bressard, Administrative Assistant at the clinic. 'I will take you to see Dr Balard,' she said.

Mary asked her if Balard was the Director.

'Deputy Director,' the woman replied. 'The Director has gone home for the evening.'

They were shown into an elegant office where a well-dressed man in his mid-thirties rose to meet them and invited them to sit.

'I believe the French police have already been here to ask about the patient we are interested in,' said Tom.

Balard nodded. 'They were here about three hours ago, looking for the Trool baby's parents. I understand the couple are wanted by the British police for questioning.'

'The Trools' daughter is here?' asked Tom.

'Yes, indeed. She is due to be operated on the day after tomorrow.'

Tom exchanged a relieved look with Mary then said to Balard, 'A transplant operation?'

'Eye tissue — a delicate procedure.'

'How much do you know about the donor, Doctor?' asked Tom.

Balard shrugged. 'Nothing at all — the operation has been arranged privately. Our clients have contracted for our theatre facilities and nursing services, but they have made their own arrangements for surgical and medical staff.'

'So the eye donor is not here?' said Mary, acutely disappointed.

Balard said not. 'I don't even know if the donor is here in Paris, or whether they are flying in the tissue from abroad.'

'Were you able to help the police with the Trools' whereabouts at all?' asked Tom.

'I know where they are staying if that's what you mean. They're at a hotel in the Marais, the Pavillon de la Reine in Place Des Vosges. But I'm afraid that's as much as I could tell the police, or you for that matter. Might I ask what these people are wanted for?'

Tom ignored the question and said, 'Presumably the police have already been to the hotel by now.'

'I would suppose so,' replied Balard.

'Would it be a terrible imposition to ask you to telephone them on our behalf?' asked Tom.

'Not at all.' Balard looked in his desk diary for some notes he had made earlier and called the number he found there. After a conversation lasting some minutes he put the receiver down and said, 'They are coming over. The Inspector would like to speak to you personally.'

'Did they say whether they have the Trools in custody and whether they had a child with them?'

Balard seemed puzzled. 'The Inspector said that they had interviewed the couple, but said nothing about holding them. He didn't mention a child, but when he heard that you were here, he seemed very interested. I think he wants to ask you some questions.'

Tom shrugged. 'Maybe it's for the best. We may as well all put our cards on the table.'

The police arrived within ten minutes, during which Tom and Mary were served with coffee and plied with subtle questions. Balard, sensing that something was seriously amiss, was becoming increasingly anxious about the apparent involvement of his clinic but Tom did not see this as a reason for telling him anything. Instead he tried to assure him that there was no question of the clinic being under any suspicion if what he had told them was accurate.

'You have come from England today?' asked the tall, rangy man introduced to them as Inspector Le Clerc.

'Wales, actually,' said Mary.

'Ah yes, Wales,' agreed Le Clerc. 'We had a call from Inspector Davies in Wales, asking for our assistance in a case of child abduction, but I think there must be some misunderstanding. We found the couple easily enough but they did not have any child with them. Apparently they came with a child but she is their daughter; she is a patient here in the clinic, awaiting an operation.'

Tom felt vindicated over his decision to come to France.

This was just the kind of misunderstanding that he feared might happen. He said, 'They arrived with their child two nights ago?'

'*Oui*,' replied the Inspector.

Tom turned to Balard. 'When was the Trool child admitted to the clinic?'

Balard checked his patient records. 'Six days ago.'

The Inspector looked bemused. Tom briefly told him the whole story, helped in places by Mary, and then he explained about the couple's earlier trip, with Charlotte. 'It wasn't really their daughter they arrived with two nights ago – it was the baby they'd abducted.'

The Inspector, who was now fully in the picture, remarked gravely: 'I'm sure there was no sign of a child being with them when we interviewed them at the hotel. But in the light of what you've just told me, we'll go back there now and question them further.'

'Maybe that's not such a good idea,' said Tom thoughtfully. 'If Anne-Marie is being held somewhere else, we could be in trouble.'

'But surely if the police turn up on their doorstep with you in tow, they'll see that the game's up and they'll confess?' said Mary.

'It's what will happen to Anne-Marie if they don't admit it that concerns me,' said Tom.

'What do you mean?'

'Anne-Marie is the key to the whole case against the Trools. That fact alone puts her in immediate danger. Without her, there is very little in the way of evidence against them. In fact, about the only thing we're left with is the money that Sonia paid into Ranulph Dawes's account, and he's now dead so they'll probably be able to concoct some story to explain it. Thinking we know why he was paid the money is a long way from *proving* it.'

'So you think they might try to get rid of Anne-Marie now if they can't go ahead with the operation?' asked Mary.

'Yes . . . I really do.'

~ *Thirty* ~

'What do you suggest?' asked Le Clerc.
'I'm trying to imagine what the Trools must be thinking right now,' said Tom. 'They've had a visit from the French police, which must have shaken them, but from what you've said, you just asked a few routine questions and then went away again, apparently satisfied with what they'd told you. They don't know anything about us being here or of the conversation we've just had.'

'So?'

'I'm hoping there's a real chance they will have seen no reason to change their plans and the operation will stay scheduled to go ahead in two days' time. That being the case, I think if your men were to keep watch on the hotel and follow the Trools whenever they go out, it's my guess they'll lead you to where Anne-Marie is being held.'

'That makes sense,' agreed Le Clerc.

'What sort of place do you think they'll be holding her in?' asked Mary.

'It really has to be a hospital or possibly another clinic,' said Tom. 'She's no doubt under deep sedation – to simulate coma conditions. Then when they're ready, they'll bring the coma to a fatal conclusion and bingo! They'll have their donor.'

'But that is outrageous!' said Balard. 'There is no question of my permitting such an operation to be carried out in this clinic. I will telephone these people and make it clear that there is absolutely no point in going ahead.'

Tom shook his head. 'You mustn't do that, Doctor. You'd just be telling them that they'd been found out, in which case they would almost certainly kill Anne-Marie and dispose of her body to save their own skins.'

'Doctor Gordon is right,' said Le Clerc heavily. 'It would be better if you were to behave as if nothing were wrong, should they phone or come here in person.'

'Presumably they will come to visit their daughter?' said Mary.

'Good point,' Tom nodded.

'Very well,' agreed Balard.

'And don't say anything at all about this to any member of staff,' Le Clerc ordered. 'Just so they behave normally too. In the meantime, I will see that a watch is mounted on the hotel.' He turned to Tom and Mary. 'Where will you be staying, Doctors?'

'I'm not at all sure,' Tom admitted, feeling stupid. 'We came straight here.'

'In the circumstances,' said Balard, 'you are both welcome to stay overnight here at the clinic. We have guest rooms for relatives of our patients.'

The couple accepted the offer with heartfelt thanks.

'Good, then I'll know where to find you,' said Le Clerc approvingly.

The policeman left and Tom and Mary were shown to adjoining rooms on the third floor of the clinic. It had started to rain outside and puddles of water were reflecting the lights of the traffic as Mary came back through to join Tom in looking out of the window. 'We're going to need some toilet things,' she yawned. Her night duty and today's mad journeyings were catching up with her. 'Maybe we can find a supermarket open?'

Tom seemed very distant. Mary asked him what was wrong.

'I'm having second thoughts,' Tom confessed. 'I'm thinking that maybe I've underestimated Trool: maybe he *will* change his plans in the light of the police visit.'

'How so?'

Still looking out of the window, Tom shuddered, 'The police may have spooked him into doing something earlier than he'd planned.'

'Like what?'

'Like getting rid of Anne-Marie.'

'But he's so close to the operation,' she protested. 'All this planning, all this waiting . . . surely he'll keep his nerve!'

'All he needs are her eyes,' Tom said. It sounded brutal and it shocked Mary.

She looked at him in horror. 'You mean he'll remove her eyes and then get rid of her body as a precaution?'

'That has to be the plan in the long run anyway,' Tom said gruffly. 'The police may just have persuaded him to do it sooner rather than later.'

'But surely the eyes alone will be proof of his guilt,' exclaimed Mary.

Tom slowly shook his head. 'I think not. By any scientific criterion the eyes are his daughter's own eyes. Anne-Marie is a clone, remember.'

'My God, do you think he could actually get away with it?' exclaimed Mary.

'He could pretend that he'd managed to clone his daughter's eye tissue *in vitro* and grown it up in the lab.'

'But I thought that was impossible?'

'It is, but he could claim a breakthrough. Without the

existence of Anne-Marie as evidence, no one could prove otherwise.'

The phone rang and Mary picked it up. After a brief conversation in French she put the phone back down and said, 'That was Inspector Le Clerc. The Trools checked out of the Pavillon de la Reine about an hour before the police surveillance team got there. They did not leave a forwarding address.'

'Oh shit!' Tom's worst fears seemed to be about to come true. 'Did he say what they're doing about it?'

'Just that they are doing their best to find them.'

Tom started to pace nervously. 'We're going to be too late,' he muttered. 'Too damned late.'

Mary could think of nothing positive to say. They were powerless to do anything, as far as she could see, but enforced inaction was not going to make the waiting any easier. 'Maybe we could start ringing round all the hospitals and clinics in Paris?' she suggested, but her voice faltered as it occurred to her just how many of them there must be. 'Maybe not,' she conceded. The suggestion however, triggered off another thought and she said, 'But we could ask their hotel!'

'Ask them what?' said Tom.

'If the Trools made any telephone calls while they were staying there. Surely they must have contacted this other clinic at some time?'

'Brilliant!' said Tom. 'But we'd better get the police to do it; the hotel won't give out that kind of information to us. You call them; your French is a lot better than mine.'

He stood by anxiously while Mary phoned the police and asked to be put through to Le Clerc. He watched her expression change from excitement to disappointment. She put down the phone and said dejectedly, 'They already thought of that. The Trools did not use the hotel phone at all.'

'Damnation,' said Tom. 'But it was still a good idea. Try to come up with another one!'

The pair of them sat fidgeting, willing the phone to ring and bring them news, while outside the rain beat against the window. It was to be another thirty minutes before the phone did ring but even then, it wasn't the police with more news; it was Dr Balard.

'Mrs Trool has just arrived to visit her daughter,' he announced in an exited whisper.

Tom's throat tightened and he felt the beginnings of a cold sweat break out on his forehead. 'We must speak to her,' he said. 'Can you arrange it?'

'Come down and wait in my room. I'll see to it that she calls in there before she leaves the clinic.'

'We'll be right down. You'll inform the police?'

'Of course.'

Tom turned to Mary and said, 'Sonia Trool is here to see her daughter. We can't afford to just let her walk away. We must try to find out from her where they're holding Anne-Marie.'

'Something tells me that isn't going to be easy,' said Mary grimly.

'It might be our only chance.'

Tom and Mary waited for over forty minutes in Balard's office before voices outside the door told them that Sonia Trool was about to be shown in. Balard indicated that they stand against the back wall to the side of the door and they did so before a knock came and Balard said, 'Come in.'

'You wanted to see me, Doctor?' asked Sonia Trool as she entered, confident and looking as elegant as ever.

'Actually, *we* did,' said Tom, pushing the door closed and standing in front of it.

Sonia turned and looked shocked, but only for a moment. She smiled and said, 'Dr Gordon, what a surprise. What brings you here?'

'This is Dr Hallam from Ysbyty Gwynedd in Wales. We've come here to take Anne-Marie Palmer back home with us. Where is she?'

'I'm not sure I know what you are talking about, Doctor. Wasn't Anne-Marie Palmer the baby who was murdered by her father back in Wales?'

'No, she's the baby you and your husband paid Ranulph Dawes to clone so that your child could have her sight restored,' said Tom evenly. 'Now, *where is she?*'

'This is bizarre,' protested Sonia. 'I've never heard such nonsense in all my life. Dr Balard . . .' She made a move towards the door but Tom blocked her way.

'Let me past,' she demanded.

'Where, Sonia?'

'Dr Balard, would you *please* call the police!' Sonia demanded.

'They are already on their way, madame,' replied Balard, ill at ease with what was going on in front of him.

His reply brought another little flicker of uncertainty from Sonia but again she recovered well and said, 'Good, then I'll be able to have these people charged with keeping me here against my will.'

'Do you deny that your child is here to have her sight restored?' Tom asked her.

'Of course I don't deny it,' retorted Sonia. 'A donor has become available and tissue is being flown in.'

'From where?'

'I didn't ask,' replied Sonia. 'I . . . find that sort of thing just too upsetting.'

'Ah you are *such* a sensitive soul, Sonia,' said Tom.

The woman's eyes flashed with anger.

'Where's James?' Tom demanded.

'Mind your own business,' snapped Sonia.

The police arrived and Le Clerc came into the room.

'Inspector, these people are harassing me. I wish to leave,' said Sonia, making a move towards the door but finding her way still blocked, this time by Le Clerc as well as Tom.

'Not just yet, madame,' said Le Clerc calmly. 'I need you to answer a few more questions for me.'

'She won't say where they're holding the child or where her husband is,' burst out Tom.

'Then perhaps you would be kind enough to empty out your handbag, madame,' requested Le Clerc politely.

'This is outrageous,' stormed Sonia, who looked for a moment as though she might explode, but on seeing that Le Clerc seemed less than impressed with her histrionics, she capitulated quietly and emptied her bag out on Balard's desk.

Le Clerc sifted through the contents that comprised mainly make-up items and paper tissues from what Tom could see from his sentry position in front of the door. 'No cards, no notebook,' said Le Clerc.

'But a mobile phone,' said Mary.

Le Clerc looked at her and smiled. He picked up Sonia's phone and started to check the call register as her face began to show panic. Le Clerc muttered to himself, 'UK, UK, UK . . . France.' He pressed the call button and put the phone to his ear. He listened to the reply without comment then he switched the phone off. Still without saying anything, he took out his own phone and said into it, 'Get me the address of the Clinique Martin, will you?'

Sonia collapsed on to a chair in front of Balard's desk and started sobbing loudly. Le Clerc said to Tom and Mary, 'Let's go. We can get the information in the car.'

As they left the room, the gendarme who had been

stationed outside was sent in to take charge of Sonia Trool. Tom and Mary got into the back of Le Clerc's car while he and the driver sat in the front, waiting for the address of the clinic. It seemed unnaturally silent, apart from the sound of rain on the roof and the driver's fingers drumming quietly on the steering wheel. Thirty seconds later the information came through and Le Clerc snapped, 'Rue Dauphine!'

The silence changed in an instant as the car's klaxon filled the air and flashing lights cleared the way ahead as the car leapt forward to start carving its way north through the evening traffic. Mary had to close her eyes on several occasions when the driver seemed to head for gaps that weren't there in her view but always – and usually at the last moment – one opened up. When they were racing up the Boulevard Saint-Michel, the driver asked Le Clerc, 'Which end of Dauphine?'

'Nearest the river,' replied Le Clerc, who had been seeking the information on his radio. They reached the head of Saint Michel and turned west along by the river to finally enter Rue Dauphine on their left. The car drew to a halt outside the brightly-lit entrance to the Clinique Martin, its sign illuminated above its ambulance bay and flanked by two red crosses. It was clearly a much larger clinic than the St Pierre and larger than many small hospitals back home, thought Tom.

They all went in together. The reception desk was staffed by two young women wearing smart maroon uniforms with their names displayed on enamel badges and with a red cross nestling below angel wings on their collar. Le Clerc did the talking after showing his ID to each in turn. He asked about Trool and was rewarded with what sounded to Tom like a comprehensive reply. He didn't catch all of it but Mary did and she whispered to him, 'Trool is here . . . He's with his patient who has been in a coma and is now close to death.

He can't possibly be disturbed at this time . . . his patient's life is hanging in the balance. A theatre has been prepared in case Dr Trool feels there is a chance that an operation might save her life . . .'

Le Clerc turned to Tom, uncertain of his ground and feeling ill-equipped to make any kind of judgement on his own.

'We have to stop him,' rapped out Tom. 'Right now!'

Le Clerc turned back to the receptionists and demanded to know Trool's whereabouts in the hospital.

'Third floor, Room 316.'

Le Clerc immediately made for the elevators with Tom and Mary hard on his heels.

'C'mon . . . c'mon!' urged Tom as he watched the floor indicator fall with painful slowness. Even the doors seemed to take an age to slide back when the lift finally arrived.

The arrows on the wall immediately opposite the doors as they stepped out on the third floor pointed to the right for 316, and with Le Clerc in the lead, they all hurried along the thirty metres or so to the room. Le Clerc and Tom listened outside the door for a moment. They heard Trool's voice saying calmly, 'She's fading fast – warn the theatre team to expect us in ten minutes.'

Le Clerc opened the door and stepped into the room. He said to the nurse who had just lifted the telephone, 'Don't bother. Other arrangements are being made for your patient.' He showed her his ID. 'Will you please leave the room, mademoiselle.'

Trool got up from the bedside, his eyes wide with astonishment. He was wearing surgical greens with a mask slung round his neck. Anne-Marie lay unconscious with tubes inserted in her mouth and nose as a bank of electronically controlled apparatus behind her did what it had been programmed to do.

'This is outrageous!' blustered Trool.

'We can certainly agree on that,' said Tom bitterly as he and Mary hurried over to examine the baby.

'Is she who you thought she was?' asked Le Clerc.

'Without a doubt,' said Tom, fighting against a lump in his throat. 'This is Anne-Marie Palmer.'

Tom's full attention was now given over to the baby as he fought to assess her condition, but he was aware of Le Clerc informing Trool that he was under arrest. It didn't really register that the policeman had stopped talking until Mary let out a scream and he turned in time to see Le Clerc's face open up in a huge crimson gash. He fell to the floor and Tom saw the scalpel that had appeared in Trool's hand. His eyes had a wild look in them as he first looked to Tom and then at Mary.

Tom pushed Mary behind him as Trool started to come towards them, exuding malice. At the very last moment, when Tom had backed away as far as he could, Trool suddenly turned his attention on Anne-Marie. He threw down the scalpel and snatched the child up from the bed, freeing her from all her tubes and lines with a vicious tug that made Tom wince. With the child under one arm, he ran to the door, removing the key with his free hand and then locking the door behind him a fraction of a second before Tom got to it.

'Help Le Clerc, he's in a bad way!' Tom shouted at Mary as he began crashing his shoulder against the door in an attempt to break it open. After a third try with no sign of success he conceded that he was more likely to break his collarbone than the door lock. He grabbed the phone and called reception, declaring an emergency and asking to be released immediately. As he replaced the receiver, he was not at all sure that reception had understood his French, which had been made worse by his state of high anxiety.

Looking about him, he spotted the oxygen cylinder standing in the corner of the room. He snatched it up to start using it as a battering ram against the door. This was a much more successful ploy, and he had broken through the panel above the lock before there was any sign of help arriving from downstairs.

Tom released himself and ran along the corridor to the fire escape to start hurtling downstairs, two, three and even eight steps at a time when he lost rhythm on the last flight and had to launch himself through the air to the bottom landing. He was lucky and landed well enough to recover and race on to the emergency exit that he opened by crashing his foot against the horizontal bar.

He found himself in the clinic's car park, looking almost directly at James Trool, some twenty metres away, still with Anne-Marie's limp body under one arm while he searched feverishly through his pockets in what was clearly a vain attempt to find his car keys. Trool saw Tom and froze for a moment before abandoning the search and turning to start running towards a narrow exit giving pedestrian access to the street. Tom raced off in pursuit but caught his foot on a low rail when, in going for a short cut, he vaulted over a dividing wall in the car park. The fall winded him but he was on his feet after a few seconds and back in pursuit. He just made it to the street in time to see Trool dodging through traffic at the head of the intersection as he ran towards the Pont Neuf.

Tom caught up with Trool in the middle of the bridge. The traffic was heavy but they were the only pedestrians on that side.

'There's nowhere to go,' gasped Tom as he confronted the desperate man.

Trool, still with the same wild look in his eye, looked first at the traffic to his right and then over the parapet at the Seine below. He gave a sort of half-smile that suggested to Tom that the reality of his situation was beginning to dawn on him, but the words that he spoke suggested otherwise.

'No baby . . . no case, Gordon.'

The horror of what Trool meant had barely got through to Tom when the other man simply threw Anne-Marie's unconscious body over the parapet. Tom was paralysed for only a few seconds but it was long enough for Trool to make a dash for the other side of the bridge through the traffic. He made it three-quarters of the way to the accompaniment of squealing brakes and blaring horns, but an Iveco truck carrying a full load of Stella Artois beer could not stop in time. It hit Trool with a sickening thud that seemed to transcend the traffic noise. The impact threw Trool briefly up into the air, his body arching backwards to land head-first on the tarmac, where his skull cracked open like an egg.

Tom turned away and hung out over the parapet, trying desperately to see any sign of Anne-Marie, but all he saw was dark, slow-moving water, punctuated with reflections of the lights on the bridge. The thought that the baby was down there somewhere was powerful enough to short-circuit all other considerations. He climbed up on to the parapet and, without pausing for further thought, jumped down into the Seine.

The fall seemed to last an eternity before ice-cold water enveloped him and instantly paralysed him with cold. Panic added to his agony, as he seemed to keep on going down into the depths with little or no control over his limbs. The rigid spasticity of his arms and legs made the eventual struggle back to the surface a nightmare, and even when he broke the surface with bursting lungs, he found that the cold was such that he couldn't breathe in properly: his chest muscles refused to work. He floundered about for fully ten seconds before he had enough control of his body again to start swimming downstream to where he thought Anne-Marie might have drifted to by now.

The sheer hopelessness of his situation was beginning to dawn on Tom as he turtle-dived below the surface for the sixth time to search by feel with his arms flailing in all directions. He was now completely numb with cold and close to complete exhaustion – so much so that he knew his own chances of survival must now be in question. It was only the fear of having to face up to the fact that Anne-Marie was dead that made him go down for the seventh time. This time his left hand touched something but he failed to grasp it at the first attempt and he had to wheel to the left to try again. His hand touched the object again and he knew that he had found Anne-Marie: the little bundle was the right size and shape. As to what condition she was in, he put such thoughts out of his head and held her close to him as he reached up desperately with his free arm and kicked out hard with both legs in what he knew must be a final effort to surface. He simply had no energy left.

Tom broke the surface and took in a huge gulp of night air, then two more before taking in another and holding it inside to give him buoyancy as he rolled over on to his back to float with the baby on his chest. He could see her face in the light spilling down from the bridge but he couldn't tell whether she was alive or dead. He clamped his mouth over hers and blew into her lungs, on the pretext that any such gesture was better than nothing at this point.

The water lapping over their faces and his own state of exhaustion prevented this measure from being either regular or correct in terms of technique, but it was all he could manage as he struggled to stay afloat and tried to kick out weakly for the bank.

The slow thump of an engine reached Tom through the water covering his ears and made him raise his head a little to look around him. Out of the darkness he could see the bows of a riverboat coming straight towards him. It was the final straw as far as he was concerned; he simply had no energy left to swim out of its way. There was nothing he could do except look up at the night sky in desperation and cry out in anguish, 'For Christ's sake! Give me a break!'

The world was suddenly filled with a blinding white light and the sound of shouting voices. Hands tugged at him and he felt Anne-Marie being taken from his grasp. He could do nothing for himself as he was pulled from the water but now he was lying on something other than water and he could breathe freely again as French voices around him said things he couldn't understand. Suddenly, he felt like sleeping. God, how he felt like sleeping! The cold was no longer a problem and he was starting to feel comfortable. There was no pain, only a delicious feeling of tiredness. The voices might be becoming more animated, even alarmed but he didn't care: they were very distant now and he was drifting off into such a comfortable sleep . . .

When Tom opened his eyes, he found Mary sitting there. She smiled at him with moist eyes. 'So you've come back to me,' she said.

He tried to speak but failed.

'This really is becoming a bad habit,' said Mary. 'It's hypothermia this time.'

'The baby?' croaked Tom.

'She's going to be fine. People underestimate how tough babies really are. Trool had been keeping her under with sedatives, pretending to the nurses that she was in an ever-deepening coma, but they've worn off now and the bath in the Seine did her less damage than it did you.'

'I never want to see water again. But how . . .'

'Le Clerc's driver saw you chase after Trool. He followed and witnessed what happened. Very enterprisingly, he commandeered one of the Bâteau Mouche boats moored at the bridge and rescued you and the baby. You were incredibly brave.'

'How's Le Clerc?'

'He's lost a lot of blood and he's never going to look as pretty again but he'll pull through.'

'It's over then.'

'Yes,' agreed Mary, running her fingertips gently along Tom's forehead. 'It's finally over.'

'Isn't science wonderful,' murmured Tom, suddenly feeling very sleepy again.

~ *Epilogue* ~

Within a week, Tom Gordon was proclaimed a hero in the press and greeted with smiles wherever he went in North Wales. One man's belief in the innocence of a friend had captured the imagination of not only the Welsh newspapers, but also the nationals, many of which requested feature-length interviews. He declined all such requests without giving reasons.

John Palmer was released from prison and reunited with Lucy, who was allowed out of hospital, although more plastic surgery would be required at a later date. Ecstatic to be reunited with their 'miracle' baby, they too were under considerable pressure from journalists to give 'their side of the story', deemed to be of great 'human interest' to their readers – something emphatically underlined with the offer of large sums of money for exclusivity – but, like Tom, they too declined.

Tom elected to tell John and Lucy himself of the facts surrounding Anne-Marie's true origins, and did so at the Manchester hospital just before Lucy's release and when John was present. It was not the easiest of tasks and there had been anger and recrimination, followed by tears and finally acceptance of the situation. The fact that Anne-Marie was still alive emerged as the most important factor and, as Tom had predicted, the Palmers' love of the child they still regarded as their daughter won the day. Nothing was going to change that and they welcomed their baby's return without reservation.

The people for whom they might have harboured hatred, and suffered the ill effects of such a cancer growing within them, were mercifully dead with the exception of Sonia Trool. She was now a virtual prisoner in her own home while the powers-that-be decided what to charge her with. Davies had warned them that proving anything would be difficult.

The refusal of any of them to talk to the media had not dimmed the media's interest however, and the Palmers' return to Felinbach with their daughter attracted wide attention. The people of Felinbach responded to the media invasion with smiles and decorations and expressions of welcome. Special mail deliveries were needed to cope with presents for Anne-Marie that flooded in from well-wishers, and it seemed as if the whole world wanted to be the friend of the tragically wronged couple and the heroic village doctor who had believed in their innocence.

With media collusion, the Palmers' neighbours threw a party to welcome them back and it was publicly announced at it that a nationwide appeal for funds to help secure Anne-Marie's future had topped £100,000 with more to come. Tom attended the party with Mary, watching the smiles and returning the handshakes but with an inner numbness. At some stage, he found himself speaking to Julie Rees.

'So you were right and I was wrong,' she said.

'No hard feelings, it was never obvious,' replied Tom. 'How are things at the surgery?'

'We're managing, but people keep asking about you. They're wondering when you're coming back.'

Tom smiled and said, 'We'll talk.' He hadn't made up

his mind about that. After a little more chat about Julie's husband and children, he moved off to where he saw Lucy detach herself from a group of friendly neighbours. He had been watching her for some time. Her mouth had been smiling but her eyes had remained cold throughout and he suspected that she was feeling the same way he was. 'All right?' he asked.

Lucy's eyes softened for the first time. 'Fine,' she said.

'Good to be back?'

Lucy looked down at the floor for a moment. 'John and I talked last night,' she said. 'We've decided to leave the village: it can never be the same for us here, now that I know.'

'Know?'

Lucy looked at all the happy faces around them and said, 'I've seen the other side of these people, remember. The insults, the graffiti, the malicious whispers, the crowds outside the court.'

'People are people wherever you go. You shouldn't expect too much.'

'I realise that,' said Lucy. 'But I'd like to go somewhere where I didn't know for sure, if you know what I mean?'

'Yes I do. I think I feel the same but I'm going to give it a little time.'

They both looked over to where John was chatting to a group of local people, his eyes bright and trusting as if nothing had ever happened. 'It's incredible. He doesn't know the meaning of the word bitterness,' said Tom. 'Maybe we could both learn something from him.'

'He *is* rather special,' said Lucy with an affectionate smile. 'But then so are you, my brave Tom, and we'll never forget you.'

'I should hope not,' he joked. 'I want to hear how you're all getting on, wherever you go.'

'Let's mingle,' said Lucy, turning her social smile back on.

As she moved off, Mary came over and took Tom's arm. 'Good heavens, you've managed to remain upright and perfectly conscious all evening,' she said cheekily. 'Can this be a day when Tom Gordon is in no need of medical attention at all?'

'Depends what kind of medical attention is on offer . . .' he responded.

Mary looked at him out of the corner of her eye and asked, 'Was there anything specific you had in mind?'

'I do feel a sudden strong desire to go back to bed,' murmured Tom. 'What d'you reckon?'

'Just what the doctor ordered,' she whispered back, and giggled.

Hand in hand, they left the party.